Photo John Sculpher

Graham Sclater lives in Devon where he is a successful businessman and active in the local community. Prior to returning to Devon in the late sixties he was a professional musician playing all over the world and working as a session musician with numerous name artists. His first novel *Ticket to Ride was* published in 2004 by Flame Books and republished by Tabitha Books in 2006. This was followed by the novella *We're Gonna Be Famous*; a third novel *Hatred is the Key* and more recently *Too Big to Cry*. *Love Shack* is Graham's fifth novel and he is currently working on several television and film scripts as well as continuing to build his music publishing company and record label.

LOVE SHACK

Graham Sclater

TABITHA BOOKS

Dedicated to Roy Montrell, New Orleans guitarist and respected session musician who died at the Sonesta Hotel in Amsterdam in 1979 while on the European tour with the author and Fats Domino.

To Lorna

Best wishes

Acknowledgements

Gerard Buckley and family, at the Castle Hotel Macroom, for their wonderful hospitality, Denise Bailey for the cover photographs, Amsterdam, Karel at the Koopermoolen, Amsterdam politie department, Barrie Cutler, Bryce Wastney, JP, all the radio presenters around the world who continue to support me, and lastly all readers who have bought my previous work.

Contents

PROLOGUE

22 August 1922

Michael Reilly played marbles in the gutter in Castle Street, Macroom, County Cork, with two of his closest friends. Their shrieks of excitement suddenly faded as a convoy of military vehicles led by the Sliabh na mBan, a 920 pattern armoured Rolls Royce car, pulled up outside the Williams Hotel. It was followed by the distinctive Leyland Eight, open top, four-seater tourer, a Crossley Tender carrying a number of fully armed soldiers, and several other military vehicles. The tyres of the first vehicle pushed the young boys' precious misshapen clay marbles deep into the mud and gravel. Michael and his friends attention was drawn to the alien vehicles, something they had never seen the like of before. The uniformed men sitting in the elevated vehicle looked up at the building behind them before they briefly acknowledged the boys. The boys took a few nervous steps backwards and stiffened to attention. They watched in stunned silence as the rear car doors opened. The military officer nearest to them opened the rear door, and stood on the pavement towering above them. He looked around furtively and while he waited to be joined by his fellow officer,

Emmet Dalton, he reached out and grabbed at Michael's cap and threw it high in the air. He caught it effortlessly and smiled to himself as he deliberately placed it onto the young boy's head the wrong way round. Michael looked up at the giant of a man in total awe. Michael Collins, Commander-in-Chief of the Irish National Army, stretched out both arms in front of him and after pushing the young boys gently aside he waltzed into the hotel. The armed soldiers jumped out of their vehicles and stood guard on the pavement outside. As Michael Collins entered the hostelry, followed nervously by his fellow officers and plain clothed attendants, the music stopped and the men filling the bar stood and stared in total silence – a combination of awe and disgust. An older man who stood at one end of the bar started to clap enthusiastically and almost immediately the whole place erupted with whistles and cheers. He scrambled onto the bar and screamed above the uproar. 'Welcome home "Big Fellow!"

That was the cue for the musicians to resume their rousing music. The noise reached a crescendo when Michael Collins effortlessly picked up the barmaid, raised her high above his head and signalled to the bar man. 'Drinks for everyone!' he shouted.

When the resulting uproar in the bar could be heard in the street outside the young boys finally relaxed. They pushed their innocent faces against the window and watched the excitement intently.

Later that sunny August afternoon the armed convoy left Macroom and drove towards Beal na mBleath, less than nineteen miles away. When it reached the S-bend on the narrow country road at Glanarouge Bridge they encountered a dray cart that had been positioned across the road to form a road block. As several of Collins's men began to remove the cart the handful of rebel forces that had remained on the rock high above them waited for their moment before they opened fire. Seconds later, on the 22 August 1922, Michael Collins, the "Big Fellow," aged 31, was dead.

The assassination of Michael Collins, the only man that had been able to bring peace and stability to Ireland, and the name he had given to his son, was the signal that Michael Reilly's father had long feared. Within a week the whole family packed their meagre belongings and made their way to join relatives in east London.

When Michael left school he initially worked in the docks with his father until at the tender age of eighteen he met and married Aileen. With no prospects or sufficient income to look after his wife and Jimmy, their newborn son, he joined the 2nd Irish Guards.

CHAPTER ONE

Take Back The night

The stench of death and burning flesh was vile.

The screams were blood curdling.

The continuous explosions were ear-splitting.

It was *hell!*

The towns of Boulogne and Calais were held by the Germans and the remaining lines of the BEF – the British Expeditionary Force – were in tatters. They now had the unenviable task of trying to survive, and return to England to fight another day.

The troops fell back into Dunkirk and fought a rearguard action with the French as the Stukas buzzed overhead and bombed and shot at them indiscriminately. The wrecked army vehicles and buildings burned and exploded around them. Although it was getting dark the flames from the blazing town was of little help to them as they blindly followed the tramline tracks through the thick acrid smoke. The confused and demoralised ragtag army were left with no alternative but to retreat. Hundreds of wounded soldiers converged on the east beach of Dunkirk to await rescue. Along with the almost continual strafing from the Stukas, the Messerschmitt's can-on positioned in the centre of the propeller boss delivered its deadly message as it dived repeatedly towards the fragment-ed and disorientated group of British. The guns strafed the defenceless soldiers killing many and inflicting fatal injuries on thousands of others. Shards of metal tore through their uniforms driving the material deep into their flesh. Private Michael Reilly and the few desperate soldiers with him bore the brunt of this attack as they desperately tried to find shelter from the unremitting attacks.

The thick black clouds from the burning oil refineries near Dunkirk hung over the beaches blotting out even the strongest sun. The oil and diesel saturated waves glowed as they lapped around the dead bodies and as the tide washed onto the beach it appeared fluorescent and gave off an almost haunting and ethereal appearance as the waves filled the boot prints in the sand. The ebbing tide left a massive expanse of horror, death and decay as the swollen and bloated bodies became marooned on the exposed sandbanks. The Stukas took their time as they continued their methodical and relentless bomb-ing and machine gun strafing of the helpless and defenceless soldiers on the crowded beaches. Although the men frequently burst into song, they all began to feel the strain and could no longer hide their fear.

Michael Reilly poured the whiskey, from a bottle stolen from a now derelict store, over his bleeding, painful arm and hand. It was much more effective than iodine and for him it was more readily available. He took the occasional calculated slug from the bottle in a desperate attempt to mask the dreadful pain. With the excruciatingly slow attempt to rescue the soldiers, it was obvious to him that it would take a long time to clear the beaches. With little or no food for several days it was a welcome relief to finally receive the army emergency rations handed out by their officers. There was poor and sometimes non-existent radio contact between Dover and Dunkirk as any semblance of a rescue looked more hopeless by the hour. The impending evacuation was still a secret back in England and everyone at home was anxiously awaiting news that would not arrive for several days. Suddenly it began to look very bleak and with the German troops massing around the perimeter of Dunkirk, Operation Dynamo was launched. Hundreds of ships, small yachts, fishing boats and paddle steamers were requisitioned to join ships of the Royal Navy to evacuate the beleaguered soldiers from the foreign beaches. A much larger vessel was used as a hospital to treat and bring back the more seriously wounded soldiers. General Brook was reported as saying that "England would be lucky if 25% of the troops would be saved from the beaches".

One of the first and most unlikely ships to arrive and approach the beach was the Medway Queen; a 180ft paddle steamer built, in 1924, in Ailsa's Yard in Troon, Scotland. She was previously used to provide excursions in the Thames and Medway estuaries but in the bitter winter of 1939 she was called up to serve with the Royal Navy as part of the 10th Minesweeping Flotilla. On 28 May 1940 they were anchored on the south coast spotting enemy aircraft and laying mines when she was ordered to proceed to the beaches of Dunkirk. As soon as they reached their destination, amid heavy gunfire and while the oil tanks blazed around them, the Medway Queen, under her Captain, Lieutenant A.T. Cook RNR and J.D. Graves RNR as her First Lieutenant, waited while their most valuable of cargoes was brought out from the beach by their motorised dinghy. Throughout the overcast day and continual shelling from the German artillery positioned all around them, two thousand wounded and shell-shocked soldiers were picked up in one trip.

Things were becoming more desperate by the hour as the larger boats were forced to use the pier, which before the war had been used to bring in the cross channel ferry, to evacuate not only the English but also French and Belgian soldiers who had organised themselves into groups of two to three hundred men.

With shells exploding around the harbour, volunteers were needed to carry the stretcher cases onto the waiting ships. The wooden jetty had been hit several times and a gap caused by a direct hit meant that it needed four men to carry each stretcher. Michael realising that it was unlikely that he would get a place on board volunteered to help the ambulance core. Although the shrapnel wounds in his left hand caused him a great deal of pain he had sufficient strength to carry one end of the stretcher with his undamaged right arm. It proved to be more difficult than he had imagined as he and his fellow stretcher-bearers were forced to dodge the shells and bombs landing in the sea near the pier and the backlash as the explosions threw up huge cascades of oily and bloody seawater. Michael joined the Medway Queen on the last of seven runs, on 4 June 1940. The wounded were taken below decks and given basic first aid attention while the more able-bodied men sought out a space on deck. Still able to walk and showing no obvious signs of life-threatening injury he was therefore not considered to be a priority he stayed up on deck. All passengers whether they were injured or not were made to hand over their ineffective antiquated rifles before the ships set sail for England.

The incessant lethal bombardment by the German artillery continued. It took more than three agonising hours to load the paddle steamer with almost a thousand men. Thomas Russell the Medway Queen's extraordinary cook and his assistant "Sec" took great personal pride in caring for every one of the soldiers with meals and hot drinks.

However the shrapnel in Michael's hand and arm had now become badly infected and unbeknown to him gangrene had set in further up his arm. The poison ravaged parts of his body and caused him excruciating pain but that was forgotten briefly when he realised he was one of the lucky ones on his way back to England and Aileen.

With the good weather and a calm sea, the paddle steamer and assorted accompanying craft moved away from the pier and beaches – a rough sea would have been suicidal for the small boats and their passengers. As soon as they were out in the open Channel the German air force intensified their bombing and strafing with machine gunfire in a blatant attempt to point out even the smallest boat for torpedo attack by the ever-present E-boats. Everyone on board the rescue ships were under strict instructions not to shoot back at the enemy but as a final act of defiance, the few troops on board who had somehow retained their rifles made a futile effort by firing blindly in the general direction of the German planes.

As darkness fell, the unlikely looking armada of pleasure boats, yachts, shrimpers and fishing boats all began to make their way at differing speeds towards England for what in some cases was the fifth or sixth trip in as many days. As it began to get light two Stukas dived from the sky with a high-pitched scream, a sound that none of the troops would ever forget. One of the gunners on the Medway Queen shot down the first plane but the second hit the Brighton Belle, another paddle steamer, with a direct hit. It sunk quickly but fortunately many of the survivors were rescued and taken on board the already overloaded Medway Queen.

The white cliffs of Dover were a bewildering yet welcome sight as the boats and ships of various sizes were forced to queue up before the tired and exhausted troops disembarked in orderly fashion at Dover and Newhaven. In Ramsgate it was much the same but the dishevelled forces disembarked in front of the Merry England funfair, a backdrop to what they were about to witness. Everyone watched with tears in their eyes and mixed emotions as row after row of tired, exhausted, dirty and disillusioned troops were commanded to march along the unnamed streets – the signs had been removed to confuse or foil the German spies – in their tattered, oil and bloodstained uniforms to the strains of *Run Rabbit Run*. Jubilant members of the public plied the troops with tea, cake, apples and Woodbines at every opportunity. In those few short days 338,000 British and French troops were rescued and brought to England.

In 1941 the 2nd Irish Guards were reorganised as an armoured Regiment, joining the newly formed Guards Armoured Division before they returned to fight once more in mainland Europe.

Michael was safely back in England but the poisonous gangrene had now spread throughout his arm and shoulder. He was admitted to Kings Cross Hospital, London and following the amputation of his left arm he was released. Despite losing an arm he was considered to be one of the lucky ones; many of his comrades who had been wounded in Dunkirk never returned home.

On Saturday, 7 September, 1940, Aileen took the bus to the hospital to bring Michael home. They were both so excited to be together again, neither of them cared about the amputation, after all they still had each other. Michael was much better off than many of his fellow soldiers and there was the consolation that he would be home for the remainder of the war and not have to fight again.

Aileen and Michael took the bus to Silvertown, in the east end of London, and got off at the stop nearest to their home in Oriental Road. Oblivious to the sirens, Aileen in her Sunday best and Michael, in his clean pressed dress uniform, with its bright red tunic, walked proudly towards their home. Aileen stopped at the butchers shop to use the amassed meat coupons in her ration book. She had been saving them for this very "special" day and had mixed emotions as she handed them across the counter to the butcher. She was excited and relieved to finally be able to use them for the celebratory meal for her family. Carefully holding her prized purchase, in a shopping bag close to her side, they walked out onto the street hand in hand. Their son Jimmy was sitting on the wall opposite the butcher's shop, with Harry, his best friend. He waved and shouted out to them but his excitement was overshadowed by the high pitched scream of the lone Messerschmitt that appeared out of the afternoon sun and fired randomly at the unsuspecting couple. Aileen and Jimmy were both hit by the first volley and fell to the ground. Aileen still clutched at the precious carrier bag while Michael tried desperately, and in vain, to reach out for Aileen's hand with his recently amputated bandaged stump.

'Ma . . . ! Da . . . !' screamed Jimmy. He so desperately wanted to approach his parents but the plane circled and returned to strafe the street for a second time. Jimmy tried to take in the horror that had unfolded in front of him in those few short minutes but unable to comprehend anything, he ran blindly into the labyrinth of lanes and streets that was the East End.

Aileen and Michael were dead before the nearest passer-by could reach them, killed a few hours before the start of the London blitz of Millwall docks.

Following the death of his mother and father Jimmy ran away, his mind in turmoil as his world was shattered and had fallen apart in front of his eyes.

Later that night the first attack by the Luftwaffe caused tremendous damage to the Docks, Silvertown and much of the East End.

Jimmy's disappearance went unnoticed until late the next afternoon. He was finally found crying in the darkest corner of an air raid shelter in Stepney. This shelter was the largest of the shelters around London and temporary home to nearly 10,000 people. The group elected a well-known local character, Mickey Davis, as leader. Mickey was an optician, hunchback and stood three foot three inches tall. Marks and Spencer installed a canteen which distributed milk to Jimmy and the other small children. Parents played cards while others watched films, and sang along and danced to a lone accordionist.

Jimmy was finally taken by Harry's parents, to Father John

Groser, a High Anglican priest, who welcomed him. Father John Groser had already taken much of the law into his own hands, stealing food from a local food depot to feed the poor and starving. He had already lit a bonfire outside his church and was cooking meals. It was almost unbelievable but for the first time in nearly three days Jimmy had a hot meal. Father John was very aware that Jimmy had been mentally damaged and adversely affected by his horrific first-hand experience and his tempestuous mood swings were proof of that. Father Groser spent a lot of time with Jimmy and gradually the young boy appeared to regain a semblance of hope. Several weeks later Father Groser felt his young charge was ready to be put on a train with a group of other young evacuees and he left London for the safety of Devon.

CHAPTER TWO

Crying In The Dark

Although many young children were evacuated from London by boat to America and other safe havens, it came to an abrupt halt when a U-boat sank a liner carrying hundreds of young families across the Atlantic.

Jimmy Reilly still not appreciating the situation was evacuated out of London to the Westcountry on one of the many trainloads of young people. His final destination was Tavistock, a small village on the edge of Dartmoor, in south west England.

When Jimmy and the other children arrived in Tavistock, cold, tired and starving, they were not expected. They were made to remain in the town hall until the following day when local churchgoers and council workers were able to arrange suitable families to take them. All the evacuees were lined up with brown cardboard labels displaying their name, tied to their jacket or coat and given a food parcel and a drink. The clean presentable children were immediately snapped up but Jimmy and a few of the less presentable kids were left to stand tired and exhausted in the church hall. Jimmy was the last child to be taken reluctantly by a farmer and his wife to a remote farm high on Dartmoor. Even in the remote and alien countryside of Devon, Jimmy could not bear to hear the thunderous sound of the German bombers, as they made their way low over the moor to Plymouth. As the sirens preceded them, Jimmy trembled with fear, as he relived that fateful day several months earlier. Life was too different, he had never understood country folk, nor did he want to. The quietness tortured him; he was never told any news or what was happening back in London. He hated every minute and couldn't wait to get back to the city, his home.

His first sighting of Dartmoor Prison in Princetown in the middle of the inhospitable moor between Exeter and Plymouth was on a cold, grey cloudy morning. Clearly visible from the road, the long, tall granite buildings capped by the long thin chimneys, surrounded by a daunting high wall, rose up out of the mist. The prison was to be a constant memory as he passed it several times a week and he often wondered what it was like in the god forsaken place miles from anywhere.

Jimmy returned to the devastated East End of London a few months after the end of the War, in December 1945, where he lived with his aunt and uncle and was brought up a staunch Catholic. But when he got in with the wrong bunch of tearaways, he started to "mitch" regular school; his future was set for ever. He finally ran away from home and joined a gang. After being caught for robbing a factory he was returned home to his aunt and uncle by the police, where he was severely beaten. The beating had absolutely no effect and he was soon caught again after committing a spate of exceptionally violent attacks and robberies, some alone and others with the gang.

At the age of 16 he was sent to borstal for the first time. It was not a deterrent to him and although he became smarter, he still got caught. With no future he was drafted into the 1st Battalion Royal Ulster Rifles and, at the end of 1950, was sent to Korea to join the war.

The six week sea journey across the world, where they were finally greeted on the quayside by young Korean girls wearing sailor uniforms and matching black bobbed hair styles, seemed an adventure for Jimmy. It was short lived as the freezing sub-zero temperatures, sometimes as low as minus forty brought all of them back to reality. He and his fellow soldiers were left in shock when they saw babies that had frozen to death being thrown into the river.

On the 23 April 1951 he found himself part of a small group of soldiers given the task to protect the Imjin River, north of Seoul. That night the discordant and eerie sound of the Chinese buglers sent a shiver through every man. Fortunately a lone bugler from the Royal Gloucester's played every tune that he had in his repertoire until he eventually silenced the Chinese. The Chinese knew that they had to smash the English and United Nations troops quickly to succeed. They succeeded as wave upon wave of Chinese soldiers continued to attack the British army undeterred until they finally broke the moral of the few able-bodied men left to fight.

On the morning of the 25 April 1951 with their ammunition close to running out the few hundred uninjured British soldiers broke out leaving the Padre and medics with the sick and wounded. Any soldier well enough to break out left in sections of five to six men. A group of tanks came to the rescue picking up fit soldiers and crushing Chinese soldiers as they drove right through them, filling the tank tracks with limbs.

The remaining fit, sick and wounded soldiers, medics and clergymen were taken prisoner and marched four hundred miles through the deep snow. Jimmy was one of the few uninjured prisoners and he soon knew it as he was forced to march with the Chinese soldiers.

Within a few days he resembled an old man as the cold wind cut through to his bones.

By contrast, in the late spring, came the intense heat and humidity followed by the start of another long winter. The survivors eventually arrived at a prison camp in November 1952 where they stayed until those still alive were finally repatriated in August 1953. When Jimmy returned from Korea he found it hard to settle down and within a few weeks he found himself on the other side of the tracks.

Throughout the fifties, bare knuckle boxing was everywhere specially at the Bethnal Green fair and he was a regular in the ring fighting for a few shillings. His love of the new Rock and Roll music, fights, coffee bars, and his involvement in regular crime made him a popular figure and by many was considered to be one of the original East End Teddy Boys. For the next ten years he spent more time in prison than on the outside and it was not unusual for Jimmy to be "nicked" on a Friday night and up before the court magistrate on Saturday morning and if found guilty he would be sent to Wormwood Scrubs for four weeks.

Gwen Maloney, born towards the end of the war in 1945 and living in the same street as Jimmy had been a young admirer of his for some time, although she was eleven years his junior. Gwen was still a teenager, aged only 19, when they met at an all-night party early in 1964. When she fell pregnant in the summer of the same year they married the following Christmas Eve. Jimmy never changed his image and maintained his Elvis quiff and greased back his hair when everyone else was transformed into longhaired hippies or stylised Mods. His pride and joy was a motorbike, a leather jacket with the obligatory chains and a painting of a skull and crossbones on the back.

Gwen doted on her husband and adored the children. Each of them was conceived immediately after his release from prison. Liam was born in 1965 followed by Bernadette in 1974 and Tommy in 1977 and she devoted her life to bringing them up.

On the 9 May 1968, while Jimmy was still in prison, everything changed. The Kray Twins were arrested for murder and the East End would never be the same. Despite short term efforts of the various gangs as they tried to get a hold of the Kray's empire, in a few short years gang rule would become almost unrecognisable.

Gwen did a good job raising her three children for much of the time on her own. The anonymous envelopes containing used pound notes pushed regularly through the letterbox helped her over what would almost certainly have left the family to suffer serious hardship. Liam, the eldest of the three children, looked after his sister under duress, but when his brother Tommy was born, he couldn't do enough for him. Consequently Tommy idolised his elder brother and worshipped the ground he walked on.

The family continued to live in the same East End Council house and Jimmy, having missed music for many years while he was in prison, rekindled his interest in music upon his release in 1976. His love of live rock music meant that he spent many evenings working as a bouncer at rock pubs: the Ruskin Arms, Hope and Anchor, and the Brecknock in North London. In 1976 following a fight at the Bridge House, Canning Town, when Jimmy broke the skull of a "would be" gang leader, he was sent to prison again.

CHAPTER THREE

Killing Me Softly

Liam grew up without seeing much of his father and would never achieve a fraction of his notoriety. Where his father planned even the easiest crime, Liam did not see the necessity, with the result that as a teenager he was continually in and out of remand homes until at the age of 14 he found himself in borstal. On his release he continued as a petty thief and burglar and when he reached eighteen he was sent to prison. Liam was the one person that every police officer wanted to nail, but defended and protected by his father at arm's length, he was to escape prosecution for many of his senseless crimes no matter how violent they were. His time incarcerated had little or no effect on his craving to take chances. He continued to flout the law but he was growing up and became easily recognisable in the East End. His jet black hair, slicked back tight to his head was in direct contrast to his pale complexion. His features were sharp but his flattened nose and chiselled jaw line conveyed the look of a boxer. His life changed dramatically when he met Kathleen in February 1986. The couple fell madly in love and were married at Newham registry office within three weeks of meeting each other. Harry was born later that year in November 1986. Although Liam vehemently denied the jibes from his friends that they had to get married, it was common knowledge that they were forced into it by both sets of their staunch Catholic parents. A year later, identical twins Michelle and Sally were born. For a short period, Liam kept out of trouble but the responsibility of feeding three small children and with no will to work in a normal or proper job, he returned to his old ways. As far as Kathleen was concerned, he appeared to have changed, but under the surface he was overwhelmed at the thought of caring and providing for a family. He returned to petty crime to pay the bills and continuous drinking to drown his depression. Sinking to lower depths he was asked to take part in a daring robbery at Mount Pleasant Post Office. For nearly a week the gang stayed at the Mount Pleasant Hotel overlooking the main sorting office as they kept a round the clock vigil noting times and shift changes as they planned their raid.

On the afternoon of the robbery Liam had already been drinking for several hours and while the remainder of his gang loaded the post bags into their waiting vehicles, Liam continued to drink heavily from a hip flask. The attempted robbery went drastically wrong, leaving one security guard dead and a second seriously wounded. Liam now almost paralytic was easy prey for the police. His fellow robbers drove away leaving him lying in the car park drunk and confused. When the procession of screaming police cars arrived he was still lying in the car park smoking and singing to himself.

The only other available witness to the violent actions was another postman Harold Simmons, who came to the assistance of his workmate and was viciously attacked by

Liam with a baseball bat. He was seriously affected by Liam's unnecessary and unprovoked attack and following a lengthy period of rehabilitation in hospital and counselling nothing seemed to be getting through. He was left deeply traumatised, a nervous wreck, confused, suffering fits and continuous bouts of shaking.

In court, Harold's condition finally sealed Liam's fate. When the jury saw the effects of the beating, Harold still unable to talk or communicate with the lawyers, it left them with no option but to find Liam guilty of the charge of attempted murder. The press coverage created a public outcry and left the judicial system with no alternative but to make an example of the only person the police had been able to apprehend and convict.

When Liam was sentenced to fifteen years in Wandsworth Prison he was inconsolable.

For fear of reprisals from the remaining members of the gang, and compounded even further because Liam, loyal to the cause, refused to grass on his fellow villains. Harold was moved to a safe house at a location known only to the police while they continued their futile investigations.

In prison, Liam, because of his father's reputation, was treated like royalty, and alcohol was made available to him whenever he wanted it. Soon he became reliant on alcohol and a hopeless wreck, completely lacking in willpower and self-confidence.

Although it was hard for Kathleen, Jimmy and Gwen saw that the children were taken care of and didn't starve. Liam was able to hide his heavy drinking for the short period during Kathleen's regular weekly prison visits.

*

Seven years into his sentence Liam heard that some of the lifers and long-term lags were planning something. He wasn't interested; he wanted his freedom.

Two prison officers were carrying out the monthly in-depth inspection of his cell when the ear splitting scream of the siren filled every inch of the prison. Almost immediately the prison officer's radios crackled into action.

'Lock down! Lock down!' screeched the voice, at the other end.

The two prison officers looked at Liam and he immediately raised his arms high in the air and shook his head – negating any threat. The prison officers mumbled to each other before Liam spoke. 'Can I suggest you both stay put?'

The nearest prison officer to the door pushed it closed and the three of them waited in silence. It wasn't long before they could smell the fire and the shouts of marauding prisoners as they made their way across the ground floor releasing the inmates as they went. Minutes later Liam and the prison officers heard them racing up the metal staircase and along the first floor balconies. Before they could do or say anything three prisoners forced their way into the cell and began to beat the hell out of the prison officers.

Liam stood and looked on until he could take no more. He tried to intervene. It was a mistake. The two prisoners nearest to him struck out, stabbing him in the stomach, legs and arms with their makeshift weapons of broken chair legs and cutlery, they had managed to steal from the kitchen. When Liam fell to the floor the prisoners resumed their attack on the prison officers.

Liam crawled to the far wall and took several deep breaths as he summoned any remaining strength. As the adrenaline pumped through his body he leapt up and grabbed both prisoners by the neck and smashed their heads together. They fell to the floor and lay motionless on top of the prison officers. The third prisoner let out a ferocious scream and pounded his chest as he flew at Liam. Liam knew that he had mental issues and he used that to his advantage. He reached for the magazine on his bed and threw it directly at the giant of a man. It distracted him for a split second and Liam, smashed his fist into his right temple. The prisoner was unconscious before he hit the ground. Liam dragged him outside of the cell and closed the door, locking it with the prison officer's key. He made sure to leave the key in the lock before he turned his attention to the two prisoners. He pummelled their bodies with his fists before using their makeshift weapons to stab them. He was badly injured and bleeding heavily. He tore his bed sheets into strips and did his best to bind the more serious wounds. He extricated the prison officers from beneath the prisoner's bodies and propped them against the end wall of his cell. He then did his best to bind their wounds. He picked up one of the prison officer's radios and exhausted he lay on his bed and waited. It seemed like an eternity but as darkness fell on the cell he heard the sound of heavy regimented footsteps of the Special Forces as they made their way along the balcony checking and securing each cell as they went. Even they were shocked at the carnage and wanton destruction as they made their way through the wing. When they reached Liam's cell they dragged the injured prisoner away and tried to open the door. Finding it locked, they beat on the door until Liam was able to make his way across the cell. He unlocked the door and was immediately thrown to the floor and handcuffed by the Special Forces.

He was initially sent to the prison hospital and after having his wounds stitched, had a catheter fitted. When he was visited the next day by the prison doctor he noticed that Liam's urine contained a great deal more blood than expected.

'Have you had any pain?' asked the doctor?'

Liam pushed back the sheet. 'What the fuck do you think?' He pointed at the bandages. He pulled the sheet up to his chin and pushed himself deep into the mattress before he spoke. 'What about the two *screws* . . . are they alright?'

The doctor lowered his head and nodded slowly as he spoke. 'They'll be fine – eventually,' he said quietly. He looked into Liam's eyes before he continued. 'But you won't be seeing them for many months . . .' He lowered his voice. 'Assuming they ever come back to work.'

Liam showed genuine concern. 'That bad eh?'

The doctor nodded and bit at his bottom lip.

'The poor . . . bast . . .' Liam didn't complete the sentence and mumbled under his breath. 'I must be going soft.'

The doctor looked at him. 'Whatever you think . . . they wouldn't be alive if it wasn't for you.'

A week later Liam was still losing a lot of blood. The prison doctor approached his bed and lifted the urine collection bag, checked it and moved towards him. He spoke softly in his ear. 'You need to go to hospital . . .' He couldn't hide his concern and his voice faltered as he pointed at the bloody bag hanging from the side of the bed. 'We can't deal with *that* here . . .'

Liam followed the doctor with his eyes as he walked to his office and watched as he picked up the phone.

An hour later, under heavy guard, Liam was moved to

St Thomas's Hospital and given an MRI scan.

That afternoon a consultant wearing a green tweed suit and a heavily patterned bow tie approached Liam's bed. Liam tried hard to hide his grin and sniggered while he waited. The consultant reviewed Liam's notes and with a grave look on his face spoke to him. 'We need to remove your right kidney.'

A stunned Liam looked at him and gasped in shock. 'What?'

The consultant shook his head as he spoke. 'You have renal cancer . . . and we have *no* option.'

Liam looked back at him open mouthed as he struggled to speak.

The consultant continued. 'If we don't remove it – you *will* die.'

Liam's face was ashen.

'You're a lucky young man . . . if you hadn't been injured we would have never known about it and . . .' He screwed up his face and continued. 'Six months.' He gazed into space. 'A year – who knows?' He walked off leaving Liam to think about his final words and repeat them over and over in his head.

Two hours later Liam was in the operating theatre, where his kidney was removed. When he awoke he was still hand-cuffed to both sides of the bed. He remembered very little of what had happened prior to the operation and tugged at the handcuffs as he glared at the prison officer. 'You thoughtless bastards, do you really expect me to break out of here?'

He looked around at the intravenous drip in his arm, touched the plastic cannula tube in each nostril, the epidural tube in his spine and the catheter in his penis. He raised his voice. 'I can't *crawl* let alone *walk* with these fucking tubes in me!' He slid his hand beneath the sheets, felt at his stomach and nervously traced the two inch wide clear tape across it and around his side. The clear tape gave the doctors and nurses the opportunity to ensure that he didn't pick up MRSA or any other infection.

Jimmy visited Liam in hospital. He knew the prison officer that stood outside the private room and he allowed him in. Much to his surprise he recognised the second prison officer that sat beside Liam's bed.

'Hello, Brian,' said Jimmy.

Brian nodded at him. 'Hi Jimmy. What are you up to these days? Haven't seen you in our place for a while . . .'

Jimmy sniggered as he replied. 'Taking it easy for the minute, Brian.' He looked across at Liam before returning to the prison officer. 'How's the missus?'

'She's fine . . . and Andy's at university now.' He shrugged. 'I got no idea what the thick bastard thinks he's going to learn there. Costing us a fortune . . . and for what?'

Jimmy smiled broadly. 'Well.' He paused and sucked in air. 'You know what they say you can never stop learnin', can ya?' He looked at Liam and smirked. 'Maybe you should 'ave gone to university, son.'

Liam shrugged and pushed himself beneath the sheet and folded it up tightly beneath his chin.

Jimmy sat on the edge of Liam's bed and looked slowly around his room. 'Seems you're in good 'ands . . .' He stopped and his mood suddenly changed and without taking a breath he spouted out his suppressed anger. 'Why the fuck did you get mixed up in that shit? Did I never teach ya anyfin'? Didn't ya listen to me?'

Brian intervened. 'Listen Jimmy, if it wasn't for your lad those fucking bastards would have been looking at the murder of George and Alfie.' He stood and straightened his uniform before settling back into his seat beside the bed.

Jimmy fidgeted nervously and pushed at his collar with his chin. 'Is that right, son?'

Liam nodded. 'If I hadn't got involved with their shit they would've 'ad me too.'

Jimmy nodded his understanding.

Liam needed to cough and pushed his hands against his stomach before coughing gently.

Jimmy exhaled a tired breath. 'You know we'll look after the kids an' that.' He stood up and squeezed Liam's shoulder. 'Look after yerself, son.' He turned and walked towards the door and turned back as it opened. 'Tommy's outside . . . he wants to see ya.'

Tommy walked in and made straight for the bed.

Brian stood up and blocked his access to Liam.

Tommy took a step back and raised his hands. 'Take it easy mate; I've been frisked by your mate outside . . . alright?'

Brian reluctantly sat down. He looked up at the clock on the wall. 'Ten minutes . . . mate,' he said, mimicking Tommy.

Tommy was buzzing with questions. 'How many did you get? What happened in there? Did you kill any of 'em?'

Brian coughed his contempt at the question and tugged at the handcuffs.

Liam took the hint and smiled at Tommy and nodded slowly as he spoke. 'Listen, Tommy, it's not the least bit fucking glamorous in there. I could have been killed!'

Tommy wouldn't let go. 'I know that . . .' He licked at his lips excitedly, 'but *how many* did *ya* get?'

*

The two surviving prisoners who had attacked Liam and the prison officers spent many months in hospital and, when they were well enough to leave, were sent to prisons as far from each other as possible, in case they tried to take reprisals against Liam. They were both given fifteen year extensions to their sentence for the attack on the prison officers and another five for being involved in the riot.

It would be two weeks before Liam was returned to the prison hospital and almost three months before he was able to return to his cell. He agreed to attend rehabilitation and while he recovered he was visited in the hospital by his counsellor. Once he was well enough he agreed to attend twice-weekly meetings in the Love Shack, a porta-cabin in the prison grounds, which to him was a haven of peace. There were no prison officers, no controls and for the first time in many years he felt free. Prisoners were able to relax in worn armchairs and settees or sit at tables where there was time for them to express their feelings without reproach. To paint, draw, write or read. Liam and other prisoners, who had drink issues, joined in twice weekly sessions with a reformed alcoholic. They were each given their own five hundred and seventy-five page book – "Alcoholics Anonymous," written by Alcoholics for Alcoholics. The plain dark blue cover had no writing or title on it but was instantly recognisable to other alcoholics, but only those who accepted their problem. During his weekly sessions, Liam marked and underlined selected sections and chapters, which he regularly read and reread.

Six months after the riot Liam was summoned to the governor's office. He stood, handcuffed, in front of the large oak desk flanked on each side by a prison officer. He stood to attention and waited while the governor flicked through his files before finally placing the signed page into an envelope and handing it to one of the officers. The governor dismissed Liam and he walked back towards his cell. Before he could reach the staircase, one of the prison officers grabbed at his arm, and told him to turn right. He was led through large double doors along the corridor where the walls displayed photographs of previous governors and old photos of the earlier prison officers. His journey continued until he was led into a room with dark oak panelled walls and three suited men, who sat majestically behind a huge carved wooden table.

The chairman motioned to Liam to sit on the wooden chair six feet from the table while the prison officers stood erect and imposing either side of him.

The prison officer passed the envelope to the chairmen, who, after reading the contents passed it to the other two men.

Liam fidgeted nervously while each of the men read the paper and flicked through their files. They then deliberated amongst themselves until the chairman looked directly at Liam. Before speaking, his demeanor changed and he gave Liam a quizzical look and coughed into his fist. 'Erm,' he paused, 'Mr *Reilly* – *Liam* Reilly?'

Liam nodded. 'Yes.'

The nearest officer kicked hard at Liam's ankle.

Liam glared up at him before turning his attention to the chairman. 'Yes, *sir*,' he said, begrudgingly.

The chairman continued. 'We've been reviewing your records,' he said, tapping the open folder on the desk.

Liam stared back at him and nodded slowly.

The chairman cleared his throat and continued. 'Could you comment on your recent rehabilitation?'

Liam screwed up his face and shook his head. He tried to reply but had no idea what he could say.

The chairman turned to each of his colleagues in turn and continued. 'Mr Reilly, as I say we have reviewed your records and, taken into account your intervention.'

Liam shot him a confused look.

The chairman continued. 'You saved the lives of two prison officers . . .' He paused and looked hard at the prisoner. 'Is that correct?'

Liam didn't reply.

The chairman continued. 'Well did you – or did you not?' he asked, firmly.

Liam coughed nervously. 'Well . . .' He pulled up his shoulders and continued. 'If you put it like that, sir . . .' He fidgeted once more and flicked at his finger nails. 'Anyone would have done *that*. The screws ain't that bad . . .' He paused and lowered his voice. 'All things considered . . .'

This time both prison officers kicked out simultaneously at his ankles.

The chairman continued. 'Well, despite your sentiments, Mr Reilly, we have decided to grant you parole.'

'Wha . . . ?' Liam leaned forward as he found it hard to hide the shock.

The chairman continued. 'Let me tell you this, Mr Reilly, none of us wants to see you back here again.' He looked at each of his colleagues who nodded their agreement. 'We're giving you an opportunity; please make sure we have *not* made an error of judgement.'

Liam sat motionless.

The two men each signed the documents in their file and passed them to the chairman. He countersigned them and handed one copy to the nearest prison officer. They closed their files and looked at each other.

The chairman spoke for the last time. 'Mr Reilly – you are free to go. Goodbye.'

CHAPTER FOUR

Fire

When Liam was released and saw the outside world, the change overawed him. The age of technology was about to replace the old ways, drug barons controlled the streets and most of the crime was attributable to drug users and addicts. He couldn't, and didn't want to understand it. Business had begun to revolve around the mobile telephone: it was too fast for him. Liam was approached on an almost daily basis by his inquisitive, growing teenage brother, Tommy, goading him to continue on the path of breaking the law. With the exception of the occasional robbery or petty burglary, which gave him his beer money, Liam was not interested. He had to stick with what he knew best even if it was unfashionable.

Harry now 12, and the twins, Michelle and Sally 11, had outgrown the father they hardly knew. They had only seen him during the occasional prison visit and consequently moved on to a life of almost self-reliance and were not prepared to tolerate his drunken regime.

Their father was almost permanently drunk; they didn't understand or know how to deal with his drunken rages and violence, or perhaps didn't want to. They soon lost all respect for him, which resulted in continuous battles whenever he was in the house, causing great distress to Kathleen, who tried unsuccessfully to calm the charged atmosphere. The house was a nightmare to be in. The three children were affected and they began to cause major disruption at school, so much so that the head teacher asked Liam and Kathleen to come to the school and discuss it. True to form Liam was drunk when they attended, and after losing his temper, punched the head teacher, only to be dragged away by Kathleen and Harry.

He stormed off to the nearest pub and returned home as it started to get dark, stinking drunk and after yet another major row he staggered back out of the house leaving everyone upset, crying and frightened. Harry fidgeted pulling at his school tie until he couldn't hold back any longer. 'Mum can't we be left alone? Does he *have* to stay here? When he's not around we are so much happier.' The twins nodded their agreement.

'Come on Harry, he is *your* father,' said Kathleen, and she tried to calm him down.

'But he's always pissed!' replied Harry.

Kathleen spun around on the spot, screaming, as she hit out at him. 'What did you say?'

Harry cowered in the corner and rubbed at the side of his head. It was the first time his mother had ever raised her hand to him and it hurt, but he refused to cry.

The twins looked on shaken and too frightened to speak; they sneaked out of the kitchen, unnoticed, and into the sitting room to stare blankly at the television screen.

Kathleen tried desperately to comfort Harry, but the damage was done. Harry regained his composure and stormed out of the kitchen slamming the door behind him. Kathleen knew she had overreacted to what was certainly the truth and she didn't know what to do. She slumped into the nearest chair, held her hands over her face and completely overwhelmed burst into tears.

Harry and the twins made it known to their grandparents, Jimmy and Gwen, what was happening but that only confirmed what they already knew. Gwen pleaded with Jimmy. 'Can't you do something? At least talk to him, you can see what he's doing.'

Begrudgingly, Jimmy went off in search of Liam. He found him in the Rose and Crown and told him a few home truths. For a few days things returned to normal, but it was short lived: they knew that it wouldn't last.

Following a particularly vicious and violent argument over the evening meal, Kathleen pleaded with Liam to go forever and leave them alone to continue with the lives that were fine until he came out of prison. Liam overturned the table throwing the food and plates onto the floor before he stormed out of the kitchen, leaving Kathleen in tears and three hysterical screaming children. Harry unable to hold his feelings in check any longer shouted after him. 'I wish he was dead!' Kathleen looked on knowing that Harry meant it, and although she would never dare to say that out loud, she quietly agreed with him.

Liam stopped, swung around and stood glaring at Harry. His fists were clenched and he was about to hit Harry but Kathleen pushed forward and shielded him. The twins screamed out at him and momentarily he stopped and stood looking at his family. After staring at them for a few seconds he thought better of it, and cursing under his breath, walked out into the cold dark rainy night.

He committed a robbery at a nearby off-licence stealing several cans of beer, a bottle of whiskey and cash, which gave him enough money to buy even more alcohol when the beer and whiskey had been drunk. He continued his bender late into the night; the tiredness masked by the alcohol and depression.

He staggered along the street in the early hours of the morning returning to the now dark house. He searched his pockets for the front door key getting more annoyed and angry as he found yet another empty pocket. The inside jacket pocket finally revealed the elusive key and, in almost total darkness except for the street light fifty metres along the road, he made a number of unsuccessful attempts to push the key into the Yale lock. He dropped the key onto the wet cracked floor tiles in front of the door and cursed as he blindly searched for it. Crawling around on all fours he slid his hand under the overgrown hydrangea and at last his efforts were rewarded. This time he focused on the lock and as the key slid in, he smiled to himself; a pathetic sight if there had been anyone around to see him. He turned the key and noisily entered the dark house kicking the door shut with the worn down heel of his left shoe. He stood in the hall swaying from side to side while he tried to light a cigarette. After successfully lighting it, he took several drags before tripping over one of the twin's bicycles. Losing his balance, he fell against the door dropping the lighted cigarette into the coats piled beside an armchair in the living room. After pushing himself up, he made his way unsteadily through the room and out into the kitchen. He turned on the light, lurched forward and fell heavily against the leg of the still upturned kitchen table. He pulled open the fridge door; his search was futile, the fridge, as always, contained little more than survival rations for the growing family. He returned to the front room a few minutes later with the only bottle of milk in the house and fell onto the stained shabby and threadbare settee with a loud thump. He sat holding the precious bottle in his hand and smiled inanely, as he gazed up at the framed photographs of Harry and the girls. He put the bottle to his lips and started to drink the milk. Realising it wasn't alcohol his whole body shuddered. He suddenly lost his temper and after tightening his iron grip on the almost full bottle, threw it towards the photographs. As it hit the wall, the bottle smashed into thousands of pieces, covering the pictures, wallpaper and fireplace in milk and fragments of glass. Satisfied with his efforts he slumped back awkwardly onto the settee and fell asleep.

The smoke from the smouldering coats soon enveloped the sitting room and Liam started to cough. Finding it difficult to breathe he woke up. At first not knowing where he was; he thought that he might be dreaming, but as the smoke filled his lungs he was suddenly and strangely sober. He pulled his jacket over his head and made his way blindly through the flames and the acrid smoke. As he approached the door, the coats, curtains and armchair burst into flames. He ran out into the hall and slammed the lounge door behind him. The fire took hold on the rest of the furniture, carpets, piles of old newspapers, thick club books and toys.

The twins' small front bedroom was already alight when he opened the door; the flames from the lounge below had burnt through the ceiling and bedroom floor, igniting the curtains, which after burning fiercely had fallen onto Sally's bed. Liam made several frantic and dangerous runs up the smoke filled staircase to rescue his family.

The fire brigade arrived to find the house well ablaze and Liam, Kathleen and the three children in the road, wrapped in blankets supplied by their neighbours. A convoy of ambulances preceded by a paramedic on a motorbike, screamed down the road, and after administering first aid took the whole family to hospital.

Kathleen, Harry and Michelle were released early the next morning and they went to stay with Jimmy and Gwen. Sally received second-degree burns and Liam suffered respiratory problems and superficial burns. They were both kept in hospital.

Liam was regarded as a hero, his photograph and shots of the destroyed house were featured on the front page of the Evening Standard and he was even interviewed for radio.

Jimmy knew the truth and was the first family member to visit Liam in hospital. He walked into the single bedded room his forehead heavily furrowed. With a look of sheer disbelief on his face he threw the Evening Standard onto the bed. 'What the fuck did you think you were doing? You could have killed those kids! Kill *yourself* if you like, but for once . . .' He shook his head violently. 'Think of *your* family!' he spluttered.

Liam pushed his head into the pillow and looked straight ahead. Jimmy continued, his voice rising to a crescendo. 'Ya might fool every other fucker!' He punched at the photograph in the newspaper of the burning house and the headlines. "Family saved by their *brave* father." He took a huge breath before he continued to vent his anger. 'But don't ya ever try to fool me!' He looked around the small room and rubbed at his reddened eyes. 'The police know it was you!' He paced the small room like a caged animal. 'They know what 'appened. You're fucked this time and don't expect me to bail ya out!' Liam didn't show any emotion; perhaps if he had his father would have understood. 'Ya can't go on like this!' He stuttered with anger. 'Ya're sssssick and it's about time ya realised that ya got a serious fuckin' problem!'

Liam looked up at him and spoke in a soft quivering voice. 'What can I do, Dad?'

His father at last began to relax knowing that he had finally got through to his son and, not wanting to waste the moment, began speaking exceptionally fast. 'The first thing ya do is to stop drinking. If ya do want to help yaself then maybe others will help ya. But, I tell ya what.' His knee flicked up and down uncontrollably. 'If Kathleen ever finds out what ya've done.' He paused for a second. 'She'll rip ya fucking 'ead off.'

Jimmy reached over and squeezed Liam's hand, and lowering his voice, moved nearer to his son. 'I'll have a word with the doctor, see if ya can go somewhere and get help.' He slipped briefly back into his Irish accent and he sighed heavily. 'God knows ya need it, so ya do.' He picked up the newspaper, screwed it up tightly, threw it into the pedal bin, and left.

Jimmy persuaded the Social Services to send Liam to a clinic, notorious for its tough regime and radical experiments into defeating alcoholism and drug addiction. That was when he realised that his son was no longer safe and could not stay in England so he made arrangements for Liam to apply for a passport while he was still in the infirmary.

In Liam's absence, Kathleen's hatred grew towards him. Although she didn't know the whole truth, upon reflection, she soon began to blame him for everything that had happened to her family and her life.

*

With the special treatment, Liam improved, but against the better judgement of his consultant; his nurse, Alison Friedman, made arrangements for him to go to the hospital and visit Sally.

Unbeknown to Michelle and Sally, Liam watched the twins through the circular observation panel in the door. At first Michelle and Sally both appeared to be normal but when Sally turned her head, Liam immediately saw the horrific scars on one side of her face. The shock was further compounded as he instantly compared the faces of the pretty identical twins. In that split second it was as though he was staring at Beauty and the Beast. Devastated, and not able to face them, he broke away from Alison and fought his way down the numerous corridors and out of the hospital. In sheer desperation he knew he had to find his "friend" the bottle.

Realising that it was her fault for the catastrophic effects that the visit had on her patient, Alison drove aimlessly around the deserted streets looking for him.

Confused and totally destroyed Liam ran along the wet, dark and windy streets, crying and screaming as he thought about the twins' childhood and happy times together. For the first time he accepted that it was him that had ruined their lives and divided the family forever as he recalled their short young lives. He knew he had failed his whole family. He blagged several drinks from punters in a pub but was thrown out when he told them he had no money to buy his round. He left the pub and attempted to rob an all-night convenience store but failed miserably. Still blind drunk he wandered off into the night. Alison eventually found her patient surrounded by armed policemen and about to be arrested for the failed robbery. She took the police sergeant to one side and spoke to him in confidence. 'It will be of more use to let him come back to the clinic, rather than put him away again,' she pleaded. She pointed in Liam's direction. 'It would destroy him totally.' She lowered her voice. 'Surely you can see that?' She paused and waited for a response. There was none, and she continued. 'He's suicidal and much too ill to go back to prison; the next time . . .' She looked towards her desperate charge and begged the policeman. 'It *will* kill him,' she pleaded, her hands clasped in front of her.

After a muted referral to each other the more senior of the policemen lowered his voice. 'Go on then.' He shook his head and sighed. 'Get the *loser* out of here.' He signalled to the armed police, who, unable to hide their disappointment, lowered their weapons and walked back to their vehicles.

Liam made a token gesture of defiance but found it hard to even stand on his own.

Relieved, Alison bundled her rain soaked patient into the car, and escorted by two police cars, the entourage, drove off into the night.

Liam, drunk and still singing was carried to the bathroom where he was lifted unceremoniously into an empty bath by two well-built orderlies. He knelt and shook until he vomited and his whole body convulsed violently. 'Help me, will somebody fucking help me?' He screamed between the expulsion of a mixture of stale food, cheap wine, beer and whiskey.

The orderly turned on the overhead shower and the freezing water jetted onto Liam's shaking, pathetic, pale naked body. He vomited again into the shallow water, blocking the bath waste, until it gradually drained away. Whilst he stood precariously shaking and covered in goose bumps, in the now empty bath, the second orderly threw a towel at him. While Liam tried to dry himself the petite female nurse passed a small clear plastic beaker containing a pale yellow liquid to the nearest orderly. Liam took a tiny sip and screwed up his face as the foul tasting concoction entered his dry mouth. The orderly, finally losing all patience, raised his voice. 'Drink it! This will do you good.' He paused, locked his eyes on Liam for a second time, and screamed at him. 'Come on, finish it – NOW!'

Liam, his eyes extraordinarily wide open, stared back at him, then at the nurse, and finally at the beaker. 'Are you sure you want me to drink this? Or are you just *playing* at being a hard bastard?'

The orderly smirked back at him. 'Think what you like . . . can I assume that you *don't* want to get out of here *alive?*'

Liam held the beaker out in front of him, stared at it for a moment and swallowed the contents in one gulp. Pleased with himself, he gave a half smile and, as he pushed the empty beaker forcefully back to the orderly, he belched loudly in his face. 'Fuck the lot of you! You won't beat me!' he cursed. He dragged his long black hair behind his ears allowing it to fall unevenly onto the top of his shoulders and smirked at them in turn.

The orderly not wanting to be outdone by his patient grinned inanely. 'Well done.' He gave Liam a mocking nod. 'We'll see you in a few hours with the next one.' Liam cursed under his breath and, now totally exhausted, lay on his bed curled up in the foetal position and went to sleep.

As a result of the intense and punishing treatment Liam began to improve and, upon his release, now sober, he could at last take stock of his metamorphosis. Liam was tall, a little under six feet, and for the first time in years showed no excess fat on his thick set frame.

Jimmy and Tommy tried hard to give Liam their support in the only way that they knew. As a token deterrent, they set him up in a bedsit next to a police station and each week the three of them would visit Arena Essex speedway and reminisce about the old times at New Cross speedway. That was how, many years earlier, Liam had fallen in love and learnt to ride motorbikes and scramble machines, tinkering with them at every opportunity between his bouts in prison.

Desperate for some peace and quiet away from his dingy bedsit, and the continual reminder that he was living next to the police station, he walked aimlessly until he discovered the transport café at the end of a large disused paint warehouse. The lorry drivers loved the place because they not only had great food but they could easily park their huge Scammells and Volvos on the great expanse of concrete that had once been the home of a thriving jam factory, alive with dozens of delivery vans.

The walls were fair-faced block work painted with magnolia emulsion, with large black boards, displaying a menu that had to be seen to be believed, fixed to every free area of wall space. Bench seats were fixed along one wall flanked by two bright, flashing, noisy fruit machines. The rest of the space was filled with spotlessly clean, olive green faded and chipped table tops. The faded light blue contract carpet was stained in places and burnt where the customers had lazily stubbed out their cigarettes on the floor instead of using the huge ashtrays strategically placed on every table.

A large wall clock had pride of place between the specials

boards. An overweight unshaven man stood feeding one of the fruit machines trying desperately to force it to spew out the jackpot.

Liam walked up to the counter. 'Tea please,' he said.

The middle-aged lady looked up to him and smiled, exposing an almost toothless mouth. 'Builders?' Liam nodded mindlessly. 'Anything to eat, son?'

He looked back at her taken by surprise that someone could at last be nice to him. He thought to himself. If only she knew me?

Nervously he stuttered his reply. 'Nnnn . . . no thanks.'

'Alright luv, but here's a nice cup of tea.' She passed him the mug. 'That'll be forty pence luv.'

He paid her, picked it up and looked around for a vacant table, the choice confused him: there were more than a dozen free tables, their chairs pushed symmetrically beneath them. He walked off towards a solitary table, beneath a large printed no smoking sign in a dark corner, well away from the fruit machines and the nearest customer.

The tea was much too hot to drink and reluctantly he was left with no alternative but to sit and wait until he could drink it. He sat looking across the large rectangular room; everyone knew each other by their first name, and the better acquainted by their nicknames. They all talked enthusiastically and freely, over a cup of tea and a sausage sandwich their troubles forgotten for a few minutes. Liam joined everyone else and lit a cigarette and watched the elderly women working behind the counter, probably pensioners, dressed in matching extra-large red short-sleeved polo shirts, and aprons embroidered with the café's name. Despite their age they both rushed about in the open plan kitchen behind the counter, preparing meal after meal from the extensive menu written in coloured chalk on the blackboards. Each portion was large but nevertheless carefully measured, cooked and then placed neatly onto the large white plates.

A prostitute flounced in and ignoring the stares and whispers amongst the young mothers with children, she ordered a tea to take away. Carrying the plastic cup and holding her head and body erect, she slowly walked towards the door, ensuring that she was now noticed by anyone that had missed her entrance.

An overweight lorry driver with cropped grey hair and a bulging bright-blue tracksuit top gave the prostitute a cursory glance before he ordered a full breakfast and picked up two Kit Kats. Before he had chosen his table he ripped open the silver paper and ate them both before sitting down to read his paper and wait impatiently for his main course. Within a few minutes, the lady behind the counter called out to him to collect his tray, piled high with his massive breakfast, plus three rounds of toast and a second mug of tea.

For the first time there was almost total silence and Liam could hear the tape machine, placed out of harm's way on top of a large glass-fronted fridge displaying cans of Coke, Pepsi and assorted cans of cold drinks. Richard Clayderman played to the undiscerning clientele, hardly audible above the buzz, but the two women had half an ear permanently cocked to the piano player's melodies that continued to play to them from the cassette, while they dealt effortlessly with the constant stream of orders.

A tall unshaven man strode in, ordered a tea and then walked off in the direction of the second fruit machine. He fed it with his hard-earned money and after swearing under his breath, returned to the counter to collect and pay for his tea with his few remaining coins.

Liam smiled to himself as he noticed that, and for some strange reason, as the largest woman working on the counter took an order, she always repeated the last word. 'A ham salad, salad, Barney? A bacon sandwich, sandwich?'

The lorry driver standing at the other flashing fruit machine finally ran out of money and hobbled nervously away from the metallic thief that had willingly swallowed his money and, after acknowledging everyone by name, without giving it a second thought walked out into the prematurely dark afternoon and the torrential rain.

Liam glanced down at his wrist, preferring the intimacy of his own reliable watch rather than the huge clock on the wall, pushed his chair back, got up and followed the man out into the rain.

He pulled up his collar and stood in the rain watching as the overweight driver dragged himself up into his cab, started the diesel engine, and pulled out of the car park and off towards the A11.

CHAPTER FIVE

Here Comes The Sun

Jimmy received an unexpected and agitated telephone call from Freddie, an old friend now living in Spain. He panicked when Freddie told him that Laurie, his other long-time partner in crime, was seriously ill. Jimmy hurriedly arranged for Liam to take a plane from Gatwick and travel over to Malaga. As Jimmy had already arranged the passport for Liam he was able to book a one week package holiday on the Costa del Sol. Jimmy smiled as he handed Liam the tickets and passport. 'See how ya get on son, ya might get to like it over there.'

Liam had never been outside of London except to visit the Kursal at Southend and the beach at Brighton with his parents, when he was a teenager. It was with trepidation he took the train from Victoria Station to Gatwick.

As he arrived at the south terminal the huge check-in and departure lounge intimidated him. Carrying only an old scratched and torn canvas holdall he handed his ticket to the young girl on the Airtours counter and, not wanting to hang around, proceeded immediately to the departure lounge. The two and a half-hour flight was hell. He couldn't smoke and to make matters worse he found it hard to resist the non-stop offers of free in-flight drinks. With an hour still to go before he reached Spain, and being confined by his seat belt, he found it to be nothing short of sheer torture. He couldn't help but remember the similar feeling when he was in rehab. Much relieved, he disembarked with the rest of the anticipating holidaymakers at Pablo Ruiz Picasso airport at Malaga. He made his way nervously through passport control and he was dragged along with the impatient crowds as they pushed their over laden trolleys towards the waiting holiday representatives. He lit a cigarette and stood watching the crowd as it gradually dispersed in the direction of the numerous exit doors. Now standing almost alone in the vast Arrivals hall, a pretty young woman, in a green blazer and a bright flowery knee length skirt, approached him. She smiled at him before speaking. 'Hello, I'm Jackie can I help you?'

'I hope so,' replied Liam, nervously.

She looked down at her clip board and waited.

Liam stood and gawped at her.

'Name?' she asked. Liam didn't reply. She continued. '*Your name?*'

He looked directly at her and smiled uneasily. 'Liam . . . Liam Reilly.'

She cast her eye down one page, flicked the paper over and checked the next page repeating his name every time she turned to a new sheet. 'Here we are,' she said, with a smile.

Liam smiled back at her with relief.

'Mr Reilly, ah yes . . .' She smiled at him. 'Oh, you're staying at Cortijo Blanco.' She appeared pleased. 'That's *my* hotel.' She looked him up and down and then continued. 'I'll see you in the morning at the welcome meeting.'

Liam looked at her blankly as she pointed to the blue wallet, that she'd already passed to him. He was holding it subconsciously in his left hand along with his passport.

She tapped it. 'It's all in there. I'll see you at twelve o'clock. 'You need coach fifty-six.'

Liam stared at her and didn't move.

She looked at him and blushed. 'I'm sorry.' She pointed him in the direction of the massive coach park. 'Over on the left hand side, coach number fifty-six.'

He thanked her and walked out of the building to be blasted by the searing heat of the Spanish afternoon sun. He took off his jacket but he still felt unbearably hot. Still clutching at his holdall he searched the vast car park until he finally found his coach. He cordially nodded to the Spanish driver. It was a mistake because it gave the driver the opportunity to direct sentence after sentence of what seemed like something from a spaghetti western directly at him. Failing to understand a single word Liam mumbled back to him before moving un-comfortably through the coach, to the most welcome air conditioning, before finding the last free seat at the rear of the bus.

Spain was very different to the East End of London and Liam was fascinated at the alien surroundings. The coach made its way from the airport making stop after stop to drop off the small groups in the narrow streets, steering between haphazardly parked cars, until it began the final part of the journey. The driver now had the opportunity to make up speed as the almost empty coach sped along the motorway towards Marbella.

The tour guide sitting next to the driver, who she had

earlier introduced as Juan, excitedly pointed out a villa on the hillside. 'Ladies and gentlemen, on the right hand side you will see a mustard coloured villa with a large satellite dish.' The passengers craned their necks and strained until they could clearly see the villa. When they acknowledged it with a mixture of mumbles and animated reactions, she continued. 'That villa belonged to Ronnie Knight.' A few of them recognised the name, but Liam had met him personally on several occasions with his father when they were doing a bit of business together up West. Neither of them liked him but business was business. The guide continued. 'It beats me why he should have chosen to buy a place that overlooks a rubbish tip when there are so many other beautiful properties in the area.' She smiled and continued with noticeable enthusiasm in her voice. 'Of course he was removed from the villa by helicopter.' The passengers gasped as she continued. 'It landed in the grounds and the armed police took him away.' There were further gasps around the coach. She waited for silence and then continued. 'He was extradited back to England a few days later.'

Liam looked up towards the hills and tried to imagine the situation. *Would Ronnie have given himself up easily? Perhaps he would have when he realised he had been conned and could no longer stand the smell.*

The guide, a mine of information, continued in full flow. 'This area around Marbella is recognised as being the home of not only the rich and famous but also the rich and *infamous* criminals. They all come down here,' she shrieked excitedly. 'But it's not cheap.'

Liam sat back and suddenly realised why his father had paid for him to visit this particular place. Perhaps he believed that he would feel at home amongst his own kind?

The coach pulled into a layby and the guide announced Liam's hotel. 'Cortijo Blanco.' With only his holdall to carry he was the first off the coach and, followed her to the hotel reception where she checked him in. The receptionist gave him his key and a map of the complex, which she marked with a pen showing the location of his room in the adjoining grounds of Pueblo Andalus.

Liam started to walk but stopped to light his last English cigarette before making his way beneath the low arches and decorative metalwork wrought into swirls. He noticed the swallows as they flew acrobatically amongst the buildings and back up into the sky and into their mud nests clamped to the eaves of the buildings. Amongst the complex of buildings were cool shaded areas, tiled seats set beneath the cool arches, and a small bar under an old gnarled and contorted olive tree. The ground floor windows were protected by ornate metalwork and with his curiosity getting the better of him; he stopped and tugged at the bars. They were purely for cosmetic purposes and he knew that if he wished he would have been able to prise them away from the wall and easily get into the ground floor rooms. He smiled to himself as he continued past the painted decorative mouldings, around the double French doors and windows and the tiled external steps that lead to the larger suites with shiny black decorative metal handrails. Three cleaners in matching pink overalls and white aprons blindly pushed modern trolleys overloaded with clean crisp white sheets and pillow cases piled precariously above their heads. A much younger girl, dressed in the same uniform and carrying a soft straw-like brush, raised her head and smiled at Liam as he walked past. 'Hola,' she said. He acknowledged her with a smile before checking his map and continuing in the general direction of his room.

The arched opening on the ground floor was very low and he needed to bend his head as he walked beneath it, before climbing a circular staircase of a dozen uneven terracotta coloured tiled steps. Although his room was considered to be a deluxe, it was very basic with a low ceiling, twin beds, and an old painted pale green cane chair with one leg shorter than the others, and a scratched dressing table and wardrobe. Although it was luxury compared to any of his prison cells, strangely he felt comfortable. He rubbed his fingers along the walls; tracing the thick brush strokes that were clearly visible, before opening the French windows onto the small balcony that overlooked the square. The cool breeze that drifted into the room was a relief and very welcome from the intense heat outside. When he opened the second, much smaller window near his bed, the chorus from the families of sparrows and swallows nesting under the eaves, reverberated around the square into his room, creating a surreal fusion of happiness, excitement and freedom. Now slowly beginning to relax, he walked out on to the balcony and stood gazing down at the terracotta paved square. The unusually designed lights, which were partially obscured by the trees, would give minimal light to anyone walking through the courtyard late at night. The square was planted with large trees heavy with bright yellow lemons and oranges strategically positioned to give shade from the searing sun. Raised beds planted with cacti interspersed the orange and lemon trees while date trees towered high above the square. Pink Bougainville had been trained up around all the windows and doors interspersed with pots of red, pink and white geraniums, which filled every available space. The high sun cast deep shadows randomly across the square creating dark shaded corners, a refuge for the plants and anyone in need of cool shelter.

After deliberating for a few seconds he finally chose his bed and threw his holdall and jacket onto the other. After checking out the strangely modern bathroom, out of place in the olde worlde building, he lay on his bed and gazed up at the vaulted ceiling before finally falling asleep. He woke with a start and took several minutes to remember where he was and to recount his long eventful journey. He ran a bath and while he lay in the deep soapy water looked around at the room, fully tiled with large white ceramic tiles. Initially it reminded him of the clinic and, for the first time since leaving England, he shivered with fear. *Perhaps he was still there? Was he dreaming?*

The coloured hand painted border tiles and the marble floors helped him to appreciate that it was certainly not the clinic. When he opened the small window and looked out onto the variegated pale dappled Roman roof tiles, with weeds and small cacti growing wildly in the deep valleys, and the pure unspoilt cloudless blue sky, he knew that it was for real. At that moment he suddenly felt free and liberated. The peace and quiet was so different to the hours that he'd spent alone in his sterile infirmary room. This time the silence frightened him but he didn't know why.

He walked back into the bedroom and lay naked on the bed reading the contents of the blue wallet that Jackie had given him. He suddenly felt alone: perhaps he was concerned that he would head for the bar and the immediate downward spiral to despair. He checked his jacket pocket for his dark blue AA book, smiled to himself and returned to the bed clutching it tightly in his wet hand.

He must have fallen asleep again and woke to a darkening room. Feeling extremely hungry he smelt his dirty tee shirt and socks before putting them back on and setting off across the square in search of the restaurant and dinner.

The restaurant manager, a well-dressed middle-aged, dark-suited man, met him at the door, asked his room number then referred to his typed list. After checking off his room number with a yellow felt pen, he showed him to a table overlooking the tree lined swimming pool and the beautiful exotic flowering plants in the immaculate grounds. Proudly, Liam refused a glass of wine from the waiter who instead returned with a half-litre bottle of ice-cold water. After pouring him a glass he pointed towards the impressive buffet.

Liam was so hungry that he gorged himself on an unusual meal of pork in a creamy pepper sauce and two pieces of fried chicken, followed by a crème caramel, a bowl of melon and three large scoops of ice cream.

He paid the waiter for the bottle of water and left.

Feeling pleased with himself, he left the hotel grounds and walked down towards the sea, passing several noisy and inviting bars, but finally after running the gauntlet, he returned to his room and an early night.

The next morning, Liam sat in the restaurant eating his breakfast. He smiled to himself as he watched the elderly couple carefully cut and fill bread rolls and wrap them in serviettes. With military precision the woman slipped the food unnoticed into her large handbag.

He finished his breakfast and walked to reception where he

made several attempts to get through to the telephone number that his father had given him. When he eventually did, much to his surprise, a Spanish woman answered in a brusque voice. Nervously, Liam asked for Freddie.

'Quien es?' snapped the Spanish woman.

He repeated his wish to speak to Freddie several times until she eventually spoke to him in English. 'Wait a moment, will you please?' she said.

Before he had time to reply she put down the phone and he could hear her shouting across the room. Heavy footsteps approached and at last he heard an English voice.

'Hello, who is it?' enquired the Englishman, at the other end.

'Is that Freddie?' asked a relieved Liam.

'Who wants to know?' questioned the Englishman.

Liam blurted out his reply. 'This is Liam, Jimmy Reilly's boy, he told me to call you.'

Much to his relief, Freddie knew who Liam was. 'I'm sorry son – but you can never be too careful over 'ere.' Freddie coughed loudly and finally regaining his breath continued. 'Where ya stayin'?'

Liam told him and they agreed to meet at three o'clock that afternoon.

Liam looked at his watch and, realising that he had several hours to kill, collected a towel from his room, crossed the tarmac road, stripped off, and lay on a sunbed beside the swimming pool. It was the first time since he was a little boy, when he fished in the many tributaries of the Thames, that he had ever been near water. Since then he had not had the opportunity because he was either in a pub or in prison. He looked up at the taller palm leaves creating amazing shadows and a strange sound as the wind tugged noisily at their extended leaves. A sparrow flew over the pool, its underbelly and wings a pale blue, reflecting from the swimming pool below it. A lone cabbage white butterfly flew amongst the trees and shrubs that surrounded the pool looking for somewhere to land and lay her eggs. Liam lay back and looked around at a proud father and two little girls who threw their plastic toys into the pool and took it in turns to "catch" them with their fishing nets.

Liam fell asleep and was woken by the massed French tourists who were noisily taking part in a quiz, while others played Scrabble at the opposite end of the pool on a huge Velcro board. He glanced at his watch. It was two o'clock. He stretched his arms and legs before sitting up. He grabbed his jeans and tee shirt and picked up his shoes. It was a mistake. The tarmac was very hot and he was left with no alternative but to dance erratically across the road before rushing up to his room for a shower.

A pair of ring necked doves flew onto his balcony looking for food and, finding nothing, they flew off again. Liam took a packet of biscuits from the side of his bed, broke up several of them, and spread the crumbs around him and sat back motionless in his chair. Immediately the same two doves flew down and picked at the crumbs until they had eaten them all. It was the closest Liam had ever been to nature and anything so exotic.

At five to three Liam walked out into the hotel car park. The searing heat pumped the blood through his whole body and he desperately needed respite. He walked back towards the hotel entrance and took shelter beneath the tall date and palm trees that had sprouted sprays of bright orange clumps of next season's fruit.

At three o'clock precisely a shiny black Mercedes saloon 450 SL swept silently in off the dual carriageway. The electric tinted passenger window slid down silently to reveal Freddie, a middle-aged balding, grey-haired man, with a short pony-tail, sitting majestically in the passenger seat. The pretty dark-haired woman sitting next to him drove the car towards Liam and stopped a few inches from his knees.

Freddie spoke assertively. 'Jimmy's boy?' Liam nodded. 'Git in, and we can get a move on.'

Liam, relieved at last to be able to escape from the hot sun and to meet a fellow Englishman, smiled, opened the rear door and slid noisily along the dark blue leather seat. As the car pulled out of the car park Freddie turned around to observe his passenger and, with the broadest of smiles, exposed an almost perfect set of white false teeth. He looked Liam up and down before turning to introduce his female driver. 'This is Juanita.' He smiled. 'She does everyfing for me, ya know.' He chuckled before he continued. 'And I never need to ask.' Freddie squeezed her right leg and, after briefly blushing with embarrassment, she regained her composure and tossed her long dark hair back with her left hand.

'Nice,' said Liam, as he nodded his understanding. He looked into the driver's mirror and when he saw that Juanita was staring back at him he smiled to her. 'Pleased to meet you,' he said, aiming his words at the mirror.

She returned his smile and flicked at the indicator. She accelerated hard overtaking a row of fast moving cars and Liam fell back into his seat.

After driving a few kilometres down the dual carriageway Freddie turned, stared at Liam, and screwed up his face. 'Wot the fuck has 'appened to you?'

'Ah, a bit of sunburn,' lied Liam. His head was thumping, his whole body was burning, and he felt sick.

Freddie pushed a cigar between his dry wrinkled lips and flicked the electric car lighter, but with the unlit cigar protruding from his mouth, laughed loudly and nudged Juanita. 'You can always tell the tourist over 'ere.' He chuckled to himself as he shook his head. 'They never learn.' After finally lighting the cigar, he opened the glove compartment, took out a small bottle of Ambre Solaire and threw it blindly in Liam's direction. 'Put that on the next time you sit out in the sun.' He laughed loudly. 'You 'ad better take more care; everybody's got fuckin' skin cancer these days.' He then removed a baseball cap from the glove compartment and threw it over his shoulder at Liam. 'You may as well have this too. Laurie won't be needing it anymore.'

Liam caught it and pulled it on.

Juanita watched him closely in the mirror and smiled back at him. 'It suits to you.'

Liam accepted the compliment, pushed himself back in the seat and tried to take everything in.

No one spoke for the remainder of the journey. They stopped briefly for fuel, at a Repsol garage. Juanita jumped out of the car, filled the tank and paid in cash. The remainder of the journey was uneventful but as they passed the raised Bull Ring Casino, Freddie became animated as he checked his thinning hair and tugged at his shirt.

A few minutes later the Mercedes swept into the car park of the Hospital Del Sol. Juanita drove as near to the front entrance as she could and parked in a space designated "privado."

The three of them walked along identical corridors until they reached the private rooms. The change was incredible. Vases overflowed with exotic flowers and filled every corner of the waiting area. On one side an elegantly dressed young lady stood behind a glass cabinet filled with trays of complimentary cakes and chocolate, and a shiny chrome coffee machine. They ignored her as they walked into Laurie's private suite and stood at his bedside. Laurie had been paralysed following a second stroke and could only blink his acknowledgement of Freddie.

Freddie moved close to Laurie before he spoke softly in his left ear. 'Hello, Laurie, me old mate. How are ya?' he said, with a forced smile.

Laurie blinked again and tried to raise his bony heavily veined right hand. The loose flabby skin was covered in liver spots that spread the whole length of his arms.

'Do ya know who this is 'ere?' asked Freddie, pointing at Liam. There was no reaction from Laurie. 'It's Jimmy's lad.' Freddie tapped Laurie's bony shoulder. 'Yer know – Jimmy Reilly?' He laughed loudly. 'You remember Liam don't ya?' There was no response and he continued. 'They soon grow up don't dey?'

Laurie tried to move but couldn't.

Freddie pulled a cheque book from his pocket and moved even closer to Laurie and held it up as close to his face as possible. 'We need to tidy up a few fings, Laurie. You alright with that . . . eh?'

There was no reply. Freddie repeated himself and Laurie blinked his response.

Freddie reached across and helped Laurie to sign five cheques. Once they were signed, he smiled and slipped the cheque book back into his pocket. He reached across and took the ludicrously large bunch of flowers from Juanita and placed them on Laurie's bed and reached down and made an attempt to shake Freddie's limp hand.

'Look after yerself, eh Laurie? You'll soon be out of 'ere,' he lied.

Laurie closed his eyes and went back to sleep.

They drove into Marbella and the Banco de Bilbao and paid two cheques into Jimmy's English account and the other three into Freddie's Swiss account. They waited patiently for more than an hour while Juanita had the cheques express cleared. They followed that with a celebratory lunch at Bar La Torre, at the tip of Puerto Banus harbour, a local watering hole for the fishermen and charter crew hands. Liam felt at home in the noisy dimly lit bar. No one took any notice of him and thankfully there were no tourists. He stubbed out his cigarette and, realising that it was his last one, tapped the table nervously as he became more and more agitated. Juanita noticed and asked the waiter for a packet of Ducados. Liam found it hard to get used to them, comparing each drag to his B and H, but he liked the feel of the soft packet, and after smoking throughout the meal he began to develop a taste for them.

During the main course of fillet steak, chips and a side salad, Freddie's mobile bleeped and, as always, Juanita answered and listened intently, before replying to the caller in Spanish. Freddie looked proudly on and winked to Liam. Juanita closed the flip of the Motorola and in a soft voice spoke to her boss.

'Laurie . . . ha muerto. Laurie . . . he has died . . .'

Freddie turned to Liam and smiled broadly. 'Perfect timin', son. It's a good job ya came when ya did.' He slapped Liam hard on his sunburned shoulder. Liam flinched and shrugged him off. Freddie ignored Liam's reaction and continued. 'Jimmy *will* fank ya for this.' Freddie raised both of his hands triumphantly, called over the wine waiter, and asked Juanita to order a nice bottle of Champagne. When the waiter appeared with the bottle of Montrachet and three ornate champagne glasses on a tray he slipped into his well-rehearsed theatrical performance of showing Freddie the label before letting him feel the temperature of the bottle. Upon Freddie's nod of approval, he undid the foil and released the cork with a loud pop. He poured the chilled champagne into the glasses and passed them around. Freddie raised his glass, followed by Juanita. Liam thanked him but pushed the delicately fluted glass away. Freddie's face reddened and he brought his fist down so heavily onto the table that the restaurant immediately fell silent. Juanita looked around and nervously stood up, raised her glass and spoke a few words in Spanish. It had the desired effect and immediately Freddie's outburst was forgotten as everyone clapped and cheered, and the excited gossip returned to the bar. Freddie clearly irritated by Liam's rebuttal to drink, poured and swallowed another glass of champagne. After his third glass he suddenly remembered what Jimmy had told him and accepted Liam's reluctance to drink. He moved close to Liam and lowered his voice. 'Sorry, son,' he said, through clenched teeth. 'I forgot.' He curled his lip in a half smile. 'Jimmy did tell me about your . . .' He faked a cough, paused briefly and continued in an apathetic tone. 'Your little problem.'

'It's more than a fucking problem! It nearly killed me!' screamed Liam, indignantly.

Freddie took a huge slug of the champagne and emptied the glass before he replied with a wry smile. 'Course, son.' He pretended to clear his throat again before he continued in a subdued voice. 'I understand.'

Freddie's half-hearted and insincere response annoyed Liam but he didn't care. No one understood his problem, except other alcoholics. He pushed his cigarette hard into the ash tray, twisted it forcefully and stood up. 'I need some fresh air,' he said. He smiled at Juanita and then turned to Freddie. 'I'm pleased it's worked out for you, Freddie. See yer.'

Juanita made to stand but Freddie touched the back of her hand, she smiled and slid subserviently back into her chair. 'Liam, you can take a taxi on the promenade,' she said, softly.

'No problem – I'll walk. I need the exercise.' He took a huge drag on his cigarette and disappeared through the smoke.

Liam arrived at his hotel just as the restaurant was serving the last sitting of the evening. After the ritual of signing in with the restaurant manager he sat at his table. He was still hungry and ate two pieces of chocolate gateaux with three scoops of ice cream. He finished his second bottle of water, left the restaurant and walked down to the deserted beach. He stood on the dark, dirty sand of the beach used mostly by the locals and looked down the coast towards Gibraltar. Thick dark clouds slowly engulfed the rock, which appeared to jut mysteriously out of the sea. The obscure random gaps in the clouds overhead were mirrored by azure shapes in the sea. They quickly disappeared and, within seconds, fork lightning lit up the dark sky in front of him followed by thunder that boomed across the sea. As the torrential rain hammered onto his body he raced towards the only shelter on the beach, an upturned boat, and slid beneath it. He shivered as he waited for the rain to stop, and as the sky cleared and the full moon lit up the beach, he walked slowly back to his hotel room.

The next morning he walked to the marina at Puerto Banus, where the multi-million pound yachts took his breath away. As he sat drinking coffee outside the Sinatra Bar, next to the Salduba Pub, in Muelle Ribera, he realised that he was no more than a petty thief compared to the headline criminals – the sheer decadence of their lifestyle and their luxurious super yachts.

He sat deep in thought and tried to take it all in.

'Hello,' said the female voice behind him.

Liam was startled and his first reaction was to reach into his pocket for his knife. He shook his head and sighed when he realised where he was and, that except for a handful of pesetas, his pocket was empty. He looked up into the sun and after shielding his eyes saw Jackie standing on the road in front of the bar.

'Oh hello,' he replied, relieved but annoyed at his vulnerability.

'Where were you?' she asked.

Liam looked at her blankly. 'When?'

'You didn't come to the meeting.'

Liam thought for a second and blushed. He had no idea what she was talking about but nevertheless he replied. 'Sorry.' He looked away from her while he tried to remember. He didn't, so he continued. 'It completely slipped my mind,' he lied.

She stood looking down at him waiting for him to invite her to sit down but, faced with silence, she asked him. 'May I sit down?'

'Of course you can,' he said, as he pulled out a chair from under the table. 'Coffee?'

'I'd prefer something stronger,' she said.

Liam grabbed the nearest waiter's attention and waited. Speaking in fluent Spanish Jackie ordered a Rioja. But as the waiter began to walk away she called him back and questioned Liam. 'Aren't you having one?'

Liam cleared his throat nervously. 'No thanks . . . I don't drink,' he stuttered. 'Www . . . well I mean . . . I *do* drink . . . but *not* alcohol.'

The waiter could see that other customers were becoming impatient and wanted to move on.

Liam looked up at him. 'I'll have another coffee, mate.'

The waiter frowned and rushed off towards the bar.

It was clear that Jackie respected Liam's honesty; she smiled and changed the subject. 'It's a beautiful day?'

'Yeah, it certainly beats the East End . . .' he looked around, 'but then anything beats that these days.'

The waiter returned with their drinks and placed them on the table.

Jackie waited for him to walk away before speaking. 'So, how come you're here in Spain on your own?'

Liam emptied three sugar sachets into his cup and sipped at his coffee. 'I needed a break and some sun,' he lied.

Jackie finished her Rioja and smiled at Liam. 'Shall we go for lunch?' Before Liam could answer she continued. 'I know this wonderful beach café. A well-kept Spanish secret,' she said.

Liam nodded.

Jackie checked the bill and left the money on a saucer and they walked to her open-top, sign-written, Seat. She drove down the dual carriageway towards Gibraltar until she reached the coast road and drove across the beach to a small shack a few metres from the sea. 'Isn't it lovely?' she asked, as she tugged at Liam's hand.

'Now you've seen Spain wouldn't you like to live here?' she asked.

Liam explained to Jackie there is no way that he could afford or would wish to live in this area. He couldn't understand the language and it made him feel very uncomfortable.

After lunch she ordered tea for two.

The waiter brought two cups, a teapot, milk and sugar.

Liam looked at Jackie. 'What's the difference between tea for one and tea for two? The pot's the same size?' he said, as he opened the pot and stirred it.

Jackie looked at him and smiled. 'It's simple; one or two tea bags.'

CHAPTER SIX

When You're Dead And Gone

Laurie's funeral took place thirty kilometres from Malaga International airport in La Iglesia de la Inmaculada, a recently restored church that nestled amongst the cobbled streets in the upper part of the "white" Andalucian village of Mijas Pueblo. The village overlooked the mass of hotels on Mijas Costa far below them. As well as a few local Spanish people, English criminals made up the majority of the congregation, along with criminals from across mainland Europe and a handful from Eastern Europe. The local police took more than a passing interest in the members of the congregation but did not interfere except to take photographs of everyone that attended.

Freddie wore a bright red polo shirt, black Italian styled trousers and a short black leather jacket, while Juanita wore a smart black knitted dress with minute hand-sewn pink flowers and a grey shawl. Liam wore the same jeans and denim shirt he had travelled in.

Freddie took a few minutes to shake everyone's hand enthusiastically and to introduce Liam to some of Laurie's closest partners in crime. Many of them saw the funeral as more of a get-together and celebration rather than a funeral with new deals being done before they left the church to go their separate ways.

Following the church service, the coffin was loaded into a black van and driven into the city and the crematorium in Velez, Malaga. Freddie, Juanita and Liam followed at a distance as did some of the local people who had worked for Laurie. Juanita parked up and followed the locals through a side door into a long narrow room with three rows of what were little more than timber bench seats. The locals raced to get the front row so Juanita, Freddie and Liam sat in the second row. The seats faced a window which ran the full length of one wall, which was veiled with pale pink curtains. The curtains slowly opened to reveal Laurie's ornate coffin, with a large crucifix and a solitary wreath on top supported on a pair of rusty trestles. Two men in pale blue overalls stood behind the coffin and, ignoring the onlookers, picked up two axes and began to chop haphazardly at both ends of the coffin until it caved in and started to disintegrate. Freddie and Liam watched in sheer horror as the men continued to smash indiscriminately at the coffin. He turned to Liam. 'Fuck me,' he mouthed.

In sheer disbelief at what was unfolding in front of him, an ashen faced Liam shook his head wildly.

One of the men opened the furnace door while the other man removed the crucifix and wreath, throwing them to one side. Together they grabbed at the riven coffin and pushed it into the blazing furnace. Everyone looked on as the flames licked around the decimated coffin before the two men slammed the metal doors shut.

'Barbaric bastards!' raged Liam. 'How can they treat a human being like that?'

'I don't want to stay *here* to die and be treated like that,' mumbled Freddie, traumatised by what he had just witnessed.

Juanita turned to him and stroked his grey veiny hands. 'It's OK. Don't worry, Freddie. I will take care of it,' she said, as she smiled reassuringly. 'We have some lunch.'

'Lunch,' mouthed Freddie.

Freddie's eyes locked on hers and he made a futile attempt to hide the terror.

She smiled and spoke softly. 'It is OK.' Freddie forced a smile but it soon disappeared as Juanita continued. 'We come back . . . in two hours . . . for the ashes . . . yeas?'

'Wha . . . ?' His contorted face emphasised his abject horror at the thought.

Liam and Freddie walked out in silence, thinking their own thoughts, and finding it hard to comprehend what they had just witnessed.

Death duties or inheritance tax in Spain started at ten thousand pounds and thereafter thirty-five percent, so in order to clear Laurie's estate they visited Mauricio Pardo, a well-known Notario, whose offices were in the centre of Marbella in Avenida Ricardo, Soriano 22. After parking the Mercedes in the underground car park they crossed Celle Juan Ramon Jimenez and took the lift up to the open plan offices. The dull yellow marble floor, two tone yellow emulsioned walls and white ceiling tiles were a stark contrast to the intricate ceiling lights, the pale orange fabric covered chairs and several matching settees and black tables with black ceramic table lights. To Liam it felt as though it was a con and everything could have been moved out in a moment's notice. Everyone smoked and Liam joined them, adding to the already smoke laden air. Little or no attention had been paid to the nondescript pictures on every wall, which were left oddly crooked. Some rooms had wooden doors while others had obscure glazed panels suspended in mid-air above the openings. Most of the employees wore jeans and casual tops. There was no defined reception area and people were milling around everywhere: organised chaos. On one desk were various silver stampers which were picked up, used and replaced for the next person to grab. Each time they were used handfuls of cash changed hands and it was immediately slipped into the secretary's drawer. A fat man sat awkwardly on the opposite side of the typist's desk smoking a cigar and filling in forms as the smoke engulfed him.

Freddie like so many of the obvious thugs was joined by his lawyer. They stood amongst the crowd of people before being greeted by the Notario with an insincere smile and hearty handshake and ushered into a small panelled room.

Juanita opened her huge designer leather handbag and flicked through the bundles of pesetas that filled much of it. She checked it and handed over a thick wad of high value notes. The Notario then checked it, shook his head and grinned at Juanita. Juanita gave him a confident wave to check it again. He did and after placing a think elastic band around it, looked up and gave her a broad smile, exposing his gold teeth. He took a triplicate book from the drawer, completed the various sections, stamped it, tore out the top sheet and handed it to Juanita. He tore off the first carbon copy and forced it beneath the elastic band. He pushed himself back in his chair and called out. A few seconds later a young smartly dressed girl raced over and waited while he explained to her what he wanted, before handing over the money.

Liam was absolutely dumbstruck that so much money was passed freely and openly around the crowded open plan office. His imagination raced. *What an opportunity for a peach of a robbery?*

Juanita regained Liam's attention and, following a round of ritualistic back slaps and handshakes, the three of them left the office.

Juanita was aware that Liam didn't understand what had happened and, once they were in the privacy of the lift, she reached into her cavernous and almost empty bag. She pulled out the stamped receipt and held it in front of her. 'Without *this* paper,' she said, raising her voice as she waved the paper vigorously in front of him. 'In a few days the government will take away Laurie's home . . .' she said, while she slipped the receipt carefully into the zipped pocket in her bag. She took a deep breath and continued, her voice trembling with emotion. 'Laurie has some friends and relatives that live in there.' Her expression changed and she frowned at Liam. 'Tú entiendes?' she said, tilting her head to one side while she waited for his response.

Liam mumbled. 'Um . . .' He shook his head clearly confused by it all.

As they walked to the car Freddie whispered to Liam. 'The police and government don't give a fuck if any bastard brings in cash providing it's less than £250,000 in any one go.' He sniggered to himself. 'Have you ever heard anything so fucking crazy?' His laugh grew louder. 'A quarter of a fucking mill, can you believe that?' he said, as he gasped for breath.

'The problem is they won't let you take it out. The bastards!' he screamed.

The next morning Liam had breakfast and went back to his room, flung open the French windows and lay on the bed. For once he relished the peace, and the natural sounds around him, and he fell into a light sleep. The telephone on his bedside table rang. He looked at it and wondered who the hell was calling him? Reluctantly he answered it in an almost inaudible voice. 'Hello,' he said.

"Hi, Liam how are you?' asked the female voice.

"Fine,' he said. He pulled the phone away from his ear and thought before he continued. 'Who is it?'

The female caller laughed as she spoke. 'It's Juanita, of course.' She muttered a few words in Spanish as she laughed a long extended laugh. 'Would you like to come for a drive?'

Liam didn't answer.

'You and myself – we go for a drive. I will show you the real Espana.'

'OK,' replied Liam indifferently.

'I come in twenty minutes . . . Please be ready.'

Liam washed, cleaned his teeth and walked across to reception.

Juanita arrived in fifteen minutes. The white Mercedes sports car skidded to a stop a few inches from Liam's feet.

'Come on – get in,' she exclaimed excitedly.

Liam couldn't fail to notice that she was a totally different person. She was vibrant and looked incredibly sexy in her figure-hugging white vest and tight fitting red shorts. Juanita looked up at the sun. 'It will be very hot today.' Without warning, she leaned forward, reached across to the glove compartment in front of Liam and pushed her breasts into Liam's chest. He pulled himself as far back as he could but, with the seat belt restricting him he couldn't help but be aroused as her firm breasts were thrust into him. She pulled out a baseball cap and handed it to him and with the broadest of grins, she spoke. 'You should put this on, yeas.'

Liam did as she asked and after fiddling with his seat belt pushed himself deep into the leather seat. 'Is this your car?' he asked.

'No, it is Laurie's.' She waited for a reaction. There was none and she continued but her mood changed. 'We will sell it . . .' She paused and stroked the steering wheel. 'Tomorrow . . . triste eh?

Liam looked at her and shrugged his shoulders.

Juanita drove along the dual carriageway past Marbella and through what was a chaotic Malaga, then northerly up the coast along the E15 to Torrox Costa. The roads were deserted and the views fantastic. It was an unspoiled Spain that Liam had no idea existed. Juanita turned off the E15 onto a narrow road that ran along the coast. On the other side of the road was mile after mile of plastic covered fields. 'What the fuck is all that?' asked Liam.

'Tomatoes – they grow much of the tomatoes here,' she said proudly.

Liam nodded and continued to stare out in disbelief at the never ending fields of plastic greenhouses.

When they reached Torrox Costa, Juanita turned away from the coast, drove inland up the narrow winding mountain road, and into the outskirts of Torrox Pueblo. She drove through the old Spanish town until she reached an ill-defined cross-road and pulled into a dusty layby near the school. She sat in silence and looked up at a property that stretched a hundred or so metres across the mountainside.

She took a huge breath before she turned and looked directly at Liam. She didn't try to hide the tears while she spoke. 'Dis is where my mama y papa lived. This was der casa, der home.'

Liam gave a slow reserved nod.

She leaned forward, took a tissue for the glove compartment and wiped her eyes. 'They died in an accident. How you say? A 'it and run.'

Liam nodded and mumbled his response. 'Um'.

'The do never catch the driver.' She paused. 'The polis think he was a *tourist* in a rental car . . .'

Liam felt guilty at being English and that was compounded further when a car, music blasting out and full of young men, hammered around the corner in a hire car, sending clouds of dust into the air.

Juanita turned to Liam. 'Bastardos!' she screamed. 'Do you see what I mean?' She fired up the engine and drove down the hill and pulled up outside a pair of open decorative metal gates. 'Come – I will show you . . .' She slammed the car door and walked towards the open gates. It only took a few minutes for Liam to realise that it was a cemetery but unlike anything he had ever seen. Row upon row of identical concrete crypts, two feet square, four rows high, spread across the hillside. Some of the newer graves had framed colour photographs, of the person inside, on the front of them. Others had fresh flowers in tiny vases. The older crypts stood out with faded photographs and sun baked distorted plastic flowers, which were almost unrecognisable. Small groups of people, mostly women, stood at the bizarre graves and affectionately rubbed at the photographs before they replaced the shrivelled flowers.

Juanita made her way to the far end of the cemetery and stopped to pray at two graves. On each of them were the identical photographs of two young people: her mother and father. Her hands shook as she pointed at the concrete crypts. 'Do you know in five years they will be removed!' she shrieked. 'We cannot buy dis!'

Liam took his time to look at the masses of graves around him. Many of them were empty. The contents cleared and relocated to a common burial ground. Liam moved closer and gazed at the photograph of Juanita's mother and father who were smiling at the camera. He guessed they had been in their late forties. He lowered his head, shuddered and took a deep breath. Juanita bowed her head and murmured prayers before she turned away and placed her arm around Liam's waist. They walked slowly towards the gates and as they reached the car she turned to face him and threw her arms around his neck. He could feel her firm breasts and this time he didn't want to hide his feelings. She felt him and kissed him gently on the cheek. 'Thank you,' she said softly.

'I'm so sorry,' he said.

She reflected before she spoke. 'I know . . . but it happens.' She wiped at her eyes. 'But why to my family? Eh?'

Juanita accelerated past the renovated houses, pavements and roads of the mountain town, upgraded with Euro money, and drove deep into the countryside until they reached a lemon grove that stretched across acre upon acre of hillside. She drove effortlessly between the terraces until she reached an area of the densest trees offering shelter from the searing heat of the afternoon sun. She turned off the engine, flicked the CD player, and gentle music filled the silence. She slipped out of the car, opened the boot, removed a huge blanket and spread it on the ground behind the car. She closed the boot, leaned against it, flicked at her long dark hair, pulled it across her almost naked shoulders and gazed down the valley. Liam joined her, placed his arms around her waist, pushed himself into her back and kissed her neck. She wiggled her waist until he reached up inside her vest and gently caressed her firm breasts. She giggled as he squeezed her pert nipples between his fingers and pushed his hard penis between her legs. He loosened her shorts and she let them slide down her tanned legs and onto the dry earth. He kicked off his shoes, pulled off his jeans and pants and fondled her naked buttocks. He kissed her neck alternating from side to side until she writhed with pleasure. Without turning she pushed a condom into his palm and helped him to slide it onto his now throbbing erect penis. As he entered her she moaned with pleasure as their bodies writhed and gyrated. Minutes later they lay naked on the blanket. The warm breeze gently swept across their still pulsing sweaty bodies while occasionally fingers of sunlight broke through the branches onto their naked skin. Liam lay with his eyes closed and stroked Juanita's flat stomach with one hand and ran his fingers gently across her still heaving breasts with the other. He finally opened his eyes, lit a cigarette and gazed up at the branches above him laden with ripening lemons. He grabbed at the nearest lemon and squeezed it gently in his left hand and smiled as he slowly began to comprehend what was a totally surreal experience in an alien world.

While Juanita concentrated as she drove along the narrow winding mountain road, down to the coast and in to Nerja, Liam pushed himself into his seat and tried to hold on to the moment for a little while longer. Juanita turned into a car park filled with locally registered cars and Liam slid the lemon into the door pocket before leaving the car.

She led Liam into the Bridge Bar, somewhere she had visited regularly with her family. The middle-aged owner recognised her immediately. He rushed towards her and hugged and kissed her. Clutching her hand tightly he guided her to the rear of the bar and the only empty table before he finally acknowledged Liam with a knowing smile. While the bar buzzed with the sound of friendly and excitable locals enjoying their lunch Liam ate in silence and waited for Juanita to speak to him. She didn't speak until the owner brought them coffee. She sighed heavily as she brushed the invisible crumbs from the check table cloth. 'Do you know *they* came here t . . . ?' She looked at Liam and waited for him to finish the sentence for her. He had been taken aback, surprised that she seemed to have ignored what had happened less than an hour earlier.

He shrugged his shoulders and shook his head before speaking. 'Retire?' he said, casually.

She smiled back at him. 'Yes.' She nodded emphatically. 'To retire. They worked so hard with their lives . . .' she clawed wildly at the table cloth, 'they sold their business . . . and . . .' She wiped at her dewy eyes with the serviette. 'Then,' she sighed, 'they are murdered!'

The journey back to Cortijo Blanco was made to the music of the *Gypsy Kings*. As Juanita drove into the hotel car park Liam had one burning question that he had to ask and suddenly blurted it out. 'Why did we use a condom?'

She looked at him, squeezed his hand and laughed loudly. 'Do you think that Freddie could make a baby with me?'

Liam blushed and shook his head with embarrassment as he closed the car door.

Juanita reached out and ran her hand sensuously down his arm and squeezed his fingers before releasing them. She spoke in almost a whisper. 'Despedida, Liam.'

Liam took his time and walked slowly towards the hotel reception. When he reached the entrance Juanita called out to him. He smiled expectantly before turning and rushing back to the car. He leaned forward to kiss her but she gently pushed him away. 'You forgot dis,' she said, handing him the lemon.

He looked at her forlornly and suddenly felt tearful.

Juanita saw that Liam was hurt but knew they could never be together. She was enjoying her rich lifestyle too much. She gave him a broad smile exposing her perfect teeth and spoke softly. 'Goodbye, Liam,' she said.

She flicked her hair over her shoulder, turned her head, reversed out of the car park and accelerated hard.

Liam was confused and found it hard to come to terms with his feelings. He stood in the hot sun, subconsciously rolling the lemon in his palm, watching the white Mercedes until it was out of sight, and wondered if he would ever see her again.

CHAPTER SEVEN

Trains And Boats And Planes

When Liam returned to England it was clear to his father and his fellow villains that they were unable to protect him any longer. Jimmy had seen his family disintegrate in front of him and continued to blame himself. His eldest son was fast becoming a liability and, following a near miss by a crow bar wielding hit man, Jimmy knew that Liam could never return to the family home.

Jimmy arrived at Liam's flat and looked furtively around before he knocked on the door. Liam took a while to answer and when he did it was obvious to Jimmy he had still been in bed. 'Don't you know it's three o' clock?' asked his father. Liam gave him a blank look and shook his head. His father continued. 'Come on, get yer coat on. Let's go fer a walk.'

As they walked the short distance to Victoria Park, they both appreciated there was little to discuss and their conversation soon degenerated to little more than small talk. The park was deserted except for two young boys fishing in the lake.

Jimmy looked across at them. 'The only fing they'll catch there is a feckin' cold.'

Liam smiled and nodded as he remembered himself doing the same thing years earlier. He lit a cigarette and unusually Jimmy reached out for one. 'You really want one of these? You know it'll kill yer,' said Liam.

Jimmy put the cigarette to his mouth and waited for a light from Liam. He took several drags and coughed uncomfortably until he managed to clear his throat. 'Ya know yer can't stay here no more? You've become a liability, son. It's too late yer know.'

Liam looked at him, shook his head and mumbled. 'Erm . . . I know.'

Jimmy looked at the cigarette in disgust and wondered why the hell he had even asked for it. 'Well, are you going back?' he asked.

'To Spain?' asked Liam. He shook his head. 'No. I could never afford to live over there, and anyway – I don't like the sodding heat. The bastards are leading such shit lives: everyone's trying to rip everybody else off . . .'

'So what's new, son? We all live in a shadow.'

'Well it's not for me.' Liam thought back to the criminals in the lawyer's office in Spain. 'They're all robbin' bastards,' he cursed. 'Nothing more than bandits . . . ?'

His father's mood changed. 'You *know* you can't stay round 'ere. Get away for a while and let things cool down.' He sensed Liam's reluctance. 'There's plenty of cash . . . thanks to you and Laurie,' said Jimmy, with a wide grin.

Liam nodded. 'I know,' he said, his voice fading. He coughed, lit another cigarette from the one in his mouth and took two huge drags before he continued. 'Like where?' He turned away from his father and dug his heals into the grassy bank and kicked the mud across the path. 'You know I'm no good with that foreign patter.'

'What about Holland – or Germany? I've still got a few contacts over there and they all speak English.'

'What the fuck? Even if I do consider it, I wanna start again.' Liam looked at his father and, seeing that he was offended, smiled and lowered his voice. 'I'm sorry dad . . . but . . . ya know.' He paused. 'I need to make it for myself, and who knows . . . the next time I might make something of it?'

Jimmy allowed Liam a token smile and pulled at his arm. 'Alright, son, I understand. But if you need any help . . . make sure you ask, right?'

Liam looked hard at his father and for the first time realised that he was now looking at an old man. He reassured his father by pressing his hand firmly and smiling at the same time. 'Course I will,' he said, reluctantly.

Tommy spent several hours watching the hospital staff car park making notes, carefully checking the time and writing it down on a scrap of paper, as he made his plans for the following night.

The next evening he took refuge under a large oak tree on the edge of the same car park and tried to protect himself from the pouring rain while he waited for a car befitting the importance of his passenger. He checked his watch and within a few minutes a car swerved into the car park, pulled in and parked out of site of the CCTV cameras. The young doctor locked it and ran towards the staff entrance. Within a split second Tommy was in the driving seat. He confidently knew he had at least eight to ten hours. He thought it was better to "borrow" a car than to steal it and he would have it back before the owner needed it, and hopefully none the wiser. A couple of hundred miles would have been added to the clock and perhaps a speeding ticket. The owner would get away with that: the unsuspecting doctor had been on duty the whole time and could prove it. Tommy having asked to drive Liam to Dover stole something special, a BMW 5 Series Convertible, from the private car park. They drove towards Dover through the heavy rain which beat down incessantly onto the canvas roof of the car. The occasional flash of lightning on the horizon initiated the need for them to speak to each other, but for most of the journey they sat silently thinking their own thoughts that they dearly wished to say, but for fear of causing an argument, decided to remain silent.

Tommy was prepared to plead with Liam to let him go with him and share his adventure. Tommy had a reason: he wondered how he was going to survive without his idol. While Liam worried in silence as to how he would survive without a drink.

Liam finally broke the painful silence. 'You know I'd give everything to take the train back.'

Tommy looked at him blankly and confused. 'What's all this about a train?'

Liam pulled his lips tightly together, dropped his shoulders and let out a huge sigh. 'I mean . . .' He paused, stretched his arms above his head and tugged violently at his hair. 'If I could take the train back in time I reckon I'd do it. I fucked up my own life and *everyone* around me.' He paused. 'Too many people for much too long . . .'

Tommy cut him short and shouted at his brother. 'I can't

believe you said that! You're a fuckin' hero! You're smart!' He thought for a second and continued. 'You've got it all!'

'No, that's where you're wrong. Can't you see? Use your fucking eyes, I had it *all* but now I've fucking lost *it* all.' Liam shook his head slowly as he continued. 'You can't possibly imagine what that feels like.'

Tommy was affected by Liam's honesty but didn't want to believe it. He'd never heard his elder brother talk like that before and it hurt. 'You've been down before and you always come back. Remember when you got shafted on that building society robbery? You were out within three weeks and – you still kept your cut of the job.'

'Tommy, *please* don't fall for that shit!' screamed Liam, shaking his head. 'They had to pay me or dad would have shot their knee caps off. It wasn't me they were afraid of it was our dad, he's twice the man I'll ever be.'

Not wanting to give Liam the opportunity to interrupt him, Tommy spoke without taking a breath. 'Don't say that Li please don't talk like that. You'll be back . . . just you see, you *will* be back. No one will ever put you down. I'll see to that.'

Liam laughed as he patted Tommy on the shoulder. 'Course you will.'

Tommy gunned the accelerator and drove the shiny convertible as close as was feasibly possible to the main terminal building. He reached around to the rear seat, grabbed the designer leather jacket left by the car's owner, and sat holding it in his hand. 'Go on have it. If you don't I'll only flog it, so you may as well.' Liam hesitated for a second and looked at it. 'Go on.'

Liam grabbed it firmly, tore it away from his brother and hung it across his bag.

The rain eased off and Liam seized the moment. 'See ya bruv, make sure you take care of things for me. Won't ya?'

Tommy smiled. 'Sure I will,' he said, without attempting to hide his total lack of conviction.

Liam squeezed Tommy's arm and pushed himself away. 'Yeah,' said Liam, with a shrug. He pushed himself out of the car and although the rain was again torrential he didn't consider covering his head, as he raced towards the welcoming front doors. He didn't look back because he didn't want his younger brother to see that he was crying. But in the darkness Tommy had failed to hold back his own tears. They were both crying. Tommy decided to wait until the ferry sailed and waited nervously in the car as the rain became even heavier and the storm moved in off the sea directly above the docks.

Liam ran out of the booking office and across to the car, he ripped the door open and jumped inside slamming the door hard behind him.

Tommy stared at him expectantly and struggled to complete his question. 'Yo . . . oo . . . ou?'

Liam answered the part finished question and nodded. 'No . . . I am going.' Tommy's jaw dropped. 'It's on time but there's a problem with the weather and it might be delayed,' said Liam.

Tommy smiled and spoke without looking at Liam. 'That's good; your luck's changing already.' But they both knew that any delay would cause them further turmoil. Liam was already having second thoughts and subconsciously played with his ticket, pushing it between his wet fingers until the ticket became almost unreadable. When he realised what he was doing he suddenly stopped and pushed it into his wet shirt pocket. He fumbled in the glove compartment until he found a cloth, which he dragged across the misted windscreen while at the same time he cleared his throat. 'I tell you what, Tommy. Why don't I go and wait inside and you can get back? The cops won't bother to look for the car in this rain.'

Tommy took the hint, nodded in agreement but still refused to move; instead he made a token gesture and pushed the accelerator down hard.

Liam took the initiative and opened his door. Tommy followed suit and they both stood in the rain, their arms wrapped tightly around each other. The rain helped to hide the tears that rolled down their respective cheeks. They tasted the salt and on cue both wiped their eyes. Liam finally pulled away from his brother and slapped him hard on the shoulder. 'Come on bruv, I gotta go.'

Tommy made one final attempt to join his brother. 'Are you sure I can't come with you?' he said, forcing out each word.

Liam desperately wanted to say yes but knew that it would be fatal to agree to his request. 'No, you stay here. Mum and dad need your help to look after things while I'm gone. Surely you understand that?'

Tommy swallowed deeply and tried to answer him but the words came out as a stifled whisper. 'I kn . . . ow . . . but . . .'

'Look at yourself, you're soaked. Come on, get back in the motor.' Liam guided him towards the car and pushed him into the driver's seat. 'Now get on. Go!'

Tommy watched as Liam ran through the torrential rain towards the pedestrian embarkation area and disappeared into the darkness of the night. He sat in the darkened car listening to the rain crashing onto the canvas roof, mesmerised by the even darker threatening clouds coming in off the Channel. His mobile rang but at first he didn't hear it. Finally, the incessant and annoying sound attracted his attention and after looking at the number of the caller he answered it. 'Hello.' He listened intently to his father's quivering voice until he broke down at hearing the news. 'No!' He screamed as he punched out at the steering wheel. After partially regaining his composure he continued speaking. 'No, it's too late; he's already on the ferry.' Tommy switched the phone off and slid it back into his inside jacket pocket. Trembling, he talked to himself. 'Sorry Liam, but it's better for you to get right away from this shit.' He remained motionless in the car staring out to sea as the ferry slowly pulled away from the dockside and into the darkness of the English Channel. Tommy turned the steering wheel and drove blindly out of the cark park while, once more, the rain hammered down onto the roof. The wipers, even at full speed, couldn't cope with the sheer volume of water. He wanted to turn the car around but at that moment a lorry overtook him, causing him to lose control. He wrestled hopelessly with the steering wheel as the car swerved and skidded out of control across the dual carriageway edging nearer and nearer to the central barrier. He struggled until he managed to straighten up and came to a stop on the flooded hard shoulder. He pushed himself back into the driver's seat and after letting out a huge sigh of relief, gathered his thoughts and cleared the inside of the windscreen. He rubbed his eyes and stared in disbelief at the flooded roads. After wiping his cheeks he edged slowly out onto the dual carriageway taking care to avoid the large areas of flooded tarmac.

Tommy pulled into the car park of the first all night transport café and for a while he sat staring through the windscreen into the darkness. Finally, he climbed out and looking back into the car noticed a small blue unmarked book on the rear seat. He stretched out, picked it up and looked at it closely. When he realised that it was Liam's "Bible," his AA book, he panicked. As the rain poured down onto him soaking him through to the skin he stood in the car park and flicked through the pages and the sections that Liam had painstakingly underlined to help him with his problem. His eyes streamed with tears as he looked back in the direction of Dover and thought of Liam and how, or if, he would survive without it.

CHAPTER EIGHT

A World Of Our Own

Liam boarded the ship for the Hook of Holland, having no specific destination in mind. He sat quietly in the lounge reading a morning paper left by a passenger much earlier in the day. But within an hour of leaving Dover a group of drunken Tottenham football supporters, on their way to a match in Amsterdam, started fighting amongst themselves. Liam ignored them until one of them fell onto him knocking his coffee off the table. He was in no mood to ignore it and he attacked two of the nearest drunken thugs and left them bruised and bleeding on the floor. The trouble stopped immediately and they made their way subdued to the upper deck. Their coach driver joined Liam at the table and handed him a fresh coffee. He thanked him for his help and offered him a lift to Amsterdam.

Liam left the coach when it arrived at Amsterdam's Centraal Station and wandered around for a while taking in the sights and mentally comparing Amsterdam with home. He eventually gave up trying when he found himself in the Red

Light District, a twilight underworld where many people have never been and can only imagine what it is really like. Exhausted and tired he sat in the late afternoon sun outside a small bar, the Red Cat, overlooking the canal, waiting for someone to serve him.

A young girl approached his table. She knew immediately he was English and took his order. When she returned with his coffee she sat down with him and lit a cigarette. Liam looked at her taken aback that she had stopped work to talk to him.

She read his mind. 'It's OK ya know, I do get a break every so often,' she said, looking at her watch.

'You're Irish.'

'So?'

Liam smiled. 'No . . . that's nice.' He smiled at her proudly. 'My family come from Ireland – County Cork.'

'Really?'

Liam blushed at her reaction 'Yeah . . .' He coughed a nervous cough and cleared his throat. 'Well . . . a few years ago now.' He kicked thoughtlessly at the worn brick paviors beneath the table before he continued. 'More like eighty . . .'

'How long?' she shrieked.

Their conversation was cut short when the same group of drunken Tottenham supporters spilled out of the nearby bar and onto the pavement. Again, Liam reluctantly intervened much to the appreciation of the young petite waitress. The English supporters were suddenly attacked by a gang of Dutch football fans that seemed to appear from nowhere. This time Liam was unable to quell what had now turned into a mini riot. The Dutch thugs pulled out knives and chains and attacked the unsuspecting drunken English fans. Scantily clad girls suddenly appeared from the upstairs rooms of the bar, screaming as they pushed their way through the trouble and out onto the street. The ensuing fight was bloody and vicious and several supporters from both sides were seriously injured and two of them lay dying beside the canal. The high pitched police sirens preceded the ambulances and anonymous vans carrying gun toting, green clad, riot police who single-mindedly dragged the hooligans and supporters into their vans.

Liam sat at the table in his bloodstained clothes and tried to ignore the chaos around him. As things began to quieten down the Irish waitress reappeared and offered him a drink. She attempted to talk him into having something stronger but he continued to hold out for coffee. Suddenly, and without warning, two heavily armed policemen grabbed him and, before he could say a word, he was dragged away and bundled towards the police van with the remaining English football fans. Liam looked back through the mêlée to see the waitress standing on the cobbled street holding his coffee and staring, wide eyed, as he was forcefully pulled into the police riot van and the doors slammed shut behind him. The van pulled away, following in the wake of several other fully laden vans and ambulances, sirens blaring and blue lights flashing.

Still holding Liam's coffee, the waitress stood on the pavement and watched until the last vehicle had gone. She looked around in dismay at the smashed and broken chairs and tables and then noticed Liam's bag beneath the only table still standing. She bent down picked it up and walked back into the Red Cat.

That night the Red Cat was closed and remained silent while around it, and as usual, the mixed music continued to blast out from almost every establishment. It merged with the relentless sound of the sirens as the police continued their twenty-four hour surveillance and sought to maintain control of the area.

Liam was held overnight in the cells with the English and Dutch football hooligans and, during the longest night he could ever remember he went to hell and back as he relived the fire. He was haunted by the sight of Sally's pretty face, as he watched her skin slowly melt and her disfigurement slowly unfolded. She stared back at him and smiled a distorted smile before she let out an ear shattering scream for help. His mind was in turmoil as Sally's screams were interspersed with abuse as the rowdy football fans taunted each other from their respective cells.

The next afternoon, Meener De Groot, the owner of the Red Cat, and the young Irish waitress, visited the police station. An exhausted Liam was released on bail and driven back to the Red Cat. The black Mercedes saloon pulled up outside and the three of them stood on the road with their backs to the canal. The driver closed the doors and sat back in his seat. De Groot walked across the narrow path and leaned on the railings, lit a cheroot and gazed into the water. He pulled a Nokia mobile phone from his pocket and fingered it lovingly. Liam took his time to look around at the damaged tables and chairs that had been returned to their positions and tried to recall the events of the previous afternoon and how he had been dragged into the motiveless violence and murder.

De Groot finally turned, eyed Liam up and down, before smiling to himself. He put his arm around the waist of the Irish waitress and turned to Liam. With the phone still in his hand he pointed at Keeva. 'You must thank this young lady . . .' He pulled her towards him. 'Keeva . . . for your freedom,' he said, with a grin.

Keeva blushed and smiled nervously at Liam.

Liam mouthed his thanks to her.

'So my friend . . . what are you going to do now?' asked De Groot. 'You can't leave the city until the polis decides how to deal with you.' He frowned and accentuated his lined forehead. '*Murder* is serious, no matter *who* has been killed.'

Liam screwed up his face and looked across the canal. 'Dunno.' He took in a deep breath and sighed. 'Have you got a cigarette?' De Groot took an unopened packet from his jacket pocket and handed it to him. Liam ripped at the packet and lit what was his first cigarette for twenty-four hours. He took a deep drag and closed his eyes until he had taken several more huge drags. He turned the cigarette and looked at the glowing tobacco as he spoke in a subdued tone. 'I suppose I have to stay here until this crap is sorted.' He shrugged and took another drag. 'Then who knows where?'

De Groot put his arm across Liam's shoulder, tapped it and pointed at the Red Cat. 'Why don't you stay and look after dis place?'

Liam turned to him in disbelief, pulled away and took a long hard look at his surroundings before he walked into the Red Cat for the first time. He was shocked at what he saw. The place was dark, dingy, smelt of stale beer and was absolutely filthy. He screwed up his face at the foul stench and it took a few seconds before he was able to focus. 'How you do any business in this shite hole!' he exclaimed.

'Godsamme,' said De Groot, as he turned to Liam and smirked. He tried to ignore the smell and continued. 'Drinks . . . they are cheap . . .' He pointed towards a hideously made-up, middle aged prostitute wearing a low cut blouse and short skirt. He smiled to himself. 'And so are the girls. Why should I worry? I make some money.' De Groot smiled. 'But we have *regulars*.' He pointed at half a dozen drunken elderly men playing cards, two toothless women, their teeth having rotted and decayed from years of alcohol and drugs, and a young junkie in the corner who looked forlornly into space. 'And, our Skunk#1 is cheap.' He stared across at the drugged punter. 'Maybe not the very best quality but . . .' He pointed directly at him and sneered. 'Do you think *he* will know dat?' He held his breath, turned and walked towards the door. 'Come with me.' He guided Liam outside before he continued. 'We are not in the central area of De Wallen.'

Liam shot him a quizzical look.

De Groot laughed and continued. 'Ah . . . I mean the famous red-light district.' He pointed a few hundred metres along the canal. 'Dis are my *special places*.' De Groot smiled with pride, pumped out his chest and momentarily revelled in his achievements. He stroked at his designer stubble and took a deep breath. 'Clubs, hotels, coffee shops, bars and "kamers" are down there . . . They make me a *lot* of money . . .' He turned towards the Red Cat. 'Here, we don't get so much business but it is cheap, very cheap.' He pulled the mobile phone from his pocket and thrust it towards Liam. De Groot grinned as he spoke. 'Dis will change my business. It is very special I can send a message with this phone.' He stroked the face of it. 'All of my special people will have this now. They are the first like dis in Holland.'

Liam wasn't interested and looked along the canal at the flashing lights and huge groups of people congregating just a hundred yards up the canal. He nodded slowly and replied stretching each letter. 'O . . . K.' His mood suddenly changed and he grimaced as he pointed towards the Red Cat. 'That place needs a total . . .' He paused and then sneered at De Groot. 'Knock the fucking place down . . .' Before he could finish his sentence the sound of crashing saucepans diverted their attention. Liam smirked at De Groot. 'Maybe it's happening already . . .'

De Groot ignored him and walked through the dimly lit bar. He pushed Liam aside and opened a door to reveal a kitchen not much bigger than a small boat's galley. A diminutive Asian woman, in her early thirties, was kneeling on the floor amongst the saucepans and woks. She looked up at De Groot and then at Liam who immediately saw the fear in her eyes. She remained frozen to the spot.

De Groot smiled at her.

When she realised that De Groot was not angry with her she breathed a sigh of relief, smiled at them and stood up. She cupped her tiny hands and bowed gracefully.

'This is Asmara,' said De Groot. 'She's been with me for . . .' He thought and looked towards the open window and the corrugated roof that covered the boxes of vegetables, and exotic fruit, much of which Liam had never seen before. A young boy pushed his way between the boxes, climbed through the window and stood staring up at De Groot and the stranger.

'Hello Rafi,' said De Groot.

The boy stood fixed to the spot afraid to speak.

De Groot smiled before he continued 'How old are you?' asked De Groot softly.

The boy bowed, cupping his hands together. 'Ten, sir, Meener,' said the young boy, his voice fading.

De Groot squinted and thought before speaking. 'That's right.' He pointed at the woman and turned to Liam. 'Asmara has been here for ten years. She is from Indonesia.' He reflected. 'I found her behind my car ten years ago ready to burst. The Greek bastard wanted to throw her in the Singel but she said she was the best cook in Amsterdam. I gave her a chance.' He nodded and gave himself a self-congratulatory smile. 'Good job I did.' He laughed loudly. 'She cooked me the best bebek betutu I'd ever tasted.' He sniggered to himself. 'Before I had time to finish it she has the baby . . . the boy . . .' He pointed at Rafi who smiled nervously back at him. De Groot continued. 'In my apartment.' He smiled at her and she gave him a reserved smile. De Groot continued. 'The rest is history. I told her she could live here at the "Cat."' For the first time there was a certain amount of feeling in his voice as he continued. 'Asmara won't be any trouble, just let her be and she won't let you down. She makes the best Rijstaffel in Mokum.'

They walked back into the bar and Liam took his time to look around. He ran his fingers along the sticky beer-stained bar and wiped them in his blood-covered jeans. He cussed under his breath and shook his head wildly. 'What the hell . . . this is fucking disgus . . .'

De Groot interrupted him. 'I will arrange it for my painters to come and see you.'

For the first time Liam raised his voice. 'Didn't you hear what I said? It needs more than fucking paint!'

'Maybe some new chairs and tables?' asked De Groot, patronisingly. He paused and watched Liam as he continued to look around in the semi-darkness.

'The lights . . . the bar . . .' Liam paused. 'And we'll need a new name.'

'Name?' asked De Groot.

Liam glared back at the Dutchman 'I'm not keeping that fucking name. I want to change that.' He snorted. 'The Red . . . *fucking* Cat!' He shook his head and repeated the name over and over until he couldn't stop laughing. 'Who the fuck gives a bar a name like that?' He swallowed hard and took a deep breath. 'Fuck me . . . the Red Cat . . . Jeez . . .'

'What difference is that to make?' asked De Groot.

'A new start . . . A new name and a new place,' replied Liam.

De Groot nodded his agreement. 'This will cost me a lot of money. How do I know it will come back?'

Liam mimicked De Groot. 'You don't know if it will "come back" but if you leave the place like this, before long it'll cost you money anyway.' Liam thought hard before he continued. 'And . . .'

He was interrupted by De Groot. 'OK.' He nodded. 'If you think you are so sure, I will agree with you.' He turned and walked towards the door but suddenly stopped and turned back to face Liam. 'OK. The first three months you keep every guilder. After that it's 60/40. Sixty percent to me, paid on the last day of every month, and I mean – the last day *every* month.' De Groot didn't give a damn what the place was called as long as it made more money than it had for the last few years.

Liam, deep in thought, stroked his chin before answering. He reached out and shook De Groot's hand. 'Fine,' he said, reluctantly.

De Groot tugged at his suit jacket and turned to the waitress. 'Keeva, your new *manager* can't stay here . . .' Keeva nodded and De Groot continued. 'Put him at the Koopermoolen and tell Karel to look after him.'

She disappeared inside returning a few minutes later with Liam's bag. 'I've been looking after it for you,' she said, lifting it high in the air without any effort. Liam thanked her with a smile. 'Come on I'll take you round,' she said, excitedly.

De Groot thrust his hands into his suit jacket pockets and walked slowly towards his car. He stopped at the open car door and turned back to face Liam. He screwed up his face and thought hard. 'Do I know you from somewhere? Eh?'

Liam shrugged his shoulders 'Dunno – how?'

De Groot called out to his driver. 'Artem, let's go.'

Artem closed the rear door and the Mercedes pulled away in virtual silence.

For the first time Liam took time to look at Keeva. She was petite, pretty with a pale complexion and short red hair. He guessed she was in her early twenties but appeared a little naive for her age.

'Keeva what the fuck was De Groot talking about? The best food he'd ever tasted . . . sounded like bebeee . . .' She laughed but realising she was laughing at Liam; she stopped and put her hand over her mouth. 'I'm so sorry.' She patted his arm. 'Bebek betutu is duck roasted in banana leaves.' She licked her lips. 'It's fantastic.' She gave him the widest of smiles. 'Maybe when we reopen we could have Asmara do us that as part of her rijstaffel?'

Liam looked at her and dismissed her suggestion with a huge sigh. 'Whatever . . .'

While Keeva and Liam walked the short distance to his temporary home she told him she came from Cork. She'd arrived in Amsterdam on the last stage of a working holiday, travelling across Europe with her boyfriend, and decided to stay for a while. That was the last she saw of him. The eldest of five children, Keeva had helped her mother to bring up the rest of the family and was feeling trapped. After losing her job at the meat packing plant and with the opportunity to travel with Rob, a safe young lad from the same street, she grabbed the chance with both hands. She didn't know what to expect, although one thing was sure; Amsterdam was it.

Liam offered Keeva a cigarette. She declined and, after slipping the packet into his jacket pocket, took her time to light his. 'Tell me about De Groot?' he asked.

Keeva looked at him, clearly reluctant to answer. He pointed a finger at her. 'Come on, you've been here for a while surely you know something about him?'

She coughed nervously. 'Well . . .'

Liam nudged her. 'Come on, spill the beans; one Irishman to another.' He laughed. 'Pardon the pun . . .'

Keeva laughed as she leaned on the railings and looked into the canal. 'I don't know much about him really. He seems to have the area sown up. He owns clubs, bars, coffee shops and runs loads of girls across the city.' She looked along the street before she continued. 'And not just in the Red Light District – all across Amsterdam and much of Holland.'

While Liam lit another cigarette Keeva gathered her thoughts. 'He's a mean bastard and certainly won't take any shit.' She looked at Liam and waited for a reaction. He took a huge drag on his cigarette. She continued. 'One night . . .' she hesitated, and relived the moment. 'He almost killed a man in the bar.' She shuddered. 'I've never seen anything like it.' She shuddered. 'He beat him to a pulp over four guilders and then his minders dumped him in the canal . . .' she pointed towards the Red Cat, 'unbelievable and right outside there.'

She swallowed hard. 'The poor bastard lived but was crippled for life.' She shook her head. 'He's in a wheelchair now . . . and will be for the rest of his life.' She wiped at her eyes. 'De Groot knows everybody. He pays off the police, judges, government people and anyone that could prevent him from doing what he wants.' She grabbed at Liam's arm. 'You must take care or . . .'

Liam took her hands in his. 'Or?'

'Who knows what he'll do . . .' she said, as her whole body shook. 'That lot yesterday were hooligans and *they* were *drunk*!' She shook her head. 'Not *professional* heavies.'

Liam nodded and at the same time smiled over her shoulder. He knew he could more than look after himself. He tugged at her arm. 'Come on, where's this hotel?'

CHAPTER NINE

Music Is My First Love

The Hotel de Koopermoolen, 5 Warmoesstraat, was once a 200-seater theatre owned by Henk Elsink – who was originally a singer and often considered to be the Dutch equivalent of Tommy Cooper. In the sixties it was renowned for its dinner and cabaret shows but with the decline of cabaret he sold the theatre and moved to Majorca, where he retired to write detective books.

Keeva led Liam into the recently renovated hotel and they stood at the desk. While they waited Liam took in the unusual surroundings. The area was surprisingly large considering the narrow entrance. An antique stove gave out a welcoming glow and candles burned on the low tables. It was long considered a tradition in Holland to burn them at all times of the day and night. At the far end of the reception a table, surrounded by matching wicker chairs, was covered with the same brown patterned carpet as that on the floor. The pretty blonde-haired girl in a dark blue suit got up from the table and smiled as she walked towards them. 'Good afternoon, I'm Anje. How may I help you?'

Keeva explained that De Groot wanted Liam to stay at the hotel. The receptionist asked Liam to fill in the registration form and pulled a key off the hook.

'That's you sorted,' said Keeva. 'I'll see you in the morning at the bar and we can make a start,' she said, brightly.

Liam smiled at her and raised his hand. The receptionist waited for Keeva to leave and took him across to the lift, pressed the button, and when the door opened she handed him his key. 'Fourth floor,' she said. 'It is a good room. If you need something please call down to me.'

The lift opened on the fourth floor and Liam's room, 2141, was immediately opposite.

He opened the door to find the flashing neon signs illuminating the pale walls. He threw his bag onto the double bed and stood looking down into the street below before walking into the bathroom. The walls were painted light grey, the same colour as the bedroom and all the woodwork was painted in a pale blue satin gloss. As he released the dark green canvas blind, it flipped up and the cord tangled around it. He shrugged as he walked back into the bedroom, lay on the bed, kicked off his shoes, edged his bag onto the carpet and fell asleep.

When he woke up he was starving so as soon as he found his shoes he went down in the lift.

From his bedroom window he had seen a café across the street, so he made for that. He ordered a burger and chips and a coffee then sat for more than an hour watching, and listening to the drunken and drug-induced ravings of young men and girls, as they roamed up and down the street outside. He ordered a second coffee and sat in silence watching the drunken Englishmen, on a stag weekend, metamorphosise into pathetic uncontrollable zombies before his eyes. They looked ridiculous and out of control, and for the first time in his life he realised what alcohol had done to him, and in turn to his family. *Could he beat his demons?* He knew that only *he* could do that. He finished his coffee, paid and walked out into the twilight world of Amsterdam: the sex capital of Europe, for the first time. As he walked down Warmoesstraat he noticed the row of police cars on the right hand side outside their station. He quickly crossed the road. He made to look into one of the shop windows and couldn't believe what he was seeing. The window of 141 Warmoesstraat was decorated with a display of condoms in every colour, fabric and design. He chuckled to himself and shook his head in disbelief before walking along the road and turning the corner. He made his way back towards the Red Cat and stopped on the nearby Armbrug Bridge. He squeezed himself between the row of bicycles, and after making himself comfortable against the railings, smoked the remainder of his cigarettes. He looked back towards the bar while he formulated his ideas. Café Centercourt a little further up the canal from the Red Cat was buzzing. *Did he want to take on the white elephant?* He would have to decide in the morning if it was really what he wanted. To him the place looked uninviting and he wondered why anyone would ever go near it let alone go inside. He threw his last cigarette end into the canal and made the two minute walk back to the Koopermoolen.

When he entered reception Anje was still on duty. 'How is your room, Mr Reilly?' she asked.

'It's fine, thanks,' he replied, as he walked towards the open lift doors.

As the lift doors closed she mouthed. 'Goodnight.'

*

Liam was awake at seven o'clock and he lay in bed thinking about the Red Cat and what Keeva had told him. He had a shower and at eight o'clock took the lift down to reception. Anje was still on duty. 'Have you been there all night?' he asked, with a snigger.

'No . . .' She laughed. 'I finish at midnight and I come back this morning at six o'clock.'

'Sod that for a game of soldiers,' he replied.

She looked at him and tilted her head to one side. '*Soldiers?*'

Liam smiled at her. 'It's an old English saying . . . I didn't really mean *soldiers.*'

She still didn't understand but nodded. 'Breakfast is downstairs.' She pointed at the staircase.

The basement breakfast room was bright and clean. The matching wooden chairs and tables were carefully positioned around the room, each with a white tablecloth and a vase of yellow silk tulips, salt and pepper and a sugar bowl. The floor was tiled and the walls once again were painted a pale grey. The breakfast buffet was laid out on a long unit on the back wall. The choice was unbelievable. Boiled eggs placed on pale yellow sand in a warm stainless steel tray, ham, salami, cereals, yoghurt, and cheese, various jams and honey, fresh fruit salad and, next to the toaster, row upon row of different looking bread. Liam looked at the bread and shook his head, He had no idea there were so many different types. There was a Still with boiling water next to row upon row of different tea bags, a coffee machine and a stainless steel urn containing cold milk. Liam stood looking at the bread and deliberated for a few seconds before picking up two slices of white bread and putting them in the toaster. While he waited for the toast he carefully picked his way through the various jams, then took his toast and made for the furthest table from the door.

As the last two people left the breakfast room Anje walked through the rear door. She had been watching the breakfast room on CCTV from the reception. She smiled at Liam and disappeared into the kitchen. A few minutes later she returned carrying a cafetière. She held it up to Liam and motioned if he wanted a coffee. He nodded. She picked up two cups and saucers from the buffet table, placed a small jug of cream inside the top cup and walked towards his table. 'May I sit with you,' she asked.

'Course you can,' replied Liam, gratefully.

She sat down at his table, arranged the cups and poured two coffees.

'Did you enjoy the breakfast?'

Liam looked down at his empty plate. 'Uh, uh.' He raised his head and smiled. 'Yeah, it was fine.' He fiddled with his teaspoon and twisted in his chair. 'How long have worked here?'

'Two years,' she said. She sipped at her coffee and continued. 'Before that . . .' She stopped herself and placed her cup in the saucer before continuing in a whisper. 'Don't make fun of me if I tell you where it was I worked before this time.' Her mood suddenly changed.

'Sure,' he replied, flippantly.

'Really? You want to hear about me?'

Liam settled back into his seat and waited.

'Well,' she said, extending each letter of the word. 'I worked at a monkey sanctuary and centre for badly hurt pets and animals in Almere.'

Liam looked surprised and nodded slowly.

Her voice changed and she suddenly began to wave her arms around wildly. 'Do you know a monkey, *not* chimp, was kept in a basement for *years*? Here in Amsterdam. He could only see feet walking past!' She couldn't hide her anger.

Liam felt uncomfortable and fidgeted nervously before he reached out, stirred his coffee and took a sip. He pulled a face. 'Urgh . . .' He shook his head in disgust.

Anje walked across to the next table, picked up the sugar bowl and returned to the table. Liam slid three heaped spoons of sugar into his cup and stirred it enthusiastically.

Anje waited until he finished stirring before she continued. 'The monkey was so stressed he threw shit at the passing people.' There was no reaction from Liam. She topped up her coffee and continued in a raised voice. '*Snakes* were used as *ashtrays* in night clubs! Turtles that were too big for their tanks were put in plastic bags and thrown over the wall into the sanctuary, or . . .' She breathed in hard and sighed. 'Sometimes they were thrown into the canal.' She wiped her eyes. 'It was so terrible – I did as much as I could to help the poor innocent creatures. Then, there was less money so I . . .' She swallowed hard, blew her nose in an unused serviette and slowly raised her head. 'Now I am here,' she said, softly.

'Wow.' Liam exhaled heavily and without taking a breath continued. 'That was a hellish job.'

She smiled back at him. 'I am sorry, Mr Reilly. I haven't told that to anyone before.'

'No, no, I'm impressed,' he said. 'Well, I'd better start *my* new job,' he said, pushing his chair under the table. 'Perhaps you can show me around this place?' He paused. 'Assuming you're not working *all the time?*'

'I would like that very much,' she said. She picked up the

cups, empty cafetière and sugar and took it into the kitchen. She called after him. 'Good luck, Mr Reilly.'

Liam didn't hear her. He was already racing up the stairs, two at a time.

Anje desperately wanted to know why Liam was working with someone like De Groot but she wouldn't ask him.

Liam arrived at the Red Cat to find four identical liveried vans parked outside and Keeva talking to a smartly dressed man holding a clipboard. She turned to Liam and raised her upturned hand in the direction of the man. 'This is Mr Matthijs Kikkert, the owner of the construction company.' He reached out and shook Liam's hand. Liam's firm handshake was reciprocated with an even harder grip. 'Pleased to meet you, Mr Reilly,' he said, as he smiled. 'Meener De Groot told me you have good ideas for this place, ja?'

Liam nodded. 'I do . . .' He sniggered. 'And it needs it, that's for sure.'

Matthijs ignored Liam's comment and turned to him. 'Shall we start out here first?'

'Would you both like coffee?' asked Keeva, as she walked towards the bar.

They both nodded.

Liam took the clipboard and was drawing on the page as he enthusiastically described his ideas to Matthijs. Keeva walked across to them with two mugs of coffee, a jug of cream and sugar bowl on a brightly decorated tray.

Liam added his usual three spoons of sugar, stirred it a couple of times and took a huge gulp. He almost choked and immediately spat it out. 'This is disgusting, I can't drink that shite!' He had compared it to the coffee that Anje had made

115

for him. Matthijs sipped at his coffee and surreptitiously put the mug back on the tray. Keeva cursed and stormed off with the tray, shaking her head.

Matthijs didn't hide his distaste at the coffee from Liam but immediately followed it with a hint of a smile and followed him into the bar. Liam let his hand glide along the keys of a neglected piano in the corner. It sounded badly out of tune. The carpenter, working on the removal of the damaged door and frame, stopped and walked across to them. He carefully placed his crow bar on top of the piano and played a few bars of music. The piano didn't sound as bad. The carpenter looked at Liam eagerly. 'I fix this for you?'

Liam looked at him wide eyed. 'If you can?' He looked at Matthijs who nodded his approval.

The carpenter pursed his lips and a high pitched whistle reverberated around the bar and four workmen arrived and manhandled the piano out of the bar and into his van.

In old Amsterdam, the majority of properties were very narrow, a direct result of the high taxes, charged many years earlier, based on the width of the buildings. Each property had a steep roof fronted by a variety of shaped gables which included, point, cornice, step, crow-stepped, bell, spout and neck. The Red Cat was five stories high with a bell-shaped gable.

Liam and Matthijs made their way to the rear of the bar and the toilets. The stench of stale urine was unbearable. Liam shook his head wildly. 'We've got to do something about that!' he screamed.

Matthijs nodded. 'And we will put a purple light, a fluorescerende, up there,' he said, pointing at the ceiling. Liam shot him a confused look. Matthijs smiled. 'Ah, in Amsterdam we put dese lights in all toilets, so dat de addicts cannot find der veins.' He looked at Liam waiting for his reaction.

Liam shrugged. 'Whatever.'

Matthijs scribbled on his clipboard before they climbed the narrow stairs to the fifth floor.

They were both out of breath by the time they reached the top floor. Matthijs pushed open the door to what would be Liam's flat. It was clear that no one had lived in it for several years. The hanging wallpaper revealed the mould which covered most of the walls. Liam reached out and tore at the wallpaper, it fell at his feet exposing the damp and cracked plaster. He walked into the bathroom and then the bedroom where he found the walls in a similar condition. Liam walked across to the window and rubbed at the filthy glass and the sun burst into the room. He peered through the clear area of glass and for the first time smiled as he looked out at what would soon be *his* view across the city. Matthijs watched him and chose his time to speak. 'It won't take too much to make these problems and with some paint it will be comfortable for you. I will arrange for the kitchen and bathroom to be replaced and we can renew the electric wires and the heating.'

Liam nodded and left the room. He'd lived in much worse conditions but this was to be his home for the foreseeable future and he wanted it to be good for him. As they made their way down the building they checked the other rooms which were equally dilapidated and the only furniture that remained was damaged.

Back on the ground floor Matthijs showed Liam the basement. It was crammed full of broken crates and boxes, old tables, chairs and signs making it almost impossible to get any further than a couple of metres from the entrance. Matthijs looked at Liam before speaking. 'If you can decide if there is anything you wish to keep please tell me and I will take the rest when I strip out the bar.'

Liam grunted his response before giving Matthijs his instructions and the ideas he had come up with overnight. The Dutchman wrote everything down on a pad on his clip board and put a cost against each instruction. Matthijs picked up the phone on the bar and telephoned De Groot. He nodded throughout the conversation but stopped suddenly and placed the receiver on the bar. It was clear by the tone of his voice that something had changed. He called across the bar to Liam. 'Mr Reilly, Meener De Groot has agreed to your ideas and the works but he would like to speak with you *now*.' He handed Liam the phone. Liam initially nodded as he listened but then began to shake his head angrily and scream into the receiver. He finally slammed down the receiver and stormed out of the bar. Matthijs and his men stood and watched in silence.

Liam leaned on the railings, stared into the canal and lit a cigarette. A few minutes passed and Matthijs approached him and spoke in a soft and sympathetic voice. 'I understand Mr Reilly and I am sorry we can't help with the other work but Meener De Groot is paying for this.' He paused and waited for Liam to respond. Liam didn't reply. 'I'm sure you understand?' said Matthijs.

Liam nodded wildly and mumbled his incoherent reply.

Matthijs continued. 'Meener De Groot is a fantastic client we only work for him and he pays very well – in cash.'

A smile slowly crossed Liam's face. 'What a surprise.' He sniggered. 'I guessed he did . . .' He put his arm around

Matthijs, threw the half-smoked cigarette into the canal and turned to face him. 'I know it's not your decision . . .' He took another cigarette from the packet, lit it and thought hard. 'So how long will *your* work take?' He didn't wait for an answer and continued. 'You will do the work in my flat for me?'

Matthijs nodded. 'Of course we will. We can finish . . .' He looked into space and scribbled furiously on his clipboard. 'Within the four weeks, Mr Reilly,' he said, with a smile in his voice. 'Then you will have a wonderful new place.'

As soon as Matthijs had gone Liam took Keeva aside. 'De Groot won't do any work to the girls' rooms. If they want it they pay or do it themselves. OK?'

Keeva looked at him. 'You don't have any girls now. You'll need to find new girls . . . and soon. If you open without them you'll have no chance.'

'Leave it to me. I know someone who can help with that.' He lit a cigarette and studied the glowing end. 'Now, let's talk about the shite excuse for coffee you gave me earlier.'

She nervously played with her fingers running them along the tips of her brightly painted nails.

'That coffee was soooo bad.' He screwed up his face. 'Have the punters been paying good money for that?' He thought. 'Mind you the people that I saw in there wouldn't know the difference anyway.' He rushed inside. 'Let's have a look at the machine that dishes out that shite,' he said.

Keeva took him across to the filthy coffee machine on the bar. He took a few minutes rubbing the casing and removing the jets before he turned and smiled back at her. 'Leave it with me,' he said, with a glint in his eye. Despite its condition Liam felt there was something very special about it.

He spent the next few hours in the basement and worked his way through the nearest rubbish deciding what he wanted to keep. After throwing out enough to give him some space he made room for a work bench. That afternoon he took the coffee machine into the basement and meticulously stripped it down.

CHAPTER TEN

God Only Knows

While the plaster in his flat was hacked off, the walls replastered and the electrical wiring and bathroom suite renewed along with a new galley kitchen, Liam spent the majority of his time in the basement. He worked his way through the remaining boxes and rubbish that had accumulated since the war and carefully checked everything. Several television sets, an old bicycle, lengths of woodworm infested timber, pots of paint, broken tables and chairs. He threw it all into the two skips outside the bar. Hidden under dust sheets and tea cases Liam found a 1950's motorbike, a German DKW RT 250. He covered it and put it aside until he had time to work on it. He kept one television and several perfect tables and chairs which he power washed outside. The matching 1970's Arkana tables and chairs, with their white fibreglass "pop" swivel bulbous bases and red check fabric seats, looked like new. He carefully returned them to the cellar and covered them in polythene before turning his attention to the dirt encrusted 1960's juke box.

The bar was a hive of activity; the electricians had stripped out the old wiring and installed temporary lighting. Decaying plaster had been hacked off and was in the process of being renewed; the remaining woodwork had been stripped and the painters made a start on the preparation of the new wood-work and plaster. The noise was deafening to him, even when he was in the cellar stripping and renovating the jukebox. Suddenly there was total silence. He straightened his back and waited for the noise to resume. He checked his watch and tapped it gently. It continued to tick. He returned to cleaning the jukebox but twenty minutes later, when there was still no sign of activity, he walked slowly up the stairs into the bar. The workmen had vanished. Their tools were where they had left them; partly sawn architrave still rested in the vice, cables hung from the ceiling and walls and a mound of wet plaster remained piled high on the spot board.

Once accustomed to the temporary lighting, Liam saw the tall well-built man flanked by two even bigger men with base-ball bats.

'What the hell's going on?' screamed Liam, 'where is everybody?' He spun around looking for the workmen before he turned back and glared directly at the visitors. 'And who the *FUCK* are you?'

The smart man shrugged and continued to stare at Liam. 'Gone?' He said in a deep voice. He paused and smiled expos-ing a mouth full of gold teeth. He held the smile while he straightened the navy blue overcoat across his shoulders. 'Ah . . . I have heard a lot about you, Englishman,' he said, drag-ging out every letter.

Liam shook his head and appeared nonplussed. He tried to understand what was happening before he finally continued. 'Me? I'm Irish! I'm fucking Irish!' he bawled.

'English . . . Irish . . . pah.' The man slapped his forehead with the palm of his hand. 'Who cares? Dis an *your* place? Da?'

Liam nodded slowly before speaking. '*Yeah,*' he growled. 'Who's askin'?'

'Unë jam *Meco* . . .' He stretched out his arms and stabbed them randomly around the bar. 'An you do dis without *my* leje?'

Liam pushed out his chest, spread his legs apart, picked up the plasterers trowel from the board behind him, and balled his other fist. 'NO! This is *my* place – we open in two *weeks*. So, FUCK OFF!'

Meco clicked his fingers and the two heavies rushed forward, grabbed Liam, pinned him against the bar and raised their baseball bats menacingly. Liam struggled but they were incredibly strong. He dropped the trowel and Meco picked it up. He nodded to his heavies and they stretched Liam's hands out on the bar. He raised the trowel high above his head but at that moment the lights flickered and, after a few seconds of complete darkness, the bar was fully illuminated. The three men heard a gun being cocked behind them. They all turned to see De Groot, flanked by Artem, his driver, and the biggest muscle-bound man that Liam had ever seen. His huge belly overhung his wide leather belt and thick black hair bulged from the neck of his white vest, his armpits and back. To the left of Artem stood a young diminutive woman in denim jeans and jacket, and a clinging olive vest. Her stance was that of a mercenary; sharp and ready for action. With the exception of De Groot, who held a pistol, they all pointed Russian AK-47's in the direction of the men.

'What the hell are you doing here, Meco?' snarled De Groot.

Meco gave him a seditious stare. 'Dis shit hole – *still* your place?' he growled.

'Of course,' replied De Groot, defiantly. 'And you know what happens . . .' He pushed back his head and as he ran the thick fingers of his left hand through his hair, he continued. 'When someone tries to take *anything* away from me . . .' He grinned and lowered his voice. 'Don't you?' He straightened his arm and stabbed his gun towards Meco and, simultaneously, all three of the AK-47's safety catches clicked to the central position ready for fully automatic fire.

De Groot flicked his head and Artem moved towards them pointing his gun threateningly. Liam seized his opportunity; he broke free, elbowed both of Meco's minders in the solar plexus with enormous force and followed that with straight finger jabs to their throats. They slumped to the ground and lay motionless. As Meco's whole body stiffened, Artem seized the shiny, razor-edged, trowel from his hand, slid it along the bar away from Meco and stepped back two paces.

Still holding his hand gun, De Groot clapped apathetically and grinned from ear to ear as he moved nearer to Meco. 'What can I say, Meco. You lot are *shit* . . . and you know it.'

Meco grunted and replied in Dutch. 'Vind je?'

De Groot ignored him and continued. 'I hear you Albanians are betting men. Is that right, Meco?'

Meco tilted his head to one side and gave a confused nod. 'Yeaaaas,' he said, nervously, the tension evident in his deep throaty tone.

The huge man and Artem stepped forward and forced Meco face down onto the bar and stretched his arms out in front of him.

De Groot had mastered the art of not needing to give verbal

instructions to his entourage and by simply moving his eyes, or occasionally using his finger to reinforce his requests, they responded immediately.

De Groot flicked his head and raised his gun. The woman raced forward at lightning speed, quickly checked the pockets of the men on the floor and removed their guns and knives. She dropped the knives into the huge plasterer's water barrel and slid the guns into her belt. De Groot raised an eyebrow and she reached out and picked up the trowel from the end of the bar before stepping back. De Groot smiled as he took a coin from his pocket and fed it effortlessly backwards and forwards between his fingers. When he finally stopped he held it between his thumb and forefinger ready to toss. 'OK, Meco.' He grinned crassly. 'I give you a chance.' He paused and stroked the designer stubble on his chin as he pretended to think. 'Ah . . . one moment.' He partially closed his eyes and peered through the slits at Meco. 'Can I ask another question of you?'

Meco glared back at him and mouthed his confused reply. 'Wh . . . ?'

'Are you left or right handed?' asked the smirking De Groot.

De Groot's henchmen spread Meco's fingers as wide as they could while still maintaining their vice like grip on his hands. They pushed his body tight against the bar, the weight of their bodies reinforcing their total control over him.

Meco tried to struggle but it was futile. He looked at De Groot and began to sweat. 'Dorën e djathtë – um . . .' His eyes flicked between each of his hands and he continued. 'Right hand,' he said, the indecision clear in his wavering voice.

'Heads of staarten?' asked De Groot.

Meco stared back at him.

'Heads or tails?' snarled De Groot. Meco shook his head from side to side as De Groot continued. 'I did say I would give you a chance. Tell me,' he snarled. 'Left or right?'

Meco knew where things were headed. 'Left!' he screamed defiantly.

'OK – *so*, you want heads or tails?' asked De Groot, pressing for an answer. Meco ignored him. De Groot walked behind the bar, slapped him across the head and screamed directly into his face. 'Luister je?'

Meco threw his head back and with a look of sheer contempt, screamed back at De Groot. 'Tails!'

De Groot stepped out from behind the bar and tossed the coin in the air. He let it drop in front of him and immediately covered it with his right foot. 'Bad luck,' he roared. 'It's heads!' He raised one eyebrow; the woman raised the trowel and brought it down onto Meco's left hand, severing it at the wrist. Meco didn't make a sound as the huge man effortlessly spun him around and thrust the bleeding stump into the mound of wet plaster on the spot board.

The young woman still held the trowel but De Groot motioned to her to hand it to him. He looked directly into Meco's face and pushed his nose hard against his. 'Rukker! Verliezer!' he screamed, as he wiped the trowel in Meco's overcoat before dropping it into the plasterer's water barrel.

Liam was mesmerised at the woman's sheer speed and precision as she pulled plastic cable ties from her jacket pocket, flipped the unconscious men over and bound their hands behind their backs. She tugged at each of the cable ties before her head darted from side to side as her eyes pierced the semi-darkness and she took in the scene around her. She leapt effortlessly over the bar, picked up a cordless drill, flicked the switch and it whirred into action. She jumped back over the bar and jabbed her boot into the neck of the nearest unconscious man, squeezed the switch and proceeded to drill through his knee cap, his meniscus and ligaments. Satisfied with her efforts she did a body flip across the two of them and landed silently beside the second man. He groaned. She lashed out and smashed the heavy drill handle into his jaw and his head fell to one side, unconscious. Once again she jabbed her boot into his neck and squeezed the switch on the drill.

De Groot looked directly at Meco and sneered as Zita drilled into the knee of the second man. 'No more "Osman Taka" dancing for you guys,' he mocked.

Meco screamed out in anger and his voice reverberated around the empty bar.

De Groot ignored him and turned to Artem. 'Toevoegen den stukadoor van.' He then spoke very slowly and emphasised every word. 'You have some *very* filthy rubbish to get rid of.'

As Artem walked towards the door De Groot shouted after him. 'Put dem deep . . . forever! I don't want to see this pathetic faces again!'

Artem smirked back at him as he walked towards the outside light. He took the AK-47's, grabbed the keys from the plasterer, slid the guns onto the floor in front of the passenger seat, and opened the side door of the van. Unable to hide his anger De Groot forgot his English and took a step towards Meco. 'Eikel! Flikker op!' he screamed. He grabbed Meco's throat with both hands and squeezed until his eyes bulged and the veins began to burst. 'If I see you within a hundred kilometres of this city, I will personally cut off your *other* hand and your feet! Begrepen?' With his anger now at fever pitch he spat into Meco's face.

The huge man and woman each dragged one of the unconscious men through the bar, loaded them in the van, and came back to take Meco. The girl tied his arms behind his back at the elbows and forced him into the second van, shut the doors and drove off.

De Groot approached Liam. 'Fucking Albanians, dey are getting everywhere.' He grinned and pushed his tongue hard into his left cheek until it reached his mouth and then he spat hard. He exaggerated every word as he spoke. 'But not in my City . . .' He shook his head before taking a minute to study Liam by looking him up and down. 'You did well. You can look after yourself, that's for sure.'

He smiled and tapped Liam on the shoulder. 'You ought to work for me.'

Liam grinned at him. 'I already do, don't I?'

De Groot sniggered. 'Touché,' he said, with a flourish.

He walked out to the remaining vans and assembled tradesmen. He opened his arms wide and raised his hands, palm up. 'Come on, we have work to do!'

They all jumped to attention and returned to the bar, where the noise of intense activity resumed almost immediately.

While the huge man stood looking menacingly on, De Groot pulled Liam aside, guided him onto the Armbrug Bridge, and lit a cheroot. He offered one to Liam who shook his head and instead lit a cigarette. The both leaned on the railings looking down towards the Oudezijds Kolk – a narrow sluice in a lock that ran from the Oosterdok – the water to the north of Prins Hendrikkade – and into the Oudezijds Voorburgwal.

'How did you know they . . . ?' He paused and shot De

Groot a confused look before he continued. 'The Albanians were at the bar?'

'Listen to me . . . my friend. A lot of shit happens here – just remember *that*.' A smug grin slowly transformed his face. 'I get a call from the plasterer.'

'The plasterer?' replied Liam.

De Groot nodded slowly as the grin spread right across his face. 'He works for *me*.' He took a self-congratulatory drag on his cheroot. 'I need to know how my business is working.' He coughed. 'Don't you agree?'

'Um,' responded Liam, with a murmur. Liam knew then that he would have to be on his guard every minute of the day and trust no one. He suddenly turned to De Groot. 'Who the hell *were those bastards*?' he asked, as he lit yet another cigarette.

'Ah . . .' De Groot roared, as he continued. 'Meco . . . is . . . or shall I say . . . was . . . an opportunistische.' Liam smiled at being able to understand a Dutch word at last. 'He thought I sold de bar to you and don't wunt de competition.' He turned and looked directly at Liam. 'We will be competition won't we?'

'What do you mean by that?'

'I mean dat place.' He pointed across to the Red Cat with his cheroot. 'It will be a success, yeas?'

Liam straightened up. 'I'll do my best,' he replied, coughing nervously through his words. He took a drag and looked back at the huge man. When the man noticed Liam was looking at him he stamped one of his huge feet and glared back at him. Liam sniggered and turned back to face De Groot. 'Who are your friends?'

De Groot looked at him confused. 'Friends?'

He slowly raised his arm and pointed his forefinger intimidatingly in the direction of the man. 'Yeah, "man mountain" over there and "G.I. Jane?"'

'Hah . . .' De Groot laughed loudly and then stopped abruptly as his mood changed. 'They are *not* my friends und never will be! Do you understand?'

Liam, clearly embarrassed, lowered his voice subserviently. 'Sure,' he said.

De Groot frowned and kicked blindly at the timber bridge decking. 'Man Mountain . . . as you name him is Skipio.' He sniggered. 'He's Greek. He was a weightlifter in the Olympics in Seoul in 1988 but was disqualified for taking steroiden.' He laughed loudly and muttered to himself at the same time. 'Idioot.'

Liam remained stony faced and nodded. 'And the girl?'

'The girl? Ah.' He smiled. 'She is Zita.' He lowered his voice. 'Israeli Mossad . . .' He lifted his finger to his tight lips and tapped them gently before slightly tilting his head and lighting his second cheroot. 'Believe me they *both* have their own reasons to be here. They needed a job and . . .' He took a drag and grinned. 'Amsterdam – is the place to come.' He looked hard at Liam. 'As *you* know so well . . . yeas?' De Groot coughed a deep cough, cleared his throat and spat into the canal, before looking back at the activity around the bar. He straightened his tie and stood erect. 'Now, let's get this place ready. It's costing *you* a lot of money.'

Liam knew what De Groot meant and that he would expect to get every penny back – with interest.

While the work continued in the bar, Liam spent his time in the cellar working on the coffee machine. He meticulously cleaned it to reveal the beautiful retro cream coloured casing and the manufacturer's eagle badge. The Fregnan family had been making Elektra coffee machines in Italy since 1947. He asked Anje to order new parts from Italy and by the time the bar was ready to open it was restored to its original condition, ready to take pride of place on the bar. Liam stood back and as he admired his handiwork he realised how much his father had taught him, when they spent those long hours stripping down and rebuilding his classic motorbikes. He looked out between the barred arched low level windows but all he saw were legs and shoes as they passed. He remembered Anje's story of the monkey and imagined what it would have been like for it, trapped in the cold, semi-darkness during the day and, during the night, the flashing neon lights as they reflected off the water.

The police sirens wailed and blue lights flashed as they raced to the infamous Museum of Medieval Torture at Damrak 33. The museum had been closed the previous day to enable contractors to carry out urgent repairs. What the police discovered was a real body stuffed in the Schandmantel – "the barrel of shame". All that was visible in the medieval barrel, delicately painted with a Chinese dragon wrapped around a tree, which was suspended in mid-air by rusty chains, was the man's head protruding from the top, a hand and a bloody stump poking out through two apertures half-way down. The display had been getting enormous interest due to the lifelike appearance of the wax model – the tormented face displaying a look of sheer horror. Cameras flashed and crowds built up around the exhibit more than any other.

An hour before the museum was due to close the curator called the police.

The autopsy revealed that the Albanian's huge frame had been agonisingly distorted and jammed into the barrel before being injected with a combination of drugs. The first would have given him hallucinations before the second took effect, forcing his vital organs into overdrive. For the last hour of his life Meco would have been in extreme agony, unable to move in the confined space, as his whole body writhed in unmitigated agony.

CHAPTER ELEVEN

Where Dreams Come To Die

Liam remained at his table after breakfast. Anje walked into the kitchen and minutes later came out with a cafetière of fresh coffee, placed it neatly on the table and sat down next to him. She held up the front page of the De Telegraaf, tapped the headlines and translated the article as she read it. She then handed it to Liam and pointed at the grotesque photograph.

Liam pushed the crusts of his toast around the plate.

'What is the matter with you?' she asked, softly.

'Dunno.'

'Has this news upset you?'

Liam sighed and shook his head. 'Nah . . . not at all.' He gave her a wry smile. 'De Groot don't mess about does he?'

Anje pretended to ignore him but she couldn't hide her nervousness and her hand shook as she poured two cups of coffee.

Liam watched her and waited until she'd finished before he spoke. 'Will you help me?' he asked.

She replied immediately. 'Of course,' she said, with a smile.

'I need to find new girls for the bar but I can't just walk up to the windows can I?'

Anje beamed a true smile and looked relieved. 'There is no way can you do dat . . . they will kill you . . .' She paused. 'For sure they will do dat.'

Liam tilted his head to one side and looked across at her. 'Not *those* girls,' he said, emphatically.

She exhaled with relief. 'God zij dank.' She laughed loudly but almost immediately a fearful look spread across her face. 'The *lady* boys and *pimps* – they protect their precious merchandise. They watch them twenty-four hours a *day* . . . *every* day. The girls are prisoners, eh?" She sucked at her bottom lip and nodded. 'They do dat for sure . . .' She forced a brazen smile. 'Do you know each of these girls can earn for them *four* or even five *thousand* guilders each day?'

Liam looked at her and mouthed the figures. He sipped at his coffee before he spoke. 'OK, so where *do* I find them?'

Anje looked at him. 'I will help you . . .' she said, reassuringly.

The next morning at breakfast Anje sat with Liam and told him she'd found eight girls who were interested in talking to him and she agreed with Karel that he could use the breakfast room to meet them.

He had never interviewed anyone in his life and, as he heard the footsteps of the first girl walking down the stairs, he felt incredibly nervous. He didn't know whether he should stand or remain seated at the table. He sat and waited and subconsciously tapped his fingers heavily on the table causing the spoon to rattle in the saucer.

Bernice Lisse, a young woman in a long black skirt, a men's black denim shirt and shiny chrome studs in her nose and lower lip, smiled when she saw Liam. As she walked towards him he stood and shook her hand.

'Hello,' he said nervously.

At first glance she appeared plain; she wore no make-up but her beautiful bone structure and short dark spiky hair made up for it. She looked like a young girl but her lined face couldn't hide the hard life she had already experienced.

'Has Anje told you about my new bar?'

She nodded and smiled.

Liam smiled back at her. 'Good.' He seemed to relax and continued. 'Tell me about yourself.'

'Well, I was born in Amsterdam, in 1971. My parents are both Dutch, broad-minded and well-educated and insisted that I had the same level of education they'd had.'

Liam nodded.

'I started playing the piano at the age of five and by the age of fourteen I played all over the city. I went to the University of Amsterdam where I studied music. When I left the University I joined the Nederlands Philharmonisch. In the first season I met Andrea Libat, a singer with the Nederlands Opera Company. At first I found it hard to understand why I felt so strange towards her but, during the euphoria of the opening night and the party that followed, I suddenly realised what was happening to me.' She took a coloured handkerchief from her pocket and fiddled with it nervously. 'Andrea was an excellent teacher and I was a willing pupil . . .' She paused and for the first time the nervousness melted away and her face was transformed into a childlike smile. 'A very willing pupil,' she said.

Liam forced a nervous smile.

She continued. 'So much so that I have never looked at a man since that time.'

Liam fidgeted in his seat, sipped at his cold coffee and motioned for her to continue.

'I left home and for a few months I shared a flat on the Leidseplein with Andrea. As our relationship grew, I experienced greater sexual pleasures by the day. Andrea renamed me Bernie, at first just for fun, but one day it gets stuck. She encouraged me to play in many of the piano bars around the city and within a few months I got to love the other side of the tracks.' She reached out for her cup and Liam topped it up. Her demeanour changed as she took a deep breath. 'Andrea left the city to tour Europe and I stayed in Amsterdam, eventually finding myself a new lover, and another, and another.' She wiped at her eyes. 'One day . . .' she paused to fold her handkerchief, 'my luck ran out.'

Liam's face mirrored her distress.

'I met Lucy.' She tugged at her hair. 'Lucy was not good for me . . .' Bernie looked down at the floor. 'She was a de opdringer van de drug and petty thief. She took me to a bad place with the drugs.' She paused and swallowed hard. 'A very bad place . . . we were always stoned and injecting anything Lucy could get her hands on.' She bent her head, rubbed at the scars on her arms and took several deep breaths as she remembered her friend. She slowly raised her head and looked directly at Liam. 'Lucy disappeared,' she said softly.

Liam fidgeted and slid the spoon between his fingers.

Bernie continued. 'Maybe she is in the Rokin or Singel.' All of a sudden her mood changed and she wiped at her tearful eyes with her handkerchief. 'I was very sick . . .' She paused, straightened her back and sat up in the chair. 'But do you know here in Amsterdam we have fantastic volunteers who spend their lives helping to rehabilitate people like me and the never ending stream of addicts in the city.'

Liam nodded. He was strangely sympathetic to the young woman in front of him, their paths had striking similarities.

Bernie continued. 'I know what you are thinking . . .' she said, as she sucked at her lips. 'Why is *she* here?'

Liam looked at her and waited.

'I want only to play piano, that is my first love and . . . maybe . . . some of your customers will like a *lesbian*. Ja?'

Liam thought for a second. 'We will have a piano – and I need someone to play it.' He smiled. 'I can give you a job but you will need to help me out when you're not playing.' He looked at her expectantly. 'Deal?'

Bernie stood up and hugged him tightly squeezing the breath out of him. 'Deal,' she said, thankfully.

The bar was to become her new home and, with the help and understanding of the majority of the resident prostitutes, she gradually regained her confidence. Whilst her lesbianism was the subject of many an in joke in front of the clients, all the girls working at the bar enjoyed her humour and music.

Anje rejoined Liam in the breakfast room. 'Well? I assume she is joining you? She seemed to be very happy.'

Liam smiled at her. 'Yes, she is and I've done my first interview.'

'Good,' she said, as she picked up the used cups. 'I'll bring more coffee.'

As she walked into the back room Liam heard footsteps on the stairs. He sat down at the table and waited.

The tall, attractive, dark-haired woman walked in, smiled and sat down in front of him. 'Hello, I'm Ruby Stern. Are you Liam?'

Liam was taken by surprise and, feeling intimidated, mumbled his reply. 'Yes . . . I'm Liam.'

Ruby was dressed from head to toe in body-hugging black leather. Tight clinging designer split skin jeans; punk influenced low strap studded ankle boots, a long-sleeved leather shirt and a plain white sheer tee shirt that accentuated her large firm breasts and protruding nipples.

She pulled her chair away from the table and moved side-on to Liam. She looked directly at him and waited for his questions.

He didn't have any and sat staring back at her, mesmerised.

She took a packet of cigarettes from her handbag, offered one to Liam, pulled her shirt across her breasts, reached across and lit Liam's before lighting her own.

Fortunately for Liam, Anje walked in with a tray of coffee. She smiled and placed it on the table. Sensing that Liam was nervous she took her time to pour the coffee.

Liam, feeling more confident to have someone else in the room, spoke. 'OK, tell me about you,' he asked, as his voice cracked with nerves.

She looked directly at him and began. 'I was born in Lubeck.' She could see that Liam had no idea where it was so she drew a map in mid-air with the hand that held the cigarette and the smoke formed a non-descript shape. 'It is a town on the coast in northern Germany.'

Liam nodded and pushed a cup towards her.

'Danke,' she said. 'It was a sleepy town and nothing for young people to do except in the summer.' She took a drag of her cigarette. 'I couldn't wait to get away from das place.'

Liam sipped at his coffee, and looked at her over the rim of the cup.

'I left home when I was sixteen and went to live in Hamburg. I loved the music scene . . . and . . .' She gave him a mischievous smile and whispered. 'And the drugs . . .'

Liam jerkily nodded his understanding. 'Um.'

'I love music . . .' She fantasised. 'Yeah . . . and musicians. Do you?'

Liam didn't reply and stared back at her. Ruby was incredibly attractive and mysterious but her face was tinged with a hard-edged look which dissolved when she smiled.

She laughed loudly. 'No. Don't misunderstand me.' She flapped her hands excitedly. 'Not musicians . . . I mean . . . do *you* like music?'

'I know what you meant,' said Liam, sloping back into his chair.

'I really love music and musicians. I loved them too much – too often.'

'I can hear that,' said Liam. He laughed loudly. 'Your scouse accent kinda gives that away.' He relit his cigarette. 'Go on.'

'I was pregnant but Johnny didn't want a baby so I tried to get rid of it. They fucked up and I nearly died. I never saw Johnny again so I moved to Frankfurt.'

'Was Johnny a musician?'

'Yeah – from Liverpool. He played guitar . . . he was great.' She lit another cigarette and tried to hide her sad face. 'Yeah he was – but he went home – and didn't come back,' she said, her voice fading. She sniffed and faked a smile. 'So guess what I did?'

Liam shrugged.

'I married Günter; he was an architect, but so different to Johnny and, do you know what?'

Liam didn't offer a response.

'He didn't like music!' she shrieked. 'He couldn't stand it.' She took a huge drag on her cigarette. 'I don't know why I married him.' She reflected. 'Yes I do.' She smiled and licked her lips. 'It was easy with him and for a while he had money.' She bit on the cigarette and sighed heavily. 'He gambled everything . . . everything.' She scoffed. 'The bastard!'

Liam refilled her cup.

'I came here to Amsterdam and worked in clubs and learned my trade. I believe I'm one of the best in this city: if not *the* best. I have a special way with some men and they love it.'

Liam stubbed out his cigarette and lit another. 'Why do you want to work at my place, if you are so . . .' He paused. '*Special?*'

The left side of her mouth curled up. 'I want to work only with my special clients and not be on a conveyor belt for eighteen hours every day and night.' She waited for Liam's response. There was none. She continued. 'Do you understand that?'

'I suppose so,' replied Liam, unable to contemplate what she had just said.

She cleared her throat and for the first time she appeared nervous. 'I have a little girl. Fleur . . . I want her to have a normal life.' She looked hard at Liam. 'If there is such a thing.'

Liam stifled a laugh and shrugged. 'Will your clients come with you?'

She licked her lips and looked directly at him. 'For sure they will. When do you open?'

Liam pushed back his chair and reached out his hand. 'Six days. OK?'

She shook his hand and then kissed him, leaving her bright purple lipstick on his cheek.

Liam pulled away before speaking. 'You will have your own room but everyone will need to decorate it themselves.'

'You didn't hear me . . .' she said, as she tossed her head back and smiled evocatively. 'My clients are very special and they will do whatever I ask them to do.' She chuckled to herself as she left.

Liam pushed his chair back onto two legs, took several huge breaths and exhaled heavily.

Anje walked back in. 'She was nice, eh?'

'Bloody hell.' He shook his head wildly. 'I've never met anyone like that . . .' He grabbed the cup and gulped at the cold coffee. 'Where on earth did you find her?'

Anje smiled. 'It is not so difficult. There are too many girls in this city and not enough places for them to work safely without pimps.'

'Is that right?' asked Liam.

Anje suddenly looked sad. 'When I have some free time I will show you the other side.' She paused. 'The sad side . . . of this wonderful city.' She turned away from Liam, picked up the tray, sniffed, and smiled back at him furtively.

He stood up, stretched his arms and straightened his back. 'Mmm . . . yeah.'

Anje cleared her throat and as she walked towards the kitchen she continued. 'So, now you have two of your girls and more to visit you.'

Liam walked around the breakfast room and subconsciously ran his fingers across the tables and thought hard about his future. *What was he getting himself into?* He knew his actions and decisions could affect so many other people's lives. He didn't have long to contemplate anything or make a decision because this third interviewee walked into the room and stood waiting for him to speak to her. He didn't hear her and continued to walk between the tables.

Peggy Rubin flicked her cassette player and the dance music filled the room. Liam startled by the music, spun round. The young woman in her early twenties was totally different to his previous interviewees and had a fresh and innocent look about her. She wore a bright yellow skirt, a yellow, dogtooth, check blouse, a light grey body warmer and a black and grey felt trilby hat which was positioned to partially obscure her left eye. She was petite but her presence was huge as she moved provocatively in time with the music.

Before Liam could speak Peggy introduced herself and flicked off the music.

On cue the door opened and Anje walked out of the kitchen with the third tray of coffee of the day. She placed it on the table and Liam motioned for Peggy to sit down. Liam felt more relaxed with Peggy and it showed. Anje smiled at him and winked before skipping out of the room.

Liam handed Peggy her coffee. 'Well Peggy, tell me all about yourself?' he said. He sat back and waited for her to speak.

'I was born in Nijmegen, not so far from here.' Liam nodded, trying to hide his ignorance. 'And I came to Amsterdam a few weeks ago.' She sipped at her coffee, placed the cup in the saucer and straightened it up. For no apparent reason she unexpectedly appeared nervous. 'I was married . . .' She paused and waited for Liam to comment. He didn't, so she continued. 'I married my boss.'

Liam gave her a knowing smile.

'He worked at the Phillips factory in Hilversum. He was the sales manager and . . .' She looked blindly into mid-air and closed her eyes. 'He was *lovely.*' She opened her eyes, turned to Liam and smiled broadly.

Liam frowned. 'So why are you here?' he asked.

'We were both sacked from our jobs and, things changed,' she said. 'He was boring when we didn't have work. And we have had no money.'

Liam looked concerned. 'What the . . . ? Why wuz yer *both* sacked?'

A smile exploded across her face. 'Noisy sex . . .' she said. Before Liam could respond she continued. 'It was at work in the office . . . Naughty eh?' She giggled.

Liam showed his concern. 'They sacked you for that?' He continued while he shook his head. 'Unbelievable.'

Her expression changed to sadness. 'It was *not* my husband's office . . . it was the office of *his* boss – on *his* desk.'

Liam wanted to laugh but maintained his composure, swigged at his coffee and reached for a cigarette but didn't light it.

'Ongelofelijk eh?'

Liam gave her a blank look and shook his head.

Peggy acknowledged he didn't understand but nevertheless continued. 'I didn't wish to stay with my husband any more. I left Hilversum the next day and went to work as a waitress at a Kasteel, near my home in Nijmegen, and within a few weeks I had my own clients. It was fantastic.' She didn't want to take a breath. 'The owner, Hugo Wessell, he told me I was his star girl.' She inhaled and pushed out her chest proudly. 'I earned more money than anyone else. My clients were millionaires, from film . . . television and pop stars: all very famous men.' She paused. 'Sometimes the girls come too . . .' She giggled brazenly and waited for Liam to comment but instead he pushed his chair back on two legs and nodded slowly, before acknowledging what she'd said.

'Um,' muttered Liam.

'Do you know what they call me?' She waited for a split second but when Liam didn't answer her she continued. She blurted it out. '45! Can you believe that?'

Liam didn't understand.

'45!' she repeated. 'I do it so quickly. Fantastic eh? They love sex with Miss Peggy.'

Liam offered her a cigarette. She shook her head. He lit his and looked at her quizzically. 'Why 45? What do you mean by that?'

'The small records play at 45! They were about three minutes long . . . 45!' she shrieked.

He nodded. 'So, if that was so good why are you here today?'

She bit her bottom lip and sighed. 'I make a mistake.'

'Mistake?' asked Liam.

'Yes . . . a grote mistake.' Liam stared at her. She smiled. 'Sorry, I know. I mean *big mistake*.' Liam nodded and Peggy continued. 'I took a holiday with a client . . . Hugo was crazy at me. He beat me!' She reflected as she gently stroked her ribs and stomach. 'And . . .' She shook her head wildly. 'He throw me out!'

Liam grimaced. 'Can you work?'

She smiled and unexpectedly gave him a mischievous look. 'You can try me if you wish,' she said, licking her lips.

Liam stood up and shook his head. 'No, no. Business and pleasure, *you* should know that. Right? Ain't that why you're here?'

She nodded slowly. 'I understand.'

Liam continued. 'We open in six days. You can have a room for four hundred guilders a week and we take forty percent of everything you earn.' He paused. 'And . . . you will need to decorate your room and supply your furniture.'

She stood on tip toes and kissed him. 'I will be there.' She flicked her cassette player and sang along with the music as she danced up the stairs.

Anje waited until she could no longer hear the music, before she sat down with Liam, and poured him a large glass of fruit juice. 'You drink too much coffee,' she scolded.

'I know. But that was hard.' He lit a cigarette.

'And you smoke too much,' she said. 'I have a break this afternoon shall we go for a walk?'

Liam interviewed five more girls and chose three of them. Helga, from Frankfurt, Saskia, from Moldovia and Vil from Ostend. All three looked very different to those he had already chosen and had varying degrees of experience but all he cared about was that he had his girls when he opened.

Anje and Liam walked out of the hotel into bright sunshine and a cloudless blue sky. Liam shielded his eyes with one hand. He hated sunglasses and had only worn them once. The effect of cutting out the light made him feel depressed and reminded him of the long months he had spent in prison without feeling the warmth of the sun.

Anje guided Liam across the road to the shady side of Warmoesstraat where they strolled slowly until he was accustomed to the brightness. They turned onto Oudezijds Voorburgwal and walked along the canal. They passed the tour boat landing stages and large groups of tourists who

145

queued excitedly as they waited for their trip. It was idyllic in the warm sunshine and Liam soaked up his surroundings like a sponge. He was enjoying his new found "home" and he felt relaxed and strangely reborn. No one knew him and he had yet another chance to remake his life although there was still a certain amount of trepidation in his mind. They passed the Munttoren on the corner of Muntplein Square, where the Singel and Amstel met, and crossed the canal bridge, taking care to avoid the blue and white trams, cars and hundreds of cyclists as they raced across the city. They arrived at the Bloemenmarkt – the only floating flower market in Europe. Liam had no interest in flowers and knew nothing about them. He'd only ever bought flowers once and that was when Harry was born. He could remember blindly grabbing a bunch from the flower seller on the stall outside the hospital and feeling extremely embarrassed as he carried them through the hospital. He passed them to Kathleen as soon as he saw her. She once told him she had a dream of a house with a decent-sized garden away from London rather than the tiny overgrown and neglected patch at the front of their house. Liam reflected. *Perhaps if they had moved away from London then their lives would have been very different.*

Anje and Liam moved from barge to barge taking in the fantastic colours and different varieties of flowers that Liam had never seen or imagined. When he saw how much Anje liked the huge yellow flowers, he bought two bunches and handed them to her.

'How did you know?' she asked.

Liam looked at her blankly.

'Van Gogh?' she said. 'He painted these beautiful flowers

146

. . . sunflowers,' she held them up and smiled with pleasure, '. . . in so many of his famous paintings?'

Liam had no idea what she was talking about. His mind was elsewhere. *What were his family doing back in London? Shouldn't he be there with them?* He lit a cigarette and wondered. *Did any of them want him there?* He looked around and took in his surroundings, shaking his head as he mumbled the answer to himself. 'Probably not.'

They grabbed the only unoccupied table outside the Ristorante Caruso on the corner opposite the flower market and ordered coffee. Anje poured Liam's coffee, stirred in the cream and returned to admiring her sunflowers.

CHAPTER TWELVE

Angel Eyes

Matthijs repositioned the bar in Liam's chosen position to the left-hand side of the front window, which allowed him the opportunity of looking onto the street and canal when he worked behind it. It also enabled him to open the large sliding front windows to let in fresh air and for the music to flow out across the Oudezijds Voorburgwal.

With the work in his flat complete Liam visited the flea market at Waterlooplein with Keeva where he bought an old CD player and radio, Balinese wood carvings and pictures for the wall of his flat; a table, two chairs and a three seater settee; and rugs to cover the wooden floor boards. Matthijs arranged for his men to use the pickup to collect everything and deliver it to the bar. Liam watched in disbelief as they used the lifting beam just beneath the roof to hoist everything up to the top floor and in through the window.

With two days left before his place was due to open there was feverish activity throughout the building. The day before the bar was due to open Liam was up at dawn. He walked the short distance from the Koopermoolen Hotel and unlocked the front door of his place. He entered and stood transfixed. He circled around several times before sitting at various tables and looking at the bar from every angle. The transformation was incredible and for the first time he was able to take in the changes that everyone had made. It was remarkable. He excitedly climbed the stairs to his flat and stood in the centre of the open plan lounge, kitchen and diner, before moving across to the window. The sun temporarily blinded him until he adjusted to it and took in the view. It was beautiful. He blindly removed a cigarette from the packet in his pocket but, before lighting it, checked that there was an ash tray on the table. It was then he noticed the vase of flowers that Keeva had placed in the centre of the table. He sat on the settee, pushed himself deep in the threadbare fabric and let out a huge sigh. He pinched himself before speaking in an almost inaudible voice. 'Well, son.' He shook his head slowly from side to side and spoke slowly. 'You've achieved something honest on your own for the *very* first time.' He wiped at his eyes and savoured every drag. He thought about what he'd just said. 'Well . . . almost,' he said, with a shrug of his shoulders. He stood up and took a final glance out of the window before he made his way through the building checking each room. Everything the girls had said to him at their interviews had been carried out. And with the help of their clients their rooms were cleaned and totally renovated, redecorated and furnished. Each of his girls had put their personal style on the décor, lighting and furnishing including the en-suite bathrooms or showers. Bernie's room was a complete contrast to all the other erotically themed rooms. With the exception of the single bed, armchair, table and chair, and several faded paintings that hung crookedly on the walls, little had changed. It had been painted, albeit badly, and left unfinished.

Liam's enthusiasm had rubbed off on Asmara and she deep cleaned the tiny kitchen, sorted out her herbs and spices and worked on a new menu. She planned the dishes for the opening night and discussed each dish in detail with Liam.

Anje had a free day and she revelled in giving Liam a guided tour of some of the numerous landmarks and museums that made Amsterdam so special. They crossed the Singel and Keizergracht canal into Huidenstraat. Anje stopped outside the Pompadour café. They both gazed through the window in silence at row upon row of intricately decorated and colourful handmade cakes and gateaux.

An elderly man pushed open the door and tapped Liam on the shoulder. 'De beste cakes in de stad,' said the man, licking at his lips before he climbed onto his rusty bicycle and cycled unsteadily away. Anje smiled at Liam and translated. 'He said, "the best cakes in the city."'

They couldn't resist and entered the tiny café. It had only four marble topped tables with four chairs at each. The chairs were upholstered with heavily patterned brocade. The décor was exquisite with its ornate plaster ceiling and coving and intricately carved pillars. The walls were decorated with suede-effect material and covered with paintings, in large antique frames, of Louis IV and Madame Pompadour.

'Pompadour was a bad French woman of Louis the fourteenth,' said Anje, shyly. Liam looked at her, thought for a minute until a confused smile slowly appeared on his face. He had absolutely no idea who it was.

Anje spoke to the young waitress and within minutes she returned with a selection of handmade cakes on individual metallic rectangular-shaped bases. She placed them neatly onto the table and took great pride as she carefully straightened up the plates. She returned with the pot of tea and milk and placed that on the table and arranged the spoons on the opposite side of the saucer to the cup handle. Liam, his mind elsewhere, paid little attention to the delightful cakes and waited for the waitress to leave before speaking.

'You remember you told me about your work at the sanctuary?'

Anje was taken aback. 'Why?' she asked, clearly stunned. 'You remember the monkey eh?' She glared at him and then frowned. 'And now – *you* are laughing to me?'

Liam appeared to be offended. 'No . . . of course not,' he replied firmly.

Anje nodded, slowly dropped her shoulders and visibly relaxed. She pointed at the cakes. Liam seemed most interested in the decorated chocolate "work of art" on the far side of the table. She slid it towards him, straightened the plate with both hands and placed the fork in his hand.

A young couple walked in and the young man held back apprehensively as the girl made for the table nearest the window. They ordered and the waitress brought the cakes and coffee before a second waitress appeared carrying a bouquet of red roses. She handed them to the young man who blushed as he handed them to the girl. He reached into his jacket pocket and took out a card. The unreserved smiles shared by the couple said it all.

Anje screwed up her nose and smiled. 'Ah . . . how lovely,' she said. 'I wish someone would do that to me one day.' While Liam grunted his disapproval the two American tourists on the next table clapped enthusiastically. Liam was visibly uncomfortable at the scene playing out in front of him and fidgeted in his seat. He waited for Anje to turn back to him and sighed. 'Well . . .' His whole body stiffened and he thrust his fork blindly into the delicate cake destroying the patisserie chef's hard work. 'I have *something* to tell *you* . . .' he said. He looked around as though everyone was listening in to their conversation.

Anje smiled and tried to ease his obvious anguish. 'It is all right,' she said. She looked bewildered. 'Why do you worry about talking with me?'

As he exhaled his whole body trembled. 'I have something that I have never told anyone.' He looked around nervously. 'Isn't it strange how you can talk about something to a complete stranger when you're in a different world?'

She nodded and looked at him quizzically. 'Am I a *complete* stranger in *your* different world?' she asked.

Liam shook his head and took time to gather his thoughts before he continued. 'What I mean is . . .' He sniffed nervously. 'When you're away from the security . . . of your own world: the real *shit* world.' He looked down at the table but saw nothing. 'At first,' he fiddled with the fork, 'you think you understand.' His eyes glazed over and he stared directly ahead as if he was hypnotised. 'Well . . . *now*, I do understand.' He rocked in his chair. 'The crazy thing is, everyone else knew except *me*,' he said, as he tried to stifle his anger.

Anje tilted her head to one side and gazed directly at him. 'What did they know?' she asked, softly.

'I'm an alcoholic for God's sake!' His raised voice resounded across the tiny café and there was an immediate silence.

Anje reached out and touched his left hand then squeezed it firmly, then as if by magic the friendly chatter resumed. 'We can help you, right here in Holland. Maybe this *will be* a new start for you in this world that is Amsterdam – your *new* liddle world.' She smiled at him and sliced her fork into the circular milk chocolate striped sponge and slid it into her mouth. 'You must enjoy this wonderful taart,' she said, as she licked her lips before she spiked another piece. 'Then I will show you around this beautiful city. It is so easy . . .'

Liam didn't taste his cake. Instead he thought hard about the challenge ahead. *He wondered if he would be able to resist his demons and live without his crutch in his new found world. After all, he was the manager of a brothel and a bar. A bar for God sake! A bar, in an area in a city that owed its very existence to sex, drugs, alcohol and extreme violence.*

Anje must have read his thoughts and gave him a puzzled look. She spoke softly. 'Can I ask how you will manage a bar when you have a problem with the alcohol?'

He sniffed innocuously. 'What choice do I have? I can't leave until the police sort out the stabbings and . . . I've already committed to De Groot.' He tapped the spoon on the saucer. 'And, in the meantime what do I do for money?' He exhaled as he sighed and realised he couldn't hold in his frustration any longer. He continued. 'If I don't take him up on his offer . . .' His whole body trembled with the mental conflict. He shook his head wildly as he spoke. 'There's NO way I'm going back inside!' He stood up and stomped towards the door.

Liam and Anje walked in silence for almost an hour as they crossed bridge after bridge and back again. Anje deliberately walked one way and then the other, confusing Liam until she felt she could talk to him. They stopped on a quiet bridge and Anje finally spoke. 'Liam, you know I can help you.' He shook his head and mumbled his response. She continued. 'I can . . . I can help you . . .' she said indignantly.

He turned to her, his face lined with desperation. 'How?' he croaked.

She took a huge breath and smiled broadly. 'It's near the Red Cat! 282A Oudezijds Voorburg Wal,' she said, eagerly.

'What is?' he asked. 'The Alco . . . ?'

He couldn't say the words but Anje understood him. 'Yes, we have this *here* in Amsterdam.' She took his arm. '*They* will *help* you,' she said softly.

Liam looked at her, his face devoid of any feeling. She put her arms around him and whispered in his ear. 'Will you go?'

Liam nodded.

Anje checked her watch. 'There is a meeting this afternoon at four o'clock . . .' She paused. 'In English . . . I will take you but I can't go inside.'

Liam attended that afternoon and continued to do so every week without fail. Sometimes he also attended the "Living Sober Group" on Wednesdays at eight pm.

Liam was deliberating with the exact position to place his pride and joy; the Elektra coffee machine. He kept flicking his long hair back from his forehead every time he bent his head or leaned forward. Keeva tapped him on the shoulder. 'You open soon and if you don't mind me saying I think you should do something about your hair.' She paused. 'And perhaps . . .' She took a deep breath before continuing. 'Some new clothes.'

'Really – what's wrong with these?' He pointed at his ripped jeans and dirty tee shirt. 'I can get them washed . . .'

Keeva cut him off with a look of disgust. 'You're the

manager, of a new bar. What will your customers think if they see – ?'

Liam interrupted her. 'Alright, let's do it.'

They walked past the Sonesta Hotel and the Magere Brug – skinny bridge – until they reached Spuistraat. When Liam saw the name of the shop he pulled back and trembled. 'I can't go in there! Did you deliberately bring me here?' he screamed.

Keeva shot him a confused look. 'What do you mean, Liam?'

'The *name*,' he replied, looking up above the shop.

'What's the problem?' she asked.

'What the hell is this place?'

Keeva lowered her voice. 'It may seem a bit weird, but it's a hairdresser's . . . one of the best in Amsterdam.'

The music blared out even before they had opened the door. *"Housewives On Fire"* was the weirdest place Liam had ever set foot inside. It was a combination of a hairdresser's, a retro clothes shop and disco. Liam's anger stemmed from the name and he was sure it had been chosen deliberately, but how could anyone know?

The DJ positioned in the window mixed 12" vinyl records on twin decks. Immediately in front of him was the bar and a row of pale green, retro, vinyl-covered barstools where customers or friends of clients could sit and have a drink while they waited.

Keeva introduced Liam to Afiza, the owner, a tall dark woman with waist length dark hair and wearing the shortest leather skirt Liam had even seen. The floor had been decorated with colour supplements from fashion magazines, glued onto hardboard and varnished. The walls were lined with quilted, off white, vinyl sheets and along the right-hand side were rails of brightly coloured clothes. The place buzzed with the combination of hairdryers, music and excitable young people flicking through row upon row of the retro clothes. The atmosphere was fantastic. Before Liam had time to think he was led to a dimly lit area at the rear of the shop by a young girl, and into a labyrinth of deep burgundy painted walls. A young gay man removed Liam's shirt and handed him a gown to put on. Liam felt extremely uncomfortable but obliged and sat in the chair. His hair was washed several times with what smelt to him like perfume. He was then guided back into the main area of the shop and the agile, pretty female apprentice, slid him into a chrome-plated barber's chair with brightly coloured vinyl flaps to rest his feet. Afiza offered Liam a glass of rosé wine. He hesitated, and then shook his head. 'I'll have a coffee . . . black,' he said.

The stylist set to work on his hair smiling throughout the "operation" which took more than an hour. The hairdresser finally dried Liam's hair and the apprentice delivered Liam's shirt which had been washed, dried and ironed. After massaging his shoulders, the hairdresser helped Liam to put it on.

Keeva remained at the bar drinking wine with Afiza as she talked excitedly about Liam, the renovation works at the bar, and how he came to be in Amsterdam. Liam's long hair had finally gone. His new style was short, sharp and cut to the shape of his head – a Steve McQueen – and was met with approval from everyone. Liam paid what was thankfully a reduced rate and as they were leaving Keeva asked if Afiza and her staff could come to the opening night. They looked at Liam and waited for his confirmation. Liam thought for a split second and pointed at the DJ. 'Sure you can . . . but I want him to come and play the music . . .' Afiza nodded her agreement and the DJ smiled excitedly at Liam.

The gay hairdresser pushed his face against the window and mouthed his response to Liam. 'Thank you . . .'

Keeva and Liam visited the men's shops in the Kalvertoren Shopping Center, took the open-sided glazed lift and raced up to the higher floors between the escalators. Liam didn't like any of the bright modern clothes so they left the busy shopping centre and made their way on to the boutiques in Nieuwe Zijde, where the prices were much cheaper and the clothes more "normal." Despite Keeva's exhaustive efforts to persuade Liam to buy something different, he chose two pairs of denim jeans, three check shirts and a tee shirt with a large Amsterdam motif on the front. They made their way back towards the bar but, after a few minutes of unusual silence, Keeva slowed down and stopped in the middle of the pavement outside the Crown Plaza Hotel. She guided Liam away from the prying eyes and ears of the tall imposing doorman, with his handlebar moustache, braided cap and long full-length grey overcoat, before she spoke. 'Liam, I'm sorry but I'm leaving. I won't be staying at the bar.'

'What?' he barked. 'What the fuck! Why do you want to leave *now*? We're about to open!'

Keeva started to walk away, feverishly rubbing her hands, before she turned back to face him. 'I really am sorry, but I have to move on . . .' she said, apologetically.

'Move on? Where the *fuck* have you got to go? You're like the rest of us!'

Keeva replied coyly. 'Robert has asked me to marry him.'

'ROBERT?' he mocked. 'He's done what?' He couldn't hide

his anger and nor did he want to. He screamed at her. 'That bastard *dumped* you here in Amsterdam . . . now you want to *marry* him! You must be out of your fucking mind!' He kicked out at the hotel planter. 'Married!'

The doorman looked up and made to walk towards them.

Liam scowled at him, raised his tight fists, took up his all too familiar fighting stance and snarled directly at him. 'Fuck off, you bastard!' he screamed.

The doorman shuffled nervously backwards until he reached his well-worn position and looked blindly ahead.

Liam repeated the threat under his breath as he stormed off.

Keeva left Amsterdam later that afternoon.

CHAPTER THIRTEEN

A World Without Love

Liam called everyone together in the bar. Matthijs's men were touching up the paintwork and clearing away their tools and materials when the girls walked in and congregated around the piano. The men immediately stopped working and gaped in awe at the collection of beautiful girls. Liam smiled to himself, satisfied he had made the right choice. He asked if the men could give him an hour and reluctantly they left. It was the first time Liam had seen all the girls together and their first real opportunity to meet each other. Liam stood and took his time to look around at his girls. Asmara stood nervously in the back and tried to be part of the proceedings. Liam sought to hide his disbelief as it slowly sunk in that it was him who was now responsible for everything. He sipped at his coffee and coughed nervously before he spoke. 'Thank you all for coming. I appreciate how everyone has worked so hard to get this place ready.' He placed his coffee mug on the bar and lit a cigarette. 'It's no secret.' His hands shook with apprehension. 'You all know Keeva has left,' he said, with a wry smile before he continued. 'She's decided to get *married*,' he mocked.

They all grinned and nodded back at him.

'Well, I'm now going to need all of you to work with me and spend time here in the bar until I find a replacement.'

They nodded their agreement once more.

'So I want you to help Bernie and work at least two shifts a week here in the bar.' He lit a second cigarette. 'As we discussed when I first met you, I expect you *all* to work *six days*, even during your periods.' There was no reaction from any of them: they had well-tried ways of continuing to work. Liam continued. 'Even if it's only drinking and entertaining clients in the bar.' He suddenly felt more confident. 'You will all need new clients, so if you all spend some time in the bar, it will be a way to entice new ones; a way for them to mingle with you, and allow you to break the ice with the shyer punters.'

While the majority of them nodded, Ruby glared at him. He looked directly at her, raised his index finger in her direction, slowly lowered it and continued. 'There will be some exceptions, but *whatever* rota *I* set I expect everyone to follow it.' He raised his voice for the first time. 'Understood?' He acknowledged their unanimous reaction, forced a smile, stubbed out his cigarette and deliberated before lighting another one. 'The good news is – we will *not* be entertaining the late night drunks or tourists through the night.'

Liam had already made the decision that to hire doormen and bouncers to control anyone too drunk to drink or buy sex was a waste of his time and money.

Every one of them gave him a shocked and relieved look. 'During the week my bar will open at midday and close at midnight, and, only stay open until one or two o'clock at the weekend. Regular clients *must* make an appointment.' He raised a large diary and tapped at it several times. 'In here?'

He waited until they all nodded their agreement. 'Alright?' They nodded and he laid it beside the telephone on the bar. 'It costs money to keep this place open and I don't want empty rooms.'

The cheers were deafening. At last someone understood them.

Liam smiled to himself as he walked outside and lit another cigarette. He mumbled incoherently as he congratulated himself with a wide grin. He looked up and down the canal, and for the first time took notice of the street dealers who were predominantly Moroccan and Moluccan men. They stood shamelessly offering and selling drugs on the bridges. He had noticed them outside FEBO, a fast food walk-in restaurant in Damrak 6, offering drugs, but didn't think they would venture into an area so heavily policed by the heavies of De Groot and his fellow criminals. For some reason he felt angry and shuddered. He stood and gave them a long hard hateful glare. It had no effect except for them to shuffle on the spot before grabbing out at the next potential customer that passed within a few feet of them.

CHAPTER FOURTEEN

Love Shack

It was a warm sunny evening when the bar finally opened on 11th May 1999. The red, white and blue neon sign above the window flashed with the new name. "The Love Shack" was finally open for business. The bar had been raised nine inches, which gave Liam a view of the whole bar on one side and the other side, the pavement and the canal. The bar had been completely redesigned and was finished in a black shiny resin that reflected the lights. Four rows of glass shelves, with discreet lighting to accommodate the spirits, had been installed behind the bar and a much smaller identical neon sign with the name flashed above the shelves. The renovated and gleaming Elektra coffee machine stood in pride of place on the right-hand side of the bar while the jukebox had been located strategically between the doors to the ladies and men's toilets. Liam had noticed that all the bars, shops and hotels had vases of tall Amaryllis flowers, red or white with red tinged petals. He went to the flower market to buy them and placed them on the bar and on the new tables and matching chairs. The renovated piano was returned the day before the opening and Bernie and the carpenter took it in turns to play it as the guests arrived. De Groot arranged with Liam for some of his girls and bar staff from his other clubs to help out for the opening.

At ten o'clock the DJ from *Housewives On Fire* took over and the place exploded into life. The girls looked ravishing and surprisingly many of their clients attended, some of them at the same time, and vied for their attention. Matthijs and most of his men attended and it wasn't long before they were dancing animatedly with the beautiful young girls that De Groot had arranged to attend. Karel from the Koopermoolen arrived alone, stayed for a few minutes, had one drink and left.

De Groot hadn't been near the bar since their last meeting two weeks earlier although Liam suspected he had been kept up to date by either the plasterer or Matthijs. Nevertheless he appeared surprised when his decorated water taxi, laden down with his special friends and dignitaries from across the city, moored up outside the bar. While the music wafted through the open windows he stood on the cobbles looking up at the flashing neon sign and the new name of the bar. The tables and chairs outside were occupied with people who seemed to be having a good time. De Groot shook his head in disbelief at the transformation and took great pleasure in showing his special guests around before finally introducing them to Liam. De Groot encouraged them to mingle with the girls and much to Liam's disgust it wasn't long before most of them disappeared upstairs.

It was almost an hour before De Groot introduced Liam to his henchmen: Skipio, who was wearing the same clothes he was wearing when Meco visited, his driver Artem, Jaap,

Luuk, Vim as well as Jan and Piet for the first time. Liam took an instant dislike to the Greek and refused to shake his hand. Instead he shrugged and turned to De Groot. 'Where's "G.I. Jane" tonight?' he asked.

'She will be here some time later. She has business to do before she can come here,' replied De Groot.

The DJ ramped up the volume and the place buzzed as his perfect pulsating music filled the Love Shack. At eleven o'clock Asmara served the banquet, a Rijstaffel that was better than anyone had seen in Amsterdam for a very long time. Martabak – pastry minced beef, Perkedel Jagung – fried corn cakes, Sambal goring tempe – fried soya bean, Ayam Setan – spicy chicken with red peppers and soya, Daging kalio – very spicy beef with coconut milk and exotic herbs, Sambal goring teri kacang – fried salty fish with peanuts, Babi kecap – sweet pork with soya sauce, Sate babi – skewered pork, Sate domba – skewered lamb, Asinan – mango salad with beansprout and spicy sauce, along with dish after dish of differently coloured rice.

The music was suddenly silent and De Groot took the DJ's microphone and spoke. 'Aan al mijn vrienden. Het is mijn eer om u bij de opening van mijn nieuwe onderneming. Een nieuwe naam en we hopen dat een nieuwe start voor iedereen. The Love Shack!'

As Bernie translated De Groot's words into Liam's ear he became more and more angry. Bernie continued. 'He said, "Welcome to *my* new place."'

De Groot raised his voice even louder and spoke in English. 'The best banquet prepared by Asmara should also have beer from her country.' Everyone cheered loudly.

Zita pushed her way through the crowd carrying two

cases of Bir Bintang, Indonesian beer, brewed by Heineken in Holland. De Groot grabbed a bottle, flicked the cap off and raised it in a toast.

'To the Irishman and den Love Shack!' The place erupted and the DJ ramped up the music even more.

Liam was so angry. He wanted a drink but instead he took himself outside, crossed the bridge, leaned on the railings on the opposite side of the canal and lit a cigarette. His anger quickly receded as he looked across at "his" bar and realised what *he* had achieved. Every table was occupied: many of the guests had spilled out onto the pavement and danced to the pulsating music. As he reached into his pocket for a cigarette he felt a tap on his shoulder. He turned to find Zita behind him. She looked so different. She was stunning. Her dark brown hair fell onto the shoulders of her diminutive frame. She wore a classic white seersucker blouse and loose brightly coloured, lightweight cotton trousers and sandals.

'Hello,' she said. 'We have not yet been introduced.'

Liam looked at her and blushed. All he was able to do, to buy time to think, was to light his cigarette. He took a huge drag and stretched out his hand. 'Liam, I'm Liam Reilly.' He released her hand. 'Pleased to meet you . . . um, Zita.'

She smiled at him. 'I like your place.' She kicked a cigarette butt into the canal. 'Nice name . . . very nice. The B52's: that is a fun record.'

Before Liam could answer Bernie rushed out of the bar and, when she saw Liam, she beckoned him to come.

Liam turned to Zita. 'I'm sure I'll see you again.'

'For sure,' she said, as she walked along the canal.

'Liam, you need to change the beer!' gushed Bernie.

*

The following morning Liam was up early and inspected the bar. It was surprisingly clean and there was little damage. He turned on the coffee machine and while he waited for it to warm up he suddenly realised that Anje hadn't come to the opening. He locked the front door and raced around to the Koopermoolen hotel. A young man was on reception reading a newspaper. Liam spoke as soon as he walked through the door. 'Have you seen Anje?'

The young man shook his head, turned the page of the paper, and continued to read. Liam reached the counter and grabbed the lapels of the man's jacket with both hands. 'I asked you a question. Where the fuck is Anje?'

He stuttered his reply. 'I don't know, sir.'

Liam released his grip and allowed the young man to reach for the telephone.

The man spoke quickly and nodded at the response. 'She is not working here anymore, sir.'

'What the fuck?'

'I'm sorry, sir but Karel said she left yesterday. We don't know where she is gone. Sorry, sir.'

Liam brought his fists hard down on the counter, turned and stormed out.

CHAPTER FIFTEEN

There Is Always A Darker Side To Paradise

The Love Shack soon gained a reputation for great food, and it thrived. On Saturday evenings it was impossible to get a table. The Love Shack was very different to the other bars, business men and office workers from outside of the Red Light District regularly came for lunch. To give him and Bernie some free time, Liam took on a young woman to help them. Magdalena was a young Polish girl and although she wore little make-up, was very pretty. She soon became invaluable to him, filling in at only a few minutes notice, even on her days off. Telephone appointments were generally taken by Magdalena but anyone near the telephone could take them. Appointments were written immediately into each girl's page in the diary and it prevented overbooking. While their clients waited they bought a drink: sometimes two or more. A week after opening they began to take bookings for lunch and dinner. Liam booked entertainment three nights during the week and alternated between the DJ from *Housewives On Fire*, tango dancers and live "Indonesian" music when the rijstaffel was served. The most popular with the middle-aged punters were the sexy tango dancers every Thursday. Couples came to eat, drink and watch the dancing or even join in. On those nights the sexual traffic passing in and out of the bar went unnoticed. Liam had telephones installed on the tables at the rear of the bar. Any girl not busy sat on their numbered tables and waited for clients to buy a drink before phoning the relevant table and joining them. For the first few months De Groot visited the bar every month to calculate his impending percentage. On the fourth month, he did the calculations in a few minutes, and without a quibble, handed Liam his 40%. The following month De Groot allowed Liam to do the tally and split the cash. The reason was simple – his take had increased from a meagre 4,000 guilders a week to 14,000 and there was no reason to see why it shouldn't continue to rise.

Liam couldn't sleep and decided to go for a walk. He pulled on his jacket, checked the pocket for his cigarettes and lighter and worked his way down the narrow staircase in almost total darkness. When he reached the first floor the flashing lights from the bars on the other side of the canal created huge distorted shadows on the walls. The bar was in almost total darkness except for the lights in the chiller and the small neon "Love Shack" sign on the wall behind the bar. Bernie sat at the piano and played as quietly as she could. She caught a glimpse of Liam's shadow in the doorway and stopped immediately. He walked towards her and gently touched her shoulder. 'There's no need to stop playing.' He smiled at her. 'You should know that by now.'

She looked up at him and smiled her appreciation.

He took the cigarette packet from his jacket pocket, flicked it open with his thumb and offered it to her. 'Want one?'

'No thanks,' she said. 'I'd rather smoke this.' She took a dirty white clay pipe from her bag and a small leather pouch. She removed a pinch of tobacco and gently massaged it into the nicotine stained bowl.

'How long 'ave yer bin smokin' dat der ting?' he asked, in an exaggerated Irish accent.

She caressed it between her palms as she spoke. 'We go back a long, long way.' She said. She paused and partially opened her palms and stared hard at her pipe before she continued. 'Too far,' her voice cracked, 'much too far . . .' She straightened her shoulders and concentrated as she packed in even more tobacco, sucked at the pipe and smiled up at Liam. 'I think you can't sleep, ja? Shall we go outside?'

Liam pulled her up and waited while she closed the piano lid.

He made two mugs of hot chocolate and handed one to her, locked the bar and sat at one of the tables outside and lit up. For a few minutes they sat in silence and looked towards the lock, a dark and peaceful end of the canal, the opposite of the noise and flashing lights to their right.

Liam lit his second cigarette and pushed himself back in his chair. 'I've never asked if you like working here.'

Bernie puffed at her pipe, tapped it and concentrated as she blew gently into the bowl. The tobacco glowed brightly and she took several more puffs before she spoke. 'Ja, I luv it. I really do.' She turned away and wiped furtively at her eyes. 'I have never been so happy . . . I like my job . . . and the girls . . .' She smiled. 'Well, they love to work at the Love Shack also.'

Liam seemed surprised. 'Do they?' He relaxed into his chair. 'Did *they say* that?'

She laughed loudly. 'You didn't know that already?' She shrieked. 'No?'

'No, I didn't. I had no fucking idea . . . that's fantastic . . .'

Three very drunk overweight German men staggered past them. One of them saw Bernie and ambled clumsily towards her, he leaned awkwardly on the table and the mugs slid towards the edge. Liam reached out and caught them and, without taking his eyes off the drunk, placed them on the floor beside him. Bernie was terrified and pulled her head back as far as she could from the revolting stench of the man's breath. Liam glanced at the other two drunks and, confident that they were incapable of any interference stood and looked directly into the man's glazed eyes. The man mumbled a few incoherent German words and staggered back to join his friends. Liam watched them until they were out of sight before sitting back in his chair. He placed the mugs back on the table and lit a cigarette. 'That's fucked that up, eh?' He sipped at the chocolate and screwed up his face. 'Urgh! I don't much like it when it's hot let alone when it's cold!' he said, before looking blindly ahead.

'Was it that bad?' asked Bernie.

'Yes.' He replied brusquely but then reconsidered and thought deeply. 'I mean . . . ugh . . . no.'

She shot him a confused look.

He shook his head violently. 'I just saw *myself* . . . I didn't like it.'

'What?'

'I'm surprised anybody did.' He sobbed. 'I was a feckin' useless drunk. That WAS ME!'

Bernie reached across the table and tried to console him. 'I didn't realise that *you* had that problem. None of us did.'

He shook his head wildly. 'Oh yeah . . . that was me alright . . .'

Their conversation was interrupted by screams that came out of the darkness. Bernie and Liam, oblivious to any danger, instinctively raced along the canal and blindly into the dark alley. They made out the silhouette of a tall man as he darted into Warmoesstraat. Liam chased after him, jumping over the boxes and black bags of rubbish dumped by the bars, clubs and coffee shops following what had been a hectic holiday weekend. He threw his lighted cigarette away and raced into Warmoesstraat. A black Mercedes accelerated wildly, tyres screeching as it raced down the street. Liam shook his head and walked back into the alley to be met by the hysterical screams of Bernie and the young girl. He rushed forward and kicked at the burning rubbish until the flames were extinguished. For a split second he remembered the fire back home. The screams of the distraught young girl regained his attention. 'Sorry about that,' he said, out of breath. He looked back at the smouldering rubbish, removed his jacket and placed it over the girl's skeletal body as she quivered and shuddered with shock. He glanced sympathetically across at Bernie.

'Shall we take her back inside?' she asked.

Liam didn't reply, instead he swept up the young girl and carried her effortlessly back to the Love Shack. He laid her on the banquette near the window and flicked on the lights. The girl sobbed and continued to shake uncontrollably until Bernie returned with a blanket, wrapped it around her and stroked at her greasy matted hair.

Liam poured a brandy, held it up to his nose and for a few seconds seemed to enjoy the aroma. Bernie called out to him and reluctantly he passed her the glass. She held the girl's head while she sipped at the alcohol.

Liam whispered to Bernie. 'Do you recognise the poor cow?'

'I've seen her around the area over the last few days,' said Bernie, 'scavenging from the bins.'

'What! Why does anybody need to do that *here* in this city?'

Bernie nodded and mouthed her response. 'I know.'

Liam shook his head. 'Alright . . . sorry.' He sucked at his teeth. 'I should have known better. I *mean* look what she's been through.' He continued to shake his head in shame as he walked across to the bar and flicked on the coffee machine. 'It looks like it's going to be a long night.'

Bernie caught his attention. 'We should call the police.'

'Yeah . . . they need to catch that evil bastard!'

Bernie left Liam to try and console the young girl while she called the police.

Within three minutes the police sirens could be heard echoing across the canal and finally the blue lights flashed outside the bar as three police cars arrived. Their blue lights continued to flash, something they did deliberately to keep people away, as they rushed into the bar. Several of them drew their guns and stood pointing them threateningly in Liam's direction. Two further police vehicles arrived, followed by an unmarked police car and an ambulance. Bernie spoke quickly and explained what had happened and finally the policemen reluctantly slipped their guns back into their holsters. While the paramedics took care of the young girl, three of the uniformed policemen left to carry out a search of the alley.

Two plain clothed detectives strutted into the bar and one of the paramedics handed the male detective a small bag. The detectives glared at Liam before they turned their attention to Bernie. Bernie explained what had happened and the two detectives nodded knowingly. Bernie then turned to Liam and introduced the detectives. 'This is Detective Pieter Ackerman and Detective Andrea Ribeker. They are from the Zedenpolitie – the Vice Squad.'

Ackerman made sure Liam had sight of his gun before he pushed the holster beneath his jacket then reached out and shook his now sweaty hand. The detective's eyes scanned the bar taking in everything around him before engaging his female colleague while he spoke. 'Have you been here before?' She shook her head. He looked at Liam. 'Nice place,' he said, as he lit a cigarette.

'Thanks,' said Liam, nervously. 'Coffee?'

They eyed the coffee machine on the bar before nodding. Their experience in foreign run bars was not good and the majority failed to serve up anything resembling coffee.

Liam walked across to the bar and returned with a tray of coffee, cream and sugar. 'Do you know *her* name?' he asked.

The detective pinged open the victim's bag and systematically flicked through the meagre contents, then removed her crumpled passport. 'Yes, we do.' He looked across at the paramedics who gave a knowing smile. 'Um.' He grunted. 'The young woman is Valentine Handel.' He looked into space and calculated her age. 'She's nineteen.' He paused. 'That is . . . if her papers are realistic . . .'

The female detective smirked.

Liam tilted his head to one side. 'Does it matter how old she is? She was *raped*!'

173

'Mr Reilly, we show sympathy to the raped victims but we do not cry or we will lose focus on the case. Do you understand that?'

Before Liam could reply, one of the paramedics crossed the bar and whispered to the male detective. He immediately waved them away. They placed Valentine on a stretcher and carried her to the ambulance.

The detectives finished their coffee and placed the empty cups on the tray. 'We will need to talk to you some more.' Bernie nodded. The male detective continued. 'We will come back in the morning – at ten o'clock, to talk to you again.' He glanced at his watch and stood. 'We will take your passports, ja?' Liam shot him a questioning look. The detective glared back at him. 'Uh. It is alright?' He paused and forced a smile. 'Meener Reilly, there is no need to worry – unless there is some secret, ja?'

Liam reached into his jacket pocket and handed it reluctantly to Ribeker. Bernie took hers from her shoulder bag and also passed it to the female detective.

The detectives stepped onto the pavement but Ackerman turned back and waved his cigarette at them. 'The passports will be returned in the morning, ja?' He pointed towards the passports in Ribeker's hand. 'That is both of you.' He looked hard at Bernie and Liam and waited for their response. There was none. He continued. 'OK?' They both reluctantly nodded their agreement.

The door closed behind them and Liam pushed himself back in his seat and exhaled. 'In all my time I've never met police like that. Christ!' He shook his head. 'Are *they* for *real*?'

Bernie poured two huge glasses of water and handed one to Liam. 'Yes, they are. You must remember they see so much bad things here . . . *every* day and *every* night. They must be in control of this area or it would not be possible for business.' She thought and continued. 'Any business . . .'

'Mm,' mumbled Liam as he nodded his understanding.

Bernie went to her room but Liam, his mind still racing from the earlier events, walked to an almost deserted Centraal Station and tried to make sense of everything. He watched in amazement as the pathetic drunks and drug addicts of all ages, mostly women more supple than the best magician's assistant, were able to contort their bodies to squeeze into the empty left luggage lockers along with their worldly belongings to sleep for a few hours of what was left of the night.

It was getting light by the time he returned to the Love Shack. He sat outside and watched the last of the drunks, dealers and pimps making their way across the city to their hotels, squats or apartments.

Liam was setting up for the day when, at exactly ten o'clock, the unmarked police car pulled up outside the bar. As soon as he saw them he stopped what he was doing, opened a new bag of roasted coffee beans, poured them into the grinder and flicked it on. He walked across to the door and unlocked it. Andrea Ribeker, in her mid-forties and overweight, with short greying hair, entered the bar followed by Pieter Ackerman who was wearing the same suit he'd worn the night before. The creases in his trousers and jacket were appalling; it was as though he had slept in it, or rather had not gone to bed but spent the night in his car. Liam acknowledged them with a forced smile and waited while the grinder noisily ground the beans. He made the coffee and they all sat down in front of the open window on the banquette where Valentine had lain only

175

a few hours earlier. Ackerman looked out across the sunlit, mirror smooth water and spoke very slowly. 'You know . . . in the daylight it looks so beautiful, ja?' He paused. 'But at night . . . imagine for a young girl . . . it is afschuwelijk.'

Ribeker translated. 'Horrific.'

Liam nodded.

Ackerman continued. 'Ja, it is *horrific*.' He offered Liam a cigarette, lit it then sipped at his coffee. 'Dis is very good coffee, Meener Reilly. It tastes better dis morning.' Liam shot him an irritated look. Ackerman raised his hand in submission before he continued. 'I mean in the morning . . .'

Liam relaxed and took a drag on his cigarette, sipped at his coffee and nodded in agreement. The door at the rear of the bar opened and Bernie hurried in. She was out of breath but she still tried to make her excuses without attempting to inhale. 'I am very sorry . . . but it was hard to sleep after dat . . . And when I did . . . I was unconscious.'

Detective Ackerman nodded slowly and smiled to reassure her.

Bernie relaxed into the chair.

Ackerman took out his note book and skimmed through the pages. 'We have made a thorough examination of the scene and there are no clues that we can work with but . . .' He paused. 'We do have DNA samples from the attacker's semen.' Liam and Bernie nodded and smiled nervously. 'But it will be several days before we maybe find a match.'

Then Ribeker spoke. 'The good news is that mejuffrouw Handel was not so badly injured and will be coming from the hospital in ten days . . .' she smiled, 'maybe nine.' Liam nodded and smiled back at her. The female detective stood up and glared down at him. 'Meener Reilly, coming from the hospital does not mean she *is* better!' She shook her head and bit at her bottom lip. She wiped the blood in her palm and rubbed it with her fingers before she continued. 'While her body will become better, her mind will be damaged for many years.' She sucked at her bleeding lip. 'Maybe it will be for her total life!' she screeched. 'Did you know that?' She paused and looked hard at Liam before she finished her sentence. 'Meener Reilly?'

Liam blushed and mumbled incoherently.

She sat down and while she continued to glare at Liam she pinched at the heavily ironed creases in her trousers running her fingers uncontrollably up and down them as far as her knees.

Before Liam could regain his composure Ackerman's manner changed. His tired eyes partially closed as they looked Liam up and down. He held Liam's passport in his hand and fanned it with his thumb. He spoke slowly, expressing every word. 'Mr Reilly that is something I think you *do* know, ja?'

Liam took a deep breath and took his time to exhale.

Ackerman continued to speak slowly. 'This morning I made a conversation with my fellow detectives in London,' he stroked at the ginger bristles on his chin, 'you spend some time in prison, ja?'

Liam nodded.

Ackerman smiled confidently. 'I think you spend a lot of time dere . . .' He paused and waited for Liam's reaction. Liam remained stony faced. Ackerman continued to wait for what seemed an inordinate period of time before he spoke, clearly revelling in the theatre. 'And often, ja?'

Bernie couldn't hide the shock as she looked across at Liam.

'Yes, I have been in prison . . . *many times* . . . ja,' replied Liam, indignantly as he mimicked the detective.

'So, I *must* ask this question. Where were *you* last night?'

'We told you! We were *both* sitting outside dis place!' screeched Bernie.

Ribeker glared at Bernie. 'We also know that you have had problems, ja?'

Bernie nodded slowly and looked apprehensively at Ackerman before she spoke. 'Ja, I do.'

Ribeker continued in a soft voice. 'Lesbische, ja?'

Bernie was happy to have her sexual preferences known, but her past? She was not. Feeling humiliated, she bowed her head in shame and murmured her reply without looking up. 'Ja.'

Ackerman jumped up. 'Why should we believe the two of you? Maybe you are both involved?' He asked, stifling a yawn.

'What?' screamed Bernie and Liam simultaneously.

Ackerman was not at all fazed. He took his time to open his cigarette packet, slid one into his mouth, lit it and took his time to exhale the smoke high into the air before sitting down. 'Meener Reilly and, eh . . .'

Ribeker flicked open Bernie's passport and checked the name. 'Miss Lisse.'

Ackerman nodded.

Liam and Bernie sat looking open mouthed at the detectives.

Ackerman continued. 'We don't believe that you *are* involved. You *see*, none of you have done dis crime before.' He coughed and looked at Bernie. 'I don't think *you* could do this? Do you?' Bernie blushed and shook her head wildly. The detective now turned his attention to Liam. 'Meener Reilly.

You are new to our city and there is something you should know about dese crimes.' He paused. 'Dese crimes of rape.'

Liam visibly relaxed and gestured his offer of coffee. Everyone nodded. While he set up the machine Ackerman walked across, leaned on the bar and spoke to him. 'In this city we do not have so much time to solve crimes of rape,' he said.

'How long?' asked Liam.

'Meener Reilly, it is two weeks.' He stared hard at Liam. 'Veertien dagen.'

'What?'

'Meener Reilly, this city has sex and drugs – with that come de criminals and . . .' He snarled as he spoke the last word. 'Animals! We need to catch dese people!' He slapped his open palm on the bar and the spoons in the clean saucers rattled. 'We are very good at our job.' He smiled proudly. 'And, often, we do catch them before that time.'

Liam wondered how many criminals they actually did catch.

'Meener Reilly, I will give you some information – there are at least four types of rape.'

Liam mouthed "four" back at him.

'Ja, there are four.' He held up four fingers to reinforce the number. 'The first is the opportunist – for sex only.' Ackerman took the first two cups and passed them to Bernie and Ribeker. He walked back to the bar and continued. 'They feel the woman, she deserves it, and "you're a whore."'' For the first time he slipped two spoons of sugar in his coffee. Liam remained behind the bar and straightened the beer mats. 'The second is anger. They are angry with the women in general – they feel they can have sex when they want it – where they want it.' Liam looked over the rim of his cup at Ackerman

179

as he sipped his coffee. The detective continued. 'The third is *power,* "I'm in control *but* I won't hurt you."' He sniggered. 'Do you know some of these bastards ask to see the woman again!' He shook with rage. 'Can you believe dat? See them *again* – after they are raping dem!'

Liam shook his head. 'The sick bastards!' screamed Liam. 'So what the fuck is the fourth reason?'

Ribeker walked across to the bar and Ackerman let her speak while he drank his coffee. 'Meener Reilly, this is often the worst of these crimes.' She reflected on the scenes she had witnessed. 'It is . . . sadistic violence! They say they will kill their victim if they scream out. And the woman will never know if that evil bastard will find them again. If we don't catch them they live forever with *fear!'* She swallowed hard. 'Meener Reilly, to rape a prostitute is the *pits* but they do it just the same.' She sighed. 'They know for the first rape they will only be in jail for two years and then they are free once more.'

Liam followed Ackerman and Ribeker as they walked towards the door. Ackerman turned and spoke to him. 'Why does any man rape a woman when he can have a verslaafde?' He paused and smiled. 'Sorry, I mean a *drug addict* for ten or maybe five guilders.'

CHAPTER SIXTEEN

Reflections Of My Life

Two weeks after the rape the young girl leaned on the railings at the side of the canal and sporadically raised her head and looked nervously towards the Love Shack. Liam dried the last few glasses and walked outside, leaned on the rails and lit a cigarette. He noticed the young girl's furtive glances in his direction and he finally caught her attention. 'Hello,' he said, softly. He could see the fear and grief in her eyes and she made to walk away. Liam continued. 'It's alright.' He smiled at her. 'Do you want something to drink? Coffee? Tea?'

She nodded but, unable to hide her fear, visibly trembled as she followed him slowly into the bar.

Liam made tea and coffee but as he approached her she began to shake and ran into the ladies toilet.

Bernie walked in carrying several bunches of flowers and laid them on the bar.

Liam whispered to her. 'She's here.'

'Wat?' she asked.

Liam didn't hide his frustration. Bernie shrugged and continued. 'Wie is hier?' She looked at his confused face and laughed loudly. 'Sorry, I can't always speak English.' Liam grimaced and Bernie repeated herself. 'Who is here?'

Liam whispered. 'The girl who was raped . . .' He moved closer to her and continued. 'She's in . . .' He pointed towards the toilet.

Bernie nodded. 'OK . . . we must wait and give her some time. She will come out for sure.'

Fifteen minutes later she walked out rubbing at her bloodshot eyes. Bernie approached her, put her arms around her shoulder, and walked her to the farthest table at the rear of the bar.

Liam felt the tea and coffee cups, shook his head, threw the tepid contents away, washed the cups, and made fresh. He placed the four cups of steaming tea and coffee on a tray and walked across to the table. He placed the tea and coffee on the table in front of the young girl. The girl looked at the two cups and, for the first time, she smiled.

'I didn't know what you wanted,' said Liam, softly.

She considered both cups and reached for the tea. Liam pushed the sugar bowl across to her and she slipped in two spoonfuls. She clasped the warm cup between her hands and briefly closed her eyes.

Liam signalled to Bernie and she nodded back to him. 'We don't know your name,' lied Bernie.

The girl sipped at the tea before placing the cup awkwardly in the saucer.

She looked down at her hands and picked at her fingers and rubbed her wrists. 'My name is . . .' she scrutinised Bernie and then Liam's faces before she continued, 'Valentine Handel.'

Liam and Bernie both smiled as though it had been rehearsed.

The girl grabbed at the cup and gulped the tea.

'Can we ask how you came here – to Amsterdam?' asked Bernie. Valentine appeared reluctant to answer but Bernie gave her a reassuring smile. 'You don't have to tell us . . .' She raised her eyebrows, tilted her head to one side and spoke softly. 'It is your choice.'

Valentine finished her tea and then, after adding three spoons of sugar to the other cup, gulped at the coffee. 'It's very good,' she said, wiping her mouth with the back of her hand. 'I am from Brugge in Belgium.' She looked at her cup and reflected. 'It is a beautiful city . . .' she said thoughtfully. Her demeanour suddenly changed as she continued. 'But it became very bad!' She grabbed at her cup and emptied it before slamming it angrily into the saucer.

Liam slid it away from her, held it up and smiled at her.

She half closed her eyes and nodded her head slowly.

Liam put all the cups and saucers on the tray and made fresh coffee.

Bernie handed Valentine the fresh coffee and Liam slid the sugar bowl towards her. She charged her cup with the obligatory three spoons of sugar and stirred it frantically.

They both looked at her in anticipation until she continued.

'I lived in Brugge . . . an' I left.' She clenched her fists and began to shake. She closed her mouth and breathed in noisily through her nostrils. She suddenly looked exhausted and slumped into her chair. 'I had to get away . . .' She sighed. 'Do you know what it is like . . . ?' She made to stand but fell back into the chair. 'To be stalked?'

Bernie and Liam both shook their heads.

'Was it so bad?' asked Bernie.

'He killed my dog!' Her whole body shook as she rolled up

her sleeves. She continued. 'He did this!' She stretched out her thin arms. 'With *acid!*' Her forearms had been grotesquely mutilated and were now covered with thick bulging areas of discoloured scar tissue. Bernie gasped with shock and horror. Valentine let out a deep sigh. 'I saved my face, yeas.' She pulled her arms tight into her chest and spread her open hands over her face. 'Like this!'

Bernie and Liam shook their heads in disbelief.

The ensuing silence was unbearable. Liam finally looked at his watch and spoke. 'Have you had any breakfast?'

Valentine shook her head.

Liam walked into the kitchen and a few minutes later Asmara came out with scrambled eggs, several slices of gruyere cheese, tomatoes and toast. Liam pushed the plates towards her and left her to eat and talk with Bernie.

Liam waited for Valentine to finish her breakfast, which didn't take long, then offered her a job at the Love Shack. At first she refused to accept his idea but Liam finally convinced her, with his suggestion that if she stayed he would try to find her attacker. She shared Bernie's room, sleeping on a camp bed, and soon settled into her job working with Bernie and Liam. She did whatever she was asked; sometimes working behind the bar and when it was busy taking orders and waiting at tables. It was good for Bernie to have a "straight" female in her life.

Fourteen days after the rape Ackerman and Ribeker revisited the bar and reluctantly told Liam and Bernie they had given up their search for Valentine's attacker. Liam couldn't believe that the police had actually dropped the case but he was now very aware of the extent of the crime in the Red

Light District and knew there was too much to be able solve all of it.

On their first free day Bernie took Valentine around the city. The sun was shining and it looked wonderful, a total contrast to that fateful night when she was raped. Bernie took her into the Oude Kerk, which was only a few hundred yards from the Love Shack. The beautiful clock, positioned up in the exquisite tower high above the sexual world of debauchery, struck out the quarter of the hour as they entered. The Oude Kerk, a huge monumental church, the oldest in the city, dominating the Red Light District with its high windows which flooded the interior with natural light, symbolised the tradition and present day of Amsterdam. Bernie took time to give Valentine a guided tour around the beautiful building and showed her where Rembrandt's wife, Saskia, was buried. The contrast outside could not be greater as the girls stood brazenly in the windows, while at the rear of the church was a multi-storey building of sexy ladies – Sexy Land. Bernie realised that Valentine was getting upset so she guided her across the Oudekerks brug, immediately outside the entrance to the Oude Kerk, and took her shopping.

Valentine gradually regained her confidence and worked regularly behind the bar most afternoons and early evenings until Liam took over.

With Valentine working in the bar Liam was able to use his spare time to work on the motorbike he had so carefully stowed away in the cellar. He carefully removed the plastic sheets and blankets to reveal the grime encrusted classic DKW motorbike. He found a manual in the rotted saddle bag and spent the next few hours sitting outside the bar reading it from cover to cover. As he turned each page his enthusiasm grew.

During the late 1920s and early 1930s DKW, based in Germany, was the world's largest motorcycle manufacturer, and in 1926 the Zschopauer Motorenwerke produced the Z500. The engine originally had an air-cooled engine but its successor was built with a water-cooled engine. The DKW Super Sport 500 with its wide sprung seat was launched in 1931 and became the dominant racing motorcycle in the Lightweight and Junior classes between the wars.

Liam stripped the bike down and methodically cleaned every part before rebuilding it. The majority of the rubber hoses had perished along with the tyres but with the help of Peggy they scouted scrap yards across the city and obtained everything they needed. Liam touched up the orange bodywork and polished it until it glistened and the large exhaust and mass of exposed metalwork gleamed. He sat on it for the first time, closed his eyes and pretended to ride it, tilting it from side to side and simulating cornering. He part filled the fuel tank and fired it up. He was shocked at the noise but he loved it. He smiled to himself and silently thanked his father for the hours they'd spent together working on his motorbikes.

CHAPTER SEVENTEEN

Ruby Tuesday

Over the next few weeks Liam became a regular sight as he dived around the city on his eye-catching, restored classic motorbike. He was liked by most people and was soon accepted by almost everyone that lived or worked in the Red Light District as he slowly came to know many of them by name. He rode past the Oude Kerk in Oudekerksplein, pulled up outside the bar and chained up his motorbike. He walked into an unusually deserted bar except for two lone drunken German tourists in opposite corners of the bar.

'Where is everyone?' asked Liam.

Liam glanced across at Magdalena who was drying glasses behind the bar.

'Upstairs,' she whispered. Without looking up she continued. 'There is a problem, ja.'

Liam rushed past another drunken punter who was walking out of the toilet. He knocked him onto the table, bringing the ash tray and empty glasses crashing onto the floor and breaking into a thousand pieces. Liam turned and motioned for Magdalena to join him. He ran up several flights of the narrow stairs jumping several at a time until he reached the third floor. Ruby had chosen that room because it gave her an advantage over her exclusive customers, who were always out of breath by the time they reached her special room, and made it easier to control them. Although most of her regulars came by appointment, Ruby picked all her new customers up at the nearby sex toy shop.

Liam and Magdalena reached the landing to find Peggy and Saskia trying to open the door. 'What the fuck are you doing?' he screamed.

They looked at him nervously.

'Stand back!' he screamed. He rushed the locked door several times until it sprang open splitting the architrave and frame.

The room was dark except for a few red candles. The trussed body of Ruby hung from the ceiling and cast weird shadows across the room as it swung slowly from side to side. Liam screamed at the three girls, who stood at the door, their mouths wide open. 'Magdalena, call the police and get an ambulance!'

The girls continued to stare into the room and, although they had seen most things working in the Red Light District, it was such a shock that it made Magdalena physically sick.

Liam screamed directly at Peggy. 'Get her out of here! Go on all of you get the fuck out!'

Magdalena continued to urge and vomit as they both raced down the narrow stairs, trying not to fall over each other.

Liam stood gazing at the grotesque contorted body in front of him before flicking the switch and turning the light on. As the red fluorescent tubes slowly came to life the flickering light made the scene even more macabre. In a split second his sober eyes communicated everything that he saw to his alert brain.

Ruby hung from a hook in the ceiling linked by a chromium climbing shackle and multi-coloured rope, which Liam knew had been tied by an expert. Her left leg was tied at the knee and pulled up towards her chest and her breasts had been tied with rope in a figure eight. The rope squeezed the breasts, forcing them to extend misshapen and erect. Her nipples were enlarged and long fine needles had been pushed through them and protruded out the other side. Red candle wax had been thrown randomly over the sensitive parts of her body leaving thick dry splashes on her pink skin. He looked down and saw that more needles had been pushed into her clitoris, while an empty syringe hung out of her vagina. Another rope placed through the black studded leather collar around her neck was tied to the main rope forcing her head to jut unnaturally forward. Her long black dyed hair fell forward obscuring her contorted face. To complete her distinct gothic look she had dyed her hair to match the black clothes – the leather that had become her trademark and, more importantly, what her clients wanted. As she continued to swing the grey roots were clearly visible. Red candles burned on the floor beneath her swinging body and each time her right foot drifted through the flame. The heat caused her skin to burn and the black nail varnish to bubble and crack on several of her toes. Liam reached up and pulled her from the hook in the ceiling. She was dead and there was nothing he could do for her. He held her twisted body awkwardly before he laid her on the floor, then extinguished the candles and half closed the door behind him before slowly walking down the stairs. As he passed Bernie's door he heard her inside. He knocked several times and she reluctantly opened her door a few inches. Liam looked inside and in the mirror saw Detective Ribeker lying naked on the bed. She smiled back at him and waved her right hand regally. He slammed the door shut and raced down the stairs,

When he walked into the bar he was ready to explode. 'What the fuck's been going on? Didn't any of you see anything?'

Nervously Magdalena and Peggy turned to each other and then looked down at the floor. Liam knew that they could name the murderer but for some reason they were unwilling to tell him. The sirens wailed and within seconds several police cars pulled up outside. Before he could ask the girls any more questions Detective Ackerman and two policemen marched in, followed by two paramedics. Two more uniformed gun toting policemen stood threateningly at the door.

Liam spoke nervously to Detective Ackerman directing his eyes towards the paramedics. 'I don't think we need them.' Ackerman ignored him and raised his left hand, pointing his index finger towards the stairs. Liam asked them to follow him and he stood at the door of Ruby's room while they scrutinised the scene and asked what seemed like a well-worn list of questions. The forensic team arrived and their female leader supervised her assistants to carefully position a number of sodium lights. When they were switched on the illuminated scene appeared totally bizarre. The lights exposed in great detail the equipment that facilitated the sordid events which regularly took place between Ruby and her clients. The forensic scientist meticulously cut through the ropes taking photographs at every stage until all the ropes had been removed. She then carried out a systematic examination of the body to establish if Ruby had been raped and what atrocities had been carried out on her before she had finally been injected with the lethal injection. When the forensic team had completed their investigation the body was placed in a white body bag.

Liam walked down to the bar; he needed a drink like never before. His whole body trembled, and his hands shook, as he stared longingly at the rows of spirits behind the bar.

De Groot, followed by Zita and Skipio, entered the bar as the detective was walking down the stairs. De Groot frowned as he asked a silent question of the detective. His action saved Liam.

Magdalena passed Liam a double espresso. He tore open three packets of sugar and poured them into the tiny cup. Without stirring it he emptied the cup in one gulp.

When Detective Ackerman saw De Groot his attitude suddenly changed. 'We will need to ask you all some questions, but . . .' He paused, 'it can wait until tomorrow.'

De Groot showed his appreciation with a nod and waited until the detective had left.

The paramedics struggled down the narrow stairs with the body bag, carried it through the bar and out into their ambulance. Liam, seeing the body bag and now unable to control his anger, screamed out to the girls. 'Alright . . . so who was it?' He spun around glaring at each of them in turn. 'What did you all see?'

It was difficult for the girls and they all wiped at their tears. They knew their jobs were dangerous, they all understood that but the reality of the danger was only brought home to them when someone they worked with was murdered.

De Groot and Skipio stared at each of the girls in turn and at that moment the tension intensified. They could all feel it and Liam knew that it was pointless pursuing his questions.

Zita found it hard to hide her disgust and her fingers twitched erratically.

De Groot lit a cheroot before he spoke directly to Liam. 'We need dat room.' He noticed the silent rebellious glare from Liam and raised his voice. 'Git it emptied as soon as the polis finish. Git it cleaned und painted! I want someone in dere next week!'

Liam glared back at him.

Zita shuffled nervously on the spot and the girls sensing that Liam was about to explode turned away from De Groot. Liam did explode. He spun around, picked up an ashtray and threw it at the optics lining the wall behind the bar. The girls covered their faces as the broken glass and alcohol flew at them.

De Groot remained unphased by Liam's actions; he stretched his body, pulled at his jacket lapels and straightened his jacket. He took a huge drag on his cheroot and walked in silence towards the door. When he reached the door he turned and scowled back at Liam. 'Remember what I said!' Liam glared at him but De Groot maintained his impassive stony faced look and continued. 'Within der week,' he said, as he emphasised every word. He smirked and turned to Skipio and then back to Liam. 'Maybe you can paint it bleck . . . uh?'

Liam moved towards him but Bernie pulled at his tee shirt.

De Groot turned and left without saying another word. He was followed closely by Zita and lastly Skipio who ambled towards the front doors. The Greek grabbed at them and pulled them wide open. He turned and snarled at Liam before slamming them shut behind him.

Ruby's funeral service took place in the Oude Kerk, just a hundred or so yards from where she was brutally murdered.

There were hundreds of people in the congregation including her family and friends, fellow prostitutes and people from the Red Light District, as well as inquisitive tourists. Liam recognised some of Ruby's regular clients who stood nervously in the shadows at the back of the congregation as they paid their last respects. While the ruby red painted coffin was carried to the exit, followed by the congregation, the song *Ruby Tuesday* recorded by the Rolling Stones filled the silence. Ruby's coffin was lowered in silence onto a barge on the Oudezijds Voorburgwal, the city's oldest canal, immediately in front of the church. The barge carrying her coffin was decked with flowers in every shade of red. A large wreath from everyone at the Love Shack had pride of place. The barge, towed by a small tug, was followed by her distraught parents on a motor launch then Liam with all the girls from the Love Shack on one of the smaller glass topped tourist boats. The remainder of the armada of motor launches, barges, and tourist boats was followed at a distance by a police patrol boat. Hundreds of people lined the route, many of them tourists randomly taking photographs of the procession as it made its way majestically along the canal. As they passed beneath one of the many bridges Liam caught a glimpse of Artem and Skipio. They looked down at Liam and grinned before both of them spat at the coffin-bearing barge. Liam glared up at them and Skipio smiled the broadest grin before he spat down onto the glass roof of Liam's boat.

The procession finally made its way to Zorgvlied cemetery on the Amsteldijk, situated on the left bank of the Amstel. With its English style garden it was the final resting place of many celebrities from the literary and theatre world. Liam, with Zita's help, arranged for Ruby to be buried next to the grave of Diana and Herman Renz, owners of a famous circus family: a couple who also died prematurely, but in their case from carbon monoxide poisoning, in 1996.

Two weeks after the funeral Detectives Ackerman and Ribeker pulled up outside the Love Shack. Liam was taking a well-earned break, leaning on the railings and enjoying his tenth cigarette of the day. Ackerman walked across to Liam and offered him a cigarette. Liam raised the hand holding the cigarette and cursed as he watched Ribeker walk into the bar.

Ackerman smiled at Liam. 'It's OK, ja. I know what you're thinking,' he said, 'it's not a problem; we all have our special needs. She is no different to any of us.'

Liam grinned and cursed. 'Yeah – sure.'

'I'm pleased you understand Meener Reilly and . . .' He stopped mid-sentence, looked enquiringly at Liam and waited.

Liam suddenly realised the reason for the detective's pause. He threw his unfinished cigarette into the canal and smiled. 'Coffee?'

'I don't think you would ask me dat.'

As they walked towards the bar Ackerman placed his hand on Liam's shoulder. 'I must say for a foreigner you do make the very good coffee.'

Liam left Ribeker in the bar with Bernie and sat outside with Ackerman. They both lit a cigarette and sat taking in the quiet of the late morning. Liam thought to himself. *Something's wrong with me. I must be going soft. I'm sat with a cop. I've finally been fucked?*

Ackerman finally turned to Liam and gave the broadest of smiles. 'I must tell you that we have some developments to the DNA tests.'

Liam stopped and looked directly at Ackerman. 'Well?'

Valentine brought them coffee and as she placed it nervously in front of them Ackerman held back. As Valentine left he turned his head and his eyes followed her. 'You take care of her, ja?'

Liam nodded. 'She's doing alright . . . Still nervous sometimes but she *is* getting better.'

Ackerman nodded and smiled before stifling a yawn.

'You need to ease back a bit, mate,' said Liam.

'Ja, ja,' replied Ackerman. He blindly looked around before regaining Liam's attention. 'Meener Reilly, you know . . . it was the same person,' he said confidently.

Liam's face lit up. 'Really . . .'

Ackerman smiled. 'It is not a surprise to me.' He lifted his cup and savoured the coffee. 'Animals tend to stay in their known territory . . .' He paused and finished his coffee. 'Until we catch dem . . . ja?'

'So, do you know who it is?' asked Liam, eagerly.

Ackerman coughed a gentle cough. 'No. I'm afraid we don't.' Liam couldn't hide his disappointment. Ackerman continued and smiled a confident smile. 'But we have sent samples across Europe . . . so if dis person is known to someone . . .' He took a huge drag on his cigarette. 'Den we will catch him.'

Bernie and Ribeker walked out of the bar arm in arm, smiling and laughing together, and making no attempt to hide their feelings for each other.

Ackerman stood up, shook Liam's hand, reached out a friendly hand to the female detective and walked towards his car. 'We will keep you up to date with any developments, Meener Reilly.'

CHAPTER EIGHTEEN

Anyone Who Had A Heart

Liam pressed the intercom of the three-storey building in Haupt straat, a building in the heart of the Red Light District that served as De Groot's Amsterdam office and doubled as his private audition room. Zita let him in and he climbed the narrow winding stairs to the second floor apartment. Zita opened the door and smiled a secret smile to him as he walked past her and into the room to reveal Skipio sitting majestically in a wide armchair, filling it with his overweight body. His head tilted back as he smoked one of his foul-smelling Arab cigarettes and blew smoke rings into the already heavy smoke laden air.

As always, De Groot stood looking down onto the area of Amsterdam over which he had total and unrivalled control. He liked the view; it helped him to concentrate his mind on business, and the noise of the crowds of tourists, voyeurs and drunks kept him on an almost permanent high. The more people around meant more money for him. He loved it.

When Liam arrived De Groot immediately handed him a palm-sized Sony video camera. 'Do you know how to use one of these?' Liam shook his head. 'Well you won't be much use to me will you? You'd better learn to use it and fast.'

Zita walked across the room and sat quietly behind the bar. Liam followed but sat on a bar stool on the opposite side and fiddled with the tiny buttons until he had them mastered. He held it up to his right eye and filmed everyone in the room, spending more time on Zita than anyone else.

She poured him a coffee from the steaming percolator on the bar and slid it across to him.

The intercom buzzed and while Skipio became animated with anticipation, De Groot motioned to Liam to answer it.

Liam slid off of the bar stool, picked up the handset and spoke into it. 'Hello who is it?'

A blurred female voice answered. 'Helena Heart.' She paused while she read the smudged name on the business card. 'I have an audition with Meener De Groot?'

Liam looked through Skipio's smoke at De Groot for confirmation and after the nod he pressed the button on the telephone releasing the ground floor entrance door.

While they awaited their visitor, Zita poured De Groot and Skipio a large glass of Jenever and turned up the music. De Groot, bored with looking down at the quiet streets, returned to his armchair and slowly sipped at his drink.

In less than a minute there was a knock on the door. Liam still holding the video camera opened it to reveal a young hard faced woman in her mid-twenties with long dyed blonde hair. She smiled nervously at him but sensing that Liam was not her appointment pushed past him and walked into the room.

De Groot did not stand but signalled to the young woman to sit opposite him. She quickly looked around at her prospective audience before answering De Groot's probing questions.

He explained that he was looking for a number of quality girls for hard porn videos which he would be showing in his clubs and selling on DVD. She told him that she was prepared to perform any sexual act except shitting and bleeding although sex with an animal was not a problem.

De Groot, satisfied with her answers, offered Helena a drink which she immediately declined. To demonstrate his annoyance at the rebuff from a stripper he got up and returned to gaze out of the window. She passed her large handbag to Zita who placed it on the nearest bar stool. She then removed her short coat and passed it to Zita who folded it and laid it on top of the handbag. Helena looked across at De Groot. He ignored her attention as he was preoccupied by the noisy late afternoon crowds building up on his patch. All that mattered to him was that the crowds spent their money in his clubs, bars, brothels and strip joints, then left.

Zita turned down the music to attract De Groot's attention. It worked; he turned to reveal a deep frown etched into his face. 'I'm ready, get on with it,' he snarled.

Helena looked across at Liam who nodded from behind the camera. 'Yeah, sure I'm ready,' he said nervously as he fiddled with the tiny controls.

Helena stood on the carpet, started to move and then stopped abruptly. She walked across to her coat, pulled it aside and threw it onto the floor. She reached for her large handbag on the barstool and moved to open it. Without any warning, Zita let out an ear-shattering scream as she vaulted over the bar, grabbed the handbag, pushed Helena onto the floor and stood with her foot pressed heavily into her chest. Skipio pushed himself awkwardly out of his chair and stood in the centre of the room waiting for his instructions from Zita.

198

While Zita flicked calmly and methodically through the contents of the handbag the room remained totally silent. After a few seconds the corner of her lip slowly curled with satisfaction and she nodded to De Groot. He lowered his eyes. Zita released her foot and effortlessly pulled Helena up from the floor.

De Groot let out a huge sigh of relief and pushed himself deep into his armchair. Helena grabbed the bag from Zita and slowly reached inside. Appearing to be unphased by Zita's actions she gave an impromptu theatrical performance as she gracefully pulled out a CD and waved it high in the air. 'Music . . . I have my own music, it helps me to work,' she said, as she licked her lips sensually.

Zita returned to her position behind the bar and Skipio slumped heavily into his armchair with his usual grunt.

De Groot demonstrated his impatience by screwing up his face. He had no real interest in anyone wasting his time, as far as he was concerned strippers were strippers; they were all the same, just money to him, a way of earning more. But for Skipio it was a different matter; already full of anticipation, he fidgeted anxiously in the enormous armchair making even him look small.

Zita took the CD from Helena, slid it into the player and turned it on. Not satisfied with the volume, Helena motioned to Zita to turn it up a little more until she was totally comfortable with the level of the throbbing rave music. She smiled and started to gyrate using every inch of space in front of the intimidating audience. The music took her to another place and she slowly and sensually removed her bright green blouse revealing a black half-cup brassiere and her firm breasts which, much to Skipio's delight, were thrust into his face several times, before she pulled back preventing him from getting his fat sweaty hands on them. Liam continued to follow her every move, closely zooming in on all her actions and movements. Her strip was perfectly choreographed to the music, her body gyrated sensually with every beat. She danced towards Skipio, gave him a false smile, and as she suggestively began to remove her short skirt, she turned towards De Groot and the video camera, to reveal a black intricate leather thong with diamante studs. As she slowly rotated a few feet away from Skipio she exposed her pale soft buttocks revealing a small purple tattoo of a heart. He wriggled in his chair and Liam pulled the camera back to include him in the frame. Helena slowly removed her bra to reveal firm and pert breasts. Her whole body moved with the music but her surgically enhanced breasts did not move in the same way that natural breasts would have moved. She enticed Skipio to lean forward in his armchair as she provocatively released her thong and pushed it under his nose, before letting it fall at his feet. She slid slowly along the carpet towards De Groot and as, she raised her head between his legs, her hands reached for his zip; he glared at her and placed both hands firmly across his crotch. Undeterred she looked across at Liam but De Groot raised his hand and pointed his index finger in the direction of Skipio. She understood perfectly and remaining on the floor, still in time with the music, crawled across the rug until she reached the sweating Greek freak. She undid his zip and slowly removed his already enlarged and erect penis; Liam had the same feeling and desperately tried to hide it by contorting his legs. Zita had already noticed, she had also become aroused.

Helena slid the Greek's penis into her mouth hiding it from the probing lens, so Liam closed in onto Skipio's closed eyes and pleasured facial expressions. Helena stopped prematurely, teasing her client who was now panting for the climax. Liam adjusted the zoom until Helena's wet mouth filled the whole screen as she manipulated her tongue between her nicotine stained teeth until she formed a perfect shape. When she was happy, she took a deep breath and buried her mouth into the side of the throbbing penis. Zita fidgeted on the bar stool while Skipio dug his thick square uneven fingernails into the arms of the chair. He closed his eyes to exclude the voyeurs and yelped with a combination of pleasure and pain. As he let out a deep 'Urgh' Helena continued to suck hard for a few seconds and then stopped abruptly. Satisfied with her efforts, she lifted her head out of Skipio's crotch, threw back her long sweating hair and pulled it away from her face to reveal her trademark and name, a perfect dark blue heart on the side of the stretched skin of his throbbing and erect penis. She bent forward, slid his penis into her mouth, and squeezed his testicles between her bony hands until the giant of a man moaned in his native Greek. Zita turned up the music, drowning out his pleasured tones until he finally reached his climax and began to yell with pleasure. Helena pulled her mouth away, her eyes darting furtively searching around the room. As she sprang towards De Groot, Zita moved instinctively to intercept her to protect her employer but stopped when Helena reached up and pulled the deep red silk handkerchief from his jacket pocket. She bent down and spat the warm semen into it, wiped her wet mouth and placed the handkerchief between Skipio's open palms, forcing them closed. While Skipio fumbled with his zip, and as if nothing had happened, Helena gathered her clothes, dressed and passed De Groot her card. 'One thousand guilders a show, OK?' she said, evocatively.

201

De Groot nodded his agreement.

Zita took Helena's CD out of the player, handed it to her, and replaced it with Robbie Williams' *Life thru a Lens*. While De Groot stood up and looked out of the window, Liam rewound the video, stopping to check it at the relevant places. De Groot turned to Liam and Zita and smiled. 'I want the two of you to go and get me a copy of that.' He sneered at Skipio, who now realised that he had been set up. Without turning back to Liam and Zita, De Groot continued. 'And try not to let that tape out of your sight.'

Zita and Liam made their exit smirking to each other.

De Groot continued to stare at Skipio, who was still too embarrassed to show any response, looking like a school child who was about to be chastised. When De Groot visibly relaxed, his austere look slowly gave way to a wry smile. '*You* owe me one . . . and a new handkerchief.' He glared at Skipio. 'Make sure its quality silk not your usual second rate Greek shit.'

Skipio replied in an unusually reserved voice. 'Sure boss.'

De Groot looked down towards Skipio's crotch. 'And, let me know how long that stays with you.' Skipio now blushed with a mixture of embarrassment and relief at finally being let off the hook.

In the sex shop and video bar Liam and Zita watched while the teenage gay assistant played the video on a wall of screens as he copied it.

Liam laughed loudly. 'Helena Heart. Can you fucking believe that? I wonder if she leaves her mark on all her punters!'

Zita looked at him. 'What do you mean?'

Liam laughed as he replied. 'Well Skipio's got a fucking purple heart on his cock!'

Liam told Zita to watch closely as the video reached the part when Helena sucked the life out of Skipio's penis. He screamed out. 'Got ya yer fucking bastard!'

Zita smiled to herself and sipped at her decaffeinated coffee.

CHAPTER NINETEEN

Heroes And Villains

Liam was crouched down restocking the bar when Artem strutted into the Love Shack, approached Valentine, and demanded a glass of genevieve – Dutch gin. Valentine shrieked and ran off in tears towards the ladies toilet. Liam stood up and reluctantly poured Artem's drink. Artem didn't hide his disdain for Liam and stepped back from the bar, stroked his shaven head with both hands and, in a bizarre show of contempt for Liam extended his body and swayed his hips from side to side like a Brazilian dancer. He emptied the first glass and demanded a second. Liam poured it and slid the glass along the bar out of Artem's reach. He growled at Liam as he stretched to reach it. Liam ignored him, turned up the music, and returned to restocking the bar. Artem picked up his drink and growled before ambling outside and sitting at a shaded table. He rolled a joint and took several deep drags, emptied the glass and stood up. As he moved away from the table he purposely pushed it over before throwing his chair towards the canal.

*

The next time Liam saw Artem it was late in the evening. Artem had dropped De Groot off at one of his clubs and driven on to the Love Shack. Valentine was helping Liam to close up for the night when Artem ambled in. He was already drunk but demanded more. Valentine poured him a drink and stood nervously looking at the pathetic man who had attacked and raped her. Artem ordered yet another drink and Valentine shook as she poured it into his glass, spilling some of it onto the bar.

Artem commented. 'I hope De Groot don't see you wasting his money . . . eh?' He let out a deep belly laugh before he emptied the glass in one huge gulp. He immediately pushed the empty glass towards Valentine. Liam carried in the tables and chairs from outside and moved Valentine aside. He motioned to her to finish and go to her room with Bernie. Liam refilled Artem's glass and slid it along the bar out of his reach. Artem stretched to reach it, gulped it down and slid his empty glass towards Liam for a third time. Reluctantly Liam filled it and walked away from the bar. Despite being very drunk Artem took the hint and after demolishing the alcohol he swaggered drunkenly outside. Liam dimmed the lights, picked up a beer towel and knife from behind the bar and locked the bar. He walked briskly along the canal and into Warmoesstraat before turning back into the alley. He fiddled with the internal lights of the unlocked Mercedes, disconnected them, and slid onto the rear seat. Artem took several minutes to stagger his way to the car. He slumped exhausted into the front seat and belched loudly. Liam waited for him to close the door. Before Artem could put the key into the ignition, Liam pulled the bar towel around his rapist's neck and choked him unconscious. He slid out of the car, crawled along the ground in the darkness and opened the driver's door. He looked around before he pulled out the knife and stabbed Artem repeatedly between his legs, cutting deep into his penis, scrotum and arteries. When he was satisfied that he had done enough damage he pushed himself out of the car. He closed the driver's door and locked it. He paused and then mumbled to himself. 'Sorry Ruby . . .' He looked skywards and continued, 'I got that bastard for *you* at last . . .'

He picked his way through the shadows and made his way back to the Love Shack. He threw the car keys into the canal and let out a huge sigh of relief before slowly stacking the chairs on the tables ready for Rafi to sweep and wash the floors first thing in the morning.

The next morning Liam opened up the bar earlier than usual. It was a bright sunny morning as he placed the remaining tables and chairs outside the Love Shack. He smiled to himself as the last few drunks staggered precariously along the edge of the canal on their way back to their hotels to sleep it off, and the lost clubbers who wandered around aimlessly across bridge after bridge as they tried to find their hotel. De Groot's car was still in the alley beside the bar and several policemen were taking fingerprints and photographs of the scene. When one of them saw Liam he walked over. 'Good morning, sir.' Liam acknowledged him with a nod. The policeman continued. 'Do you know this car?'

Liam took his time to walk around the car before he answered. 'Um . . . Yeah, I think it belongs to my boss, Mr De Groot,' replied Liam in a subdued voice.

The policeman scribbled a note in his pocket book. 'Do you know how long it has been here . . . like dis?'

Liam shook his head and took a deep breath. 'I have no idea . . .' He paused. 'Why? What's happened?'

The policeman looked directly at him. 'There was an attack here last night . . .'

'Really,' replied Liam, feigning shock.

The policeman continued. 'A man was stabbed . . .' He shot Liam a knowing smile. 'It could have been a jealous girlfriend.' He shook his head slowly. 'Or maybe . . .' He paused and gave the widest of grins. 'A jealous husband? Whoever it was, they made sure he won't be able to do the sex thing again . . .'

Liam smiled, turned and walked back towards the bar. He stopped outside, picked up a chair and placed it as near to the edge of the canal as he dared, sat down and lit a cigarette. He was at peace and he loved it. The peace didn't last for more than a few minutes; it was broken by the thumping dance music that boomed up the canal from the clubs as they opened their doors to attract their first customers of the day. He shook his head and smiled. 'Welcome to Amsterdam,' he said.

Artem was taken from the hospital later that day and was never seen again, dead or alive. De Groot's blood drenched Mercedes miraculously disappeared from the police compound and was found several weeks later burnt out on an industrial estate near Nijmegen.

For De Groot the whole episode had come too close to contemplate.

CHAPTER TWENTY

I'm Your Puppet

Liam was tidying the bar when the phone rang. He picked it up and sipped at his espresso, nodding animatedly as he listened to the caller before replying. 'What? You want to come over now . . . . But I'm just . . .' He slammed down the receiver, removed the cloth from his shoulder and threw it down onto the nearest table before he vented his anger at Magdalena and Valentine. 'Can you get this place looking like it should be? It looks like shit!' he screamed.

Magdalena looked across at him and nodded subserviently. Liam set up another espresso and lit a cigarette while he waited for the thick dark liquid to flow through. He grabbed at the cup, took one large gulp and slammed the cup onto the bar and left. He had second thoughts and returned. 'I'll get back as soon as I can,' he shouted.

Liam arrived at De Groot's flat and found it hard to hide his anger but, as always, De Groot had a knack of disarming him with his smile. 'Good morning, it is good of you to come so quickly.' He paused and took his time to look Liam up and down. 'I like dat.'

'Um,' mumbled Liam. He hated not to be in control but for the time being he had no option. He needed De Groot.

Skipio stood looking out across the canal and took a large drag on his most foul-smelling cheroot. He turned briefly to acknowledge Liam with a shrug and then returned to the window.

'Well?' asked Liam. 'What's so urgent that I have to come running?'

De Groot settled himself into his armchair before speaking. 'You are taking a holiday my friend.'

Liam screwed up his face. 'Holiday? Now?' he paused and thought. 'Where the fuck am I going?'

At that moment a young woman opened the bathroom door and stood looking at him. 'Marlene will look after you,' said De Groot.

She gave Liam a comforting smile and held the door open for him. She could see that Liam was unsure. She was used to that.

'Go on, she won't bite . . .' barked De Groot. 'And don't take too long, you have a plane to catch in four hours.'

Liam walked slowly towards the door and the two of them disappeared inside.

Marlene cut, styled and washed his hair, gave him a manicure, pedicure and massage and left him to take a shower. As soon as he climbed into the shower she returned and took his clothes.

A few minutes later a very confused Liam walked dripping wet back into the room wrapped in a thick white dressing gown. 'Where are my fucking clothes? Will someone tell me what the fuck is going on or . . . I'm out of 'ere.'

Skipio turned, gave a wide grin and mumbled to himself.

Liam tried to contain his rage but finally flipped and lunged towards Skipio screaming. 'I'm gonna shove that shit you're smoking up your ass where it belongs.'

De Groot stood up. 'Take it easy, my friend,' he said, with a disarming smile. 'This is a simple situation, you are taking a holiday and I need you to be one hundred percent correct.' He stopped and stared hard at Liam. 'A professional like you surely understands what is required. I can't take any chances. Can I?'

Liam looked at him, shivered and nodded slowly.

'Get dressed and I'll tell you what this is all about, but . . .' He looked at his watch. 'Be quick or you might die with the cold . . .' He smiled. 'Oh, and your old clothes will be washed and delivered to your flat before you return.'

Skipio smirked and nodded slowly to further antagonise Liam.

'Just go, my friend,' said De Groot. Liam didn't budge and De Groot continued in a soft voice. 'Please.'

Liam returned to the side room. A few minutes later he was dressed and stood in front of the mirror for the first time. He spoke to himself. 'Morning . . .' Marlene ignored him and made a few final adjustments to his hair.

He knew he was ready and returned to De Groot.

'You look good my friend. How does it feel to you?' asked De Groot.

Liam couldn't lie. He felt different and very good.

The transformation, although small, was incredible. Liam stood upright and confident, the best he had felt for a very long time. Gone was the unkempt hair and uneven finger nails. He was wearing a pale green Quiksilver check shirt, chino designer trousers with a wide embossed leather belt, Chatham deck shoes, and a light brown leather jacket.

'Take a seat my friend and we will tell you about . . .' He paused for several seconds before he continued. 'Your holiday,' said De Groot, knowing that at last he had gained Liam's confidence.

Liam sat down and Marlene, unable to hide her self-congratulatory smile of satisfaction, handed him an espresso.

'That will be all Marlene . . . You did well as usual,' said De Groot. His complement was confirmed by a wide grin from Liam.

De Groot coughed loudly. 'OK, down to business. You are going on a short trip to the Canaria Islands. We have given you a new name.' He paused for a reaction from Liam. There was none and he continued. 'Robert Webster?' He waited for a response and yet again, there was none. 'Everything you need is in dat bag.' He pointed to a brown travel bag and a larger suitcase beside it. 'And your clothes are in the larger case . . . And one very important thing . . . be sure you can recognise your case.' He pointed at the red, white and blue straps wrapped around the case and smiled. 'That will help you.'

Liam looked at him. 'Everything I need?'

'Yes, absolutely everything.' He could see that Liam was ahead of him and he continued before he could be interrupted. 'There is nothing in the bags that will be of interest to the customs or police here or in the Canaria Islands. You must give us *some* credit.' He paused before continuing with a smirk. 'Mr Webster is a very boring man, ja.'

Skipio sat down and after he forced his huge overweight body into the armchair near the window, coughed loudly and sniggered. Liam fired him a hard stare before De Groot immediately regained his interest with a cough. He reached down to the table, opened a large brown envelope and handed the contents to Liam. Here is your passport, tickets and a mobile telephone. Do *not* use it to make any calls. You will be called and if you do have an emergency you must press 1.' He waited for a response. There was none, Liam flicked through the passport. De Groot continued. 'Do you understand?'

Liam slowly raised his head. 'Yeah . . . but what's the point of going through all this if there isn't anything in the case?'

'All will be revealed.' De Groot hesitated and pushed himself deep into his chair. 'Robert, listen carefully.' He smiled at Liam, waiting for a response before he continued. Liam looked at him blankly before he suddenly realised that De Groot was talking to him. De Groot took a sheet of paper from his pocket and handed it to Liam. '*Robert,* you need to read this and learn everything about yourself before you reach Schiphol and then you *must* destroy it.'

Liam started to read. De Groot checked his watch and immediately raised his voice. 'We have lost so much time. You must leave now! Your plane leaves in three hours and you cannot miss it. You will have time to learn everything about Mr Webster before you reach the airport, ja?'

Liam rose from the chair and stopped suddenly. 'What about my own passport?'

De Groot reached into his jacket pocket and slowly removed it. 'I will retain this and if all goes to plan it will be returned and . . .' He slipped it back into his pocket. 'The new one will make you . . .' he lowered his voice, '*invisible* . . .' He grinned. 'If you *ever* wish to return to England unnoticed.'

Liam turned and as he walked towards the stairs, De Groot shouted after him 'Remember my friend when you use the credit card that it is *my* money.' He repeated it slowly. '*My* money . . . Use it carefully and I want you to come back to here in six days.'

Liam had coped with a lot in his life but this time he was doing something that he had not instigated himself and he didn't like it.

Liam made his way to Centraal Station and took the first train to the airport, choosing to sit upstairs. The urgency to learn about Robert Webster was eating away at him and slowly he began to read. Robert Webster lived and worked in south London where he ran a café in the infamous East Street market on the Walworth Road. Liam was surprised at the background chosen for him because it was the exact opposite to his previous life. Did the Dutchman have an ulterior motive? Liam suddenly became agitated. He had ventured across the river a few times but not out of choice. South London? What an insult. He read on: a Crystal Palace supporter. Liam wasn't a football fan but – Crystal Palace? Another insult followed: he was also a season ticket holder. If he had liked football then Millwall would have been his team of choice. He continued to read and memorise the information before re-reading it for the final time and ripping it into as many pieces as he could and carefully disposing of it in the various waste bins around him. He now turned his attention to his wallet. It contained a Visa credit card, a Booker Cash and Carry card, Matalan and Next store cards – a contradiction in shopping, a Blockbuster video card, a return Eurostar ticket to Waterloo, a tube ticket to the Elephant and Castle, a MacDonald's receipt, his Crystal Palace season ticket, and cash. He carefully counted it: four hundred and ten pounds, seventeen thousand pesetas and two hundred guilders. He felt inside his jacket pockets and found loose change in mixed currencies. He laid it out on the table in front of him and sorted it out before placing it in different pockets.

As the train approached Schiphol he pulled out his passport and tickets. His passport had been issued in 1997, and although it didn't have any stamps in it, was slightly soiled and worn.

Liam checked in, slipped the boarding pass into his pocket and walked away from the check-in desk. As he walked towards the escalator the check-in girl called out over the tannoy. 'Mr Webster . . . Mr Webster . . . Could you please return to the check-in desk.'

Liam continued to walk towards the escalator. Two security guards briskly walked towards him and, although he tried to avoid them by turning away, they continued to close in on him. When they reached him Liam pushed them away until one of the guards finally stopped him and, taking his arm, turned him around until he was facing the check-in desk. Liam now beginning to lose his temper gave a sigh of relief when he noticed that the girl on the desk was holding his passport above her head. She smiled at him. He thought to himself. *If you're going to be someone else it would help if you knew who that was.* He swore not to make that mistake again.

He smiled nervously at the security guards who walked beside him as he made his way back to the desk. He took his passport from the check-in attendant then, after thanking her profusely, turned and thanked the guards before heading off up the stairs and into the departure lounge for a much-needed cigarette, one of several before boarding the plane.

Once seated on the plane he searched through his bag and found a copy of the Evening Standard. That was a week old, nevertheless he read it from front to back, even the sports section. Much to his satisfaction he saw that Millwall was more successful than Crystal Palace and he wondered if De Groot was trying to upset him. He smiled to himself and for the first time began to relax.

Zita flew to Frankfurt before flying on to Lanzarote, landing at Arrecife airport 45 minutes before Liam. She collected the Wrangler 4 x 4 grey open-topped sports jeep with a 2.5 litre engine from De Groot's private lock-up. She preferred this to a hardtop because if the weather was warm, which was highly likely this time of year, then she could remove it. Lanzarote was positioned on a similar latitude to Florida and the Bahamas and although it was not as warm, she was determined to make the most of it, knowing that the temperatures at home would be much cooler.

Zita waited in the jeep until ten minutes before Liam's flight was due to land. Then she slowly made her way to the exit doors of the arrival lounge, ordered a coffee, sat and waited.

The 747 from Schiphol, touched down at Arrecife airport and Liam was the first passenger on that flight to reach immigration. He switched on the mobile phone, collected his case and followed the passengers from his flight into the Arrivals hall. He walked slowly. He had no choice: he was waiting for

something but he didn't know what. As he reached for a cigarette, he felt a hard object pushed into his back and he lurched
forward. He turned and, with his fists clenched, was ready to
attack his assailant. Before he could land a blow he realised
it was an elderly man with a trolley that was out of control.
His suitcases had fallen on to the marble floor and the trolley
had raced towards him. Liam smiled and was helping him to
re-load his trolley when his mobile bleeped. He flicked it and
read the text message. "Go to the bus park – stand 15."

He followed the lines of tourists pushing their overladen
trolleys out to the bus park until he reached stand 15 where he
sat on his suitcase and lit another cigarette. A jeep approached
and screamed to a halt in front of him. He stood up and was
about to vent his anger when he noticed that Zita was driving.
Relieved, he smiled the broadest of smiles.

'Come on get in,' she shouted.

Zita looked very different and more relaxed than when she
was in Amsterdam. She wore a navy NY embroidered baseball cap, a black vest, white shorts and trainers. Liam threw
his case and bag in the back and she raced away.

'I am glad to see you,' said Liam. 'Do you know what this is
all about? Why all the secrecy?'

'You'll be fine – just sit back and enjoy it.' Zita flicked in a
CD and drove out of the airport towards the open country.
'Hold tight and put this on.' She passed him a matching base-
ball cap and reluctantly he put it on.

They didn't speak until they were out on the LZ-2, the
recently completed main road which led to the south of the
island. Zita flicked out the CD, turned on the radio, tuned into
one of the many local Spanish stations and began singing along
with the local tunes, which although Liam tried desperately to

216

recognise from his one and only trip to mainland Spain earlier in the year, they meant nothing to him.

After a thirty-minute drive they reached Playa Blanca. Zita drove into a Supermercado car park, returning a few minutes later with two plastic 5-litre bottles of water. She threw them onto the rear seat before driving the last few hundred yards to the four star hotel. The Playa Dorada hotel was situated on the southernmost tip of the island. Recently refurbished, it was the only hotel on the island with an indoor swimming pool, sports centre and modern gymnasium, squash courts, Jacuzzi, steam room and sauna all of which suited Zita.

The jeep pulled into the large car park and she motioned to Liam to take his bag, suitcase and a bottle of the water, and check-in. As he walked away she called after him. 'Don't forget to hire a safe for your bag.'

Once through the automatic doors, the opulence of the hotel reception overawed him. He walked towards the long reception desk and nervously handed his booking confirmation to one of the pretty young dark-haired receptionists. She smiled politely and read the details on his sheet before speaking to him in almost perfect English. 'Good afternoon, Mr Webster, welcome to Lanzarote and the Playa Dorada. May I take your passport?' Reluctantly he handed it over.

His room had been pre-booked by De Groot. Perhaps he had arranged that deliberately so that he could keep tabs on his every movement. She read his details and tapped them competently into the computer before passing him his electronic door key. 'Thank you, Mr Webster . . . Room 183. I hope that you enjoy your time with us. You can have your passport again this evening.'

He moved away from the main desk, hesitated and flicked

through the rotating rack of picture postcards of the hotel and the island. He took a while, flicking the rack backwards and forwards until he selected four cards. He glanced out into the car park. When he saw Zita climb out of the jeep and walk in the direction of the hotel, he paid for the postcards, turned and walked away in the general direction of his room. Wherever he looked the hotel walls displayed large bright abstract oil paintings and, in every available space, stood large pieces of Artisan bronze sculptures, clay and terracotta pots.

Zita went through the same procedure but was given a room on the third floor on the opposite side of the large hotel complex.

Liam walked down the never-ending labyrinth of corridors, past the exotic plants and giant cacti until he found his room on the ground floor at the far end of the hotel. He inserted his security card into the door and, as soon as the green light came on, he turned the handle and entered a large dark room. The room was lit only by the late afternoon sun which struggled to find its way between the outer and inner curtains. He panicked for a second until he realised that he had to insert the card in the box beside the entrance door, which once in place automatically turned on the lights and air-conditioning.

After checking the bathroom he threw his bag onto one of the twin beds, pulled back the curtains, slid the large windows open and walked out onto the balcony. He stood leaning on the handrail looking out across the desolate sea of volcanic rock and the lava mountains which formed an uneven backdrop on the horizon. The whole area was still very barren, the nickname it was given by the tourist guidebooks of being a lunar landscape was more than apt. It was impossible for any plant life to live and sustain its existence on its own; instead every tree or shrub had to rely entirely on water fed through mile upon mile of black plastic pipes or on effluent from the leaking drains.

The craggy coastline had been rearranged by the constant blasting of the volcanic rock in preparation for bigger and better hotels. The extensive man-made breakwaters were constructed from the black volcanic rock found all over the island. They reached out into the Atlantic in readiness for more and more golden beaches and hotels to satisfy the insatiable hunger of the thousands of tourists from all over Europe and the Nordic countries, all trying to escape the cold wet winters and unpredictable summers.

CHAPTER TWENTY-ONE

Life In A Bottle

Although they had arranged to meet in thirty minutes at the pool bar, Liam had hardly finished unwrapping the complimentary toothbrush and toothpaste, razor, sponge and other assorted items when Zita startled him as she let herself into his room. She entered the bathroom unheard and slapped his back. 'Come on, let's go.'

It took Liam a few seconds to get over the shock of how she could get into his room without him hearing her. 'Go where?'

She gave an unusually cheeky smile. 'Explore.'

Liam was about to close the door to his room when Zita pushed him aside. He resisted until he realised that he had forgotten the security card he needed to open his room door. He couldn't hide his embarrassment as she removed it and handed it to him.

Zita stopped in reception to read the weather report before tapping on the barometer. 'Fine weather, not too hot for the next couple of days and then it will get hot . . . very hot.' She looked at Liam. 'Don't worry . . . we'll go somewhere *very* nice,' she said, with a smile.

They walked through the exotic hotel grounds in the late afternoon sun, between the clear sparkling swimming pools, until they reached the arched gate which lead directly on to the tiled promenade overlooking the Atlantic. They both stood for a moment deciding which way to walk. To the left was a rocky coastline, a made up dusty uneven path and, in the distance on the headland, large cranes jutted up into the clear blue sky from the numerous construction sites.

Zita took the lead and tugging at Liam's arm she dragged him to the right. 'We'll go this way.'

They had only walked a few metres along the promenade when Liam saw the man-made Playa Blanca beach below them. The golden sand was unexpected and strangely out of place amongst the black volcanic lunar wasteland and huge chunks of lava that had been positioned to protect the coastline from the occasional wild Atlantic storms. They weaved their way down towards the beach following the steep winding paths reinforced by recycled railway sleepers. Zita ran ahead onto the beach, kicked off her sandals and threw her beach bag on the nearest sunbed. The beach was almost deserted except for two small children who took it in turns to build and then demolish sand castles, and a few elderly couples who wandered aimlessly along the shoreline.

The late afternoon sun was still warm, a stark contrast to the cooler late summer weather back in Amsterdam.

Liam caught up with Zita, sat on the edge of a sunbed, and lit a cigarette. Zita proceeded to remove her pale blue patterned wrap to reveal nothing but a black thong. Without a word to Liam she ran towards the clear blue sea and, after taking a few short paces in the shallow water, she dived and disappeared from view. For Liam it was several painful minutes before he was at last able to relax as she reappeared nearly a hundred yards from the beach and well outside of the protected swimming area. He smiled to himself, relit his cigarette and sat soaking up the last of the warm afternoon sun.

Zita didn't stop. Instead she continued to swim out to sea, her strong arms slicing alternately in almost perfect rhythm through the much deeper azure blue sea. When she eventually reached the distant outcrop of rocks she turned and effortlessly swam back towards the beach. She looked perfect as she walked out of the sea, her wet olive skin glistening in the sun, her small but beautifully shaped breasts with projecting dark nipples. Liam, now aroused, reached for the towel, stood up and placed it around her shoulders. Unable to resist, he lifted her breasts and gently dried the soft pale area of skin beneath them.

For a moment she shivered but, as the sun warmed her body and she dried herself, she smiled at him. She tucked the towel around her body, reached down, picked up a smaller towel and vigorously dried her curly dark hair which, now wet and heavy with the water, touched her shoulders. Before reaching down to remove her wet thong she pulled her wrap around her and her nimble fingers, as if by magic, tied it around her body creating a mid-length dress. 'That's better,' she said, as she smiled. 'Now I feel as I should after that flight. Let's take a drink.'

They walked the short distance across the sand and up the path to the bar overlooking the beach. While Zita sat under a large yellow umbrella near to the wall constructed of variegated volcanic rock, Liam ordered the drinks in one of the few phrases that he had been taught by Juanita in Puerto Banus.

'Kaffee solo y descafeinado con leche por favor,' he said nervously.

The barman smiled and motioned Liam to take a seat. Liam walked to the table where they both sat in silence and took in the view before occasionally tilting their heads back to enjoy the last hour of warm sun. He sipped at his coffee and when Zita's eyes were closed he looked nervously across and thought about his actions on the beach.

'Look at her,' said Liam, pointing at the badly sunburnt woman in a bikini as she walked past.

Zita looked at him confused. 'What?'

Liam continued and pointed at the woman 'The white patches look like she's still wearing her clothes.'

Zita ignored him and sipped at her coffee.

A quad bike, steered accurately by its young rider, methodically made its way between the straight rows of empty sunbeds and umbrellas. A younger boy lined up each remaining pair of beds either side of an umbrella before the quad bike drove between them grading and raking the sand as it went.

The volcanoes of Fuerteventura thrust up into the darkening sky and the Fred Olsen ferry made its return journey from the adjacent island to dock in the tiny harbour, a short walk along the coast.

Zita finally spoke. 'Wolf Island.'

'What?' asked Liam.

She pointed out to sea towards the darkening shadows. 'That small island between here and Fuerteventura is called Wolf Island.'

Liam shrugged his shoulders and thought before answering her. 'I can't imagine how anything could live on these god-forsaken places. Mind you, if De Groot's involved perhaps they already know something we don't.' He pointed along the coast at the cranes and shook his head. 'When will they ever stop building?' he paused and thought. 'Perhaps well after we are dead and buried.'

Liam turned his head to one side to catch the last of the sun, thought, and then smiled. 'Well who cares. This is perfect for me. Maybe I've already died and this is heaven.'

Zita stood up. 'Come on let's go.'

As the sun finally disappeared behind Fuerteventura they walked along the promenade, fronted by shops bars and restaurants, as it wound its way around the coastline towards the town.

Throughout Playa Blanca the majority of buildings were single storey and the highest no more than two-storey, with their whitewashed walls and roofs and pale green shiny glossed woodwork, a pleasant contrast to Puerto Banus and Torreleminos.

The beach along the promenade was very different to the man-made sandy beaches. Natural large smooth black boulders, the rough edges of the lava worn away by thousands of years of tides, waves and rough seas, protected the island. They crossed the wooden bridge set within the promenade and walked along Avenida Maritima until they reached the many restaurants that followed the coast. They stopped at the Almacen de la Sal and Zita guided Liam inside.

The restaurant was luxurious compared to any restaurant Liam had eaten in before, open plan with a balcony, a baby grand piano suspended in mid-air on a steel platform, and the frame of a small boat perched high up in the ceiling. The waiters standing at the entrance wore white shirts, black bow ties and high-necked white starched jackets with gold epaulettes on their shoulders. They all lowered their heads as Liam and Zita entered. Zita knew exactly where she wanted to sit and chose a table that looked out across the narrow channel and the lights of Fuerteventura. The nearest waiter handed each of them a menu and ceremoniously lit a small turquoise oil-filled lamp.

Zita studied the menu and when she raised her head the waiter rushed across to their table. Liam couldn't resist gazing at Zita as she ordered their dinner. Speaking in faultless Spanish, one of the many languages that she spoke fluently, she joked with the waiter.

Liam knew Zita was good for him; she didn't drink alcohol or want to. She did nothing that would affect her athletic performance; she knew alcohol would slow her down and affect her . . . the main reason De Groot had her around and kept her on his payroll.

They sat in silence and took in the atmosphere and the soft piano music.

Two waiters approached their table with the starter. The first waiter placed the white plates in front of them and the second waiter, carrying a sizzling frying pan, served the starter. *Lapas con Mojo* – a plateful of limpets cooked quickly on a hot griddle and served with a sauce of ground garlic, parsley and cumin, salt and white vinegar. Zita had given specific instructions that the white wine usually used in the dish was replaced with the vinegar.

Liam had no idea what he was eating but followed Zita's lead and seemed to enjoy every mouthful. She waited until he had cleared his plate and was eating the last piece of bread before she spoke. 'Did you enjoy that?' Liam swallowed hard and smiled back at her as he emptied his water glass. 'Very nice,' he replied.

'I love sea food especially limpets . . .' she said, wiping her mouth with the soft white napkin.

Liam nearly choked. 'L . . . l . . . limpets?' He caught his breath. 'What the hell are they?'

She smiled back at him. 'Does it matter what they are if you enjoyed them?'

Liam shook his head and picked up his empty glass and tried to drink from it. The second waiter rushed over and refilled both glasses before the first waiter cleared the plates.

Zita had chosen the table for a reason and she periodically checked her watch and timed the arrival and departure of the Fred Olsen ferry and Volcan de Tindaya, the much smaller ferry, as they took it in turns to make their way in and out of the harbour.

Liam looked at her. 'You are full of surprises aren't you? What's next?' he asked.

She blushed. 'Wait and see,' she teased.

The waiters returned with a large terracotta casserole dish and warm clean plates. As soon as one waiter lifted the lid, the head waiter ceremoniously placed a sole fillet on each plate and laid a large portion of baked baby Calamari to the side of it. The second waiter carefully served noodles, placing them delicately around the fillet.

Zita looked across at Liam who was clearly very nervous at what he was expected to eat. 'Try it. I'm so sure you will like it.' She immediately speared one of the calamari and sucked it into her mouth. She momentarily closed her eyes as she savoured the flavour. 'Wonderful . . . I've been waiting for this moment.' She paused. 'Come on Liam . . . try it,' she said, enthusiastically.

He nervously raised his fork and prodded at the calamari before choosing a chunk of the soft sole fillet. His eyes couldn't hide his pleasure and he smiled as he reached for more of the sole and noodles.

Zita cleared her plate and reached over and ate the remaining calamari on Liam's plate. 'Um . . . heaven isn't it?'

Liam nodded.

The waiters cleared the table and reappeared with two menus.

Zita refused to take hers and looked at Liam who had already placed his on the table. 'You can choose now,' she said.

Liam turned page after page until he reached the desserts. He mumbled nervously to himself until he saw something he recognised. He smiled and pointed it out to the waiter.

The waiter nodded and walked off.

Zita looked at him expectantly. 'Well?'

Liam pushed himself back in his chair and stretched. 'Wait and see,' he teased.

It wasn't long before the waiter returned with Liam's choice of dessert. He placed two huge portions of apple pie and ice cream in front of them.

Liam smiled at the shocked expression on Zita's face. 'How can I eat all of this,' she said.

'Eat as much as you want,' replied Liam.

Much to his surprise she cleared it all and smiled with satisfaction. 'Sometimes it is good to eat so much, yes?'

Liam nodded.

As dusk approached, a lighthouse, precariously positioned on a narrow finger of projecting rock, flashed sending strobes of light across the darkening ocean, and as the illuminated Fred Olsen moored in the harbour for the night it reminded them both of Amsterdam.

While they ate, the promenade came to life as tourists of all nationalities ambled up and down soaking up the atmosphere.

Zita's mobile beeped with the receipt of a text message. She read it, tapped in a response and smiled at Liam. 'It's tomorrow.'

Liam took a large gulp of water. 'OK.'

Zita now switched into gear and spoke with authority for the first time since arriving on the island. She looked at the bill resting under the ashtray, counted out the exact amount, pocketed the receipt and stood up. 'Let's go.'

CHAPTER TWENTY-TWO

Night Fever

Zita asked Liam to wait in reception while she went out to the jeep. She returned in a few minutes and handed Liam a bulging travel suit cover and a shoebox. 'Wear this tomorrow – it's a very special day.'

It was already dark when Liam returned to his hotel room. The soft white hand towels had been folded to resemble swans and carefully placed in each of the wash-hand basins. He turned on the television, made himself a black coffee and flicked through the channels until a song on one of the many radio channels attracted his attention. The Gypsy Kings sang to him for the first time this trip. He sat on the bed and opened the black cover to reveal an oatmeal, lightweight, handmade suit, and the box containing a pair of brown Masseratti ostrich skin shoes and matching belt. He laid the suit on one bed and sat on the other. He stared at it and smirked to himself before his mood changed to anger. He noticed the colourfully wrapped chocolates that had been placed on each pillow. He grabbed at them and put both into his mouth; while still chewing he subconsciously danced his way out onto the balcony to be overwhelmed by the soft warm breeze. He grabbed at one of the cane armchairs and fell back into it. He sipped at the coffee and looked out across the bizarre dark volcanic lunar landscape, broken only by a single light from a cottage in the distance and the lights on the dozens of small fishing craft close to shore.

He finished his coffee, looked out into the moonless sky and started to count the stars. He talked to himself. 'What a different world this is?' He suddenly realised why the music was so popular with English tourists who visited Spain or the islands. The Gypsy Kings gave way to *Something* by the Beatles, a cassette tape he remembered buying for Kathleen when the twins were born in 1988.

He began to cry uncontrollably and looked back into the luxurious room. On the bedside table he noticed the bottle of Brut on ice. He dashed in, grabbed at it, ripped off the foil, released the cork and thrust the bottle into his salivating mouth. He emptied the bottle and let out a loud belch. Within an hour he had consumed every miniature in the mini bar and fell unconscious onto the bed.

Zita was up before dawn and after taking a quick shower she ran to the beach and swam for over an hour until the sun began to rise out over the sea. Small groups of oyster catchers joined her to begin their search for breakfast, darting up and down the deserted shoreline. In Liam's room, the telephone rang repeatedly to itself. He didn't hear it and continued to snore loudly. He was finally woken by the frantic banging on his door. Zita finally let herself in to his room to be hit by the stench of stale vomit. She held her nose while she took in the wrecked furniture and the sight of his clothes strewn everywhere. She screamed as she hammered at his contorted body. 'Sie dreckige Bastard! Come on! Clean yourself up!'

Liam was unable to move and shook violently. She took a deep breath and reluctantly pulled a hypodermic needle from a small yellow bag, charged it and thrust it into Liam's right buttock. He didn't feel it. She threw the duvet over him, watched passively and waited. Within a few seconds his whole body went in to spasm and he slowly regained consciousness. Minutes later he rolled off the bed and stood quivering in front of her. She checked her watch and glared at him. 'Sie dreckige Bastard! Shower NOW!'

Liam staggered blindly towards the bathroom where he was violently sick. While he showered, Zita found a clean space on the unused bed, laid out the suit, cleaned the vomit from the shoes and unbuttoned the pale blue cotton shirt.

With his hair still wet she helped him to dress. He looked in the mirror and began to rip off the jacket. 'Who the fuck do you think I am? John, sodding, Travolta!' Zita shot him a confused look but Liam continued. 'John Travolta?' He laughed hysterically. 'You don't know who the fuck he is do yer?' He continued to stare at her and waited for her to respond. She didn't, so he continued. *'Saturday fuckin' night fever?'*

Zita shot him a confused look and he suddenly realised that the film was released in the seventies and that she had probably never seen it.

Liam tugged wildly at the jacket before slowly raising his head to face her. 'Sorry. It's only . . .' He tilted his head back and flicked his wet hair. 'Well my mother loved that film and us kids were forced to watch the video every Saturday night and . . .' He cursed. 'Sometimes Sundays.' He paused and refocused his bloodshot eyes. 'What about . . . ?' He thought hard. 'Fucking . . . James Bond . . . 007?' He turned and looked into the mirror. He trembled as he spoke. 'Listen . . .' His voice faded to a whisper. 'I can't go out looking like this . . . Please . . .'

Zita had already lost patience with him. She knew they were running out of time. 'We don't have time for any shit . . .' She stiffened up, took a deep breath and slapped his face. Liam, unaffected by the powerful blow, swayed blindly in front of her and tried to focus. Zita stared directly into Liam's eyes and jabbed her fingers into his chest before continuing. 'Just . . .' She didn't finish the sentence; instead she grabbed him and dragged him down the corridor. She stopped when she saw the cleaner. She whispered in her ear and handed her 10,000 pesetas. As Liam passed the cleaner she looked him up and down and shook her head disapprovingly.

When they finally reached the jeep, Zita checked her watch, flicked the key, accelerated hard and skidded noisily out of the car park, forcing Liam's head to fly back as she raced away. She stopped at a farmacia, returning a few minutes later with a bottle and a straw hat. She manhandled him out of the jeep, shook the bottle and carefully opened it before she pushed it towards him. He smelt the liquid and pulled his head back at the foul smell. 'Drink it! I don't want you to erbrechen on to me.' She looked across at him and thought for a minute. 'Or,' she lowered her voice, 'over your *beautiful* suit.'

He swallowed the whole bottle and shook his head in disgust.

Zita reassured him. 'You will feel human once more in a few minutes.'

Liam crawled back into the jeep. He looked like death.

Zita reached onto the rear seat and pulled out a bag. She

opened it, pulled out two dry bread rolls and handed them to him. 'You must eat these . . .'

He pushed them away.

'Now!' she screamed.

He responded by tearing tiny pieces from the bread rolls and slowly chewing it.

She waited until he had eaten both of them before taking a capsule from her pocket. She handed it to him along with a bottle of water and waited for him to take it.

Reluctantly he swallowed the capsule and emptied the plastic bottle.

Once Zita was satisfied he wasn't going to vomit she started the vehicle and pulled out of the car park. She continually checked her watch as she drove along the deserted road and after exactly fifteen minutes she pulled off the road and waited.

Liam jumped out and retched violently.

'Take care of your suit . . .' she said. She waited until he had finished vomiting and threw him a box of tissues. He wiped his mouth, walked slowly back to the jeep and climbed in.

Zita flicked the ignition and drove away in silence.

Liam finally spoke in a subdued voice. 'I'm sorry, Zita . . . I tried . . . but couldn't resist it . . .'

She snarled at him. 'You must learn to take care of your own shit!'

He nodded and sighed heavily. 'I feel better now.' He exhaled noisily and sighed. 'What the fuck did you give me?' He smiled at her. 'How did you know that would work?'

She looked directly at him. 'Don't ask,' she said. She grinned and continued. 'I kept a few from before . . .' she smirked, 'De Groot needs my expertise . . . that's why he hired me.' Her smirk suddenly vanished and she spoke sternly. 'Remember, I trained to use drugs for everything – life or death . . .'

Liam looked confused.

'Come on. We have not the time,' said Zita. 'I will maybe tell you one day . . .' She gunned the accelerator and raced away.

Liam grunted at her and closed his eyes.

The mist still hung over the sea and it was partially overcast as they drove towards what was the first ferry of the day. She drove along the concrete apron of the port, into the car park and left the jeep next to the Red Cross centre. Liam remained in the passenger seat while Zita jumped out and walked across to the car park office, returning a few minutes later with their tickets.

The Volcan de Tindaya, the smaller of the two ferries, docked, and after disgorging its mix of multi-national passengers, tourists and locals, Zita was signalled to drive into the cavernous metallic belly of the ferry, passing the already positioned delivery vans, lorries and tourist coaches. Their jeep was the last vehicle to board the ferry and after parking and furtively checking the steel padlocked box beneath her seat she led Liam upstairs. 'Come on, you need to eat something or the dose won't have total effect.'

Zita walked up to the counter and returned carrying a tray with two black coffees, three croissants and two bottles of water. She motioned for Liam to follow her up onto the deck before she placed the tray carefully on the table. They ate and drank in silence and took their time to take in the different perspective of the port and harbour and the small fishing boats overloaded with rust-encrusted lobster pots and their patched archaic fishing nets.

This was Liam's first trip on a commercial Spanish ferry and as each day passed he realised that he had wasted so much of his life spent in captivity or in a drunken stupor. He was becoming more and more aware that there was a lot to see and discover outside of captivity or his self-inflicted alcoholic prison in England.

Liam watched two young girls in silence as they chased each other between the tables and round the deck. He could feel tears welling up inside him. He pushed his chair away, stood up and walked along the deck. Zita followed and grabbed at his arm. 'Did I ever tell you alcohol killed my mother?' she asked. 'She died of a broken heart.' She paused and swallowed hard. 'The American . . .' she choked off her emotion, 'do you know she waited for him all her *life* . . .' She paused and thought hard before she continued in a soft voice, a tone that Liam had not heard before. 'Until the day she died.' Zita looked out to sea before turning back to face Liam. He gave a half smile. She glared at him. 'This alcohol could kill you too . . .' She shook her head very slowly and wiped the tears from her eyes. 'Be careful . . . be very . . . very careful.' She looked hard at him. 'To some people life is very precious, eh?'

Liam shrugged and walked across the deck.

As the ferry approached Fuerteventura, the nearest inhabited island to Lanzarote, Liam leaned heavily against the handrail watching the fingers of early morning sunlight reaching down onto the sandy beaches. He looked at Zita. 'It's beautiful. How come De Groot sent me and didn't come himself?'

Zita smiled. 'What do you think? De Groot is like everyone else in Holland they love the sun. He will come back again in the summer or maybe even in the spring.' She shrugged her shoulders. 'But he is a little bit strange . . . he doesn't want to be brown from it.'

The ferry passed the Fred Olsen jetty and docked in Corralejo, the northernmost port in Fuerteventura.

'Come on, we must go downstairs,' she said, grabbing at his arm.

He followed her down the stairs but she stopped abruptly on the half landing, turned back and frowned. 'I say to the hotel not to restock your mini bar,' she said, in a stern voice. 'I cannot save you or your life . . . it is for you to want to do that.'

Liam shrugged and walked on down the stairs towards the jeep.

It was not until the ferry docked and the hangover remedy took full effect that Liam realised how different Zita looked. Her hair was pulled back off of her face and tied back in a single plait. She was wearing a white blouse, fitted olive skirt and short matching jacket and light brown designer ankle boots.

Zita handed Liam the straw hat. 'Put this on . . . you will need it.'

He held it in his hand before pushing it discreetly behind his seat.

Zita drove the jeep carefully down the ramp onto the quayside and immediately into a hive of activity. Tourists and locals alike took it in turns to dodge the lorries and delivery vans as they buzzed in and out of the narrow streets servicing the needs of the numerous tourist shops and restaurants. The diverse mixture of old and newer buildings of similar style made it very difficult to tell the difference between what was new and those that had been built many years earlier, when the old town was a vibrant fishing harbour and port. Corralejo was very different to Playa Blanca and the small sandy beach was almost deserted except for a group of young surfers sleeping on the man-made beach, still stoned from the night before and oblivious to the activity going on around them. Fuerteventura had clusters of smaller buildings built in a haphazard way between new construction sites and, as in Lanzarote, cranes rose up towards the clear blue sky.

They drove along the rugged dusty gravel roads for nearly an hour before reaching a cliff on the west of the island. Zita stopped and they climbed out and looked down at the view below them. What they saw made them realise that what they were watching had happened so many times before throughout the Canary Islands and mainland Spain when commercialism finally began to overtake the peace of a barren and untouched part of the coastline. The feverish activity seemed strangely out of place amongst the white single storey fishermen's cottages close to the shoreline.

Zita drove down the steep road onto a beautiful beach fringed with clusters of tall palm trees, and continued until they reached the luxurious hotel complex. As they pulled into the landscaped car park a tanned man in his early sixties walked out to welcome them. Zita shook his hand and introduced Liam before they took one of the four lifts up to the penthouse suites with their own rooftop infinity pools and breath-taking views which took in the harbour, the unspoiled bay and mountains behind it.

Before they sat down at the large carved table, covered with plans of the complex, Zita introduced Liam formally to Juan Martisco, the architect. He was in his early sixties and wore a cerise long-sleeved shirt, an off-white linen suit with heavily creased trousers, interlocking leather belt and highly polished brown leather shoes. His fine wavy grey hair, long at the back, fell over his collar. As he walked towards the table Liam realised why he was required to put on the suit that he had been so reluctant to wear.

Juan then introduced his assistant, Francesco Raphael, an overweight and obviously gay man in his late fifties. He had tried to hide his greying hair but the dye hadn't taken and left ginger patches all over it. He was also wearing a white suit but instead of a shirt he wore a black tee shirt with the motif "Bad boy" across the chest. Liam grinned to himself as his eyes were drawn to the ridiculous undersized tee shirt stretched across the man's fat stomach distorting some of the letters.

They all sat at the table and a young tanned gay man, wearing the briefest of shorts, brought in a tray of coffee and almendrados – almond cookies – and attempted to place it on top of the drawings. Juan hurriedly reached out and rolled up some of his designs to leave space for the tray. As he left the room the gay man smiled nervously at Francesco.

Zita spent the next hour asking probing questions in fluent Spanish before she left with Juan to check on progress and take photographic evidence for De Groot. Taking great care not to include any people in the photographs she took on the new Pentax IQ Zoom digital camera.

Liam remained at the table, took a cigarette from his top pocket and offered one to Francesco. The gay man refused, took out a cigar and lit it. He took a long hard drag before blowing a huge plume of smoke. He sat back and sipped at his coffee and spoke for the first time. 'You are English, Mister . . . yeas?'

Liam shook his head. 'Irish . . .'

Francesco nodded and continued. 'Senorita is a very sweet piece of fruit yeas?' He paused. 'How you say . . . a peach.' He paused before he continued. 'I think yeas?'

Liam didn't reply.

The man sniggered. 'Ah . . . maybe you like her . . . Yeas?' He took another long drag from his cigar and leaned forward. He stroked Liam's leg and waited for a reaction. Without warning Liam pulled a knife from his jacket and stabbed it through the centre of the man's other hand pinning it to the table. The man screamed in agony and tried to pull the knife out but it had penetrated deep into the wooden table top.

Liam grabbed at the knife and grinned inanely at the Spaniard. Without any compunction, he twisted it vigorously before yanking it out. The gay man let out an even louder scream and, clutching at his bleeding hand, ran off towards the lift and the first aid station.

Zita continued to make notes throughout the tour of the complex but when they reached the last of the three luxury swimming pools she stopped and spoke sharply to Juan. She took the lift down to the jeep and sent a text to De Groot. While Zita sat in the jeep, Francesco returned to join Liam at the blood stained table and glared at him while he continued to apply pressure to his heavily bandaged hand. The architect, choosing to ignore the altercation, sat beside Liam, and played nervously with his fingers beneath the table.

Zita drummed her fingers on the steering wheel impatiently while she waited for a response. A few seconds later her mobile bleeped. She feverishly pressed a few of the buttons, read De Groot's response and took the lift up and rejoined the group. She briefly glanced at Francesco's bandaged hand and then Liam before turning to smile at Juan. 'OK,' she said. The tension was immediately broken. She signalled to Liam to join her at the jeep where she unlocked the metal box beneath her seat and passed the bags to Liam.

She stood on the terrace beside the table, signed the papers and handed them to Juan. He countersigned them and passed one copy back to Zita. She nodded and Liam placed the bags on the table. Juan quickly opened them and started to count the Dutch guilders and German marks. He stopped before he'd counted it all. Smiling and visibly relieved he looked at Liam and Zita. 'I'm sure is no need to check it, eh?' Zita shook her head. Juan closed the bags and smiled. 'Lunch?'

Liam and Zita responded simultaneously. 'Sure.'

The four of them walked to their respective vehicles and pulled away.

Zita could sense that Liam was angry and as soon as they were alone in the jeep she spoke to him. 'Liam, what is the matter with you? What did you do to him?'

He snarled at her. 'What you probably wanted to do.' She nodded. 'Another minute with that slimy bastard and I would have killed him.'

Zita shuddered. 'Yeah, I know what you mean, they are both creeps, they make my body crawl.'

Liam burst out laughing. 'They don't make your body crawl.'

Zita looked at him and appeared to lose her temper. 'You say that I am telling lies? I tell you they do!'

Liam raised his hands in submission and tried to reassure her. 'OK, OK. I know what you mean, but it's not right.'

Before she had time to interrupt him he continued. 'What you should say, is that they make your *skin* crawl, not your *body*.'

She giggled and laughed loudly before she accelerated hard throwing him back into his seat.

The vehicles followed each other back to Corralejo and through the cobbled side streets of the port that wound between the low level buildings. This soon gave way to dozens of restaurants, the majority of which served seafood. The restaurateurs had carefully set their tables in the shade amongst the trees that punctuated the side streets to protect their clientele from the heat of the sun.

Zita knew exactly where she was going and chose a limited parking area to the rear of a small local beach-side restaurant. The Cofradía de Pescadores was a very basic restaurant run by the local fishermen's guild where the fish was guaranteed to be fresh and perfectly cooked.

Liam was made to feel like a stranger as Zita took control of everything including the ordering of the food and drinks. Lunch was kept formal despite the surroundings. Zita had carefully chosen the restaurant and table so she could see the jetty. When their ferry docked they said their goodbyes and left.

They joined the small queue of vehicles and Zita pulled on the handbrake. While they waited for the ferry passengers to disembark Liam jumped out of the jeep and rushed into a small artisan shop next to the Café Latino, an Internet café, beach bar and restaurant situated near the port. He knew exactly what he wanted and bought the leather saddlebags for his motorbike. He returned to the jeep and smiled proudly as he held his trophy in the air.

As the Volcan de Tindaya left the harbour for the return

journey to Fuerteventura, the Bougainville, four times the size of their ferry, docked at its own mooring. Relieved to be back on the ferry for the return journey, they both stood at the bow enjoying the warm sunshine. As the ferry cut into the calm sea the cool spray blew into their faces. At last the atmosphere had changed and with the business complete the two of them were now able to relax.

Zita looked across at Liam. 'Well, De Groot will be happy,' she said, with a sigh as she looked over his shoulder and out across the sea. 'And now we have a little time to enjoy ourselves.'

Liam moved closer towards her, squeezed her shoulders and kissed her on the forehead. 'Were you really angry with me for this morning?'

She nodded. 'You will kill yourself . . . maybe the next time you *drink* so much? Do you want to *die* – to kill *yourself*?' she said, sternly.

Liam looked directly at her, the blank look on his face clear of any indication of a response.

Zita continued. 'You know . . .' she paused, 'you *will* die . . . for sure. Do you want dat?'

Liam looked at her coyly. 'Of course I don't for f . . . .' He kicked blindly at the deck. 'Is that why you spoke to those bastards in Spanish *all day* – so I couldn't understand? As a punishment?'

She smiled and closed her mouth. She wet her lips and pushed her tongue out between them. 'Of course not, it was easier for me to make the business.' She ran her hand through Liam's hair, parted his fringe and kissed his forehead. 'The less you know the better.' He frowned and shook his head slowly. She ignored his reaction. 'No, believe me, it *is* better,

242

much better,' she said, trying to reassure him. 'Not a secret . . . but trust me – it is better.'

Liam visibly relaxed, dropped his shoulders and offered a smile.

Zita continued. 'De Groot doesn't trust the Spanish, especially Martisco and the gay bastard. Trust me, it is *strictly* business,' she said.

'So, in that case, why is De Groot so keen to build things on these Islands when Spain is nearer?' quizzed Liam.

'The Canaria Islands have tourist business all year and as you say they *are islands*. The mainland of Spain attracts the low life, crooks trying to hide. It is too easy.' She looked to him for confirmation.

He remembered the Ronnie Knight fiasco and smiled at her. 'Yeah, I understand.'

Zita continued. 'Here it is more selective, the people are different and they rely totally on tourists.' She reflected and smiled. 'Oh . . . and . . . maybe bananas.' De Groot has many plans. She looked around. 'He will be building one of the best hotels over there.' She pointed to building work on the land up the coast from their hotel. 'It will be so luxurious and his best investment. He will sell the new hotel in Fuerteventura keeping one penthouse suite for himself, and the clean money from the sale will pay for this.' She paused and pointed in the other direction. 'And over there will be a marina but he will only do the deals on that, he doesn't want to be too conspicuous.'

Liam laughed. 'Does he really believe that he can do all of this without drawing attention to himself?'

Zita smiled. 'That's why he doesn't come here himself so often. He stays in Amsterdam and comes here only for holidays.' She laughed loudly. 'He's much like *you*.' She laughed to herself. 'He likes the sun but gets burnt so he often comes in December or January. Sometimes he will come in the summer but not so often anymore.'

Liam blushed. 'I didn't say, I *didn't* like it, it's just that *I burn.*'

They left the ferry and Zita turned in the opposite direction to their hotel and drove along the coast. She stopped on a hill overlooking a lighthouse. 'Come on I want to show you something.'

They left the jeep and walked across to what was the slope of a now defunct volcano. In front of them was a huge construction site, cranes towered high into the sky. 'De Groot wanted that site.' She pointed slowly across the bay from the lighthouse to the headland on the other side. 'This is Flamingo beach.' She briefly fantasised. 'What a beautiful name?' She pointed at the cranes below them. 'And this will be the Natura Palace, with two hundred or more bedrooms. It is now being built by Hipotels.'

Liam nodded as he took his time to look across the bay and the local men fishing, oblivious to the feverish activity going on around them. 'So why didn't he? I thought he got everything he wanted.' He paused and tilted his head back to catch the last sun of the day before he continued. 'One way or another.'

Zita kicked at the dry path. 'He wanted a hundred percent of it. As always he wanted total control. He got greedy and it backfired on to him.'

Liam watched spellbound as the waves crashed onto the rocks. 'What a fantastic place for a hotel.'

'It really is and when they build the holiday apartments and bungalows around here it will be worth a lot of money . . . but . . .' She paused and remembered the meeting six months earlier. 'He wanted it all and it is something he can never learn. De Groot would never have that much money to build a hotel of that size, although it was something he so desperately wanted to do.' She turned. 'Come on let's go to the hotel for a shower and have dinner.'

CHAPTER TWENTY-THREE

Postcard From Heaven

There was an early morning chill in the air, reminiscent of early autumn in Hamburg, as Zita jogged out of the hotel grounds. Beginning at the promenade she turned right towards the port but, irritated by the pseudo foreign joggers, she turned off towards the slopes of the nearest dormant volcano and the rough terrain of the volcanic ash and gravel. It was much harder and more demanding for her athletic physique.

The bright morning sun gradually crept around the walls filling every inch of Liam's room until it woke him up. He pushed himself out of bed and stood out on the balcony looking across the alien landscape towards the sea. The sky was incredibly blue and for a second he stood on the tiled floor totally overawed and mesmerised by the view. The cold tiles finally brought him back to earth and reluctantly he walked back inside and into the shower. An unsuspecting spider crawled out between the ceiling and the wall tiles. Liam grabbed the shower, turned it on to full power and holding it like a gun, posed as he obliterated the defenseless spider out of existence. He pulled on his jeans, new boots and a tee shirt and went for a walk to the nearest Netto supermarket. They were everywhere and had become the mainstay of self catering tourists. Liam bought a newspaper, the Sun. He sat at a nearby bar and ordered a black coffee but rather than read the paper, watched a little girl struggling with her dad. Liam muttered under his breath. 'You lucky bastard you should appreciate what you've got.' The man looked across at Liam and mouthed a response. Liam glared back at him and made to stand. The man took his daughter's hand and walked briskly away. Liam smirked to himself and drank his coffee before throwing the unopened newspaper into the bin.

Liam saw Zita sitting at a table on the patio outside the restaurant and joined her. A pair of peacocks that lived in the hotel grounds scrounged tasty morsels from the guests who sat at the tables nearest to the plants and shrubs. After breakfast Liam and Zita left the hotel for the short drive a few miles along the coast to Papagaya beach. Zita confidently drove towards the dunes maintaining incredible control over the vehicle as it bounced over the rough terrain. She passed a few cars in the makeshift car park and still continued on into uncharted territory until any signs of a track disappeared. The fine golden sand flew high around them as the tyres dug in hard for traction. She suddenly pulled up, jumped out, grabbed her well-worn rucksack from the back seat, pulled it across her shoulders and, after picking up a few packages from the floor in the back of the jeep, she ran out into the dunes.

Within a few minutes she was out of sight swallowed up by the ever-changing isolated sands transformed almost daily by the sometimes violent winds from the Atlantic Ocean.

Liam sat in the passenger seat and lit a cigarette while he tried to understand what was going on. His curiosity finally got the better of him and he climbed out of the jeep. Finding it extremely difficult to run in his Cuban heeled boots, he walked in the general direction that Zita had already taken. He continued to walk slowly in that direction but after a few minutes he was totally lost. Unable to find her he sat down in the sweltering heat, lit a cigarette and looked across the dunes and out towards the crystal blue sea wondering what sort of a game she was playing. He lit a second cigarette and waited, it was the best thing he could have done as in the distance he saw a wisp of smoke. In the still air it floated up into the clear deep blue sky. He didn't rush. He finished his cigarette and walked through the dunes until he reached the top of the highest one desperately hoping that it was a signal to him from Zita. When he looked down a smile passed across his face. Zita had set up an almost perfect camp and was kneeling in front of the small fire she had built in a sunken well excavated in the sand. She had erected a huge umbrella, which took pride of place, arranged the large hotel towels beneath it and tied the portable CD player to the pole to protect the plastic case from the sun.

Liam tried to run down the soft dunes but fell awkwardly, at first sliding down the steep slope then falling the last twenty feet to land in a heap, his hair clothes and pockets filled with fine sand.

Zita was laying naked on one of the towels. Liam landed beside her but before he could catch his breath she got up. 'I'm going for a swim. Going to join me?' she asked, licking her lips.

Liam raised his head, looked towards the sea, and shrugged his shoulders. Zita didn't wait for his verbal response, instead she laughed and ran towards the sea shouting back to him as she crashed into the sea.

Although he was lying beneath the umbrella the sun gradually began to get to his pale body. He finished his cigarette, removed his boots and jeans, and now dressed only in his underpants and tee shirt followed her into the sea.

While he walked along the shoreline Zita burst up out of the water and splashed him. Liam splashed her back until his underpants and tee shirt were soaked. Zita pulled him through the waves and into the deeper water. They swam for a few minutes and then stopped to tread water. Zita disappeared beneath the surface, pulled off his underpants and resurfaced holding her trophy. She let Liam catch her but as he reached her she threw his underpants out into even deeper water. He grabbed her shoulders and when she turned to face him she kissed him gently on the lips. Zita disappeared once more under the water, eventually resurfaced and swam back towards him. Without saying a word she pulled him close to her and guided him towards the shore. As Zita removed Liam's tee shirt she pulled him down onto the warm wet sand and, now further aroused by the hot sun and each other's naked body, they lay at the edge of the sea. They rolled together along the soft sand between the waves and with the water gently lapping over their bodies they made love in a way that Liam had only dreamed of during his many years in prison.

The larger waves crashed onto the black stone breakwater drowning out their shrieks of pleasure. As they both reached a climax the friendly waves lapped around their bodies. After lying for a while, Zita dragged Liam back into the water where they washed each other before walking hand in hand up the beach.

They lay beneath the umbrella and giggled uncontrollably for several minutes until, following a lengthy silence Zita
spoke. 'You swim well . . . very well,' she said.

'Yeah, it was a case of having to. If you couldn't swim at
school you got picked on and there was no way that was going
to happen to me. My dad made sure of that.' He nodded and
offered a smile. 'He was right. They left me alone,' he smiled,
'and . . . picked on others.' He reflected. 'Poor sods.'

Zita was the first to speak. 'Come, I will put on some cream
or you will burn.'

Liam retorted. 'Why me? Don't you ever burn?'

Zita tried to appease him. 'Of course I do. You can put the
cream on me, all right? My father was black so that means
that I am black.' Liam shot her a confused look. She tilted her
head to one side and continued. 'Maybe not on the outside –
but inside – my *soul*.' Liam looked at her unable to hide the
confusion in his face. Zita continued. 'I am sometimes.' She
shook her head excitedly. 'I can *feel it*,' she said proudly.

Liam didn't want to argue and lay back on his towel.
While she massaged the cream into his burning skin he subconsciously twisted the hair in her armpits between his fingers.

They stretched out beneath the umbrella but, still sexually
charged, Zita moved nearer to him and began to slowly stroke
the top of his back and shoulders in small circular movements,
moving ever nearer to his buttocks. She kissed his shoulders
running her tongue up and down his spine before she grabbed
him and pulled his arms nearer to her before kissing him hard
on the lips.

She whispered in his ear. 'Let's dance?'

He stood up to join her on the warm sand and they moved
slowly to the hypnotic rhythm of the reggae music, pushing

their bodies hard against each other. Liam's penis was hard and seeking. Zita now pulled him even closer to her and once more guided him slowly down towards the shore. On the beach she feigned a slip and fell into the foaming shallow water. He fell on top of her and silently entered her. After long, slow rhythmic sex on the edge of the water, Liam sat up and looked out across the beach towards the blue mirror sea. Zita looked at him strangely and then began to laugh. 'You've not been circumcised have you?'

Liam flinched. 'So what?'

Zita tried to undo her question by making it appear less important than it really was. 'It's not a problem for me.'

Liam was offended and it showed. Zita looked at him and immediately changed the subject. 'You know we shouldn't be here, De Groot would go crazy if he knew it.'

'How is he going to know what the fuck we're doing, when he's back in Holland?' He thought and then looked at Zita. 'How many miles away?'

Zita thought about his reply for a moment and shrugged. Satisfied with his answer she relaxed again and, after laying her head on the sand, she looked up at the blue sky before getting up and grabbing at Liam's hands. She smiled and sighed with pleasure. Liam smiled and together they walked hand in hand up the deserted beach towards the welcoming shade of the umbrella. They caringly covered each other in sun cream and while Liam lit another cigarette Zita was up again. She assembled a spear gun from a handful of assorted innocent pieces of metal that she took from one of the side pockets of her rucksack.

When Liam saw what she had made he flinched and covered his penis. She lifted the gun and pointed it directly at him and simulated firing it. He feigned fear. 'Be careful with that will yer,' he screamed. Once more she reached into her bag and pulled out a small roll of silver paper, which she threw to him. He caught it effortlessly and unwrapped it. After smelling it, a smile spread across his face. 'Thanks.'

'That's OK.' She smiled back at him, pleased that she had made him happy.

Zita's firm buttocks and perfect body glistened in the sun as she walked effortlessly down the beach, carrying the spear gun at her side. She dived silently into the sea to disappear beneath the waves. Liam pushed himself up onto one elbow took a drag on his hastily made joint and watched. He couldn't believe that he was really here. While Zita was in the sea he thought he would write his postcards but his efforts were futile and two joints later he lay back and fantasised. For the first time in his life he had lost any thoughts of self-consciousness.

He lost all track of time and was oblivious to Zita walking slowly up the beach with two huge fish impaled on her spear gun. She stopped halfway, tilted her head to one side and after a moment continued to walk towards him. When she reached the shade of the umbrella she dropped the fish and, without saying a word, pulled a stiletto knife from another much smaller pocket of her rucksack and disappeared into the dunes. She made her way across the dunes until she was within a few metres of the voyeur's beach buggy but, as she prepared herself for the dash across the open sand towards her unsuspecting victim, he opened the buggy door. She threw her knife and he screamed out in agony as it penetrated deep into the calf of his left leg. With the knife still embedded in his leg, he gunned the accelerator. When the wheels found a compacted strip of sand he was able to pull away. Zita read and reread the registration number until she had memorised it. She watched as the buggy threw up the sand and disappeared into the distance. Frustrated by her failure, she kicked at the sand before returning to the spot where the vehicle had been parked. She knelt down and meticulously searched every inch of the area before walking back to Liam.

Liam looked at her. 'What the fuck was that all about?'

Zita replied – not even out of breath. 'I think maybe someone was looking at us.'

Liam laughed loudly and sneered. 'I would have thought every perv on the island comes here.'

Zita's expression changed. 'Liam, that is not so funny . . .'

Although feeling cheated, she said nothing as she picked up the fish and walked down to the shore. She washed them in the warm sea, gutted them on the shoreline and begrudgingly threw the guts to the noisy impatient lone black-backed gull that gorged himself before flying off in search of his next meal. As Liam sat watching her he reflected. He thought that *he* was a fisherman, but a woman with a spear gun – catching fish that you can *eat*?

Zita walked up the beach, pulled some large green banana leaves from her bag, wrapped the fish in them and, after tying them with lengths of tough wild grass, she placed them into the fire and lay down beside Liam, resting her arm across his sunburnt back. He no longer felt any pain the hashish had the desired effect, but with his raised awareness he could sense that she was now preoccupied and spoke to her in a quiet voice. 'Is there anything you can't do?'

Zita looked down at him. 'I wish that I catch that bastard. What we did was wrong. My training would never allow me to do what we did. You could have been shot. I never lose a client before . . .'

Liam looked at her in disbelief, anger etched deeply into his ever reddening face. '*Client*! *Is that all I am your fucking . . . client!*'

He pushed himself awkwardly into a kneeling position and was violently sick. Zita moved towards him. 'Get away from me!' he screamed.

There was a difficult silence for several minutes while Liam walked down to the sea and washed his face. He relit his joint and lay back smoking it slowly and thoughtfully. When it was almost finished he moved closer to Zita and whispered to her. 'I'm sorry . . . I really am sorry . . . It'll be alright.' He took a final drag. 'I shouldn't worry, it was probably a Gerry perv.' As he finished the sentence, he immediately realised what he'd said but it was too late.

Zita took immediate offence and glared at him. 'Why do you say these things when you know that my mother was German?'

For the first time Liam felt bad. 'I'm sorry.' He changed the subject. 'Who do you reckon it was?'

Zita poked at the parcels in the fire, turned them over then reached deep into her bag and took a chunk of schwartz brot. She pulled her head back and thought hard. 'I don't know, maybe you are correct and it was a German. We will see.'

Liam, now physically and mentally exhausted, dozed while Zita poked at the fire and sat mesmerised by the flames. He was woken by the smell of fish. Still not fully conscious, he watched as Zita removed the parcels from the fire and cut them open to reveal the perfectly cooked white fish. She unwrapped the schwartz brot and cut it with her hunting knife but, before serving the mouth-watering food, she reached up under the umbrella and turned up the volume of the CD player.

Liam was enjoying every minute and he mumbled to Zita. 'Tommy would love it here.' He had second thoughts. 'But it's not much like Brighton is it?'

Zita looked up at him confused.

Still laughing, he explained. 'I'm sorry – Brighton *has* got a nudist beach . . .'

'FKK?' she asked.

He stuttered embarrassed at what he'd just said and continued. 'I went there one summer with me mum and dad.'

Zita screwed up her face. 'But you told me that you have never been without your clothes before this time?'

'That's right. Do you imagine that my mother and father would strip off in front of us kids?'

After eating every piece of the fish and bread, Zita pulled oranges, pears, bananas and grapes from her bag and they took it in turns to feed each other with them.

Liam lay back and Zita tenderly traced the scars on his body. 'You have been in many wars, I think?' She stopped, amazed at the long scar on his stomach that extended around to his right side.

'That was when I was in prison . . .' He reflected. 'That's how I came to be here.' He lowered his voice. 'Can you believe that I.' He sniggered. 'Me, saving two screws?'

Zita shot him a confused look. '*Screws?*' Liam touched her hand and guided it around his body. 'Yeah, I mean *prison officers*. We were locked in a cell together.' Zita frowned. Liam laughed and continued. 'Not by choice. Eh . . .' He

255

smiled. 'The funny thing is if I hadn't saved them *none* of us would still be alive.'

Zita smiled at him and continued her exploration of the scars.

Liam suddenly sat bolt upright. 'Fucking cancer! That's what that scar is . . .' he said tracing the scar himself.

'Cancer? You had the cancer?' shrieked Zita.

Liam shrugged. 'So what's the big deal? It's gone now. It went with the fuckin' kidney.'

Zita stood up and looked down at him. 'I would never have thought to know that.'

'Ain't it the disease of this generation?' said Liam.

'It is,' she said, before looking out across the beach and turning back to him. 'But I would never have thought . . . *You* with cancer.'

'I said it's not a big deal. I was one of the lucky ones. Save your worry for the others who aren't here now.'

Liam changed the subject, rolled over and tapped the towel. Zita lay down beside him and he traced the scars on her body. 'You've got your share of battle scars.'

She huddled close into him. 'Like you I am lucky to be here but not from my injuries.' She sighed heavily and Liam stroked her naked back. 'My Jewish mother lived in Berlin. She loved music and spent many nights at the Liverpool Hoop Club.' She smiled. 'One evening, in 1967, when the Manchester Playboys, a group from England, played there, she met an American G.I.' She heaved a big sigh and all the muscles in her body tensed before she shook with anger. 'The black bastard raped her!' She wiped at her eyes. 'Do you know she was seventeen years old?' Liam stared at her and tried to imagine but couldn't. 'Within a few weeks she knew she was pregnant. My mother could not stay in Berlin so she moved to Hamburg and that is where I was born in 1968.'

Liam stroked at her hair. 'Fucking hell! That is some tough shit.'

Zita continued. 'I know,' she said, dismissively. 'Can you imagine a teenage Jewish girl with a baby that is not fully white?' Liam shook his head and sighed. 'She worked so hard, she had three jobs and still took care of me.' She rubbed at her eyes. 'When I was in Israel they checked out my story and even traced my father.' She thought deeply. 'Maybe I'll go one day and meet him.'

Liam yelled at her. 'Yeah, kill the bastard? Or shoot off his balls?'

Zita ignored his comments and stared into the distance. 'Maybe . . .' she said, before lurching forward and hammering her hands in the sand. 'Do you know my mother always believed he would come and find her?'

Liam reached out his hand. 'Did he?'

'No . . .' said Zita, softly. She shook her head. 'I did tell you this before.' Liam showed his embarrassment and chewed his finger. Zita continued. 'She drank too much . . . and died very young . . .' She punched out into the air. 'She was crazy to see him one more time. She always believed that one day he *would* come to find her.' She feigned a smile, looked out to sea and continued. 'When I was seventeen I went to Israel and joined a Kibbutz.' Zita daydreamed and spoke slowly. 'I loved it.' She took a deep slow breath. 'I was treated the same way as everyone else and within a few months I joined the Kibbutz Ma'abarot.'

Liam rolled over and pushed himself up onto one elbow and stared blankly at her. 'Wha . . .' he mouthed.

'I was a member of the military guard – I was trained to use a gun.' She smirked at him. 'To shoot, clean and repair it and . . . how *not* to waste the ammunition.' She screwed up her face, slowly raised her head and peered at him through her narrowed eyes. 'It is expensive you know.'

Liam nodded. 'Is it? I've got no fucking idea about that.' He shrugged his shoulders. 'We just get hold of 'em when we need 'em.' He took his time to roll and light a joint. 'So what the hell happened then?'

She pushed out her naked breasts. 'I was recruited to join the Mossad: the Israeli *elite*.' She emphasised the "t".

'Fuck me,' yelled Liam. He took a huge drag on his joint and exhaled the smoke as slowly as he dared.

Still totally naked, Zita stood to attention in front of him and saluted. '"*Without guidance do a people fall and deliverance is in a multitude of Counsellors. Proverbs XI/14,*"' she said.

Liam was left speechless. With his mouth wide open he tilted his head to one side. 'So, are *you* a fucking fanatic?'

She looked down at him, stroked her body sensually, and smiled. 'What do you think, Mister Liam Reilly?'

He looked up at her and for some weird reason felt proud.

Zita continued. '*You*, the British, have your SAS . . . and America has Delta Force, so why not Israel?' She lay down and pushed her feet into the sand and let it slip slowly between her toes. 'Do you know the Mossad was formed soon after *your* SAS?'

Liam shook his head. 'I got no idea . . . it's fucking scary if you ask me.'

Zita kissed him and whispered in his ear. 'I'm sorry liebling, but you did ask . . .' Liam nodded. 'Shall we leave now or do you want to swim some more?'

Liam smiled at her and stubbed out his joint.

They swam for more than an hour and then lay on the beach. Liam dug his hands into the sand and felt the tiny finger nail sized white shells. He collected several handfuls of them and slipped them into his jean pockets.

While Zita took in the last of the hot sun, Liam finally had the time and opportunity to write the postcards that he had bought in the hotel the day they arrived. He wrote the first card to his mother and father, then one to Tommy, and the third to Kathleen and the kids. He suddenly stopped, contemplated and began talking to himself. 'This one to?' he paused and sat looking at them. 'Why the fuck did I buy four?' He held up the remaining card and continued talking to himself. 'Do you know I've got no one to send this to?' He sat in the shade contemplating until, in disgust, he flicked the remaining unwritten postcard across the hot sand. He sat deep in thought and after stretching his body began to rub his legs; the few varicose veins in the calves were aching, heightened by the lack of efficient blood supply. 'I'd love to get rid of these.'

Zita was lying quietly with her eyes closed, but, when she heard what he'd said, she opened her eyes. She slid towards him and gently massaged each leg in turn. 'I wouldn't. In case you get thrombosis.'

Liam stopped her. 'Thromb . . . ?

'What you need is to treat yourself. Whenever you take a shower you must put your feet under cold water. The blood will race to your feet and increase the blood supply and help it to flow, stronger and much better.' He thanked her for the suggestion but had absolutely no intention of doing it.

As the sun began to descend on the horizon it created a blinding mirror near the beach and it was impossible to look towards the port. Zita screwed up her face. 'I can't see through the "sea shine."'

'Sea shine?' questioned Liam.

'Well, what else can you call it?' retorted Zita.

He immediately lost interest and still feeling relaxed from his massage lay back. 'You know, I can't believe it's almost September.' He turned his head to one side and thought. 'It'll be Christmas soon.' He sat up and looked up and down the beach. 'Ya know I never knew anywhere like this existed.'

Zita could sense that Liam was becoming affected by the day and, seeing his burnt shoulders, started to break down camp. 'You can go to the jeep if you wish . . . I will finish here and catch you.' Zita took the postcards from Liam. 'I will post them for you.'

Liam nodded and pulling his still wet tee shirt around his red sunburnt neck climbed slowly up the dunes.

When he was out of sight she burnt the postcards in the fire before extinguishing it and covering the embers with sand. 'If I posted them who knows who would read them?' she said.

CHAPTER TWENTY-FOUR

Highway To Hell

Zita drove Liam to the hotel and sat in the jeep with the engine running. Liam jumped out and stood holding the door open. She reached across and pulled the door closed. 'I'll meet you for dinner at eight o'clock. OK?' she asked.

He looked at her. 'What?'

She repeated herself. 'I'll meet you at eight . . . OK?'

He frowned at her until he realised that she wasn't getting out of the jeep. 'OK,' he replied, and made his way, head down, across the car park to the hotel entrance.

She shouted after him. 'We'll go somewhere special this evening . . .'

Liam ignored her.

The apartment block was nestled high up the mountain over-looking Playa Blanca. Pink bougainvillea was trained up the building and across the roof. De Groot bought the block of six apartments on three levels in 1988 when he sold on his first consignment of drugs from North Africa. The top floor consisted of two identical luxury apartments but only one had

De Groot's personal effects and that was solely for his use. The other apartment was tastefully furnished for use by any of his "guests", which invariably included judges, politicians, government ministers or business partners, for as long as they saw fit to entertain their mistresses, wives or boyfriends. He didn't care as long as he benefited from their visits. In an emergency he could be at the heli-pad within six minutes, off the island and away. The rooms at the rear, with no sea view at all, were for use by Zita or any of his bodyguards, while the sparsely furnished ground floor rooms were for his house-keeper, maintenance man and local driver when De Groot was on the island, or for the carriers of drugs back to Holland. De Groot had a secret staircase linked from his apartment to the basement garage but fortunately he had only needed to use it once and even then the problem was dealt with by Zita and Artem, allowing him to escape unscathed.

Zita drove past the apartment block. After checking her mirrors she continued down a side road and turned into a gravel lane. She flicked a remote control and the security doors glided open allowing her to drive into the underground car park. She glanced at the other vehicles: De Groot's black Mercedes convertible, another black Mercedes saloon, and a small and dirty family car sometimes used as a decoy. There was no sign of the beach buggy she had seen earlier at Papagaya beach. Suddenly it appeared from behind the Mercedes saloon and accelerated towards her. The driver continued to race directly at her and to avoid it Zita pulled hard at her steering wheel. The vehicle clipped one of the concrete pillars, damaging the offside wing and indicators as it drove away. By the time Zita had reversed and closed the garage door it was gone. She continued to drive until she finally caught a glimpse of the beach buggy. It was speeding towards the built-up area on the outskirts of Playa Blanca. She was within a hundred metres of it when she saw two tourists step onto a pedestrian crossing. The driver continued to accelerate, hit the tourists and didn't stop.

The pedestrians were both killed instantly.

Zita turned around and drove until she saw a phone box. She called the police anonymously and gave them details of the vehicle. The driver was arrested an hour later at Arrecife airport.

Liam climbed into the bath and screamed with pain as the hot water burnt his already sunburnt skin. He relaxed for a while, washed his hair, lay back in the water and looked down at his penis. 'You've done well, son.'

He remembered the first time he came out of prison when Kathleen had told him that she loved every part of his body. But it wasn't for long. He was back inside prison within three days.

He lay on his bed, shivering one minute and burning up the next. The sunburn had now become very painful. His fair freckled skin had always been susceptible to the sun. Liam didn't hear Zita jump over his balcony and, without any warning she appeared beside his bed with a thick piece of prickly Aloe Vera. She carefully peeled back the thick skin with her knife and, taking care to avoid the rows of sharp barbs, rubbed the soft green sticky flesh into his red and inflamed back and legs. It immediately soothed the pain and relieved the burning sensation of the sunburn. While he lay back being gently massaged he could feel the tingling on his top lip, a sure sign that a cold sore was developing under the surface.

'Any place else that hurts?' she asked.

Liam had already become aroused and as the pain subsided his penis became erect. Zita noticed it and giggled. 'I don't think this will help you with that,' she said, as she waved the sharp piece of cactus around his penis.

When Liam reached out and pulled the sheet across him Zita jumped off of the bed and punched playfully at the mattress. 'Come on get dressed. I'm hungry.'

Half an hour later, Liam sat in reception flicking through one of the many glossy tourist magazines. He heard footsteps and looked up. He couldn't speak. Zita looked ravishing in a white cotton fitted dress that complemented her beautiful tanned legs, tight plaited hair and long gold earrings. She grabbed his arm. 'Come on. I did say I was hungry,' she said, licking her lips.

Zita drove the jeep past the Lanzarote Princess as they made their journey to the port for dinner. 'That's where we stayed the last time.' Liam felt a pang of jealousy and quizzically looked at her. 'Did *he* try it on?' Zita laughed. 'De Groot? No, of course not, he has a Spanish girl on the island. I will show you.'

She parked the jeep and they walked into the precinct and sat on one of the bench seats outside a shop displaying shiny silver ornaments of every conceivable size and type of animal and bird. Zita pulled out her mobile phone, sent a text to De Groot and waited for a reply. It only took a few minutes before the phone bleeped and after reading the text message she slipped the phone back into the pocket.

She pointed towards the shop and a young girl with long dark hair. 'That's her,' she said. Liam looked on unable to decide or establish which girl Zita was referring to. Zita became a little agitated and tried to point out De Groot's girl-friend without making it too obvious. 'That's her . . . in the shop . . .' She pointed towards the open door of the jewellery shop and whispered. 'The girl in the blue jeans.' Liam was still confused but he nodded. Zita continued. 'This is De Groot's shop and, now we are here we have one more job. You must go in, give her your credit card, and she will sell you some-thing.'

Liam felt in his pocket for the credit card, stood up and walked towards the shop. After spending a few moments pretending to look at various articles in the window he finally walked inside without making eye contact with De Groot's girlfriend. He feigned interest in several small silver animals until the shop was empty and then passed his credit card to the young girl who took it from him and read the name on it. Liam watched her closely as she stretched up to the top glass shelf in the cabinet high above the counter, revealing her flat tanned stomach. She lifted down a small ornate silver elephant, which she carefully wrapped before handing it to him.

With an innocent smile and a soft voice she thanked him. 'Gracias, Senor.' Liam picked up the beautifully wrapped package, nodded to her and left the shop. Zita walked across to meet him, reached out and took his hand. 'OK, now that business is really finished for today, let us have dinner.'

They walked down to the promenade and, with only the light from the cliff above them to illuminate the beach, they stood for a few minutes watching a group of teenage boys dressed in matching striped lime green and yellow shirts and blue shorts, as they warmed up before breaking into pairs to practice Taekwondo.

They walked up and down the promenade studying the menus displayed outside every restaurant until they decided to eat in the Casa Pedro, a small oldie worlde restaurant on the edge of the new port. Throughout dinner Liam was not himself, fiddling with his knife and fork and hardly listening to a word Zita said. Unable to keep quiet any longer he blurted out. 'What the fuck is inside this elephant? I hope it's not dope.'

Zita looked at him, smiled and started to laugh. 'No, of course it isn't. De Groot's not interested in anything like that this trip. But, if you must know what is inside . . . ?' She gave him a rare look while she calculated whether or not she should tell him. But having made her decision, she moved closer to him and spoke in a whisper. 'It is diamonds.'

Liam slowly shook his head in disbelief. 'I can't believe it.' He shrugged. 'De Groot's fingers reach every fucking where.'

She nodded. 'I know.' She pointed at the wrapped package. 'Be sure to put that in the room safe until we need it.'

It was red hot when Zita parked the jeep in the huge car park of Teguise old town market; a gravel and dust covered area on the outskirts of the mountain town. She paid the attendant and they walked into the town square with row upon row of stalls that sold a collection of the same things; jewellery, tee shirts, soap, CD's of local music, shoes and towels. A wizened old man tried desperately to sell carved wooden bird whistles which he repeatedly blew in the face of everyone he came into contact with. Illegal African immigrants desperately tried to sell watches from plastic bags as they weaved their way between the stalls, taking care to avoid the police. Liam didn't want to be there or to be associated with the many English tourists who wandered aimlessly from stall to stall. He failed to show any interest in the stalls or street vendors but they still continued to harass him.

Zita stopped to buy Liam a tee shirt with a logo of the Prince 1992 album, *1999*. He thanked her with a squeeze of her hand. As they made their way back towards the car he was drawn to a display of designs laid out by a tattoo artist who worked out of the back of a van. Liam spent several minutes deliberating over the various designs before he finally spoke to Zita. 'What do you think about that one?' he asked, pointing at a Chinese dragon wrapped around a tree.

Zita dragged him away before replying. 'No way should you have a tattoo!'

Liam looked at her confused. 'Why? What's the big deal?'

She marched him away from the market and pushed him onto a large rock in the nearby car park. 'Do you know why I don't have one of those?' She said as she pointed in the direction of the tattooist's van.

He shook his head. 'I dunno . . .' He made to stand up but she pushed him back. 'What the fuck is up with you?'

'Listen, Liam. Can I tell you this?' She paused and rubbed her hands up and down her olive skin. 'You can be recognised . . . Identified!' she said, raising her voice. She paused again. 'Yes?'

She waited for his reply.

Liam stared at her until he finally understood and nodded wildly. 'Fuck me . . .' He sniggered and subconsciously rubbed his own bare arms.

She smiled back at him. 'Do you understand that now?

He grinned back at her. 'Fucking clever these Chinese,' he said, as he raised his arms at the invisible onlookers.

She leaned forward and whispered in his right ear. 'I know nothing of the Chinese but in my world you don't have anything drawn or painted on your body that can show others who you are. It can save your life if you don't have them.'

Liam stood up and continued to smile as he wandered towards their jeep. Zita started the engine and accelerated away leaving a huge cloud of the dust behind them.

'I'd never have thought of that ya know . . .' said Liam. He grinned at her. 'Fuckin' sharp . . . you are . . .'

She grinned back at him and screamed at the top of her voice as she accelerated away. 'Y . . . ah!'

CHAPTER TWENTY-FIVE

Diamonds Are Forever

The next morning Zita took Liam for a drive around the island and it was mid-afternoon before they reached the hotel grounds. Liam sat beside the pool, removed his tee shirt and stretched out on the sunbed. He raised his head, tilting his face towards the sun. Zita looked at his body, Liam had a strange love hate relationship with his body. But still it looked good, no excess weight, despite the torture that he had inflicted on it.

Liam pushed himself up onto one elbow. 'You know my wife and kids would love it here.'

Zita turned to look at him somewhat put out. 'Your wife?'

Liam then lay back on the sunbed and had second thoughts. 'But perhaps not. I fuck up everything I touch.'

Zita tried to reassure him. 'I don't believe that.'

The waiter approached them and Zita looked across at Liam. 'Would you like to drink something?'

Liam nodded. 'I don't find it too difficult not to drink here.'

Zita smiled. 'Water is easy, everyone drinks it. I know the different bottles and tastes as most people know their wine.

No one can poison water, I know how it should taste.' Liam smiled and felt so much better. Zita looked up at the waiter. 'Dos aguas sin gas, por favor.' She paused and continued in English. 'No ice.'

The waiter nodded and left for the bar.'

Zita smiled again. 'You know ice is cold and drugs can be covered by the cold. It kills the senses.'

Liam looked at her and nodded slowly, trying to work out how she had discovered that. 'Don't you ever relax?' he asked.

Zita slowly shook her head as she tilted it back.

The waiter returned with their drinks and Zita waited to reply until he placed them on their table and left. Zita took her glass and immediately drank the contents.

'Well?' asked Liam, as he sipped at his water and desperately tried to taste it.

'I did on the beach with you . . . yesterday,' she said, coyly.

Liam looked at her but didn't understand.

'You asked if I ever . . . relax.'

Liam smiled.

Zita looked at him and slowly emphasised each letter. 'Yes.' She giggled and repeated it. 'Yes, I did . . . OK?'

He licked his lips erotically. 'So did I.' He leaned towards her. 'OK?'

Zita blushed for the first time since Liam had known her. She reached for her glass which, although empty, she pretended to drink from it.

Surprised at her reaction Liam also blushed. He turned on his sunlounger and looked towards the poolside bar and the holidaymakers who were enjoying every minute of "happy hour". He noticed the barmaid's erect breasts beneath the short red crop top and fidgeted. Zita detected he was preoccupied with the barmaid. 'You've changed,' she said softly.

Liam slowly turned to look at her, hoping to hide his blushes. She spared him any embarrassment. 'It is the heat, ja?' She thought hard and sighed. 'Tomorrow we must return to Amsterdam.'

Liam took a minute to answer. 'I know.' He thought for a moment. 'Maybe we can come back next year?'

'I doubt it. De Groot only lets people come here together once.'

Liam thought, and with a quizzical face replied. 'But – you've been here before.'

'That's right. But I speak the language, De Groot needs me.'

'That's fine. But why is he building a hotel when *he* can't speak Spanish?'

'It is very simple. When it's finished perhaps he will sell it. It's close to Africa.' Liam looked at her strangely. He still didn't understand. 'You really don't get it do you?' Zita picked up a napkin and drew a map on it. 'Drugs.'

Liam finally understood and nodded forcefully. 'The sly bastard. What a great cover . . . The tourists?'

'That's correct . . . and De Groot will keep a few of the best apartments for himself and his friends; politicians, senior policemen and couriers who work for him. They'll take it into Holland or anywhere else that wants to buy it.'

Liam stared at Zita. 'Why doesn't De Groot come here himself?'

'He did. He came here three months ago when the days were longer and the nights warmer. In the winter he prefers to stay in Amsterdam, unless of course he knows that it will be worth his while.'

Liam, confused by the day's events, was overcome with

emotion and the extent of De Groot's wealth and size of his empire. He felt like he was a loser. Looking and feeling depressed he stood up, pulled on his tee shirt, and with his head bowed walked away from the pool.

Zita got up from her sunbed and joined him.

Subconsciously, as he walked, he reached out and dragged his hands through the huge poinsettia bushes. He stopped and looked at them and turned to Zita. 'Fuck me. We buy those at home as pot plants. My wife gave me one of those for Christmas in '97.'

Zita smiled. 'That's nice.'

'Yeah?' Liam briefly feigned a smile. 'For me fucking prison cell?'

After taking a shower in their rooms they agreed to meet in reception. Zita asked Liam to bring the package he had collected from the jewellery shop. As they walked towards the promenade Liam saw two parrots in a large cage in the hotel grounds next to the hotel bar. He felt angry, very angry; he remembered the years he had been held in captivity, caged like a bird in his cell.

Liam muttered under his breath. 'The poor bastards.' He began to hurry. *'Come on.'*

Zita could sense the tension building. 'You know what, Liam . . . they don't know any different.'

'No? Perhaps not . . . but I do . . .' he cursed.

She knew that moments like that would be hard for him to handle.

Liam continued to walk along the promenade ignoring all the passers-by and his gaze alternated between the sea and the marbled sky. Zita caught up with him but she may as well not have been there. She spoke softly. 'Well who knows? Once De Groot's built his hotel then maybe your family will come and stay.' She deliberated for a second. 'De Groot's not all bad.'

Liam looked at her, shrugged his shoulders and laughed loudly.

They sat at a small bar overlooking the Playa and waited. A black Mercedes pulled up beside them and Juan Martisco, the architect, walked towards them. He kissed Zita on the cheek before shaking Liam's hand. 'It is good to see you both once more,' he said, with obvious indifference.

They both sensed it and nodded reluctantly.

Zita signalled to Liam with her eyes.

'Shall I walk with you to your car?' asked Liam

'Certainly,' said Juan. He pursed his lips. 'Um. Goodbye, Zita. I hope to see again . . .' He smiled broadly. 'Very soon.'

Juan and Liam turned and walked towards the Mercedes.

Liam sat next to Juan in the rear seat. 'I believe you came for this?' he said, as he handed him the elephant.

Juan reached out and grabbed it from him. 'Gracias,' he said, as he faked a smile. 'Please tell Senor De Groot it is good doing business with him.' He spoke to the driver who gunned the accelerator hard and signalled for Liam to get out. Liam had one foot out of the car when Juan grabbed his arm firmly. Liam balled his other fist and waited. Juan spoke. 'Please be sure to tell Senor De Groot our work will finish in four weeks and we expect to be paid the remainder at that time.'

Liam pulled his arm away and straightened his tee shirt.

Zita guided Liam back to the Almacen de la Sal restaurant on Avenida Maritima. Liam paused and smiled when he realised where they were. Zita looked at him. 'You enjoyed it before – why not come here once more?'

Liam smiled his agreement.

Zita chose the traditional Canary Island food: papas arrugadas – wrinkled salt-covered potatoes – served with two delicious "mojo" sauces. Mojo picnón – spicy sauce and mojo verde – green sauce, with sautéed turkey and mixed salad. For dessert she ordered "bienmesabe", a mixture of honey, almond cream, eggs, without the rum.

Liam watched as the waiter poured a brandy for the man on the next table. 'Look at the size of that shot.'

Zita smiled. 'The seven second pour,' she said.

Liam's face lit up. 'Bloody hell maybe I should be drinking after all.'

Zita glared at him. 'I don't think that's a good idea? Do you?'

Liam recoiled with embarrassment.

She looked at Liam and sensed that he wanted to ask her a question but waited until the coffee was served. 'Liam, what is bothering you?' she asked.

He pushed his coffee away and placed his elbows heavily on the table. 'Why didn't we get the diamonds earlier? We could have taken them with us on the ferry.'

She smiled and replied slowly emphasising every word. 'De Groot likes to split the payments.' Liam nodded his understanding and Zita continued. 'It's safer. Juan or Francesco could have arranged to rob us during our journey and De Groot would have lost both of the payments.'

Liam thought about it. 'Yeah.' He nodded slowly and grinned. 'Yeah, I'd have had the lot . . .' He laughed to himself. 'There's no doubt about that.'

After dinner Zita bought Liam a RAD Swiss watch with a blue enamel face, gold hands and matching strap, and in the next shop a woven silk polo shirt. At first he turned his nose up at it until she held it against him. 'It's supposed to look creased and you will not need to iron it,' she said.

Liam looked at her and smiled. 'Thanks.'

They felt good as they walked slowly along the poorly lit promenade, the silence frequently broken only by the invisible waves that crashed noisily against the volcanic rocks laid to protect the coastline from erosion. The moon suddenly appeared from behind the thick clouds and the silhouetted cranes seemed to reach high up into the warm night sky. They looked out to sea and tried to count the number of tiny boats in the fishermen's armada by counting the single lights a few hundred metres offshore. When they approached an unlit section of promenade where the lights were broken Zita placed her arms around Liam while he lit a cigarette. They stood silently looking out across the smooth flat dark sea lit only by the full moon. Zita looked up into Liam's eyes. 'Just look at it. Isn't it . . . ?' She paused and flung her head back. 'Beautiful?' She smiled with total contentment before speaking 'Now that's what I call *moonshine*.'

Liam placed the cigarette in his mouth, took a large drag and held it in his lungs before finally exhaling a thick cloud of smoke. 'Yeah, I suppose you could call it that.'

They both stood in the silence enjoying the moment.

Liam felt Zita's body stiffen but before he could do anything a group of men surrounded them. Zita pushed Liam aside and while one attacker grabbed her around the neck another grabbed her arms and pulled them behind her back.

She allowed him to pull them down but suddenly she forced them back up and when her firm hands reached his collarbone it snapped with a loud crack. At the same time she raised her leg up between his legs and kicked out behind her before throwing him over her shoulder. He fell to the floor in agony. The shadow in front of her still held her head and now that her hands were free she brought her straightened fingers up under his rib cage puncturing his lung and breaking his ribs. As he fell, she grabbed at his left arm and effortlessly broke it.

When Zita pushed him, Liam subconsciously filled the hand in his pocket with coins. At first he punched and kicked out blindly at his four attackers who had overcome him. Luckily he was still on his feet when Zita moved across, grabbed the shoulder length hair of the tallest attacker and swung him around, her foot now above chest height clipped his jaw and he fell away screaming in pain.

Unsuspecting couples out walking after dinner, seeing the altercation ahead of them, turned back along the promenade to avoid getting involved in the violence.

Liam head-butted his nearest assailant, before kicking him in the groin, and he fell heavily to the ground. Zita took care of the next attacker and Liam, with the adrenaline pumping through his body, punched accurately until the last of their attackers fell to the ground. Liam's anger now took over and he kicked out at the dazed and broken bodies groaning on the floor around him. When Zita noticed Liam's blood-covered tee shirt she ran towards him panicking until she realised that it was not his, but blood from their attackers.

Zita then surprised Liam by returning to their assailants. She stood on each of their arms in turn and twisting her heel, systematically broke their fingers and wrists. She counted their assailants and realising there were only six, she ran into the darkness until she found the remaining mugger who had crawled away. She reached down, pulled his head off the ground, and pivoting on her right foot she swung around and clipped his jaw with the edge of her left foot. The contact seemed little more than a tap but her victim screamed in agony and slumped to the floor. She then proceeded to break his left wrist in the same way that she had done to the others. Then as if nothing had happened, she turned, pulled Liam away and walked towards the hotel. She stopped under the first light and reached towards Liam. While he tried to light a cigarette she grabbed at his jacket. He flinched and tried to pull away from her. 'Come on, you can't walk into the hotel like that. You look like a rover,' she said.

'Fucking rover?' He took two paces away from her. 'A fucking dog!'

She touched her lips with her forefinger and lowered her head subserviently. 'Sorry. I mean . . . robber. It is hard sometimes to speak in the correct language.'

His face exuded happiness. 'OK, I understand. If it's any consolation – I find it hard speaking *one*.'

Although he still tried to light his cigarette, he let her remove his jacket and reverse his tee shirt to hide the bloodstains, before helping him to pull it back on. They walked a few yards and as Liam finally began to enjoy his cigarette, he stopped. 'Why did you do that?'

Zita looked at him. 'What?'

'I mean we gave 'em a bloody good hiding – you didn't need to break their fucking hands? Did you?' asked Liam.

Zita froze, her blue eyes searing deep into his, something that he had not seen in her before, and it totally surprised him.

'What do you think they would have done to us if we were defenceless tourists?' Before he could answer she continued. 'Probably killed you and . . .' She suddenly raised her voice for the first time. '*Rape me*! The only way to show any cowardly bastard is to be sure that everyone can see that they met their match and for once they have been beaten and they are not infallible.' Her anger continued to build. 'Do you realise that we have probably saved hundreds of tourists by teaching those bastards a lesson?' She started to walk away from him and then stopped, 'I think that in London you beat people the same, yeas?'

Liam looked at her, nodded thoughtfully, moved closer towards her and tried to put his arm around her but she shrugged him off. He lit another cigarette and reflected. 'I'm sorry, Zita. Yeah. You know you're right.'

They were distracted when they heard the police sirens in the distance and saw the police cars and their flashing lights eventually arrive at the scene. Zita looked at him and for the first time since dinner she smiled. 'You know . . . we are both bad . . . but we must survive in our different worlds.' She paused and looked directly into his eyes. 'Or die.' Liam nodded his agreement. 'Surely you know that?' she said.

'Of course I do, but it seemed . . .' He didn't finish the sentence. She pushed her fingers against his lips; he stopped speaking and kissed her passionately.

They walked slowly back to the hotel and took their time as they strolled around the pool, through the illuminated grounds and into the large airy hotel bar before choosing a leather settee amongst the large tropical shrubs. They sat in silence and listened to the elderly Spanish pianist positioned on the other side of the glass while he played songs they both recognised. When the pianist stopped for his break, instead of going to their respective rooms, Zita guided Liam towards the indoor spa. She whispered to the attendant in Spanish and after looking at the clock, he reluctantly handed her a towel. She smirked as she walked past him and made for the Olympic sized pool. Liam then reached for a towel but the attendant pulled at his arm and once more looked at the clock. 'I am sorry, Senor . . . we close in fifteen minutes.' Liam shot him a threatening look. The attendant gave the clock a cursory glance. 'Um . . .' He tapped his fingers on the desk and looked around apprehensively for help but he was on his own. 'I think then it is alright, but please tell the reception when you leave. Security, you know?'

Liam pulled at the towel, walked inside and stood watching Zita, who was already naked and swimming effortlessly up and down the pool. When she saw Liam she stopped and shouted across to him. 'Come on get in . . . it's fantastic!' Although he shook his head she persevered. 'Come on, this will help you to relax.'

Liam declined to join her, instead he stripped off and while he sat naked in the steaming, bubbling Jacuzzi he wondered how she had so much energy. After swimming more than fifty lengths Zita climbed out of the pool, joined him in the Jacuzzi and examined every inch of his body for bruises and cuts.

'Do you know that when your adrenaline is high it can take more than one and a half hours for your body to become normal once more?' said Zita.

Liam gave his usual response – a shrug.

They dried themselves, dressed and sat outside the bar on the patio. She ordered coffee and while she waited for the waiter to bring it Liam went to his room and returned with the leather bag. He spoke as he handed it to Zita. 'Do you realise there's 10,000 dollars in there?'

'Yes.'

'What's *that* for?

'Shall I say,' she paused, 'insurance.'

Liam frowned. 'Against what?'

She didn't want to reply.

Liam stared at her and waited. 'Come on . . . insurance for what?'

She sighed. 'Liam, this is not London or even Amsterdam. The Spanish are unpredictable.' She bit her bottom lip. 'I think you say, "just in case" – you never know when you might need to pay someone.' She winked. 'You know what I mean, yeas?'

Liam smiled broadly. 'Yeah, 'course I understand.'

Zita stood up and stroked Liam's knee as she spoke. 'We meet in the restaurant for breakfast in the morning at seven thirty prompt. Then we travel to the airport.' She grabbed the bag from him. 'I will put this somewhere safe for the next time,' she said.

Liam couldn't hide his disappointment.

She turned to him and spoke softly. 'Goodnight. Sleep well.'

He nodded and lit a cigarette.

Liam drank another coffee before walking back to his room. He forced his blood-stained tee shirt down the toilet and flushed it, then ran a bath. While he waited, he turned on the television and scanned the channels until he found something that he could understand that was worth watching. By chance he found the three porn channels and, after flicking through them all, caught a glimpse of Helena Heart performing her infamous blood tattoo on Skipio, her unsuspecting victim's penis. Liam smiled and talked to himself. 'You bastard . . . De Groot.'

He fell asleep on the bed and when he woke it was still dark. He grabbed his cigarettes, pulled on a shirt, sat on the balcony and watched the sun rise.

Even though it was her last morning Zita maintained her strict training regime, which meant she was also awake before dawn and ran along the beach towards the port. As the sun began to rise, she heard the first ferry from Fuerteventura sound its horn as it glided into the harbour and manoeuvred alongside the quay disgorging the first cars of the day. She loved this time of day, she was alone, and as the mist rose from the sea she took time out to watch the plovers and other sea birds as they searched desperately for the tiniest of edible morsels. Birds were scarce on the island and she felt extremely privileged to be able to see them. The tourists were lucky if they caught a glimpse of anything wild on the barren island.

By the time she ran back from the port the early morning swimmers had already left the tell-tale signs – their footprints, in the virgin sand after the tide had come in and gone out during the night.

Liam and Zita were the only guests at breakfast and after toast and coffee they checked out and left the hotel. Neither of them spoke for the whole of the journey to Arrecife airport. Zita dropped Liam a hundred yards from the Departures entrance and drove off to park up the jeep in one of De Groot's private lock-ups near the airport.

Liam filled his cup at the coffee machine and sat quietly at a table near the window looking out across what appeared to be a chaotic scene of airplanes landing and taking off. He reflected on the last few days and the new experiences. He was already wondering if he had been dreaming when his peace was broken by an ear piercing scream. He turned to see a small boy crying. He'd been burnt. The man at the checkout stood shaking as he turned to his wife. 'It was an accident!'

'You should have been more careful,' shouted his wife.

Liam remembered graphically the look of Sally when he saw her for the first time in the hospital. He started to shake violently and broke out into a sweat. He shook his head and wiped a tear from his eyes. 'The poor bastard,' he mumbled, as he walked towards his plane.

CHAPTER TWENTY-SIX

Help

Liam sat on the train from Schiphol and thought about his 'holiday' in Lanzarote. It was late in the afternoon when he walked out of Centraal Station and he was immediately accosted by people trying to find him accommodation, drugs or whatever he needed or didn't want. He pushed them aside. 'Do I look like a fucking tourist?' he fumed. He had second thoughts and then continued. 'Maybe I do, dressed like this.' He smiled at the nearest man. 'Sorry mate – it's been a weird week.' The man shrugged and turned away looking for his next target.

Liam walked slowly along the canal and for the first time realised how much he had missed Amsterdam. When he arrived at the Love Shack the place was bustling. Everyone was pleased to see him, including some of his regulars. He walked behind the bar dropped his bags, gave Bernie a huge hug, and made himself a coffee. Within an hour De Groot walked into the bar flanked by Skipio and a tanned Zita. De Groot approached the bar, smirked and smiled broadly. 'Congratulations, you did good, ja? You must go away more often.

The girls have worked their zitvlak's off while you were away.'

Liam smiled and congratulated himself. 'Yeah, course they have, we're a fucking team.'

De Groot was taken aback but had already pulled a rolled up bundle of notes from his suit pocket and it was too late. He reluctantly handed Liam the money. 'Here is your bonus.'

Liam was surprised and it showed. 'Bonus?' He held the notes tightly in his hand and slid them into his trouser pocket.

De Groot had a wide grin on his face. 'It wasn't so bad was it? Um?'

'No . . . it wasn't . . . but what if they'd got me for carrying the cash?'

'No way could they have done that . . . We have used that process many times before but we have to use a different carrier each time. So you see . . .' He lit a cheroot and enjoyed the first few drags. 'I don't lie to you and I understand you had a very good time.' He looked across at Zita. 'And you both had a little sun.' Liam lowered his head nervously and made De Groot an espresso. They sat down at the only empty table in the depths of the bar. De Groot leaned on the table and eyed Liam up before he continued. 'Unfortunately things will be a little boring for you now but I would like to see the bar increase the takings. You need to work the girls a little harder – they've had it easy while you've been away.' He finished his espresso and stood. 'Thank you my friend . . . and you can keep the clothes.' He shook Liam's hand and walked towards the door. He stopped suddenly and turned. 'Oh, there is one thing . . .'

Liam blushed and felt at the roll of cash in his pocket.

De Groot continued. '*My* credit card?'

Liam nodded his oversight, reached into his back pocket and handed it to De Groot. De Groot slid it across to Zita, straightened his jacket and left.

Liam and Asmara made one of their twice weekly visits to the Albert Cuyp Markt in the Pijp district. With its three hundred plus stalls, mostly of food, it was not only a wonderful place for locals to shop but was also packed with tourists. They arrived back at the bar to find Detective Ackerman sitting outside talking to Valentine. Liam flicked his motorbike onto its stand, removed his bulging saddle bags and hung them across Asmara's shoulder. He walked towards Ackerman and Valentine, leaving Asmara to struggle to the kitchen with the fresh vegetables, spices and herbs. While Ackerman reached out to shake his hand Liam looked over his shoulder at Valentine, who lowered her eyes, signalling to him.

Liam didn't understand and was none the wiser.

'A nice relic,' said Ackerman, looking across at the motor-bike.

'Relic,' said Liam, raising his voice and showing his indignation. 'That's a Classic . . . a real classic . . . that's what that is.'

Ackerman raised his hands in submission. 'OK. Where did you get the *classic,*' he mocked.

Liam lovingly stroked the shiny metalwork. 'In the cellar – been there for years – probably forty or more.'

'You did a good job, ja?'

'Thanks,' said Liam, glancing across at Valentine. 'So what are you doing here today? She's not in trouble is she?'

'No.' He smiled. '*She* is fine – she likes it here.'

Liam walked Ackerman towards a table as far along the

pavement and away from the entrance to the bar as he could. 'Coffee?'

The detective nodded.

Liam returned with a tray of coffee and two pieces of homemade apfel cake. Liam passed the coffee and a plate to Ackerman. While Liam was waiting for Ackerman to tell him what he wanted he finished his cake and drank most of his coffee. Unable to hold back his curiosity any longer Liam forced a cough. 'Surely you didn't come just to see how *she* is?' He looked at Ackerman's empty plate. 'Or to drink my coffee and eat my food?'

Ackerman shook his head, lit a cigarette and took several drags before speaking. He looked directly at Liam. 'Do you know we have found something strange?'

Liam could feel his body tense but managed a smile. 'Like what?'

The detective smirked, pursed his lips and wiped the crumbs from them. 'We have made a match of the DNA.'

'Ah,' said Liam.

Ackerman smiled the widest of smiles. 'Can you guess whose it is?'

Liam shook his head – he didn't like games and he showed it with his reply. 'No fucking idea,' he said.

'You know the car belonged to Meener De Groot?'

'Yeah.'

'And you know he had a driver?

'Uh, uh. Yeah, Artem – '

'And he was attacked, ja?' He paused and pointed. 'Around de corner . . . very near to dis bar.'

Liam nodded. 'Yeah, I spoke to your men when they found the car,' he said, in a matter of fact way.

'When he went to hospital we took a sample from him.' The detective lowered his voice. 'Without permission, you understand?'

Liam shrugged. 'Yeah, well . . . who gives a f . . . ?'

Ackerman raised his hand and stopped Liam in his tracks. He moved close to Liam and spoke slowly, emphasising every word. 'Well, I think you know who it is.'

Liam could feel his face colouring up. 'Another?' asked Liam, reaching for the cups.

Ackerman made little effort to suppress a grin and, after studying Liam's face, he nodded. 'Ja, bedankt.'

Liam took his time making the coffee; he wanted to speak to Valentine but she had gone to Bernie's room. He took as long as he dared before walking back to the table. 'Sorry about that.' He smiled. 'I had to grind more beans. It always happens when I'm not around.'

Ackerman grunted his reply. 'Um. So . . . I must ask you one more time. Do you know who it is?'

Liam tried to buy time by stirring his coffee.

'Doe je?' pushed Ackerman.

Liam took a cigarette from his pocket but didn't light it. 'I guess it was Artem,' he coughed, 'De Groot's driver?' He lowered his head and pretended to turn his full attention to lighting his cigarette.

Ackerman waited patiently until Liam finally lit it and took a few deep drags, then smirked at him. 'That is the correct answer, Meener Reilly.' The detective watched Liam visibly relax. He continued. 'The question is – who do we think did that thing?'

'Dunno.'

'Let me tell you something more, Meener Reilly.'

'Um,' said Liam, raising his head and giving Ackerman his full attention.

The detective straightened his back, leaned towards Liam and whispered. 'It was the *same man*.' He pushed his tongue behind his teeth until it physically hurt him. 'He did those things to Valentine and Ruby.'

'The bastard!' yelled Liam, as he stood up.

Ackerman pulled at his arm and signalled to him to sit down. 'I still have a question for you, ja?'

Liam nodded.

'Who did it?' asked Ackerman.

'Did what?'

'Attacked the driver – in de car,' he barked.

Liam struggled for an answer. 'Like your man said, "a jealous husband – or girlfriend" . . .'

Ackerman shook his head. 'I don't think so, do you? It was very violent and how do you say, um . . . berekend . . . calculated?'

Liam shuffled nervously in his chair.

The detective continued. 'Well, luckily for his attacker,' he looked at Liam and grinned, 'Meener Artem Luka has . . .' he paused, 'disappeared.'

Liam looked back at him. 'Disappeared?'

'Ja, he was taken from the hospital . . . so we can't question him – we leave the case open until he maybe arrives.' He reached out and firmly shook Liam's hand. Still holding Liam's hand Ackerman looked towards the motorbike and smiled. 'Ja, a classic, eh?'

As Ackerman drove away Liam let out a huge sigh of relief, sat down and gazed blindly into the canal.

*

Anje drove several kilometres from Almere until she reached
the outskirts of the village and finally saw the tiny cottage
swathed in pink and red roses, and huge sunflowers that
almost reached to the top of the windows. Only the front
door and tiny windows were exposed. She parked her car in
the lay-by, pushed open the small wooden gate and walked
up the winding path between the beautifully scented flower
beds of carnations, lilies, agapanthus and fuchsias of every
conceivable colour. Her coat brushed against the lavender
bushes and, as her feet crushed the rosemary and oregano
that peppered the gravel path beneath her feet she could smell
the mix of beautiful scents and herbs. She stood briefly at the
open front door and watched the bees and butterflies darting
from plant to plant.

'Kom binnen,' said the frail voice from inside.

Anje entered the tiny sun-filled cottage and a world of
plants and flowers that took her breath away. The elderly
woman beckoned her to join her at a small table and pointed
to several small carved boxes. Anje tapped on an ebony box
and the woman lifted the lid and removed a pack of seventy-
eight tarot cards wrapped in a deep-blue silk handkerchief.
She handed them to Anje and asked her to shuffle them. She
then asked her to choose ten cards and the woman laid them
out face down in the shape of a Celtic cross in front of her.
The reading took half an hour and Anje seemed pleased with
the comments given to her. As she was about to stand the
woman shuffled them again and asked her to choose one final
card. Anje selected the "nine of wands". The man depicted in
the card had a bandaged head and was bleeding. The woman
suddenly appeared nervous and upset and grabbed Anje's
hand. She held it firmly as she spoke in little more than a

whisper. 'Someone who is close to you will have trouble . . . very soon.' She looked directly into Anje's eyes and continued with desperation in her voice. 'You must try and warn them.' Anje tensed and pulled her hand away. The woman continued. 'Please, my dear . . . take care. Everything I have already told you is important but . . .' She tapped the card. 'This is the most important thing to you now.' Anje paid her and left in silence. She couldn't drive and sat in her car and pondered what she should do next. Finally, she started the car and drove like a woman possessed until she reached a telephone box. She opened the door and dialled.

Liam stood in the bathroom cleaning his teeth. Mornings were his time, his reward for getting through the night without a drink. He would often reflect on London but at this time of the morning everyone would be sleeping back home – he would always call it home. To him Amsterdam was an interlude but he had no idea what would follow this period of his life. *He wondered what his father would say when he received the post office transfer from him for Kathleen and the kids. Liam's bonus, earned almost legitimately.*

The telephone on the bar rang. The bar was closed. There was no one to answer it.

The bathroom mirror was covered in condensation from the hot water when he had taken his long relaxing bath. He generally took a shower but sometimes when he felt tired he preferred to add a few drops of aromatherapy oil that Zita had bought him in Lanzarote. After soaking for nearly half an hour, and now feeling relaxed, he climbed out of the bath, dried himself, tied the damp towel around his waist and began to clean his teeth. The bath gurgled as it emptied.

The mirror suddenly cleared as the door opened and the cooler air from the sitting room burst into the confined space. In the mirror he saw Jaap and Luuk.

Jaap grabbed Liam's left ear and left arm simultaneously and pulled it forcefully behind his back while Luuk grabbed his hair and right ear. Skipio pushed awkwardly past them and with the toothbrush still in Liam's mouth, grabbed at his elbow, raised it up as far as he could, splitting the cold sore scab on his lip. Liam watched as blood spurted onto the mirror. Although he struggled his efforts were futile. There was no doubt that Skipio had carefully chosen his moment because Liam was now at his most vulnerable. He struggled in vain to reach them as they pushed him hard against the edge of the wash-hand basin. Skipio pushed the toothbrush deep down Liam's throat, the grotesque smile on his face confirming that he was enjoying every minute. Liam urged, vomited and screamed with pain as the toothbrush first cut his mouth, his windpipe and then pierced the vocal chords at the back of his throat. Skipio grabbed at Liam's wrist and twisted it violently, forcing him to release the toothbrush, leaving it embedded in his throat. Liam attempted to speak but the pain was excruciating and, as he struggled in vain, Skipio's henchmen inflicted even more torturous acts on him. Skipio glared at Liam's face in the mirror pulled a long thick cigar from his shirt pocket, chewed off the end and spat it at the mirror all the while gauging Liam's contemptuous face. Skipio looked back at him in the mirror and smiled through his recently grown moustache and beard, cultivated to disguise the thick rolls of fat that had built up since he'd virtually ceased his daily strenuous training and bodybuilding. His fat neck coupled with his stance and movements, made him appear more apelike than ever. Continuing his slow torture, Skipio turned on the hot and cold taps simultaneously and his moustache began to quiver with pleasure. As the water splashed over Liam's bare torso tortuous pain crossed his already agonised face. The sweating Greek suddenly leant forward, ripped the towel from around Liam's waist, and after wiping his sweating face in the driest corner threw it into the sink to cover the vomit. He stood back and looked at Liam's naked body, contorted with pain, as it twisted from side to side. Slowly becoming aroused he stroked Liam's tense bare buttocks and thighs with his short stubby fingers, while he licked his lips as he imagined what might be. Liam was now delirious with a combination of pain and anger. Pain was no stranger to him but at least in the past he had been able to defend himself from his aggressors. Skipio took his time to light the cigar before he studied the flame and after a deep drag blew the thick smoke into Liam's hair. For a split second his reflection was obscured by the smoke. He patted Liam's bare buttocks while still maintaining eye contact in the mirror. He repeatedly stabbed the cigar hard into Liam's left buttock. Liam writhed in agony, his eyes cutting into Skipio's merciless face. Skipio smirked back at him before he took another huge drag and turned his attention to the right buttock, repeatedly stabbing it with the cigar. Skipio stood back to take in his handiwork and the raw bleeding letters on each buttock; "N" on the left and "O" on the right. Skipio threw the cigar into the bath, reached for the soap and lathered his hands before he moved close to Liam. He smiled condescendingly into the mirror before placing his fat arms around Liam's waist and grabbing his scrotum and penis in his large soapy hands. He sneered into the mirror at Liam's contorted and anguished face. Liam tried to wrench himself free but with every movement Luuk and Jaap tightened their hold on him and kicked out at his feet forcing his legs even further apart. Skipio now removed his hands and washed them again making more lather. When he was satisfied with the thick foam in his hands he took his time to rub the thick soap into the burning flesh on Liam's buttocks. As the searing pain shot through Liam's whole body he tried to scream but the toothbrush cut deeper into his throat. Skipio dried his hands and undid his zip. He pulled out his penis and pissed onto Liam's soapy buttocks, all the while staring at him in the mirror. He knew Liam wanted to kill him but *he* was in total control. Skipio grabbed Liam's robe from behind the door and threw it over his head covering his shoulders, back and buttocks. The Greek's expression suddenly changed and he turned his attention to the chrome shower head and hose. He reached out, ripped it from the wall and smashed it across Liam's head, around his neck, back, ribs and buttocks. Skipio's relentless beating had the desired effect and Liam slumped on the wash-hand basin. Skipio reached into the inside pocket of his jacket and pulled out a chrome cosh, shaped to resemble a large penis, held the scrotum-shaped handle firmly in his right hand, and motioned to his cohorts to spread Liam's legs wider apart. He tore the robe from Liam's head and stood watching Liam's reaction in the mirror as he brought the cosh down hard into his open left hand. Liam didn't flinch. Skipio, enraged at Liam's reaction, walked directly behind him and pushed it hard between his open legs. The anger in Liam's eyes was murderous and intense and for the first time Skipio felt nervous. He gave a defiant smile before wiping the cosh in Liam's towel and slipping the cosh back into his pocket.

The pain in Liam's throat was now almost unbearable and as he moved his tongue he could feel the furrows in the roof of his mouth where the toothbrush had scored it. But he was not prepared for what followed. Skipio reached into another jacket pocket, pulled out a handful of photographs and fanned them before pushing them into Liam's swollen face. Liam tried hard to focus through his pained watery eyes until he could see that some of the photographs were of Zita. He shook his head as much as he could in the vice like grip of his attackers until he could see that the photographs had been taken of the two of them at Papagaya beach in Lanzarote. Skipio selected one photograph of Zita, standing naked at the water's edge carrying the spear gun and fish. He pushed it into Liam's face, pulled it away, bent forward, opened his mouth and slid his long cigar stained tongue across it. It drove Liam crazy. He was helpless and the torture was to continue. Skipio reached forward and like a man possessed brushed everything off of the sink top and laid the photograph on the wet surface beside the wash-hand basin. He grinned at Liam before pulling out a flick knife. He released the blade and brought it down between Zita's legs and slowly sliced through the photograph as far as her throat. Liam, trying to control his breathing exhaled a muffled scream at Skipio. 'Go to hell you bastard.' They stared at each other, the anger visibly overflowing into rage.

At that moment Liam vowed that one day, if he survived, he would treat Skipio in the same way.

Skipio threw the rest of his collection into the empty bath onto his cigar, undid his zip, and pissed over them before aiming at the cigar which hissed as it continued to smoulder. He signalled to Jaap and Luuk, who both released their grip simultaneously before wantonly and blindly punching and kicking Liam until he fell forward hitting his head on the wash basin, cutting his chin and nose.

After stamping purposefully over his bruised and bleeding body they left.

Liam lay exhausted on the bathroom floor. He found it impossible to swallow and difficult to breathe as the cigar and singed photographs smouldered in the bath and the room quickly filled with thick acrid smoke. He pulled himself up and in unbelievable pain crawled into the sitting room and slumped awkwardly in front of the settee. While he fought desperately to breathe, unable to take the pain any longer his body shut down and he fell unconscious,

The unexpected arrival of Zita saved his life. She crept silently up the stairs until she reached the top landing and noticing that the door had been forced she summarily reverted into how she had been trained to perform. She pulled her elbows in tight to her body, crouched, and slowly pushed open the door, her eyes taking in every part of the room, before she continued to crawl silently across the floor. As soon as she saw Liam lying motionless on the floor, in front of the settee, she made her way into each of the other rooms. Having already detected the stench she finally entered the bathroom where she noticed the burnt and wet photographs in the bath. She was not surprised and knowingly nodded to herself as she stamped out the smouldering cigar and photographs before rushing back into the sitting room. She jammed the door shut before returning to Liam.

'What the hell has happened to you? Who did this?' she screamed. The sight of blood was not a problem, she had been trained to ignore it and instead assess the seriousness and the cause.

Liam slowly came round and stared up at her pitifully. Unable to speak, his throat gurgled uncontrollably while his mouth foamed with dark red blood. His grey, pain racked face, unable to hide the agony every time he took even the shallowest breath.

She tried to prise his mouth open to assess the damage but when his whole body convulsed in spasm she knew immediately that her field training would be useless. She spoke in a calm voice. 'You need to go to hospital.'

Liam tried to answer but Zita put her hand over his mouth causing him to cough and scream out again with pain as he tried desperately to breathe. Zita finally lost her temper and screamed at him. 'I told you that it was a mistake to get so close to each other!'

Liam blinked his response but didn't care.

Zita dialled 611 and asked for an ambulance, which fortunately arrived within a few minutes. Liam lost consciousness once again as he was lifted into the ambulance and taken to the Sint Lucas Ziekenhuis hospital in Jan Tooropstraat.

It was dawn before the teams of surgeons completed their complex operations to repair his throat, voice box, oesophagus, thyroid muscles and nerves and to repair the extensive and debilitating damage to his body. By mid-morning Liam's condition had stabilised and Zita was finally prepared to leave his bedside. She took a taxi and made her way across Amsterdam to De Groot's flat. It started to rain as she left the taxi. As she psyched herself up Zita stood on the pavement paying little attention to everything going on around her. She eventually pressed the bell using her own identifying number of rings before she climbed the stairs and let herself in.

De Groot was sitting in his armchair having a manicure from a young blonde, semi-naked, beautician. He motioned to her. 'Go get a coffee. Come back in half an hour.' The young woman pulled on a short revealing dress and left without acknowledging Zita. De Groot gave one of his insincere smiles; something Zita had seen him give to others many times before but never to her. 'This had better be important . . . you know I don't like to be *disturbed*.'

Zita looked at him, her face firm and hard. 'I think it is. What did you do to . . . Liam?'

De Groot gave her a curious look and screwed up his face. 'Liam? I have no idea.'

'I think you do. Why did you take it so far? He was almost killed.' She crossed her arms and waited. He didn't answer. Zita continued. 'Why? What has he done to *you*?'

De Groot's expression changed and he raised his voice. 'Young . . .' He muttered the other word to himself. 'I think *you* could have been more discreet? Yeas? Do you remember when you came to me for a job? Do you remember what I said to you, eh?' Zita nodded. 'I told you that if you work for me then you must give up everything. I pay you well, ja?' He paused and then continued as he spat out every word in anger. 'Very . . . very . . . well. But what do you do with that *flapte*? You *fuck him* . . . at *my* expense.' He thought before he continued. 'He is dispensable.' He looked Zita up and down. 'But you?' De Groot thought again for a second and lowered his voice. 'Well, I didn't want that oily Greek sonofabitch to have the pleasure of doing anything to you.' He took a cheroot from the case in his shirt pocket. 'You abused my trust. I thought you were a professionele!'

Zita replied immediately. 'Would you *never* take a break? Even professionals . . .' She didn't finish the sentence.

'I can't afford to do that!' snarled De Groot.

'What?' questioned Zita.

'I don't mean the financiële cost, I mean my empire.' He lowered his head, looked at his nails and lit the cheroot. He fiddled with his nails until a smile tugged at his lower lip. He raised his head and his whole body stiffened. He pushed himself further into his chair and gave Zita a stern look. 'How do expect me to command respect if my employees are fucking each other behind my back? UH!' He brought his clenched fists down onto the arms of the chair. 'Before long you will all want to fuck up me and my business.' De Groot continued. 'Do you know how much I paid to get him off?' He bellowed.

'Who,' asked Zita.

'My *guide! He* took the pictures of *you* on the beach . . . *naked*!' He slouched awkwardly in his chair. 'Do you know how much I pay to get him off?'

Zita shook her head; she didn't care.

'I'll tell you. More than either of you earn in a year . . . That's how much!'

Zita took a deep breath. 'Did he tell you he killed two innocent people . . . on a crossing?'

His gave her an ingratiating look. 'Life can sometimes be very cheap . . . you know *that* more than anyone . . . It's what you were trained to do . . . isn't it?'

Zita silently agreed with her boss with a slow nod. She had killed many times and agreed with him but she had to defend herself. She looked him directly in the eye. 'But surely you don't consider *him* a threat to your business?'

De Groot stubbed out the cheroot and lit a cigar. After

filling the room with smoke, he replied. 'Never underestimate anyone. And . . . I mean *anyone*!' he roared.

Zita interrupted him. 'You didn't want him killed?'

De Groot looked at his cigar, tapped the loose ash into the ashtray and blew the end of it until it glowed a bright orange.

Zita needed an answer to her question. She continued. 'Come on, tell me that you didn't order that treatment?' There was a knock at the door. 'Come in,' growled De Groot.

The beautician walked in and ignoring Zita removed her dress and sat down in front of her client. De Groot settled himself into his armchair, rested his free bare arm limply on the wide arms of the chair and, without looking up at Zita, continued speaking to her. 'I will talk with Skipio. You know he sometimes gets a little over excited.' He pushed himself even deeper into the armchair filling it as he relaxed and spoke to the beautician. 'Can we get on . . . now?'

The beautician took his left hand and began to shape his nails.

Zita left the room and as she walked down the stairs she knew that her initial thoughts had been confirmed. Although De Groot had wanted to make an example of Liam, the extent of the beating was solely attributable to the fat Greek bastard.

Liam had a tracheotomy inserted into his throat to help him breathe and was placed in an enforced coma in intensive care for several days. He had tubes everywhere to keep him alive, and for several days his life was in the balance. It wasn't only his throat that was affected, but his whole body, from the vicious beating and torture he had endured.

When Liam was finally considered to be out of danger and conscious he was moved to a different ward. Mr Felix de Klerk, one of the consultants responsible for his survival, accompanied by several trainees, visited him. The consultant was very unorthodox. He wore a bright check shirt, red tie, chinos and open toed sandals. After talking to the trainees he finally spoke to Liam in perfect English. 'Hello Mr Reilly, you have been very poorly.' Liam blinked. 'How are you today?' Liam blinked once more. 'If you don't mind I would like to explain to my colleagues about the various problems we had following your attack.' Liam blinked and forced a painful nod. 'I won't hurt you but if these young people are to learn I do need to explain what we did.' Liam licked his dry lips. The nurse in attendance poured some water, lifted Liam's head and gently poured a few drops carefully between his lips. The consultant thanked her and gestured to her to leave. He waited while she walked along the ward before he gently pulled back the white sheet exposing Liam's pale brutalised body. He traced the lengthy scar across his patient's stomach and continued to speak in perfect English. 'This scar is from an open nephrectomy.' The trainees looked closely at the scar and they all nodded. 'I suspect Mr Reilly has had his right kidney removed – I believe because of cancer – possibly a year or so ago?' Liam blinked and the consultant smiled proudly before continuing as though Liam was no longer there. 'We have repaired the massive damage to his throat and reconstructed much of it.' He smiled and looked down at Liam. 'We expect that you will be able to speak again – with some pain, but in time it should heal.' Liam blinked back at him. 'We have applied skin grafts to both buttocks.' The trainees continued with their ritual nods. 'We took the skin from the patient's inner thighs.' He pointed at Liam's bandaged thighs. 'With any burns there is a high risk of the patient developing posttraumatic stress disorder so we will treat him with anti-anxiety medications.' He turned his attention to the dark blue bruises across Liam's torso and stomach. 'The broken ribs will heal and fortunately so will his remaining damaged kidney – but it will take time.' He reached down and touched Liam's hand. 'Thank you Mr Reilly. I will come and visit you again but in the meantime please try to rest as much as you can. You are in safe hands and we will soon have you up and about.'

Liam dozed until he was woken by a soft voice he recognised. 'Hello, Liam. How are you?'

He opened his eyes, focused and smiled. He reached for the note pad and pen and scribbled excitedly. "Hello, Anje. I've missed you. Where have you been?"

Anje ignored his question. 'What the hell has happened to you?' She paused. 'It is my fault you are like this now. I wanted to warn you. She told me something terrible would happen.' She covered her face in shame. 'I called you at the bar . . .'

Liam didn't write anything; instead he looked at her with sad enquiring eyes.

She began to sob but noticing that Liam was getting upset she controlled herself and wiped her eyes. 'I'm sorry I left without saying goodbye,' she said in a whisper.

Liam nodded.

'I didn't want to leave . . .' She swallowed hard 'You must know that.'

Liam blinked.

'I lost my job . . .' she said.

Liam scribbled two words on the pad but didn't hand it to her.

'Come on show me,' she pleaded.

He passed her the pad.

She read it and traced the letters with her finger before she spoke. 'Karel said I wasn't needed any more. He said he'd had a complaint of me.'

Liam looked surprised and smirked but almost immediately gripped by severe pain in his throat pressed both hands against it and shook his head wildly.

'I'm sorry. I know I shouldn't have come, but when I heard what had happened, I had to.'

Liam closed his eyes before he scribbled on his pad. "I blame the same person."

Anje took the pad from him and read it. 'Do you really think so?' she asked.

Liam nodded wildly and took the pad from her and scribbled. "Where are you working now?"

She smiled for the first time as she read it. 'You'll never guess?' she said.

Liam scribbled excitedly but instead of writing he did a childlike drawing and pulled the pad into his chest. She tried to reach it but he held it tight. He slowly turned the pad and showed her his drawing. She shook her head and laughed loudly at his sketch of a monkey. 'Yes, that is right. I'm working once more at the animal sanctuary.' She looked hard at the drawing. 'Is that supposed to be a monkey?'

Liam nodded and smiled before writing once more. "I'm sorry you left."

Anje walked towards the bed and placed a pale green tee shirt at Liam's feet. He didn't have the energy to open it so she did it for him. She unfolded it and Liam gazed at the logo advertising the animal sanctuary on the front. He forced a painful smile, nodded his appreciation and scribbled on his pad. "Will I see you again?"

Anje lowered her head and wiped the tears. 'I don't know.' She shook her head. 'Liam . . . I really don't know.' She wiped at her eyes again. 'Maybe,' she said. 'Maybe . . .' she stood up and walked towards the door. She turned back to face him. 'Maybe I will, but it's not a good idea . . . for either of us. Goodbye Liam.'

After nearly three weeks in hospital Liam was well enough to leave. Zita collected him by taxi and he made a welcome return to his flat above the Love Shack. Liam had not been able to eat or drink normally since the attack; his only intake of liquid, food and medication was dispensed intravenously through tubes in both of his arms and stomach, from bags suspended on an adjustable chrome frame which he carried around with him. His throat was still extremely painful, and haemorrhaged if he spoke more than a few words or was put under any undue pressure. His voice had changed dramatically and it was difficult for anyone to hear or make out what he was saying when he did attempt to speak.

CHAPTER TWENTY-SEVEN

No Regrets

The day after Liam returned from the hospital the sunny autumn weather gave way to heavy rain which soon made him feel very miserable and depressed. De Groot and Skipio chose that day to pay him a visit. He was by no means well enough to see them and Zita, the only person able to protect his privacy, had been conveniently sent out of Amsterdam on business for De Groot.

De Groot, followed closely by Skipio, opened the unlocked door and entered Liam's redecorated flat. De Groot motioned to Skipio to wait on the stairs. The Greek demonstrated his contempt at the order by taking out a cigar, lighting it and blowing clouds of smoke into the room, before sitting on the top stair and slouching against the wall.

Liam unshaven pale and drawn, lay on the settee dressed in ill-fitting track suit bottoms and the green tee shirt Anje had given him in hospital. His throat still heavily bandaged and the plastic nasal cannula which was connected to a portable oxygen tank lay beside him. A second cannula, covered with a bandage, remained in the back of his left hand in case he needed to be hospitalised again. As De Groot approached him Liam, with his senses razor sharp, enhanced by the strong medication, smelt the polish on his recently cleaned shoes. For a split second Liam realised he was totally defenceless. Unable to get up he blinked his acknowledgment to De Groot, who walked past him. After staring out of the window for a few minutes, De Groot turned, looked down at him and with an expressionless face spoke out. 'You look zoals shit.' He walked towards the coffee table immediately in front of Liam and flicked through the boxes of painkillers and medication. 'You should have a licence for dese,' he said. He turned to Skipio and let out a ludicrous raucous laugh.

Skipio looked across at Liam and sneered before taking another drag on his cigar and blowing the thick smoke in Liam's direction.

Liam's whole body tensed. He so wanted to get at the Greek but having no energy slumped back into the settee before adjusting the plastic tubes in his nose. He turned towards De Groot and struggled to speak. 'What do you expect?' he asked, managing only a whisper. He paused to take another shallow breath. 'I can't eat, drink or sleep at the –' He heard someone running up the stairs and much to his relief, Zita pushed past Skipio, jabbed the cigar hard into his hand and slowed down before walking calmly across to the window and pretending to look out of it.

De Groot paid no attention to Liam's response, instead he glared at Zita who turned and smiled innocently back at him. De Groot cleared his throat. 'If all my labourers acted as you do I would become very weak to my enemies!' He snarled at Zita. 'And I then would begin to lose everything I have worked all of these years to make!' Before Liam could reply De Groot continued. 'Denk je?'

Liam looked at him and took a painful breath before finally answering him. 'I know,' he said, his voice hardly audible.

De Groot's fingers flicked uncontrollably in all directions before he finally controlled his feelings enough to be able to speak. 'Do you know why I bothered to spend money for the two of you to stay at de hotel?' He didn't allow Liam to even try to reply. '. . . so you are lost between the tourists.' He paused and took an unusually long drag on his cheroot. 'If I wanted to protect my money I could have put you in a shit hole! Luister je?' He paused and waited for a response from Zita and Liam. There was none so he continued. 'Eh?' His bottom lip curled as he glared at Liam and then at Zita before he continued. 'Maybe dis is all you *deserve* . . .'

Skipio eased his way into the room and smirked at Zita before turning to Liam. Liam pushed himself up onto his right elbow, glared at Skipio and pointed his forefinger menacingly at him before slumping exhausted into the thick pillows that had been propping him up.

Zita could imagine what he was going through but was powerless to help him.

De Groot looked at Liam and grimaced. 'It is not good to mix *my* business with *your* pleasure.' He turned and glared at Zita. 'Remember that my young *friends*.' He sniggered and scratched slowly at the stubble on his chin while he deliberated before glaring once more at Zita and then Liam. 'I remind you . . . pleasure don't come cheap,' he said, his words deliberately protracted and intimidating. He slid a finger into his mouth and tilted his head to one side as he tried to remember something. Finally, unable to recollect what it was, he pulled back his sleeve, checked his watch and grunted. He waved his arm wildly at Skipio. 'Ik moet weg,' he said, as he marched towards the door. He turned to Liam and screamed at him. 'Try gargling with salts!' he said, before emitting a deep unrestrained belly laugh.

Skipio sniggered at Liam and spat onto the carpet and naively tried to copy De Groot's swagger as he left the room but his massive misshapen body looked ridiculous.

Zita initially set Liam a simple training regime to regain his strength and asked Asmara to prepare a diet that was not too harsh for his slow healing throat. Zita visited him for at least two hours each day and, with the help of the girls at the Love Shack, gradually speeded up his rehabilitation with more demanding exercises. As well as having received extensive physical injuries Liam had been mentally affected by the torturous treatment meted out to him by Skipio and De Groot's henchmen. Zita knew that it could take several months or even years to heal. She had witnessed it first hand when captured Israeli soldiers were released from imprisonment and torture.

Liam was a determined and model student and persevered with rebuilding his strength continuing with the innovative vocal exercises to strengthen his damaged throat. Within a month he was able to talk and eat normal meals but was very aware that his voice would never totally recover and his throat would always be sensitive and vulnerable to infection.

His favourite part of the recovery regime was to take walks along the canal. During those walks, which grew longer every day, he discovered a more conventional side to Amsterdam, something he hadn't contemplated ever existing outside of his bubble in the Red Light District. He regularly spent time in the Koppel Café, part of the Sonesta Hotel, in Kattengat, before walking across the timber, Magere Brug – the skinny bridge – opposite the Carré theatre, and along the Amstel and back. It was quieter there and, away from prying eyes, he drove himself harder than anyone knew. His strength and energy levels slowly returned to what they had been before the attack – which for the time being was to be his secret.

Christmas came early in Holland and was marked by the arrival of Sinterklaas. He arrived in Holland mid-November – the first Saturday after the 11 November – allegedly on a ship from Spain. Sinterklaas was a serious man with white hair and a long white beard. He wore a long red cape and carried a red mitre and a long shepherd's staff with a fancy curled handle. Along with his entourage, which included Zwarte Piet – black Pete, Sinterklaas would parade through the streets on his white horse. While children cheered and sang traditional songs his assistants would throw sweets and gingerbread biscuits into the crowd. A few weeks later on the night of Sinterklaasavond, 5th December, before going to bed, children would put their shoes next to the fireplace or chimney of the coal-fired stove, and in modern homes close to a radiator. The next morning they would be rewarded with sweets, or a small present in their shoes, with larger gifts beneath the Christmas tree.

At the end of November, when Liam returned from an extended walk with Valentine, he was surprised to discover that the windows of the first two floors above the Love Shack had been decorated with coloured flashing lights and brightly coloured tinsel. Still shaking his head in disbelief he walked into the bar to discover it too had been transformed and decorated for Christmas. Matthijs and some of his men and the girls screamed their excitement at seeing Liam's beaming smile. He forced back his tearful appreciation until he had summoned enough breath to be able to speak. 'Thank you so much,' he said. He swallowed hard and continued. 'Me and Valentine were wondering how we could do something to decorate the place and . . .' He swallowed again. 'But you've *done it*.' He shook his head in disbelief. 'It's wonderful, thank you. Thanks everybody.' Bernie passed him a coffee and he sat down at a table and tried to take everything in.

Following what was a fantastic Friday evening at the Love Shack the girls talked Liam into going out after work. He was getting depressed and they all knew what would happen if he didn't get away from his surroundings occasionally. They took him to the Paradiso Club, in Weteringschans 6–8, which was housed in a converted church just off of the Leidseplein. The Paradiso had been in existence for many years and was popular for its eclectic programme of punk, rock, underground, experimental and occasionally acoustic music.

When Liam first opened the Love Shack, he had made a decision to keep away from clubs: the smoke, noise and drugs made it difficult to resist a drink when his mind was unoccupied.

Liam hadn't seen Urchin, the East End rock band, since 1988 when they played a reunion gig at the Brecknock. They regularly played around London in the late seventies at the Brecknock, Ruskin Arms and the Bridge Inn at Canning Town, and to see them in his adopted home of Amsterdam was a rare treat. One of the true 70's rock bands split when lead guitarist and vocalist, Adrian Smith, left to join Iron Maiden in 1980.

The band took to the stage and the double bass drums filled the club: Barry was at his best, hammering every skin in sight. Liam suddenly felt homesick but it was short-lived as Andy Barnett crashed chords to an original song, the coloured lights flashed and the strobe created a feeling of pure ecstasy. Liam thought he saw Tommy, his younger brother, but before he could focus the image was gone. Liam continued to shake his head to the music and joined the already eager crowd until, after two rousing encores, Urchin left the stage. Liam joined the girls and between records he heard the voice he couldn't forget. Tommy was singing as he swayed at the other end of the bar, but strangely not in time with the music.

Liam pushed his way through the crowd towards him but a split second later his brother shook violently and crashed towards the floor. Liam tried to pick him up but he was too heavy and there were too many people around them. He tried to scream but the pain was too great. 'Call an ambulance will yer,' he mumbled. No one heard him. He punched out at the people around him and, once he had their attention, he pointed at his brother.

Bernie raced across to the bar and dialled 611. The ambulance and paramedics arrived in a few minutes and after resuscitating Tommy they gave him emergency treatment before racing him to the hospital. Bernie and Liam followed the ambulance in a taxi.

Tommy lay unconscious in intensive care for the next four days and Liam spent the whole time waiting for some sign, any indication that his younger brother was going to recover. On the fifth day Tommy finally opened his eyes. 'Hi Li . . . where the hell am I?' he slurred.

Tears of relief filled his eyes as Liam grabbed at his hand.

In a broken voice he tried to answer. 'Amste . . . you're in Amsterdam.' He shook his head wildly. 'Amsterdam – in hospital.'

Tommy looked up at his brother and after recovering from the confusion, finally spoke. 'Nah . . . is this for real? What are you doing here? How did you find *me*?'

Liam didn't reply and nervously rubbed Tommy's arms and hands and gave a quizzical look. 'Who did this to you? Who sold you the bad shit?' he mumbled.

Tommy didn't want to answer.

'Come on tell me . . .' Tommy looked at him unsure if he should answer. Liam took as deep a breath as he dared before speaking. 'Fuck me, Tommy, we've all done it. Now who sold it ya?'

'Don't know their names but one had a split nose and his mate was a huge geezer – fucking huge – like a gorilla.' Liam managed a tired smile and gave him a knowing nod. Tommy stopped mid-sentence and looked up at Liam. 'Your voice . . .' He shook his head in disbelief. 'Fuck me! What the hell's happened to it?'

'It's a long story,' replied Liam, 'a very long story.' He paused for a moment to catch his breath. 'Coffee?'

'Tea please,' replied Tommy.

Liam got up and walked slowly towards the machine in the corridor. He returned with the drinks. 'What are you doing here anyway?'

'It was Dad's idea. He suggested I came over with the band,' he sniggered. 'I'm one of their roadies.' He laughed loudly. 'Mad innit? Me a fuckin' roadie . . .'

Liam nodded. 'A great band though. They should have made it instead of that fucking Iron Maiden.'

Tommy nodded. 'Yeah I suppose they should have. They're brilliant.'

Liam sipped at his coffee and screwed up his face in disgust before putting the paper cup on the table in front of Tommy. 'How is everyone?' asked Liam, as he handed Tommy his tea.

Tommy looked into his cup and took his time to answer before replying in a whisper. 'Mum . . . she died . . .'

'Died?' Liam gasped with shock.

Tommy rubbed his watery eyes and wiped them in the sheet. He looked directly at Liam, shook his head and sobbed. 'Yeah.' He swallowed hard and sipped at his tea. 'She fell . . . broke her hip.' He sighed and took a deep breath. 'Got blood clots in her lungs . . .'

Liam looked into mid-air and tried to remember the last time he'd seen her. He shook his head wildly and broke down. After recovering from the initial shock Liam questioned his brother. 'How's Dad coping without Mum?'

'Coping,' replied Tommy, before taking another deep breath. 'It hit him hard. He's a shadow of what he was . . . sits in the chair most of the time . . . won't go out.' He coughed. 'He's not eating.' He reflected as he shook his head. 'He's doing nothing – not a thing.'

'Fuck me. I don't know what he's going to do without her. Do you?'

Tommy shook his head. 'I know.'

Liam coughed. 'What about Kathleen and the kids?' Liam asked, nervously.

Tommy smiled. 'Dare I say they're doing fine? Harry spends time with me – '

'What?' screamed Liam, forgetting his throat.

Tommy raised his hands in submission. 'Don't worry Li; I'm taking care of him. He's fine. He's a smart lad . . . just like you.'

Liam cussed, sat down in the chair and rubbed at his pained throat. He sighed. 'OK. Just you be sure . . . Don't let him learn any of your ways.'

Tommy smiled. 'I won't . . . but he needs somebody around now that Dad's shut himself away.'

'Are you all alright for money?'

Tommy smiled. 'Yeah.' He nodded slowly. 'We all are. Thanks to that mystery trip of yours to Spain . . .'

Liam remembered Juanita and smiled. 'Yeah, it was a fucking mystery alright . . .'

Bernie arranged to borrow a friend's car and drove Liam to the hospital to fetch Tommy. As they walked slowly across the car park Tommy stopped. 'Are you coming back for Christmas, Li?' he asked.

Liam looked at Bernie who also waited for his response. 'I can't,' he said, choking back his feelings.

Bernie smiled with relief.

Liam continued. 'I have a new life here. There's no way I can.' He thought long and hard. 'I *will* come back when I'm ready – but not yet.' He coughed, pushed his hand against his throat and struggled in agony as the stabbing pains raced through his whole body. He pulled a small phial of liquid painkiller from his pocket and swallowed it.

Tommy reached out and gave his brother a hug. 'Alright . . . but Li you haven't told me what you're doin' 'ere . . .'

Liam squeezed him as hard as he dared without breaking into a coughing fit. 'The less you know the better.' He choked back the emotion. 'I'm OK . . .' He swallowed hard. 'I'm OK, Tommy . . . *really* I am . . . I'm fine.'

Tommy looked across to Bernie and she confirmed it with a slow nod.

'Can't I stay here with you then?' he pleaded.

Liam rubbed hard at Tommy's shoulders and raised his voice. 'No way, Tommy! You can't stay *here*.' He shook his head wildly. 'It will destroy you . . . this place takes no prisoners. Shit really happens here. Surely you can see that?'

Tommy tried to reply but Liam held his hand across his mouth and, while he stifled his brother's answer, he took the deepest breath he could before handing the airline ticket to him. 'Come on . . . let Bernie take us to the station and you get the plane home.'

He helped Tommy into the car.

Bernie drove them to Centraal Station, removed a bag from the boot and passed it to Liam. She waited in the car and watched them stroll through the front entrance before driving away.

Liam and Tommy walked slowly onto the platform where the train to Schipol airport was ready to leave. Liam moved close to Tommy and put his arm around him before handing him the bag. 'These are from me.' Tommy stared at him and Liam read his mind and tapped the bag. 'Presents . . . OK. Give everyone my love but please don't tell them where I am, or –'

'How the hell do I do that, Li?' Tommy asked.

'I'm sure you'll think of something,' said Liam, sniffing heavily. 'Oh . . . and give Dad a special hug – tell him I'm fine . . .' His voice faltered. 'Please . . .'

Tommy nodded as he climbed reluctantly onto the train.

'See you soon,' he said as he closed the door behind him. His whole body trembled as he stood gazing at his brother through the glass. 'Happy Christmas, Li,' he mouthed.

Liam waited on the platform until the train pulled away, wiped the tears from his eyes and continued to wave erratically as it disappeared into the distance. As he turned he talked to himself. 'Happy Christmas Tommy.'

He sighed and swallowed hard as he supressed his heightened feelings: something that had been difficult to cope with since his life changing injuries. The surgeon told him that it might take a year or more before the general anaesthetic that had flowed through his whole body during the numerous and delicate operations was totally out of his system.

He walked out of the station and stood on the wide pavement. He looked across at the front of the Frans Beekwinder building, decorated with dozens of Christmas trees and flashing multi-coloured Christmas decorations. He attempted to light a cigarette and cursed to himself before sliding the cigarette back into the packet. He tried to force a smile but failed. He knew he couldn't smoke, he had been banned from smoking for the foreseeable future and that hurt him as much as his damaged throat.

CHAPTER TWENTY-EIGHT

So This Is Christmas

As on every other day, Liam was up early on Christmas Eve. After buying yet another Christmas tree from one of the many passing barges, he walked down Oudezijds Voorburgwal turning into Grimburgwal, Langegrug and down Rokin towards the Munttoren, the gate of Amsterdam's medieval city wall, until he reached the Bloemenmarkt. The barges were very different from his previous visits. As well as masses of tulip and daffodil bulbs they had displays of painted wooden tulips along with assorted flowers, massive amaryllis bulbs and, in pride of place, numerous vases of very expensive tulips. At the rear of their displays hung bunches of dried roses that they hadn't been able to sell in the summer. He ignored those and turned his attention to the rows of potted poinsettias and immediately remembered Lanzarote. He couldn't hide his excitement as he walked on and off the numerous barges buying armfuls of the best plants.

After stopping at a coffee shop for a double espresso he walked back towards the bar passing barrow upon barrow of street vendors selling hot sticky sweet snacks. Unable to resist the aroma of the freshly fried olliebollen – dough balls, covered with icing sugar and the appelflappen – a cross between an apple pie and a doughnut, he stopped to buy one of each. After placing the poinsettias beside the barrow he stood and ate both of them. He brushed the sugar off his hands and wiped them on his jeans before buying a bag of Pannenkeok met kaas – Cheese pancakes, for the girls at the bar.

When he walked in he was stunned to be met with vases of flowers, filling every available space, and gifts from the girls stacked neatly at one end of the bar. Liam completed the decoration with the potted poinsettias which he strategically placed around the bar.

Rather than working, the girls spent the early afternoon celebrating. They stood round the piano singing song after song, none of which Liam recognised. Strangely their clients were happy to sing and drink with them. Maybe the girls had planned it that way? Liam stood behind the bar which for him formed a barrier, protecting him from the unwanted opportunity of having to join them in a drink. He was surprised how ordinary the girls seemed as they laughed and joked with each other.

They left early to allow themselves enough time to get back to their families in Germany and the smaller towns in Holland.

Liam locked up and sat alone in the dimly-lit bar half listening to the music on the juke box and tapping subconsciously on the table. He alternated his gaze between the plants, flowers and presents, which he said he wouldn't open until Christmas Day, and row upon row of alcohol behind the bar. He was finding it unusually hard to resist but after taking a deep breath he reluctantly pulled himself away, walked behind the bar and ground half a bag of coffee beans. He made himself an espresso and walked out into the freezing night. For once the whole area was strangely deserted and eerily silent. While the Christmas lights reflected and flashed on the canal, Liam couldn't help thinking about Ruby's young daughter, Fleur, who no longer had a mother. But then nor did he. He thought about his family back in London. *Would they miss him? Who knows?* He wasn't to find out any time soon.

The clock on the tower of the Oude Kerke struck out sending a shiver down Liam's spine as it cut through the surreal silence. Still carrying the empty coffee cup he continued to walk, oblivious to the sub-zero temperatures. When he realised that he was still holding the empty cup he threw it towards the frozen canal. The cup slid across the ice until it disappeared into the darkness beneath the nearest bridge.

Liam woke up early on Christmas morning, totally alone. The building was deserted and silent. He talked to himself while he moved the flowers around the flat and placed the largest poinsettia on the windowsill. 'You wouldn't stand a chance in Lanzarote. You look like a Bonsai compared to them,' he said, stroking the red leaves.

He reached down and switched on the Sky channel, his only link with England, except for the occasional newspaper left by a tourist, and looked out of the window across the icy canal. The ice on each side of the canal, immediately outside the bar, had become much wider and thicker, almost meeting in the centre. As the Sky channel transmitted Christmas scenes from around the world, it finally visited St Paul's Cathedral in London. He immediately felt homesick. The intercom buzzed but instead of answering it he walked down the stairs past the open brandy bottle on the bar and let Zita in the front door.

The weak winter sun partially blinded him and as he turned to look around the empty darkened bar a blank look crossed his face.

Zita pulled at his arm. 'Eine mark fur was du dinke.'

Liam looked at her. 'What?'

Zita replied. 'I'm sorry Liam; I mean a Deutsche mark for your thinking.'

He scratched his head, thought for a moment and then gave her a grin.

Zita pulled away from him.

'I'm not laughing at you,' he said, trying to reassure her.

She didn't attempt to hide her annoyance. 'Then why do you laugh at me?'

Liam reached out to her. 'You mean a penny for my thoughts.'

Zita looked at him. 'Only one penny? That's much less than a mark. Surely, your thoughts have more worth than *that*?'

Liam sighed and responded to her question. 'Who knows? He looked across to the open bottle on the bar. 'What I'd give for –'

Zita stamped her foot angrily. 'Your life! I think so!'

Clearly won over by her innocent smile and perfect white teeth he smiled back at her. 'Oh well, perhaps not.'

She gave him a long kiss and then passed him a beautifully wrapped present. 'I hope that you like it. It will remind you of the sun and your time on the island.'

Still holding her close with one hand and using the other hand to tear at the paper, he unwrapped *Islas,* a CD from the Canary Islands, and *Postcard from Heaven* by the Lighthouse

Family. Liam kissed her and then spoke softly to her. 'Happy Christmas Zita.' He held her close to him and then still holding her hands pushed her away. 'But . . . I didn't buy you a present,' he said, looking and feeling embarrassed.

Zita looked up at him. 'No problem. If you don't drink that filthy . . .' She pretended to urge and looked hard at the open brandy bottle, replaced the cork, placed it on the shelf behind the bar, and continued. 'Then . . .' she gazed into his eyes and smiled the broadest of smiles. '*That* will be *your* present to me, yeas?'

Liam felt uncomfortable because for the first time in his life he felt that someone understood his problem and really cared for him.

When they reached his flat she pulled him close to her and whispered in his ear. 'Happy Christmas Liam.' She smiled at him and continued. 'That wish is for *your* Christmas – but *we* celebrate Hanukkah – remember?' He gave her a bemused look. She continued. 'A few weeks ago, yeas?' Knowing he had forgotten, she pushed him towards the bathroom. 'Es spielt keine Rolle. Go on, have your shower.'

He left the room shaking his head, embarrassed that he had forgotten such a recent event that Zita had celebrated with him.

To remind Liam of Lanzarote, Zita put on the Islas CD and turned up the volume so that Liam could hear it while he showered.

He smiled at the music and muttered to himself. 'At least now I can remember what happened yesterday – and the weeks before.' He reflected. 'Well, some things anyway . . .' He thrust his head under the warm water and held it there.

Zita cleaned and refilled the coffee percolator and while the water heated she looked out across the rooftops. She shouted to Liam above the music. 'Maybe it will snow tonight.'

They had an early Christmas lunch in a tiny café in Leidsekruisstraat, off of the Leidseplein, before leaving for Zita's houseboat.

Liam slowed down near the bridge, on the corner of Berenstraat, and glanced up at "Crumbs", a dilapidated coffee shop, before turning into Brouwersgracht and onto Zita's houseboat. The deck was a mass of plant pots of all shapes and colours, filled with primroses, pansies, snowdrops, crocus and hellebores, with abstract wood carvings positioned amongst the larger plants. On the roof was a small Christmas tree with one solitary star on top, Zita's only concession for the time of year. Her bicycle was stored on the outside deck of the boat chained to a wooden bench. Liam deliberated for a few minutes as he looked for somewhere to leave his motorbike and by moving a few of the pots he was able to find a spot for it. He reached onto the roof and grabbed at the folded dark green tarpaulin and threw it over his motorbike making sure it wasn't immediately distinguishable to anyone who passed.

While Liam was up on the roof Zita went below and lit the stove. Liam had no idea what to expect as he climbed down the timber staircase into the sitting room. He stopped on the third step and looked around, unable to speak. Soft classical music played from speakers in every corner of the room. The last of the afternoon winter sun cut through the rooflights that were positioned the length of the room, shedding a bright light onto the thick brightly-coloured rugs that covered much of the shiny heavily-grained timber floor. The ceiling was painted pale grey and the walls a very pale blue. Almost every inch of the walls were covered with large black and white framed photos of old Amsterdam. There were no Christmas cards but near the open-plan galley kitchen was a large poinsettia which took pride of place on an antique dining table complete with two odd chairs. An array of pots and pans hung from butchers hooks above the worktops and stacked at one end were dozens of jars, of all shapes and sizes, containing herbs and spices. At the other end of the room were two well-used misshapen settees covered with brightly covered throws, a coffee table, a large carved giraffe and several retro chrome standard lights which Zita had carefully positioned for maximum effect.

Zita continued to prepare the coffee but turned to gauge Liam's reaction. 'You like it,' she asked, expectantly.

'Wow . . . I love it. I can't believe it . . . It's fantastic,' he gushed.

'So do I,' replied Zita. 'Can you believe we are on the canal – floating?' she shrieked.

Liam bent down and gazed out of the nearest window and then the next until he had looked out of all of them. 'What about the tourist boats? Don't they cause problems?' He moved his outstretched flattened palms wildly to emulate a rocking motion.

'No. There is a speed limit . . . a very slow speed limit . . .' She laughed loudly. 'Is that sense?'

Liam smiled and looked over her shoulder at the cafetière. She blushed and turned to pour it.

They made themselves comfortable on the largest settee and while they sipped at the coffee Liam tried to take in the fact that he was on a boat. He suddenly jumped up and scrutinised the room. 'You don't have any *Christmas* cards.'

Zita looked at him and tilted her head to one side. 'I work

for De Groot,' she said, grinning back at him. 'You must remember – I don't wish for anyone to know where I am. I must remain invisible.'

Liam slowly nodded his understanding. 'A bit like me, eh?'

Zita replied. 'Now do you understand?'

'Of course I do,' said Liam, sitting down beside her.

They spent a few intimate hours making love on the thick rug in front of the stove.

Liam lay mesmerised by the random shapes of the flames as they reflected on the walls and ceiling around him. He suddenly began to tremble. Zita knew instinctively something was wrong. She slid her fingers through his hair and as she massaged his neck she felt him begin to relax.

Liam moved closer to her. 'Do you know this is my first Christmas away for my kids?' He sighed. 'Well . . .' He thought hard. 'No it's not . . . but it's the first one when I weren't banged up in prison.'

Liam exhaled and took his time to tell Zita the reason *he* was in Amsterdam.

Zita wiped at his tearful eyes and kissed him lovingly on his bare chest 'I never knew. It must be very hard to live with such a thing?' She continued to stroke his neck. 'I am sorry.'

She changed the CD and made toasted muffins and hot chocolate. They lay on the setee, their bodies intertwined, and enjoyed each other for the next few hours while they remembered their time a few months earlier on Papagaya beach.

Zita sat up. 'Liam, I have something to tell to you.' She took a breath. 'This is *my* secret.'

Liam sat up next to her, pulled her in towards him and waited expectantly.

Zita swallowed hard and forced a cough. 'I said a lie to you . . .'

'Really,' replied Liam.

'Yes, I did.' She licked nervously at her dry lips and wiped the corners of her mouth. 'I did meet my father . . .'

Liam's eyes opened wide. 'You did?'

Zita nodded slowly. 'Ja, I travelled to America.'

'Wow.' He took his time to exhale.

'He was with a young woman – a *very* young woman.' She stood up. 'Do you know she was the same age as my mother when he . . . met her!' she shrieked.

Liam motioned to her to sit down beside him. She shook her head violently and tried to force a smile but failed.

'Did you tell him who you were?'

'Of course I did – he laughed into my face. He called me a liar – a lying BITCH!'

'Fuck,' said Liam. He continued but spoke quietly to himself. 'I bet that went down well?'

'I thought of my mother and how that bastard ruined her whole life . . .' Zita, ashen-faced, looked at Liam and lowered her voice. 'I have had no choice . . . you understand?'

Liam looked up at her. He had never seen her like that – her face twisted in anger. He waited for her to continue with baited breath.

She managed a demented smile.

Liam had only seen a look like that once before – when he saw Reggie Kray mercilessly stab a rival in an unprovoked and frenzied attack. Liam understood and nodded. 'You killed the bastard – right?'

'Ja, I killed him – and he died very, very slowly,' she said, in a subdued voice.

Her face was immediately transformed as the relief of sharing her long-held secret flooded across it. She sat next to Liam, nuzzled into him and fell asleep.

At midnight Zita, dressed only in her Chinese silk robe, walked up on deck with Liam and waited while he guided his motorbike off the houseboat.

He reached out and kissed her before firing up his motorbike. 'To *our* secrets, eh?' said Liam.

She raised her left hand. 'Our secrets, ja.'

She stood on the deck shivering in the freezing night until Liam was out of sight and she could no longer hear the engine.

At first Liam raced along the almost deserted canals but then slowed down to take in his new found world as he rode the last kilometre across Amsterdam and back to the bar. He'd enjoyed the day and although he missed his family and London, he smiled to himself as he recalled his first Christmas out of prison, away from England, and how different it had been. And – this time, he was sober.

It had suddenly gotten much colder. Zita was right, maybe it would snow. If it did it would be a perfect ending to a very unusual and special day. He arrived at the Love Shack and took his motorbike into the cellar. Now feeling wide awake, relocked the front door, walked along the canal and past the Oude Kerke. He was confused and felt cold but continued to walk. Unbeknown to him he was walking farther and farther away from the lights still flashing onto a virtually deserted canal. At first he felt the rain on his face but then noticed that it had started to snow. He looked towards the nearest street light for confirmation and saw the flakes blowing around it. He stood for a moment enjoying the total silence. It was as though, for a brief priceless moment, the snow had killed the filth and degradation around him.

Liam loved the snow. He recalled the long winters in prison when he used to long for the pure snow to mask the unholy and depressing prison yard, barbed wire and surrounding buildings. And when it did snow he looked through his cell bars and wanted to be in it: the sheer purity and freedom. As it became heavier he could hear the larger flakes falling onto the canopies, and the plastic bags and boxes strewn around the almost deserted streets. The snow quickly covered the ground and it crunched beneath his boots as he walked. He raised his face skywards to feel the snowflakes brush across his cheeks as he walked slowly back along the canal towards the Love Shack. As he got nearer, the dirty pavements and the rubbish of broken bottles, fast food containers, wrappings and empty boxes had disappeared, to be covered with a thick blanket of virgin snow, beautifying the whole area. The neon lights flashed across the white innocent world as though nothing obscene and dirty had ever existed in this part of the city. It was as though the snow was putting on a show for him and him alone, and he didn't want it to end.

When it snowed in Amsterdam it was much different than the East End. In this part of the city there was little or no motor traffic whereas back in London the incessant flow of cars, lorries and buses continued until was impossible to go any further.

The few prostitutes still waiting patiently at the windows stood fascinated like small children, their thoughts a million miles from the real reason they were standing there. Some of them naked, others clad only in skimpy underwear, came outside. Looking oddly out of place and laughing like innocent young children. At first they threw snowballs at one another until they noticed Liam and he became their target. Any punters who dared to venture towards their windows were bombarded until they retreated. The frivolity was soon brought to an end when their pimps noticed and, realising that they were losing money, lashed out and forced the now shivering and giggling girls back into the windows.

A nervous punter looked odd in the new snow. It was clear that he had found it hard to talk to the girls and having finally approached the windows, he turned away. The only proof that he had been close to walking across the threshold of promiscuity were his lone footprints.

Liam reached the Love Shack and stood at the front door dreading the morning when the rubbish might resurface through the alien purity and it would become slushy and grey, making the whole of the Red Light District even uglier than usual.

Liam could still not believe that he was free and no longer in captivity. He never closed his curtains and was woken by the sun streaming through his window. Much to his surprise the snow had frozen and everything was just as it had been when he had eventually gone to bed. The canal had totally frozen over and was now covered in thick snow, obscuring the frozen water beneath it. In the past it had not been unusual to see skaters racing on the canals during the winter but, following accidents in the past, skaters were not permitted to venture onto the frozen canals until the green light flashed, signalling it was safe for them to skate.

CHAPTER TWENTY-NINE

Race With The Devil

On Boxing Day, it took Liam less than half an hour to ride from Amsterdam to the coastal resort of Zandvoort aan Zee. He accelerated across the almost deserted beach over the sand dunes and down onto the wide beach and the wet compacted tidal sand. Zita held onto him with an iron grip as he skidded and broadsided in figures of eight and back again. When they reached the water's edge the large waves filled with dark sand churned up from the bottom and stoked, by the strong, biting northerly wind, roared menacingly onto the beach. The strong wind took the top off of the waves, causing a fine spray, before they reached the shore. Out at sea, the sandbanks periodically broke through the waves as the tide continued to ebb, before returning to cover them once again. Gulls picked amongst the driftwood and debris looking for any tasty morsel pitched onto the beach by the waves. A lone jogger ran along the sand, into the wind, and tried desperately to maintain his speed. The only other people on the beach were several couples who had braved the severe weather to walk their dogs. Once on the beach, they released their canine friends to race wildly along the waters edge, across the deserted beach, and up into the dunes. The braver dogs jumped the smaller waves in the freezing sea while the more timid preferred to chase their coloured balls blown along by the strong wind.

The noise from Liam's bike broke the peace and quiet as he raced along the vast stretch of deserted beach. Dry loose sand blew into their faces as the rear tyre sank into the thick, wave-soaked sand, exposing the dry sand beneath. The thick grey rain clouds, which would soon turn to snow as they reached inland, rolled in off the North Sea. Fingers of weak sunlight illuminated the dark sea highlighting the horizon with silver flashes of brilliance.

Liam accelerated hard and, to beat the rain, raced to the only open beach bar.

They sat at a table near the window and Zita ordered two bowls of thick ertensoep – pea soup.

Liam poked at the soup and appeared reluctant to try it.

'You must try this, Liam. It is fantastic,' said Zita.

Zita took her time to describe the ingredients: split peas, soaked overnight, smoked Dutch sausage, bacon, spare ribs, celery, leeks and celeriac finished off with parsley leaves and a plate of pumpernickel bread and Dutch butter.

Liam screwed up his face.

She offered him a spoon of her soup and much to his surprise he took an instant liking to it. They emptied their bowls and ate all the bread. As they slowly thawed out they hugged each other. The restaurant was momentarily empty and Zita gazed lovingly into Liam's eyes and gently smoothed the back of his hand. They spent the rest of the afternoon watching the storms rage out to sea and the clouds dumping their contents onto the already saturated beach.

It was almost dark and, being the only customers left in the bar, the owner, tired of hinting his wish to close by cleaning the tables and then returning to clean them all over again, finally told them that he wanted to lock up.

As Zita and Liam walked back to his motorbike they disturbed a handful of pigeons drinking rainwater from the deeper puddles amongst the uneven brick paviors in the car park.

CHAPTER THIRTY

Smoke On The Water

By New Year's Eve it was much milder, the ice had begun to melt and in the afternoon tourist boats were once again making their ritual tours along the canals. Skipio sat alone in the Blue Parrot bar. He had already drunk the best part of a bottle of ouzo but was still very aware of everything going on around him. The bar wasn't full but was made up of misfits and people who had no real interest in New Year's Eve or Christmas. At 11:15 pm his mobile phone buzzed and a text flashed across the screen. *"Meet me at the Waalseilandsgracht Brug at midnight. You must wear fancy dress. Cat woman xxxx."*

Skipio hurriedly finished the bottle and ambled out of the bar without acknowledging any of his fellow drinkers. He took a taxi to his bedsit – no one would live with him. He quickly changed and continued the journey to his rendez-vous at Waalseilandsgracht. The area was dark and deserted when Skipio left the taxi and turned the corner. Thick mist swirled around the canal obscuring the pavements and much of the bridge. He stood briefly and squinted until he made out the bridge in the moonless sky. He shivered in the pale flowing Arabic robes and keffiyeh headdress held in place by a rope circlet – the only fancy dress he could possibly wear to accommodate his gross overweight body. He took a huge breath and sauntered excitedly towards the only light nearest to the bridge. Through the mist Cat Woman seemed to be elevated in mid-air, her face obscured by her trademark mask. She wore a black ankle length coat and body hugging black latex catsuit which highlighted her full breasts and slim body.

As Skipio approached she pulled back her coat and slipped her hand sensuously towards the zip and slid it down from her neck to her naval exposing her firm breasts and hard nipples. Skipio licked his lips in anticipation and shuffled awkwardly towards her. At that moment the first of many premature fireworks lit up the dark night sky illuminating her pale body and breasts. He reached out to her and grabbed her breasts, squeezing the nipples hard. She winced with pain but, while the Greek was preoccupied with her body, unnoticed, she took the syringe out of her pocket and, with it still hidden in the palm of her latex-gloved right hand, effortlessly flicked off the plastic cover. Simultaneously she reached beneath his headdress with her other hand and walked her fingers around his fat neck until she felt his pulsing jugular vein. She squeezed it between the fingers of her left hand and after lining up her other hand jabbed the syringe deep into the enlarged throbbing artery.

Skipio immediately slumped onto his right knee, trans-fixed, his body frozen by the massive dose of tranquillizer. She looked towards the shadows and nodded. Batman raced towards her carrying a tarpaulin in his latex-gloved hands. He placed it beside Skipio and they rolled him onto it.

The skies were suddenly filled with sky rockets lighting up the cold night sky. Cracks, pops and bangs filled the night air reverberating off of the walls. His attackers knew that everyone in the city was looking skywards on this very special night. Cat Woman removed another syringe from her coat and continued to inject directly into Skipio's cardoid artery. His vacant eyes looked back at her, while his whole body convulsed out of control, and his paralysed muscles and nerves reacted to the concoction of Haloperidol, Droperidol, PCP and Acepromazine – "Ace". He knew what was going on but was unable to react to it. Batman removed a carpet trimming knife from his pocket and slit the Arabic robes from head to toe exposing the Greek's gross body covered with thick black matted hair. They looked at each other in disgust as the fireworks continued to fill the night sky. Batman slit Skipio's underpants to expose his penis and testicles. Cat Woman tied a tourniquet around them, to stop the blood flow, before slicing into his scrotum with a scalpel. She looked at Batman before making a deeper incision and removing his testicles. Batman prised open the Greek's mouth and she pushed them into his gaping mouth, positioning one testicle in each cheek.

Batman pushed his face hard into Skipio's vacant visage and glared into his traumatised eyes. He screamed in his high pitched voice, his vocal chords stretching painfully. 'Got ya . . . ya bastard!' He grabbed at the Greek's pulsing neck and pushed his gloved forefinger hard into his throat.

With tremendous agility Cat Woman jumped off the other side of the bridge into a motor launch and started the engine. Batman pulled a "rotje" – a banger – from his pocket and forced it into Skipio's anus before lighting it and hurriedly covering his body with the tarpaulin.

The firework exploded causing the Greek's huge body to lift briefly off the ground.

Batman watched Cat Woman as she guided the motor launch beneath the bridge and let it glide towards them. She threw the rope to Batman who tied it to the bridge. She threw him a second rope which he tied tightly around Skipio's ankles and, as the boat edged along the canal, the Greek slipped into the canal with a massive splash. Batman retied the boat and they ran into the shadows, stripped off, and changed into black workmen's overalls. Cat Woman carefully placed the syringes into the pouch in her overalls and ensured it was sealed before racing back to the boat.

They jumped into the boat, piled their fancy dress costumes in the centre of the craft, and the woman poured petrol over them. She reached out and poured the remainder over Skipio. While the man thrust another rotje into Skipio's mouth the woman strategically placed dozens of fireworks and homemade explosives amongst the clothes. They untied the boat and jumped onto the canal side and watched as it chugged down the canal dragging Skipio behind it. They raced into the shadows. The woman took several pairs of overalls from a black plastic bag, pushed them into a nearby rubbish bin, and deliberately threw several syringes behind the bin before she ran to the next bridge. She waited until the boat was directly beneath her and dropped a number of lighted fireworks into the boat. The boat continued its journey until the fireworks ignited and detonated. Skipio's head exploded, skin, hair and bone flying high in all directions and simultaneously blowing the boat high into the air. The explosion was just one of thousands of explosions that night and went unnoticed.

The man raced out of the shadows on a motorbike and as the woman climbed into the pillion seat she flicked Skipio's mobile phone and sent the text to the police station.

"Help! Help me . . . Please!!!!!!!!"

She waited for confirmation that the message had been sent and threw the phone towards the rubbish bins.

The motorbike raced off into the night and disappeared into the darkness while above them a huge wave of thumping acoustic shockwaves resounded in the air sounding like a massed army firing machine guns and mortars at the same time.

Zita knew the Dutch have a unique way of celebrating New Year, preferring to stay at home to celebrate quietly with their family until the stroke of midnight, when they dashed out onto the streets and indulged in a freestyle orgy of pyrotechnics. Holland is probably the only country where so many fireworks are let off in such a short space of time in the streets and public areas, reminiscent of a war zone.

She and Liam had made the decision to act during their trip to Zandvoort on Boxing Day, and spent the next few days setting up clues to implicate De Groot and his men. She knew De Groot would be alone at the Kasteel on New Year's Eve and Luuk, Jaap, Vim, Jan, Piet and Skipio would be left to their own devices. She collected hairs from their brushes and combs and carefully threaded them into the linings of worn and creased overalls. She took fingerprints from cups and glasses with lifting tape and then imprinted them onto the syringes and scalpel. She hid some of them, along with a few identical fireworks, lighter and small vials of the lethal concoctions she had used to inject into Skipio, in their drawers and wardrobes at De Groot's house.

The motorbike slowed down near the bridge on the corner of Berenstraat before arriving at Zita's houseboat. Once inside the houseboat, they stood in silence looking at each other, until simultaneously they let out huge sighs of relief before releasing their feelings with ear shattering celebratory screams of satisfaction. Their euphoria was short-lived when Zita looked towards the clock. Realising they needed to rush, Liam quickly changed into his normal clothes while Zita cut the studs and zips from the overalls, opened the stove and one at a time pushed them into it. While they burned, she went up on deck and threw the studs and zips high in the air where they scattered as they fell back into the canal.

CHAPTER THIRTY-ONE

Millennium

De Groot's mobile rang incessantly at midnight with New Year wishes and, as he walked to his suite with Lutya and Bobbie, he scrolled through his texts. He reached his suite and the girls immediately removed their dresses and poured three glasses of champagne. He was preoccupied and didn't even notice as he continued to flick through all the texts.

One text was very different. *"Skipio's gone. The police are coming for you."*

He read and re-read it several times. The colour drained from his cheeks and he began to sweat profusely. The girls lay provocatively on the huge bed, each of them vying for his attention, but his mind was elsewhere. Lutya stood up and walked towards him and attempted to remove his shirt. He growled at her and pushed her away. He grabbed his jacket, raced out of his suite and, deep in thought, made his way to the walled car park. He started his Mercedes and accelerated hard, his tyres pitching the gravel onto nearby vehicles, as he speeded between the open electronic gates before they closed behind him. He had been drinking heavily but knew he had to get away. He gunned the accelerator and made his way towards Amsterdam. He turned onto the deserted N326 and drove a hundred and thirteen kilometres until he reached the A10 on the outskirts of Amsterdam. He left the A10 at Ringweg Zuid and drove until he reached Beethovenstraat, a side road which ran beneath the A10 and the main railway line to Schiphol airport. He drove across Water Street, an area of private land owned by a mysterious consortium of developers, until he reached the insignificant and dilapidated rows of arches beneath the main railway lines and the A10. He took a remote control unit from his inside jacket pocket, clicked it and waited. An electronically-operated door in the railway arch opened in exactly one and a half seconds and he drove into his most secret place – De Groot's "bunker" – a converted double railway arch. He turned off his lights and sat in the darkness waiting for the external door to close. As soon as it was closed he flashed his headlights four times and the inner doors opened to reveal a brightly-lit area with white tiled floor and walls. He had it built in the early eighties, using tradesmen from Germany, Belgium, Poland, Serbia and France for each part of the works, to ensure that only he knew what it was. He had used it once before, for an extended period, when the police carried out a purge around Amsterdam and he needed to disappear for a while. He had maintained this hideaway for almost twenty years and only he knew it existed. He wondered if he would ever need it but something told him that his luck would not last forever and he had to have a guaranteed exit route.

Once inside he parked the Mercedes beside a BMW and telephoned the plasterer who immediately made his way to Centraal Station. He opened the designated locker, removed a fake passport and credit card in the name of Meener De Groot, and immediately left for Schiphol airport. He took a one way flight to Malaga and an unexpected holiday at a five star hotel. He would fly back to Amsterdam a week later using his own passport.

De Groot took a key from behind a wall tile and unlocked the metal clad door at the far end of the room, entered the self-contained flat and undressed. He carefully folded and hung his clothes neatly on hangers in the air-conditioned room. He rubbed the shaving foam into his face and began to shave, taking care to leave a thin line of blonde bristle above his top lip. He showered and cleaned his teeth before unlocking a second area and carefully choosing his change of clothes. He turned on the television and briefly watched the Millennium celebrations but shook his head when he realised he was wasting valuable time and turned it off, preferring to listen to a CD by Klaus Mertens. He pulled on a pair of neatly-ironed chinos, pale olive polo shirt, light socks, brown shoes, a beige jacket and a dark brown, well worn, knee length leather coat. He took a small case from the top shelf and carefully fitted soft blue contact lenses before finishing off his look with a pair of silver framed glasses. He smiled briefly at himself in the mirror, closed both cupboards and locked the metal door before returning the key behind the wall tile. He walked across to the dark blue 1985 BMW and flicked up the boot. He slid his hand deep inside and opened a secret compartment beneath the rear seats and removed a metal case. His fingers carefully skimmed through the contents and removed a German passport. He flicked it open and compared the picture to his *new* look and once more smiled at himself in the mirror.

*

While he was in prison De Groot spent much of his time learning to speak German. He shared a cell with Hans Feldman, a notorious drug dealer from Hamburg. Hans taught him German with the distinct Hamburg dialect and twang. He told him stories of the heady sixties, when the Beatles played at the Star Club and Top Ten on the Reeperbahn and Hamburg was home to dozens of English groups.

When De Groot was released from prison in 1978, he decided to stay in the Hansa city of Hamburg and, using the contacts given to him by Hans, worked as a barman in various clubs and bars in St Pauli, on the Reeperbahn, the notorious Red Light District. As Hans suggested, De Groot changed his name; he chose Dieter Stange – the name of a boy, who had died at the age of five. At the same time he changed his appearance – but only slightly, with blue contact lenses, a carefully-sculpted pencil moustache and silver-framed glasses with clear glass. It was all he needed and was very simple and easy to change his persona when required. In Hamburg, he took on the identity of Dieter Stange and gradually built up a new life for himself. He spoke with the instantly recognisable Hamburg intonation and within a few months, opened two bank accounts, passed his driving test and secured a German driving license. He bought the second-hand BMW the follow-ing day and a few weeks later, with the help of Hans, he took over ownership of the bar in Hein Hoyer Strasse. It was perfect, with two flats immediately above the bar which he rented out, and a bedsit on the top floor where he lived. It had a fire escape which gave him access to the roof and, if needed, an exit route to adjacent buildings. He obtained a national insurance number, made his annual tax returns and obtained a German passport, along with several credit and debit cards. He learnt a lot about the underworld in Hamburg and, when he felt he was ready, he returned to Amsterdam and put much of what he'd learned into practice.

He continued to return to Hamburg, in the HH registered BMW, on a regular basis and built up a business that was the envy of many people in St Pauli. Amsterdam was his first love and he was proud of his reputation and the power he had gained and he regularly returned to the city. He would park his BMW in his secret underground garage before emerging as Bram De Groot, driving the Amsterdam registered Mercedes.

His Dutch mobile bleeped with a message. "*We resign . . . Happy New Year . . .*" He read and reread it and smiled to himself. 'We'll see . . .' he said, with a strong German accent. He stood erect before talking to himself. 'I remember you from *Malaga* . . .' He stabbed his index finger into the air and laughed loudly. 'Even if you don't remember me – Meener Liam, fucking, Reilly!' His whole body stiffened as he took himself back to the previous year at the funeral and then to the present. He tightened his fists, raised them high in the air and screamed out. Suddenly, he seemed revitalised and ready to complete his transformation. He turned off the Dutch mobile and removed the German phone from the box, and clipped in the battery, before turning it on and placing his other phone back in the boot. He played the message on his German phone. "Hello this is Dieter Stange . . . I'm unable to take your call at the moment, please leave a message." He smiled to himself and repeated the message to himself several times. It was his way of becoming Dieter Stange.

He slipped the mobile into his jacket pocket and opened a separate compartment in the metal case, removed the small quantities of German marks, Dutch guilders and euros. He didn't need to carry much cash but felt that he had to have some money on him. He flicked through each currency, removing any notes that looked new and returned them to the case. He checked the dates on the German credit and debit cards and placed them, along with the notes, in a worn wallet. He completed the contents with two business cards from his Hamburg bar, a card identifying his blood group, some recent receipts and a receipt for the second mobile phone paid for with his German credit card, and a few odd coins, which he placed in his trouser pockets. He pulled a well-worn leather holdall from the compartment and removed the contents, placing them neatly inside the boot. He looked at them and concentrated on what would be reasonable items for his trip before he repacked the holdall. He opened the leather wash bag and took everything out. He carefully checked the part-used items. The toothpaste, toothbrush, shampoo, shaving foam, razor blade, aftershave and hair brush he had bought in Hamburg. He meticulously replaced it every time he went there to ensure that it had recent dates and price stamps on it. He could leave nothing to chance. He opened the German passport and held it near the mirror. As his forefinger traced the moustache he compared himself to the photo. Without any doubt it was the same person. He checked himself for the third time in the mirror before he locked both cars, turned off the light and walked out into the New Year.

He walked along the deserted street towards the railway station and stopped at the phone box. He made three calls before making his way up onto the platform of Amsterdam

Zuid WTC and bought a single ticket to Schiphol airport from the machine.

He had always expected to make this journey, but not in this way.

Zita and Liam arrived at the Love Shack, on the motorbike, a few minutes after midnight. The lights were on but they had been deliberately kept low. Liam had made the decision to close for the evening and didn't want any unwanted drunks or customers descending on them. Inside the bar all of the girls, along with their favourite clients who had paid highly for the extended privilege, plus Matthijs and his family, and Detective Andrea Ribeker, sang along with Bernie as she played a never-ending selection of traditional Dutch and German tunes. Even Liam whistled tunelessly to himself as he stored his motorbike in the basement.

Zita bought three bags of olliebollen, in various flavours, from a street stall, on their way back to the Love Shack, and placed them neatly on plates on the bar. Everyone rushed excitedly to grab and eat theirs while Bernie continued to play. Zita put two on a separate plate and took them over to Bernie, placing them on the piano for her.

Liam returned from the cellar and smiled to himself when he saw how much everyone was enjoying themselves. He stood behind the coffee machine and waited for the hot water to filter through the freshly ground coffee. He made himself an espresso and sat down at the table, decorated earlier by the girls. On cue Rafi and Asmara carried in her speciality rijstaffel, placed the dishes on the candle-lit tables and joined them in the celebrations.

Liam lifted his cup high in the air and exhaled with a sense of deep satisfaction and relief, before finally speaking. 'Happy New Year to all of you,' he said, as he took a sip of the espresso. They all smiled back at him and chattered excitedly as they deliberated over their choice from Asmara's fantastic New Year banquet.

CHAPTER THIRTY-TWO

Live And Let Die

Acting on the text message, the police raced to De Groot's house in P.C. Hooftstraat, situated in the exclusive suburbs of Amsterdam, and surrounded it. While they arrested Jaap, Luuk, Vim, Jan and Piet, other detectives were investigating the explosion, the remains of the motor boat and mutilated body in the canal. They found hairs, fibres and fingerprints that matched the DNA of De Groot and all of his men. They would soon be charged with Skipio's murder and a warrant issued for De Groot.

When Dieter Stange arrived at Hamburg airport on his flight from Schiphol he made his way to the check-in desk. Without saying a word he was given an automatic upgrade to First Class. He walked into the departure lounge, bought a copy of the Hamburger Abendblatt, a magazine, a bottle of Asbach, a bottle of Kirsch and a Mozartkugeln – a ball-shaped, chocolate-coated cake with a pistachio and almond marzipan centre and an outer layer of nougat coated with bittersweet chocolate.

He sat in the executive departure lounge and repeatedly checked his watch while he crunched his way through the Mozartkugeln.

The lights in the packed clubs and bars in the Red Light District were burning bright celebrating the dawn of the new Millennium. Two motorcyclists, dressed from head to toe in black leather, pulled up unnoticed outside the dimly-lit bar. They each removed two Molotov cocktails from their jackets, lit them, nodded to each other and threw them simultaneously. The flaming bottles crashed through the windows and fire immediately engulfed the Love Shack.

Four hours later, on 1 January 2000, Dieter Stange arrived at Arrecife airport in Lanzarote. He passed through customs and sat at the café in Arrivals, drinking a large coffee.

A hand gently touched his shoulder. He turned and smiled. 'Hello. I'm so glad you're here,' he said.

'Me too,' replied the young girl.

He left the table and they kissed as they walked to his car.

'I didn't expect to be here until the spring. Did you?' asked Dieter.

The girl put her arm around his waist and purred in his left ear with her soft Irish accent. 'Why not?' Keeva rubbed his shoulder lovingly and giggled. 'The sooner the better, eh?'

He kissed her passionately. He removed his jacket and threw it on to the rear seat. He flicked the CD player, turned up the music and smiled to himself as the two of them drove down to Playa Blanca, onto the early morning ferry to Fuerteventura, and the penthouse suite at his new hotel.

Love Shack

To Be Continued . . . ?